CANDLE

AND

CLAW

THE WITHERCLAW TRILOGY
BOOK ONE

STEPHEN TAYLOR

For my parents, who read to me.

TABLE OF CONTENTS

HUNTING

They say they're ruled by leaders they chose for themselves. The truth is that they're ruled by witchcraft.

—The Witherclaw Witch; a letter to Golkorun.

HUNTING A WITCH wasn't as frightening as Giovel had expected. He found a familiar rhythm in sneaking around the crumbling corners of North Hold, keeping weapons ready, tripping on tree roots and dark rubble, never pausing to think too hard about the dangers ahead. Just like any other night, really.

Not that it didn't scare him. But he'd been afraid every day for twenty years or more.

The night tasted like autumn, with faint smells of wood smoke and frozen grass wafting through the broken streets. It was a red night too, red like fire and turned leaves. Only Yulen offered much light in the wreckage that was North Hold, a crimson glow from the south sky. Giovel used the red darkness to his advantage as he jogged across another street and climbed a teetering rooftop to scout ahead.

The witch was still moving east. Still looking over his shoulder every score of steps. Giovel gritted his teeth. Did the witch know they were hunting him like hounds on a bleeding hart? Or was he simply as afraid as Giovel was?

Elínla signaled from across the ruined street. She, too, crouched on a rooftop with her eyes on the witch. Only pale hair and a bit of her face were visible beneath a gray cowl.

"He's speeding up," she hissed.

Giovel nodded and dropped to the ground to run around the next corner of moldy wood, fallen stonework, abandoned slate, and slanted cobbles. He might be new to hunting witches, but his experience in the Candleguard had taught him to act quickly when the quarry caught on. They'd followed the witch for hours already. Not about to let him get away now.

The streets twisted inward, cutting Giovel off where two immense shopfronts appeared to have collapsed on one another. Too risky to clamber over. So Giovel doubled back, looped around an oblong pond, quickening to a full sprint when he got past the wreckage. Earlier in the war he would have paused to wonder at the devastation in the streets. Not now, though. It was just another example of Redremel handiwork, too widespread to be repaired, too common to be noteworthy.

That street ended abruptly with a turn into a mossy stone wall. The witch stood there, waiting with his back to the barrier and three glyphs glowing red in the dirt. He had a wild look in his eyes. Not mad. Just hungry. Curious, almost. Giovel slid to a halt, ignoring the protesting ache in his knees.

"I thought I saw someone," the witch said. He inched sideways to see whether Giovel was alone. "Are you a Gray? A Lance?"

No time for new fears.

Giovel raised his hands slowly away from his sword. "I didn't come here to fight you."

"I don't drink the lies you people piss. How'd you find me?"

"We find every witch," Giovel said simply.

Witch. As soon as Giovel said the word, the witch's face twisted violently. He threw his whole body forward as if he were trying to shake a hawk from each arm. The closest glyph flared as bright as Yulen, and a jet of dark something burst from the glyph and shot at Giovel's chest. So much for the offer of peace.

Giovel dove to the ground, snapping his right arm out to launch a dart from his concealed wrist-thrower. The witch dodged too, releasing another spell almost as quickly as he'd cast the first. Cobblestones and chunks of frozen dirt exploded beneath Giovel, showering him with debris and hurling him forward in a cloud of dust and smoke.

He rolled behind the rotten shell of a barrel, whipping his sword from its sheath as the witch unleashed his third glyph. This spell shattered the old barrel and hit Giovel just below the knee. An intense itch shot to his thigh before he could even gasp. Then the joints of his leg began to swell like bloated worms. His eyes watered and stung, and sweat poured down his face despite the chill of the evening.

"I've got more glyphs ready for you!" the witch shouted from somewhere near the edge of the street. "Call off your hunt or I'll slice you in half right now."

But he didn't have more glyphs ready. There'd been no time to draw or imbue more. So Giovel pushed himself upright and rushed forward on his swollen, stinging leg.

The witch saw him coming. He narrowed his eyes and fled the way Giovel had come.

It was all Giovel could do not to trip on his own boots. He could hardly hobble with his leg as swollen as it was. His eyes seemed to be streaming extra liquid as well, blurring his vision and making him wince and grunt in exertion. Damn spells. The witch was probably half again as fast anyway.

I'm not so young anymore, Giovel thought. I can run if I think of Iremni, though. I know this isn't one of the witches who ruined her, but I can push myself to forget it.

So he thought of her, how witches had spirited her off and driven her mad. And he ran.

The street twisted up a small hill with still-tidy copses of trees cutting through the roads and slashes of toppled wall intersecting the trees. Giovel veered off to dodge through the thick darkness of the forest. If he aimed true, he could cut the witch off ahead. And if not? He'd probably trip and break the leg that hadn't been spelled.

His estimation worked. He burst through the frosted leaves on a stretch of clear road barely five paces from the witch. Then he spun around and tackled with all his might, slamming into the witch so hard his own watery sight went black a moment before they crashed into the dirt.

They rolled over one another in a flailing barrage of fists and kicks and jabbing elbows. Something sharp connected with Giovel's right boot, not piercing but sending a bolt of pain through his already burning leg. He retaliated with the pommel of his sword, managing to smash the cold metal straight into the witch's chin. Blood and spit sprayed onto Giovel's face. The witch screamed and stumbled a step out of reach.

Giovel regained his feet just as the witch began drawing another glyph. No hope of dodging it in such close quarters. So Giovel launched another dart from his thrower, taking the witch hard in the neck, while he stabbed above the witch's knee with his sword in his left hand. The witch gave a shout and toppled over. Blood pooled in the dirt beneath him. And still his eyes looked hungry.

Before the witch could do anything else, Giovel yanked his blade back and raised the witch's chin with the red tip. The witch howled in pain but held half-still when the sword tapped against his skin.

"Elínla!" Giovel called. "I've got him."

The witch shuddered, gripping his red knee. "You brought a Divine Mage with you?"

"You could say that." Giovel tapped his sword upward again. "Hold your hands in front of you."

A dazed emptiness began spreading in the witch's eyes. The dart Giovel had launched was miniscule, no bigger than a fingernail, but the serum on its head would be starting to spread, slowing the witch's reflexes and loosening his muscles. Another few minutes and he'd be helpless. He did manage to push himself half upright, spitting more hot blood at Giovel before he extended his arms away from his torso. As he turned his body upward, he slid one foot through his half-finished glyph. It mangled the shape of whatever pattern he'd meant to draw, but the glyph flared to life as soon as it connected with the witch's foot. Giovel flinched.

There'd be no telling what the spell did, no way for the witch to control an unknown glyph like that. But unknown, unshaped spellbuilding was a witch's mark. And Giovel was too close to escape the effect of this spell as it erupted from the witch's haphazard glyph.

A flare of gold. Snapping sounds like ropes pulled in half. Giovel's sword broke into pieces, hurling steel upward right past his face. The ground split like a crust of hot bread. Liquidy torrents of violet *something* spewed out between Giovel and the witch, and fiery waves of pain shot through Giovel's swollen leg, his chest, his neck, his face.

It was what he'd feared. Spellbuilding he couldn't anticipate, dying at the hands of a witch the first time he really faced one.

Would Elínla be near enough to avenge him?

The hissing spout of liquid magic tore off up the street, shooting away from both Giovel and the witch. The witch screamed in frustration and tumbled to one side, clutching at his wounded knee. He must have lost control. Couldn't have anticipated the spell's effect anyway, not with his glyph so misshapen. Little wonder it had broken free of his command, as even known spells often did. The flare of energy blasted through the trees and dissipated with a loud crack against the side of the nearby hill.

Giovel didn't wait. He dropped the pommel of his broken sword, rammed another serumed dart into the witch's neck, and pushed the witch hard down on his face. Then he twisted the witch's arms to hold his hands apart, pulled both ankles off the ground, and locked his own feet under him to hold the witch in place like a landed fish.

He almost felt a thrill of triumph, as if he'd caught the one he was looking for in the first place. The feeling faded as quickly as it had come, because this witch was new to his power, so new Giovel and Elínla hadn't even got proper authorization to track him down.

Not the one who spirited my wife away and left me behind.

Elínla skidded around the bend in the road a few breaths later. She had her sand tablet out with a glyph Giovel thought was the Tremor already drawn. Her face looked like a mask in the darkness, the blue threads of her sept tattoo slashing across her cheeks in a twisted pattern.

"That's a lot of blood," she said, slowing to a halt.

"There'll be more if we don't stitch him up," Giovel said. "Help me."

"You think you can capture me and make me talk?" the witch shouted. "I'll bite my own tongue out before I work with the Divine and their dogs."

"You hear that?" Elínla asked. "He's going to kill himself if we don't Tremor him and tie him up. What a gutsy fool."

"Go ahead, then," Giovel said, still straining to hold the witch in place. The strain was lessening, though, as his leg recovered from the witch's spell and more serum spread into the witch's blood.

"You do it. You need the practice," Elínla said.

Not more magic practice. "Is this really the time for that? You've got the glyph, so use it. Or just tie him up and be done with it."

Elínla grabbed the witch's ankles and wrists, shoving her tablet into Giovel's hands as she did so. "Protocol is to Tremor first. And I order you to do it."

The witch gave one more twitch of effort, trying to break free of Elínla's grasp. "You're a Gray?" he spat at Giovel. "And you never even tried to hex me?"

"More than a Gray, witch-boy," Elínla said. "New member of the Divine Order. Giovel, *Tremor him.*"

He hated orders like this. Pointless, misguided ones that steered subordinates—like Giovel, as the newest and most junior member of the Order—in what their commanders only thought was the best way to proceed.

He'd followed orders for twenty-five years with the Candleguard. Now was not the time to stop.

He touched the glyph with his fingers, careful not to displace the rivulets of magnetic sand in Elínla's tablet. Then he reached out to Yulen in his mind, imbuing the glyph with life from the red orb in the southern sky. It began to glow.

The last part was the most difficult one. Controlling the spell. And not hating what it felt like to use Yulen's power. So Giovel thought of Iremni again and wrenched his mind around the glyph, bowing his head sharply in time with his efforts. The glyph flared and winked out, pushing the tablet's sands out of shape as the spell took form and hit the struggling witch.

The Tremor made Elínla's part easy, especially with two darts' worth of poison already spreading through the witch's system. His whole body began to shake violently. His mouth sloshed open. His head rolled back and forth against the ground. His knees jittered. He soiled himself loudly a moment later and went still.

"*Now* we tie him and bandage that leg," Elínla said. "That's how we hunt them, Giovel."

Maybe for now, Giovel thought. But when I lead my own hunt, I'll do it without shows of authority, without degrading orders, without glyphs.

He promised himself so ten times over as he returned Elínla's tablet, feeling dirty all over.

SPIRITING

At first I thought they simply couldn't describe what spiritings were because we spoke different languages. I realized, with time, that they know as little about spiritings as I do.

—The Witherclaw Witch; a letter to Golkorun.

THEY DEPOSITED THE witch at the Divnum barracks just as a yellow glimmer of dawn touched the walls. The Candleguard there tipped their heads respectfully when Giovel handed him off at a suspension cell. The barracks was totally awake despite the early hour, with smells of simmering broth and warm milk coming from the little kitchen and shouts of drill calls echoing in the frosty yard behind. The candle never falters for the guard, as the saying went. That was what Giovel liked about places like these. Candles were the kind of people he'd known and depended on all his grown life, people much more like him than the High Optate's Divine Order of Mages were.

"Let's get back to Sur," Elínla said when a few Grays arrived to ensure the witch was safely contained.

"I suppose we're late for our lambasting," Giovel said.

"That's a grim view of us stopping a witch. What makes you think we'll be reprimanded?"

"Just that we didn't get permission before we did our duty. It means no one above us can take credit for it."

Elínla raised an eyebrow. "You figured Order politics out quickly. The important thing is that we caught him before anyone got hurt."

"Anyone but me, you mean."

"He barely bruised you. Sur won't be that angry."

Giovel wished he could share Elínla's optimism. Years in the service had given him a sense for when punishment was imminent. Especially one as pointlessly unjust as theirs was likely to be.

From the barracks, he and Elínla followed the grassy shore of Cloud Lake toward the Candlespire. The flat commons around Cloud Lake was filling with people for some reason. Giovel saw why when a huge gout of flame shot up over the western shore. It must be Fire Day. An official excuse for people to dress in reds and golds and yellows, smell like smoke all day, and . . . light fires. Giovel and Elínla dodged a crowd of merchants arranging lantern displays along the edge of the lake, but a tall gray-haired woman broke off from the group to follow them.

"Lord Giovel! A moment or two of your time?" she asked, pulling a scroll and charcoal from a voluminous robe that looked as fire-like as anything.

"Not now, Birenlu," Giovel said. "I need to report in the Candlespire."

Birenlu matched his pace. "Perfect. Perfect. I was about to walk this way myself. I wondered if you could tell me more about the selection process for members of the Divine Order. I think it would supplement the research I'm doing on mystical septs."

"We're neither mystical nor a sept. Ask Elínla if you want to learn about that."

"My sept isn't mystical," Elínla said.

"And I've interviewed Elínla a score of times," Birenlu replied, already setting her charcoal to her parchment.

"What are you writing? I haven't even said anything—and I can't because I'm afraid I don't have time right now."

"How much warning did you have that you'd be appointed to the Order?" Birenlu asked.

"Aren't you supposed to be twice-burning some criminal's ashes or something?" Giovel asked, trying not to sound as beleaguered as he already felt.

"That's Ash Day, Lord Giovel. What about you, in your own opinion, qualified you to join the Order despite not having any training in Yulenic arts?"

They'd almost reached the great doors at the Candlespire's outer wall, so Giovel pretended to be yawning until he cleared the lintel. Obviously too long, though the sleepless night made his fatigue real. "Apologies, Birenlu. We'll have to continue this some other time. Or possibly never because I'm very busy."

Birenlu just scribbled more notes, as if he'd given her a wealth of wisdom in his responses.

The grounds within the Candlespire's outer wall were quiet, empty, with only the spire itself sprouting at their heart. It was a massive structure, built in the age before the Order existed, back when magic did more than kill people and waste cities. The walls were pale, scarred stone that looked like snow at midnight. Walkways, stairways, colonnades, and enclosed halls twisted around its great base, drawing in toward the tower's point high overhead. The Candlespire rose above everything else in Divnum. Even the Optate's Citadel seemed small in comparison to the great tower and its crown of watch posts and walkways. Before being chosen for the Order, Giovel had often walked beneath it, admiring the ancient structure. It still felt oddly dreamlike now to walk inside it daily, but in he went, through the grass-scented Sanctuary filled with river stones, a pair of trickling streams, and knee-length brush that was still green somehow. Mirrored stairways spiraled on the outside of the Sanctuary, leaving a long slant of sunlight cutting across the room from high windows overhead. The open entrance hall gave a moment of calm — the clean smell of petrichor before a storm hit.

"I didn't mention it last night, but thank you for coming so quickly with me," Elínla said, walking right to the stairs.

Giovel grunted and followed.

"I mean it, Giovel. I could have rounded up some Grays with more time, but it's always better to have a fellow member of the Order with you on these kinds of things."

"You make it sound like a picnic with the Optate. Let's hope Sur is as relaxed about it as you."

It was Sur whose authority they'd snubbed directly by running off without authorization. Much to Giovel's annoyance, though, it wasn't Sur who met them in the council chamber above the Sanctuary. It was Adni himself, Councilor to the Optate and Illumined Knight of the Divine Order. The one person with the most authority to punish them and least equipped to be decent about it. Adni was a little younger than Giovel, perhaps forty now. His hair still had brown in it, though the weight of leading the Order had lined his face and tinted his brow with white. He scowled over the round stone table in the council chamber when Giovel and Elínla walked in.

"I'd wondered where you were when you didn't report last night," was all he said at first. He didn't even look up at them.

Time to get this over with. Giovel gave a slight bow. "My apologies, Lord Adni. We were hunting a witch."

"So I hear. On whose authority?" Adni asked.

"I got the lead as he fled from his home," Elínla said. "If we hadn't acted quickly, he would have vanished."

"I'll ask again. On whose authority?"

"We acted on our own authority as members of the Order," Giovel said, stiffening. "As Elínla was saying, the witch likely would have escaped if we delayed after she discovered him."

"That's your damn defense for violating the rules of the Order?"

"We're not here to invent excuses, Lord Adni. We can give a full report, if you're amenable to hearing it."

Adni turned to look at them, his mouth twisted at the edge like a hook. "I have questions first. Who went with you?"

Elínla shuffled on her feet. "It was only the two of us."

"No Grays? No requests for help from outside arms?"

"There was no time to gather any Grays," Elínla started to say.

"And our report will answer questions like these," Giovel added.

"Then answer them now so your report can be shorter," Adni said. "How did you discover this so called witch?"

The reprimand had begun.

It was a typical debriefing, if a little long. Adni asked his questions, waited long enough for Giovel or Elínla to try answering, then pressed on before they could finish speaking. Had they prepared for a possible ambush? Had they considered that the witch Londir might have allies? Had they left word with any Grays to follow them for support? They were questions worth answering, but Adni's method of digging on without pause made his opinion clear. Perhaps it was his way of pushing them toward a wall, denying them any time to formulate a defense for their actions. Effective if paltry.

"Did you at least consider warning any of North Hold's Candles or asking them to join you?" Adni asked.

A trick question, since securing the assistance of any Candleguard or other fighters outside the Order's purview would have required at least a note from Sur, Adni, or some other senior member of the Order.

"We couldn't have diverted any Candles without asking them to violate their own orders and patrol duties," Giovel said, losing patience.

"So you left them blind to the dangers you'd brought their way instead. Perhaps you had to be sure any praise for finding this witch went to you and you alone, even while you were splitting ranks."

When would this be over? Sighing inwardly, Giovel said, "*We* acted of our own accord. Neither Elínla nor I coerced each other to go, and nor were we willing to push Candleguard into a situation that conflicted with their responsibilities."

"And what do you say for yourself, Elínla?" Adni asked. "You've been oddly silent."

She flinched visibly. "We didn't go out there on a whim, Lord Adni. We knew Londir was a witch, and that he'd already killed using Yulena. It was only a matter of time before it happened again."

"And you thought that taking along a mage as fresh as a dewdrop was a good way to handle the situation," Adni said.

"I'm not exactly defenseless," Giovel said.

"Yet while Elínla emerged unharmed, your clothes are in tatters, your leg is bleeding on that chair, your face is scraped like an old cobblestone, and you seem to have lost your sword."

This had gone far enough. "You say we're violating rules of the Order, but if you don't allow us to give our report, then you're preventing us from following those rules now," Giovel said. "May I report?"

That at least shut Adni up for a moment, if only because Giovel's lack of consternation threw off the rhythm of his attack. Then he stared for a long moment, no doubt willing Giovel to break his silence again and give more evidence of recklessness. When Giovel resisted the bait, Adni finally sighed and stood to pace around the room.

"Giovel, I'm assigning you to investigate the new spiriting."

"Another one?" Elínla asked.

Adni ignored her. "You'll find her in the maps room with Uri."

Not another spiriting. How were there so many? Now Giovel really wanted to argue, but he found his voice catching, keeping him from acknowledging the new assignment.

Adni pounced. "Does this task make you uncomfortable, Giovel? Beneath your talents, maybe, or does it just remind you of something unpleasant? Well, swallow that thought and be grateful you're trusted with anything."

And there in Adni's naked cruelty was the footing Giovel needed, normalcy enough to push past his loathing for the task at hand. "I'll proceed right away," he said with a half bow. "Unless you have more to discuss before I leave."

"You're such a pompous fake," Adni said. "And no, there's nothing more to discuss. Just know that Suresni and Dlenar got reports of more skirmishes in Yeren and North Hold. Suresni thinks multiple witches were involved in each, witches working together. The sort of thing you'd like a go at unraveling, Giovel, if I'm not very much mistaken. Not that you'll be anywhere near them, since your blatant disregard for Order law merits some consequences. Now leave this room and get on with your duties."

That was that. Giovel and Elínla both stepped out of the council chamber and filed along the Candlespire's rounded second level. Giovel was about to go his own way without another word, but Elínla grabbed him by the arm almost as soon as they were out of echoing distance from the council chamber and Adni.

"Why did you mouth off back there?" Her face twisted so sharply the blue threads of her tattoo nearly obscured her own eyes. "I risked my life for *you* specifically more than once last night! If you wanted to rattle the flagpole, the least you could do is back my argument."

Giovel pulled his arm from her grasp. "If you wanted someone who would lie for you, you chose the wrong companion."

"But you know we were right to go after Londir, and to do it quickly!"

"Which is why I came when you asked. What more do you want me to say?"

"I want you to go back and make peace with Adni! Our standing among the Order depends on him accepting our decisions and respecting them."

Ah. So this wasn't about duty or efficiency or even something as touchy as Elínla's perceptions of right or wrong. Just her own way of clawing for rank and power. Giovel supposed he shouldn't blame her. She was young and ambitious. Unlike him, she'd made a name for herself quickly—first as a paragon among the Gray Order, now as the youngest person ever to lead them, even younger than Adni himself had been when he directed the Grays fifteen years before. Elínla had something to live up to.

Giovel almost laughed to realize Elínla now stood almost exactly where she had when she'd thanked him moments before they met with Adni. Some poisons worked quickly, and Adni's ire was one of them.

Giovel cleared his throat and said, "I don't particularly care what Adni thinks about my 'position' in the Order. He has his own work to do, as I have mine."

"Adni's right. You are a pompous fake. You never would have climbed so high in the Candles without caring half a sack of grain how your commander sees you."

Wrong again, but Giovel knew better than to argue with people who had no desire to listen. So he said nothing as Elínla left him at the end of the stairs.

The spiritings were still a new occurrence. As far as Giovel knew, there had never been one before last year. And now the Order had counted over fifty, each as unexplainable as the last. They always appeared suddenly, often miles from their homes without any idea why or how. Giovel understood the experience better than most, since he'd woken to find Iremni gone and had to hunt and search and wait and fear until they found her, five days later, bruised, half-starved, and delirious in North Hold.

Let this one be different. Let it be easy to send them back home alive and sound. And let a loved one be waiting when we do.

He found the spiriting woman high in the Candlespire's maps room, as Adni had said, earnestly scanning the long wall chart of the region while alternately raising smaller maps for comparison. She wasn't a local, that was sure. She had paler skin than the bronze of Foneth or Redrem, and her hair was dark as char, like someone had dyed it in buckets of ink. Her eyes too. Lacian, maybe? But Giovel had never seen one with eyes or hair like that. The spiriting stayed focused on the maps as Giovel entered, barely glancing in his direction.

"Lord Giovel," Uri the translator said from a bench at the side of the little room. She stood and clasped her hands together in greeting.

Giovel nodded to Uri, though he avoided her eyes. Seeing her often brought back unbidden memories of Iremni. Just as meeting spiritings did.

"I take it our friend here doesn't speak much Medín?" Giovel asked.

"Not a word when she got to me," Uri said. "Smart woman, though. She learned 'map' and a few conversational words faster than a baby learns to wail."

"Where did she come from?"

"No telling as yet. Her language isn't one I know, and she can't seem to read any of the characters either. I rattled off as many city and mountain names as I could, but she didn't recognize any of them from what I gather. Now she's looking for land markers she might know."

That was an unfortunate first. Spiritings almost always came from nearby. Most were from Divnum, Belnum, North Hold, or Yeren at the farthest. Giovel had never heard of one from a region unknown to the Order. Then again there was no telling how many there really were in the first place. The Divine likely only found a handful, since witches often got there first.

Though the Order had to assume the witches were responsible in the first place, no one really knew that either. They just knew that when the spiritings began—people vanishing in one place and turning up leagues apart—witches swarmed to the spot like flies on a piece of rotting fruit. They always knew when to look for one, often where. Yes, they had to be the ones responsible. Damn them all for that.

"What's her name?" Giovel asked, trying to wave his anger aside.

"Varan," Uri said. "She kept asking me about something called Dundal. I'm assuming it's the name of her home, but I can't say whether it's a village, a city, or even some far-off queendom."

"Keep trying to find out. Have you given this info to anyone else?"

"Not yet. I'd planned to speak with a few archivists if Varan can't find this Dundal on a map."

Giovel nodded. "Keep it just to yourself and them. I'd rather no one else knows we have her until we determine where she comes from."

Uri met his eyes but asked no question. She had to know what he was thinking about.

Witches came for Iremni. They might come for this Varan as well. And no one deserves to go through the hellish experience my Iremni did.

When the Candleguard had found her, they all thought Iremni would recover. She'd been hurt, but not direly. She stayed skittish and confused for weeks, though, always peering into corners and shadowed holes as if afraid of finding glyphs there, then holding on to steady surfaces as if she expected to be spirited again unless she kept a hard grip on something. Iremni wouldn't talk about what had happened to her. Never said whether witches had found her after the spiriting. Wouldn't even mention what had occurred in the days between her disappearance and an old Candle finding her in a stinking hovel by North Hold's watch tower. In a way, it was like she never came back at all.

Then she took ill. After that she stopped responding to either Inorovel's or Giovel's voice. Soon the madness took hold; they had to tie her down to stop her from throwing her own head against the floor. Then she died.

So Adni's right, Giovel thought. I can never face another spiriting without wondering what Iremni went through, or whether—even when we get you back to your home—you'll find yourself broken like she was. It's why I hate seeing people like you.

He stepped closer to Varan to examine the same maps she stared over. She still focused on them, not even glancing up until Uri said, "Varan," and, indicating to him, "Giovel."

Varan blinked her dark eyes, said, "Giovel," then repeated her own name while looking Giovel in the face. After that she was back to looking at the maps, peering across the surfaces in search of something neither Uri nor Giovel could find.

Giovel sighed. Almost no indication where she might hail from. The only marker that gave him any hope was a crest on the back of her dress, what looked like a red claw emblazoned in thick stitching. The cut of her dress didn't look like livery, but the claw at least formed a distinct shape.

"Ask your archivists about this claw sigil as well," Giovel said to Uri.

"Planning to. I'm thinking it might at least give us a point of comparison somewhere in their records."

"Let's hope so. Have you gathered any other information as to why she might have been spirited?"

"That's the question worth a crown. But no crown for me, I suppose. Varan doesn't act like she expects rescue, so I'm doubting she's a noble. She does seem educated. Might be an advisor to someone powerful. A potential ransom, perhaps?"

"Try to find out," Giovel said.

"I'm sure I'll come up with something once she and I understand each other enough to converse. Anything else you'd like to know?"

"Where did she appear?"

"Here in Divnum. Not five hundred paces from the Candlespire, actually."

That was news. Giovel had heard of spiritings from Divnum, but never of spiritings arriving *in* Divnum, right on the doorstep of the Order. Their appearances in North Hold and Belnum offered the strongest evidence that witches were responsible. But witches spiriting someone right into the corner of the Divine Order?

One more thought to brush aside for now, since Giovel had no way of finding such answers.

"Varan," he said. He waited until she turned and looked him in the eye again. "I promise to help you find your home, back to your people."

He knew she couldn't decipher his words any more than he could see her thoughts. From the softening in her face, though, he hoped she could comprehend some splinter of what he meant.

As you should. As anyone would who knows something of your experience like I do. I won't leave some brother or sister or husband wondering about you like the witches left me. I'll get you back where you belong.

Uri said a few words, some in Medín and some Giovel assumed she'd already learned of Varan's own language. Varan nodded in turn and clasped her hands clumsily, like someone who had just learned the gesture. So even that was new to her.

While Varan returned to her study of the maps, Giovel stepped outside and waved for Uri to follow him out of earshot. "If it takes time to find her home, I want you to assess her skills and see about getting her some kind of work."

"Work?"

"It's what people do who aren't highly learned translators."

"No need to insult my profession. How will I go about finding something for her, though?"

"You have the Order's approval to situate her somewhere. That ought to be enough."

"But where? I seem to recall you not wanting many others to know about her."

"Here in Divnum, then," Giovel said. "I'm sure you can find something."

After all, there was a war on. War made work for everyone.

SEARCHING

They talk about Yulen, but it means so many different things. It's the red moon that never leaves the south sky, day or night alike. It's like a mystical religion. It's also the source of their witchcraft.

—The Witherclaw Witch; a letter to Recia.

YULEN GLOWED MORE brightly than usual that night, a blood-colored lamp in the southern sky. Apart from its shadowed haze, only dim, greasy lanterns lit the streets of North Hold below. Perhaps that was for the best. North Hold—North Old as outsiders had started calling it—tended to look worse the more closely one observed it. The red dimness also let Etelier move more freely than he might otherwise.

Etelier waited near the corner of an abandoned rope shop and what might once have been a grain house, judging from the sweet rot wafting from it now. He breathed into his hands to stave off the cold. Every few moments he turned to scan nearby streets and the long shadows stretching from stone and wooden walls.

Nothing moved. Claravena was late.

Maybe she'd been caught. Etelier always had to wonder nowadays. He doubted the Divine could find or pin a crime on her without help, but he'd been wrong before. He'd doubted they'd find *any* of his fellow witches. Three of them were dead now. Claravena was smarter than the others, to be sure, but they were all vulnerable.

And I might be the most vulnerable of all, Etelier thought as he breathed into cupped hands again.

He shifted position and tested a wrist-thrower, just in case anyone else came along. At last Claravena appeared in the distance, dressed in a cowl of rusty brown and ash gray. She'd almost be invisible if her copper hair didn't reflect so much of Yulen's light.

"Were you followed?" Etelier asked when she came close enough to speak.

"Maybe at first. I couldn't tell."

"You lost someone?"

"Tranin and I left a trap for them."

"I don't know how you keep yourself hidden when you're building spells left and right and letting strangers see them like you were selling pictures of the Citadel."

"No one ever knows it's me."

Etelier wasn't going to win this argument tonight, so he just grunted. "Let's forget it. We're not far from the place I'd like to search."

"You really think the Divine would hide a library out here, of all places? It would be hard to visit without someone being suspicious."

"Not when they raid North Hold every few days," Etelier said. "They spend more time here than in Divnum now."

"Maybe. At least it would be easy for them to hide here."

Claravena was right, of course. Never mind that Etelier had searched half the wrecked buildings on this street while waiting. There were more than enough hiding spaces in North Hold for all the city's vagrants, whores, poachers, thieves, and cutthroats. Enough for Redremel, rebels, and dissidents too. Maybe even enough for witches and Divine alike.

"Where is this place you want to check?" Claravena asked.

"Just a few turns away. Follow me. And keep your head down. If there is someone there, I don't want anyone recognizing us."

"You're the one in danger of that."

Right again. Etelier had the disadvantages of unusual height, pale gray eyes that stood out against the clay color of his face, and a memorably deep voice. He'd never blended in well. It made it hard to lead a coterie of witches; first meetings usually had to be final ones for him, no matter how costly or violent that might make the meeting.

He led Claravena up two sagging side streets, across an overgrown square, through a plot of brown grass and out again between a few tall houses and trees with turning leaves. The streets smelled less like refuse and more like autumn here, with the scents of grass and earth diluting North Hold's usual stink. Perhaps someone had cleaned the nearest streets, even if only a little. Some patch of civilization the Redremel war hadn't scarred. Or some hidden bunker surrounded by ruins.

"That's the one," Etelier said softly and pointed ahead.

The street split three ways, with a jagged wall of wood and crumbling stone arching around two alleys. A side street stretched between rows of mismatched hovels, leaving one leaning, connected mess of stairs and doorways that might have been a guild hall once.

"What a death trap," Claravena said. "We'll lose them if we start bursting into the wrong places, and it would be easy for anyone to see us coming from this direction."

"I'm counting on that," Etelier said.

He strode forward and drew a large glyph in the road—a half circle broken by five equal lines. He connected to Yulen and the glyph flared red, brightening the street visibly.

"You're a risky fool," Claravena sighed as Etelier began outlining another glyph.

He planned to stay a risky fool until they found the Divine's library. "I'll keep them distracted when they show themselves," he said. "You get inside."

Claravena darted to the side to find a way over the wall, while Etelier moved carefully around his two full glyphs to outline another.

His risk worked. Before his third glyph was done, the sounds of shuffling feet and mumbled orders echoed in one of the alleys. Three figures appeared in the shadows, right arms curled back as if to ready wrist-throwers. They left a door exposed behind them, a clear entrance to their lair. Etelier rushed toward it.

Sure enough, all three figures snapped their arms out and back, hurling darts in Etelier's direction. They loosed all at once, though, giving Etelier time to skid and roll right beneath their missiles. Not Candleguard, then. Not trained fighters at all. Just fools with weapons and something worth keeping under cloak and guard.

Etelier threw his own arm straight to launch a return dart, sending his attackers stumbling back for cover. Then he lashed out with his left arm to activate his first glyph. A puff of dust rose as the force of the spell pushed the dirt-carved glyph apart and the spell flared to life. Half a breath later, a fist-sized globule smashed into the nearest figure's shoulder, spinning him around with a crunch. The Hammer, Etelier called it. It was barely visible, a blurred projectile like a disc of clear glass that vanished on impact.

He struck with two more Hammers before the first fool could recover. One Hammer broke free from his control and punched into the stone wall, but the second took a tall man in the face in a splash of blood. The spells' residue hummed faintly as they dissipated in the air.

The last defender turned to run the direction he'd come. Etelier snapped his arm out again and darted the fleeing man right between the shoulders. It didn't slow the man yet, but the rustwood on the dart's head would do that soon enough.

Two more guards exited the corner building from another doorway, these ones with swords and twin-shot handbows. So it wasn't all fools guarding this place after all. Etelier dove for cover behind a tree. Four bolts thudded near enough by him to be sure these two knew how to aim.

Etelier dropped to the ground and outlined one more Hammer before his attackers could reload their handbows or advance too far. Then he snapped his right arm out around the tree to hurl another cover dart. The two new guards flinched but kept moving in his direction as the dart stuck harmlessly to a wall.

"Where'd the woman go?" one of the guards called. It was the one Etelier's first Hammer struck in the shoulder, now limping and clutching his side but joining the other two in their advance. Not much time to shake them away, then.

Etelier clambered up his cover tree, swinging himself out between two splits in the trunk where he could see his attackers but they'd have trouble spotting him. It provided just enough cover as they loosed their handbows again and the wounded one launched another round of darts.

"Step any closer and I'll light your skins on fire," Etelier announced, scraping a second glyph in the soft bark by his face.

"Prove it, witch," the wounded man called back. He kept advancing as his companions paused to reload their handbows.

Etelier swung his left arm out again, this time aiming his ground-drawn Hammer right at the head of the man whose shoulder he'd already hit. The spell smashed into the side of his skull where his ear met the line of his jaw. It was a grazing blow, really, but it still hit with enough force to send the man's head whipping back and to rip half his ear off his face. He went down without time even to howl in pain.

The two with handbows hesitated. Then Claravena leaped out behind them and struck with a massive Dimmer. A bubble of shadow crashed into their backs and hurled them off their feet. They didn't stumble far, but they were slow to rise, clutching at their faces and turning wildly around. Blinded for the moment.

Etelier jumped to the ground and hit each of their necks with a dart. Then he planted a foot on one's back and pulled both their weapons out of reach.

Easy as that. He hadn't even needed the Hammer he carved in the tree.

"I hit one more with a dart," he said. "We need to find him before he signals anyone."

"Done," Claravena replied. "I got him in the alley."

"Dead?"

"Bleeding out. Immobile at the very least. I couldn't see any others."

Etelier nodded and pulled one of the remaining guards aside to bind him. The man managed to spit in Etelier's face before Etelier forced his hands behind him and bound them together. Definitely not Candleguard, judging by the taste of sour vinegar in the man's spit. That was a shame.

"Who are you?" Etelier asked as Claravena tied the other one.

"Drop yourself in Cold Lake," the man said, trying to spit again.

Etelier pulled his captive's arms upward toward the shoulder blades. The man cried out and writhed in pain.

"I'll ask again. Who are you?"

"Wait, wait!" the other said, trying to raise his hands defensively. Claravena kicked his wrists aside and shoved her prisoner against the stone wall. "We're nobody!" the man all but whimpered.

"So nobody tried to dart, bow, and threaten us tonight?" Etelier asked. "Nobody spit on me? Nobody refused to answer my question? Maybe nobody will be missed in the morning when the Candles find these bodies."

Claravena finished binding her prisoner and pushed him onto his stomach, ignoring his pleas for another chance to speak. "Let's look inside nobody's little fortress."

They dragged their prisoners to the edge of the building, gagged them, and stepped inside in quick succession, Etelier with his arms curled back to throw another dart or loose his last Hammer. The building looked deserted. If it could be called a building at all. More like a ramshackle addition to two neighboring structures, a sort of wooden tunnel leeching off the walls. It was windowless, lit with sputtering candles and an oil lamp, and smelled like pickled tubers. A few sacks and barrels lined the walls. It was empty otherwise.

"I'll check the side where those three first emerged," Etelier said. "You take the upstairs corner."

The creaking wooden hallway led him to what appeared to be an old moneylender's shop, with dusty scales and logbooks lining shelves along the walls and a scarred table barring the way to the exit. It too was deserted, though Etelier made sure to check outside before turning back toward the prisoners and Claravena.

No Divine secrets. No hum from past glyphs lingering. No well-protected records.

He'd spent nearly a week scouting the site, paying for information, watching men ferry goods in and out, hoping this, at last, really was the Divine's hidden library. Instead it looked like nothing more than a cutpurse's hideaway. A complete waste.

"Anything, Claravena?" Etelier called.

"Some cheap contraband," Claravena replied down a narrow stairwell. "I think what we have here is some smuggler's bolt hole."

Damn. She'd been right after all. Etelier's source had insisted that the Divine Order moved in and out of the spot every few days, always under cover of nightfall and seldom at the same time twice. Well, of course they did. This was just the sort of place bandits or Redremel spies would hide. No wonder the Divine had been sneaking around too. They might be back any minute, snaring two witches when they'd come for a band of lowlifes.

Claravena returned downstairs with a small pouch, which she tossed to Etelier. He smelled pungent herbs as he caught it.

"They're making this upstairs," she said. "Either a poison or a drug."

"So they really are nobodies."

"North Hold's commonest kind."

Outside, the two prisoners gave muffled shouts in unison. The wooden wall of the bolt hole shuddered. Then the street was quiet.

"What was that?" Etelier asked.

Claravena raised a hand to her lips. She inched toward her edge of the room, where holes in the wooden slats might allow a shallow view of the streets. Her eyes went round when she looked out. Then she dropped to the floor and waved for Etelier to do likewise.

None too soon. A flare of green light cut through the walls around them just then, sending stone, splintered wood, chunks of mortar, and clouds of dirt showering across the chamber.

That would be the Divine.

Etelier spat dust and crawled for the stairs, signaling to Claravena to move as he did. Another spell tore through the walls as they went, causing the entire structure to buckle precariously inward.

Etelier cursed himself for not moving sooner, especially when Claravena might have been followed. Such an easy trap—find some fools' hideout, tip an informant that the Divine were interested, and wait for witches to arrive. Now we're the fools, Etelier thought. Fools with waves of Yulena erupting right beside us.

Claravena reached the stairs and raced upward. Etelier was just beginning to follow when a splash of pale light hit the center of the stairwell in front of him. The spell snapped the stairs' support beams like twigs. Bits of rotted wood rained across what was left of the room, and the entire building began to cave in with a wrenching creak. Etelier had nowhere to go but out. He scrambled to his feet and leaped through the holes the last few spells had opened in the outer wall.

The building collapsed behind him. Brick and rock scraped together and tumbled into the center, while the leaning staircase snapped outward like a loose pennant in the wind. A few panes of filthy glass shattered at Etelier's back, sending a spray of shards over him. He rolled on the ground and waited for more debris behind or a torrent of magic in front.

All he felt was the crunching glass, followed by a wave of dirt as the collapsed building settled. The Divine Order wasn't waiting for him. It was just one figure in the street—a bony, filthy woman with round eyes. And a dozen glyphs glowing in the dirt around her.

Strike while you have the chance. Hurl a piece of broken wood. Dart her in the face. Use that last Hammer carved in tree bark. Etelier thought of ten more moves in the moment he saw her. But he didn't know this woman, didn't know who else was nearby, didn't know whether Claravena had made it through the collapse or not. So he made the patient move and raised his arms slowly as if to show he was unarmed. Would that she didn't notice the loop where his wrist-thrower connected to one finger.

"On your feet," the witch said.

Another chunk of stone and wood dropped nearby, making Etelier jump. The woman flinched too. So she was not in so much control that her own destruction couldn't startle her. He might be able to use that.

"On your *feet*," she said again. Her voice shook. "And step away from the building."

Etelier pushed himself upright and walked gingerly over shards and heaps of debris. What if he seized one of the woman's own glyphs from her? It wasn't difficult in concept. Didn't matter who made the glyph—just who summoned Yulen's power by it. The cluster of exposed glyphs marked the woman as a new witch, or a secluded one at the very least. The thing was, Etelier didn't recognize any of her shapes and patterns. Trying to wield ones he *did* know was challenging enough; seizing unknown glyphs had killed more witches than anything else had. So Etelier did as she said and backed away, praying Claravena was somewhere upstairs in the neighboring structure, watching and ready.

"Are you one of the Grays?" he asked to distract the witch. "I didn't know they sent you out alone."

"I'm asking the questions," the woman said, though her voice still shook as if her own words startled her. "Where's the other one? The woman you send around recruiting for you."

Etelier made a show of glancing around. He found the two bound smugglers by the wreckage heap, both dead now. No Claravena.

"She was out here a moment ago. I sent her to follow the smugglers who escaped."

"That's a lie! I watched her go into that building with you."

"I sent her out the back when we found another exit," Etelier said. "She must be nearby. Everyone from here to Tovómil will have heard that ruckus."

Sure enough, voices echoed in the distance. The witch glanced sidelong down the streets, just as Etelier hoped she would. Once again he thought of striking. Using his Hammer would be difficult from this angle, since he'd have no line of sight from his glyph and might hit himself if he missed the witch. Perhaps he could take her in the neck with his thrower, though. At this close distance, one dart might even be enough to kill her. He hesitated too long, and the woman looked back in his direction. She kept her eyes on him as she moved sideways and ducked behind a pile of broken crates.

"Call her," the witch said.

"What do you want with us?"

"Call her or I'll hit you with every spell I've made!"

Etelier knew better than to argue. His foe might be a fool, but her spells would kill the same as anyone's. After all, they'd demolished half a building in only a moment.

So Etelier called, "Claravena? Can you hear me?" and hoped she'd heard enough not to answer. If she was still alive at all.

Claravena appeared farther up the street a moment later. Dirt covered her, and she moved with a halting limp. It looked like she'd twisted an ankle, though she seemed unharmed otherwise. Etelier wasn't sure whether to sigh in relief or curse that she'd answered him.

"Etelier?" she called back. "Etelier, I can't see you. There's something in my eyes."

"I'm here," he replied.

And you'd better wipe your eyes clean or we might both be dead.

Claravena limped in his direction, murmuring softly as if in pain each time she put weight on her leg. Etelier began shifting one foot on the ground, trying to slide toward cover. He'd need to strike as fast as a spear of lightning in summer.

When Claravena was just ten paces from Etelier, the witch stood from behind her crates.

"Stop where you are."

Claravena halted, still murmuring and wiping at her eyes.

"Do you know my voice?" the witch asked.

A pause. "No. Who's there?"

"You visited my home yesterday. You burst into my house and threatened me and my family if I didn't join you."

A look of recognition crossed Claravena's face. "Unalis. I remember your voice now."

Unalis raised her hands but pointed them at Etelier. "You, witch. You send people like this woman to do your dirty work? To drag people like me to your side?"

He did indeed. And he always wondered if he should rein his recruiters in a little more.

"Yes, Etelier sent me!" Claravena said, now dropping to her knees. "Please, don't blame me! He would have killed me if I hadn't followed his orders!"

"Prove it," Unalis said. She tossed a knife into the street. It landed nearly halfway between Claravena and Etelier. "One of you is going to help me find someone—someone who *left me* because of your visit last night. The other one stays here. You decide who is who."

Was she fooling? Etelier might have laughed if the witch wasn't so reckless, not to mention unusually powerful. But she seemed to mean what she said. Etelier and Claravena met each other's eyes. Then Claravena dove for the blade.

That was all Etelier needed to know they'd be alright. The limp was gone now, Claravena's seeming blindness too, and Unalis seemed not to realize it. Imbecile. All she saw was a servant willing to stab her master to save her head. So Etelier played along and leaped for the knife too, pretending to trip while Claravena fumbled with it. Only her fumbling was very controlled, outlining a tiny glyph, no bigger than a handsbreadth. It flared to life almost immediately.

They unleashed their glyphs at the same time, Etelier's bark-carved Hammer and Claravena's Talon. The Hammer hit Unalis's upraised arm aside while Claravena's Talon sent a tiny bolt of shadow springing up at her. It cut right through Unalis's chest, spraying her front with blood. She only had time to open her mouth in shock.

It was how Claravena usually killed. She worked Yulena without delay, without even a tell. It made her so fiendishly effective, especially when accompanying a tall, obvious witch like Etelier, whose thrashing tell was the perfect misdirection for Claravena's imperceptible one.

Unalis's body slapped to the ground. Claravena tossed the knife onto it and wiped dirt from her face. Calm as ever.

"What a waste," was all she said.

It always was. That was the price of fighting the Divine Order.

Etelier let out a pent-up breath. "Are you hurt?"

"No. You?"

"Just a week's worth of worry. I didn't know you tried recruiting this one."

"Raf and I tried together. I didn't think it was worth even mentioning," Claravena said with a tiny shrug. "Her husband hadn't known she'd awakened. I doubted he'd let her live after I revealed Unalis's secret."

And Claravena had left, accepting the woman's death as a possibility. Etelier wondered if he should hate her for that. Or if she had done Unalis a favor in some twisted way. Being a witch tended to drain whatever well of mercy they'd possessed before Yulen awakened them, and being hunted by the Divine only sped the drainage up.

"Let's get out of North Hold," Etelier said. "I've had enough close calls for one night."

They left the smugglers' den open. What was left of it anyway. They also left the bodies in the street as they turned to leave.

It was early morning when Etelier reached his home in Belnum. The streets were empty. Smoke was just beginning to rise from bakeries and smithies as their inhabitants coaxed fires to begin their work. Etelier had a few hours, at best, before he reported to Tovómil for his own work on one of the new manor houses. Claravena had tried to persuade him to abandon day labor. You're a witch, she'd say. The rest of us can get money for whatever your family needs. But Etelier had to believe he wasn't like Tranin, Claravena, Noru, or the others, that he wasn't a witch because he enjoyed having Yulen's power.

His little house pressed against two others at the end of a dusty road, facing the east edge of Foneth and the yellow waves of field, pasture, and grassland beyond. It was dark when he arrived, but Pramél sat by the door with a faded blanket over her shoulders. Waiting for him, as always.

"Are you hurt?" she asked as he closed the door behind him.

"Not this time," Etelier replied. It was their normal greeting now. If anything could be normal since he'd awakened.

He removed his coat and boots and walked to Mota's tiny room behind theirs. Mota was sound asleep, with waves of hair obscuring her face and one arm thrown wildly across her own forehead. Her breathing was so quiet Etelier barely heard it, yet steady as a pendulum. He slowed his own breath to match so he could feel his chest move in time with Mota's little body.

It always comforted him, hearing her breathing while she slept. After her sickness last winter, he and Pramél had worried she'd never breathe again. It had taken Mota weeks to do so without rasping and sputtering, even after they scraped together enough coins to have a decent healer tend her. Maybe that was why the steadiness of the sound relieved Etelier now. A small life grown in part from his own, continuing to draw breath in and out each day even after all she'd experienced. She was a strong little girl. His strong little girl.

After a little while, Etelier ducked into his own room to undress for bed. Once again Pramél waited for him. Her eyes seemed to be on the rough stone wall rather than on him.

"Did you find anything?" she asked.

"Criminals. A witch Claravena tried to threaten into joining us. Nothing else."

"Thank you for trying, Etelier."

Pramél said it every time. It was hard to tell if she really meant it.

"You don't believe we'll find anything. Do you?" Etelier asked.

"Not anymore. Even if the Divine had some secret library, they'd never store everything there or let anyone else close to it."

"There has to be something. They've kept in power too long not to have a record somewhere."

"So people say."

The Divine had that old goat Hirnu Pala experimenting with new spells every day, fifty Grays out using Yulena to corner awakenings, not to mention seven hundred years of time rediscovering magic like people had worked before their Order came to be. There had to be more to it than just Hammers and Talons, Dimmers, Nettles, and Tremors. The spiriting spell alone proved that.

"By all means, keep looking," Pramél added. "Just know that I hate to see you waste every night and trudge through every day exhausted for nothing."

"I don't really have much of a choice."

Pramél's fingers brushed over his hand, but her touch seemed void of desire or warmth. "You're on a fruitless hunt," she said.

He thought of Mota. He couldn't believe his wife. For Mota's sake, he wouldn't let himself.

HOME

HOME WAS A narrow old house by the edge of the Featherwood Forest. Even late in autumn, smells of red pear blossoms wafted from the trees, and starlinnets sang from the shadowed branches most nights. Only a few other homes stood nearby.

Giovel wondered sometimes if he should move Inorovel somewhere new. They could live nearly anywhere they wanted now. The Order didn't compensate for his work much more than the Candleguard had, but no one would deny a Divine Mage a safe, comfortable home wherever he wanted one. It might be nice to live closer to the Candlespire, or even the Citadel. Somewhere with no memories of a sick, distant Iremni.

But in the end Giovel never thought he could leave the quiet trees by the Featherwood, because it was a place he and Iremni had settled and made home together. The house had plenty of garden space behind it, despite not being a large structure itself, plus the beautiful Sanctuary Iremni had designed—a square mirror pool fed by a tiny waterfall from the Iceflow. It was the only place left that Giovel felt truly free from politics and positioning, from knives in the shadows, from scrutiny and judgment and public expectation. The one place left where he could stop being a Divine Mage, at least for a few still moments.

Inorovel was sitting by the mirror pool when Giovel arrived home. She was fourteen, skinny, with pale hair like Iremni's. Black dirt covered her face, and she had ink spattered over her hands, but she smiled as brightly as ever.

"Another night on duty?"

"Something like that," Giovel said, hanging his cowl behind the door. "Not that my superiors were pleased to find out what I'd been doing. What happened to your face?"

"I was climbing."

"There's mud in trees now?"

"I fell into Cloud Lake," Inorovel said.

"Wonderful. Now I don't know whether to punish you for being reckless or praise you for having the sense to keep a lake under you for a safe landing."

"What happened to *your* face, da?" Inorovel asked, indicating the long scrape past his left eye.

"Just a shard of my sword snapping off in an explosion. What do you feel like eating tonight?"

They talked about nothing as they cooked rice with dulin bulbs. Then they laughed when Inorovel burned a pan of peppers and Giovel scorched half the rice. Giovel poured the crusted remains of his cooking in the back of the garden, and they ate what portions they could salvage while watching the sun sink over the forest and Yulen's dim red glow spread across the ground.

"I might be getting a new assignment of interest to you," Giovel said.

"None of your assignments are interesting."

"This one's different. I might have to participate in a play for the Optate."

Inorovel sputtered while drinking mintwater. "You?"

"It's just a rumor for now," Giovel said. "Apparently each of the Optate's councilors has to send someone to be part of a performance every year. I never heard anyone mention it in the Candleguard, though, so it might be something Lord Adni made up just to scare me."

"Maybe the Candles just wanted to keep it secret to stop anyone from coming to see them. What play are they doing?"

"It's called *The Golden Swan of Spring*."

"That's a play for four-year-old children. What if someone recognized you? I'd be so embarrassed."

Giovel grimaced. "I'm glad you understand the gravity of my responsibilities. If they do assign me, I'll try getting a costume that covers my face."

"Da, I mean it. If you're in a child's play and anyone else finds out, I'll be laughed at for months. Years."

"Well, I think being in the Optate's play will buy me some amnesty from normal decorum. I can probably arrest anyone who laughs."

"Why would they waste a Divine Mage's time with something like that?" Inorovel asked.

"Probably as a way to keep us in line," Giovel said.

The Divine Order had almost total freedom to fulfill their mandate; they could bring in any Lance, Candle, Lawrit, or even elected official that showed real evidence of using Yulena without authorization to do so. But put them on a stage with children in animal costumes, singing songs about eating your fruit and drinking your broth? They'd be as weak as a trowel against a mountain.

"I thought you were supposed to be . . . researching magic or something," Inorovel said.

Giovel sighed. He'd thought so too.

But his short hours at home weren't the time to worry over that. It was time to talk to Inorovel and enjoy the last few evenings of half-warmth before winter set in, so they scrubbed char and burnt vegetable from their dishes, sat in the Sanctuary together to meditate, then put on cloaks and walked beneath the old Divnum walls beyond the forest, admiring the same carvings and symbols they'd seen a thousand times before.

Sometimes Inorovel looked so much like Iremni that Giovel would almost stumble, would almost want to look away, even run away. But sometimes he remembered there was no time for that. Her years as a child were ending all too fast. Giovel steeled himself, pushed Iremni from his mind, and tried to hold on to the days he had then and there.

ASSIGNMENTS

*People here who awaken to magecraft have three main pathways open to them.
First, they can reveal themselves and submit their powers to the Optacracy.
Second, they can try quelling their own abilities, keeping them hidden in exchange
for the semblance of an ordinary life. Third, they can use their magecraft in
opposition to the Optacracy. I seem to represent an aberration to all these paths.*

    —The Witherclaw Witch; a letter to Golkorun.

As a child, Giovel had learned that the Order's chief design was to
safeguard the world from untamable magic. He felt the weight of that
responsibility from the moment he was relieved of his duties with the
Candleguard and named a Mage of the High Optate's Divine Order.
The worst part of his appointment wasn't the great scope of the work,
however. It was the endless meetings. Most represented nothing more
than a requirement to detail *something* Adni could relay to the Optate's
other councilors, so it was much like the sequence of communication
Giovel knew from the Candleguard. And just as onerous as ever.

After bringing Varan to meet with Uri again, Giovel joined
meetings on suspected witch sightings, the general state of training for
the Gray Order—the circle of lower mages Elínla directed—and even a
deadly dull meeting with the Lawrits on compliance and certification
procedures for new mages in Foneth. Then there were coordination
councils with the Spireblades and Citadel Guard each in succession,
which entailed more sitting and silence and repeated announcements
of things Giovel doubted he needed to know, since the Order had no

real say in what anyone else did, and since he had no real say in the Order anyway.

His penultimate appointment was the most daunting. It was his personal session with Hirnu Pala, second-most senior member of the Divine and Observer for the Order. They called it a council meeting. It was really just Hirnu's way of training Giovel in how to use the Yulena to which he'd recently awakened. Like drill, but with no one there but him.

"Shouldn't I just practice with the Grays?" Giovel asked, entering the stone-walled yard behind Hirnu's home. "This hardly seems worth your time, and their grasp of Yulena is just as good as mine."

"Their grasp is probably better than yours," Hirnu said. She sat, as usual, on a thin mat at the center of the yard, sketching shapes on her sand tablet. She couldn't be much older than Giovel, but she managed to appear as if she had three hundred years of wisdom to her. Perhaps because she never looked anyone in the eye when speaking. It made Giovel think Hirnu was conversing with the clouds and had to descend to see who was interrupting her elevated discussion.

"We're going to start with the Rod today," Hirnu said, holding out her tablet with the glyph drawn for reference.

Not again. They'd worked on the Rod across the last four sessions. Giovel still wouldn't be any good at it, and it didn't matter, did it? As far as he could gather, he was chosen for the Order because he was a decent Candle who just happened to awaken during this war with the Redremel. Learning a glyph or two wasn't going to change him.

Giovel said nothing, though, not to Hirnu. He just pulled his own sand tablet from his deep coat pocket and traced the shape of the Rod, pushing his tablet's magnetic sands aside with a finger.

"Again," Hirnu said.

He smoothed the iron sands by sliding the flattening bar across it. Then he sketched the shape again. And again. And ten times more without any change that he could tell. At least Hirnu trusted him to practice on the tablet itself. He'd heard that new Grays had to use charcoal and paper for weeks before they'd be entrusted with a valuable tool like a sand tablet, all to make doubly sure no witches got their hands on such devices.

When Giovel had produced the glyph forty times, Hirnu slid the flattening bar across her own tablet. "Make it from memory," she said.

Giovel did so.

"Again."

Was this what she did every day? As Observer for the Order, her primary responsibility was to research and expand Yulenic lore—to study new ways to utilize magic. Since her methods suggested much more caution than imagination, Giovel understood why the Order hadn't discovered anything useful in five centuries.

They hardly touched the real practice of breathing Yulenic life into the glyphs, let alone activating them to cast the spell. Then again, even wielding well-known spells was dangerous. People died doing it, or lost control of botched glyphs and killed passersby. Perhaps Hirnu took the risks especially seriously since she alone was exempt from the laws restricting magical experiments.

After what felt like an hour of Giovel drawing the same shape, Hirnu finally ordered him to cast a completed spell. He failed.

He was able to connect his glyph to Yulen after a few focused tries, bringing red light flaring through the outline in his tablet, but activating that finished glyph was another matter altogether. When Giovel finally did manage to activate the spell, he miscast it. The spell jetted out from his tablet and hit him in the stomach. It was like being whacked with a spear butt. Giovel tumbled back, clutching his side and grunting through the blunt pain.

Hirnu watched in silence, patient old bat. She voiced no criticism over his failures to work the spell correctly and proffered no advice on how to do it better. After a pause she simply said, "Practice this before we meet again."

Then she dismissed Giovel so they could both go to yet another meeting.

Adni and Elínla were already seated in the Order's council chamber when Giovel arrived, and Ralden followed soon after. Ralden was third in seniority among the order, an austerely immaculate woman who never seemed to have a hair straying from her head or a wrinkle in her gray cape. Hirnu appeared a moment after Giovel, though he had no idea how she had caught up so quickly.

"Dlenar and Suresni won't be with us today," Adni announced. "I'll share their reports after we hear our guest. I believe you've met Giovel, Commander?"

Their guest appeared to be Zuris Medín, Vermilion Commander of the Lances. Zuris met Giovel's eye and nodded while fingering his enormous mustache. He was a broad-shouldered man about Giovel's age with a brilliant tabard that glittered like golden fire and seemed to make his copper face glow even in the cold light of the council chamber. Giovel returned Zuris's nod. He didn't know Zuris well, but they'd crossed paths in Giovel's last two years with the Candleguard. One of the few Giovel knew who bore the Medín family name without being an utter ass.

"And what does our esteemed guest have to discuss with us?" Ralden asked, eyes narrowing.

"He's suspicious about some of your textile guild's dealings," Adni said.

Ralden stiffened. "How dare you. Commander Zuris, I assure you that my guild does everything in line with the laws of—"

"That's not why he's here," Hirnu cut in. "Zuris, please explain to the rest of the order."

"You're as droll as drama, Adni," Ralden mumbled. "And a river of piss too."

Zuris gave a slight bow before he began. "I'm here to ask your support in an unpleasant measure of the Lances' war effort. To be quite clear, it has to do with an idea I've formed of removing a number of Foneth's Sanctuaries."

Silence. He'd been right. It was an unpleasant idea.

"Will you hear me out?" Zuris asked before going on.

No one seemed eager to speak first. Giovel certainly wasn't, but he hadn't known Zuris to put forward an idea that wasn't well-formed, so he said, "Go on, Zuris."

"It comes down to this," Zuris said with a frown. "I know we all value the Sanctuary spaces we've preserved for so many generations. In fact, you're right in the heart of some of the finest Sanctuaries in all Foneth. But the fact is that the size of our city makes it nearly impossible to defend. If we were to consolidate more of the city, especially within Divnum's walls, we'd stand a much better chance against the Redremel."

"You mean cut down forests?" Ralden asked. "Clear meadows out? Drain our lakes?"

"Many of them can stay just as they are," Zuris said. "The lakes and rivers are defensible already. It's the other Sanctuaries we can't adequately cover."

"We've done it before," Ralden said. "We've done it a thousand times or more."

"That's true. But we've failed another thousand times as well. Look at North Hold."

Silence again. Giovel had often thought of how difficult it was to watch over Foneth's massive districts with so few Lances to counter the Redremel and even fewer Candleguard for street patrols. Divnum had its walls, of course, and each of the estates to the south had hills, rivers, moats, and trenches, not to mention fighting forces of their own. But Belnum crowded outside Divnum's walls like a clump of wild mushrooms, and North Hold spilled far out into the open, indefensible edge of the city. Too much ground to guard.

Zuris's point rang true to those thoughts, that they might well have kept North Hold if it weren't spread so far afield. Furthermore, the Redremel were just as good at killing in Foneth's Sanctuaries as elsewhere.

"You're not just talking about spots of land, Commander," Elínla said. "These are sacred places. Half the septs here have a unique history with ten or more of the city's Sanctuaries."

"And many more individuals as well," Hirnu said quietly.

"I know I'm asking you to consider immense sacrifice," Zuris said. "But please give it serious reflection. We don't know whether the Redremel will wait until spring to strike again, and even if they do, we'll likely be woefully outnumbered. If, however, we consolidate the city into Divnum's walls, we can protect thousands of those civilians most vulnerable to Redremel reach."

"Let me see if I understand you," Adni said. "You're saying we could crunch Foneth closer together. Maybe clear out some of the city's open spaces and somehow move whole streets, whole districts of buildings?"

"You understand me correctly."

"It's a preposterous idea," Ralden said. "It'll take years."

"More than twenty years, by my estimations," Zuris said, now looking at the ground.

"And what about the costs?" Ralden asked. "Who will pay for it? Just consolidating a worthless pit like North Hold would cost hundreds of thousands of spans."

"Tens of millions, I estimate," Zuris replied. He pulled a set of scrolls from his orange tabard. "I've drawn a phased plan for how it might be done, so I'm well aware it would be an arduous undertaking."

They leaned around to see what this mad idea might look like. Giovel found himself curious as well, despite how distasteful the whole notion was to him. He had too many memories in too many Sanctuaries to like the idea of removing even one of them. Memories by himself, with Inorovel, and with Iremni.

Zuris's plans were detailed and well-organized. He'd charted a modest approach to clearing the edges of Belnum and North Hold first, pulling residents and a handful of buildings all the way to the center of Divnum. It looked as if later stages of his plan would involve building new walls to encase a tighter, more compressed Belnum—not just Divnum itself.

"We can repurpose many materials both from buildings to be abandoned or trees to be felled where it's useful," he explained. "My plans also ensure that no family, workshop, guild, or any structure would need to be moved more than once in the course of this project."

"The logistics behind your plan are impressive," Giovel said, now looking over a suggested calendar of major tasks beside Lilywater Lake. "Can you explain why you're coming to us, though? We can't help you with something like this."

Zuris glanced at the ground again, looking defeated for the first time. "I know granting any sort of permission for this project is far outside the duties or authority of the Order, but I'm asking everyone under the Optate's Council to voice their support for a consolidation. It needs to be done if we're to defend this city in the years ahead."

"Years ahead?" Elínla growled. "Half our Order will be dead before this plan makes a dent in the outer districts."

For a moment Zuris said nothing, but Giovel knew what he himself would say. All the more reason to begin. All the more need to do something now. Foneth's way of life was suited for contemplative peace, not siege. Perhaps that way of life was too old to last now.

"Consider this," Zuris went on after a moment. "Right now we have more than two hundred Candles patrolling North Hold each night. Their routes are immense—far too large for them to reach everyone in the moment of need. If we consolidate just North Hold into Belnum and Divnum, we can give more than twice as many people close access to Candleguard protection. A consolidation of the outer districts will also make it more difficult for Redremel cells to hide in our very midst. Or witches, for that matter."

"And what do your Lances stand to gain from this?" Ralden asked. "Military authority over those Candles or over our Order?"

"The Lances would gain a safe haven of retreat so fewer of them have to die on Redremel blades," Zuris said, still somehow maintaining his aura of tranquility. "That's why this plan matters. Until the war with Redrem ends for good, no one can remain safe outside Divnum's walls, be they Candle, Lance, Lawrit, Gray, or even a Divine Mage."

Zuris let his words hover a moment before asking, "Will you tell me plainly what you think?"

"I think it's totally impossible," Ralden said. "Our guilds pay for enough of the war effort as it is. We can't pay to move entire cities five miles to the west."

Elínla nodded. "Ralden's right. You'd need every worker in every district and every family to agree simultaneously. The Optate would be removed from her position if she even suggested this to the people."

"I think it's an interesting idea," Adni said. "I, for one, will give it serious consideration."

"What do you think, Giovel?" Zuris asked.

The others fell silent and looked Giovel's way. He knew why Zuris looked to him, of course. Yes, Adni seemed to like the plan, and, yes, he at least could advise Optate Olura as well, but Giovel doubted Adni's abilities to persuade the rest of the Order. Ralden's textile guild stood to lose a great deal of money if such a plan required them to move. Dlenar, though not there, would likewise disagree because his family would also lose property. Elínla's entire sept would likely oppose the motion out of respect for Sanctuaries they regarded. But Giovel knew firsthand the wisdom in what Zuris said, knew the immense difficulty the Candleguard faced just in protecting the streets, not to mention the city's many vulnerabilities to outside attack. Foneth needed a change if they were to survive against Redrem, and this plan might just help the Order's mission too. Less holes for witches to hide in, less secret corners of the city where awakenings could build their first spells. Giovel just had to wonder whether saving half of the city's Sanctuaries would be worth willfully leveling the rest.

"I will think on it, Zuris," he said. "I promise you that."

"That's only fair," Zuris sighed. "But give your answer soon. I intend to approach the Optate directly before winter begins, and I'll need to know who all will support the measure."

"I'll answer by then," Giovel said.

"And we will discuss this again before your meeting with Optate Olura," Adni announced. "Thank you for your commitment to Foneth, Commander."

Zuris bowed and led himself out.

He'd barely left when Ralden began talking loudly about his idea. "He'd ruin everything sacred between here and the Empty Hills. I can't believe he'd even offer an idea like that to us."

"He's only doing his duty, Ralden," Adni said, leaning back in his seat at the head of the table. "Besides, it's clear that no one else supports him yet. He would have told us so, otherwise."

"Suresni might," Ralden said.

"Suresni isn't everyone, and neither am I," Adni snapped. "Zuris will need more than just two of us to favor his plan if it's ever going to happen. Let's put it behind us for now and hear Elínla's report on the latest witch in our custody."

Elínla kept her eyes down as she summarized the events of the witch hunt two nights before. Ralden and Hírnu granted Elínla the dignity of asking only clarifying questions, despite Adni offering a subtle reminder or two that she and Giovel had gone witch hunting without the rest of the Order's knowledge or approval.

"Was this witch Londir alone?" Ralden asked.

"He seemed to be alone both before and after he awakened," Elínla replied. "If he was working in concert with other witches, he hid it very well."

"Some time in custody will loosen his tongue," Adni said.

Ralden nodded. "Still. I'm concerned about the number of reports of witches banding together. I don't know of many instances like this before, and I can't think of a worse time for them to wise up and gather their own pack to counter the Order."

"We still don't know that they *are* working together," Hirnu said.

"We know multiple witches have surfaced simultaneously in close connection with one another," Ralden said.

"We know that multiple witch appearances have been *reported*," Hirnu replied. "It could be the same witch running from place to place, wearing different clothes each time. Or telling the Candleguard that they've seen multiple witches."

"Sounds unlikely to me," Ralden said.

"Maybe if Elínla spent more time supervising the Grays—like I assumed she was—we'd know a little more," Adni said mildly.

"I've stretched them as thin as I can," Elínla said. "They can't be everywhere at every time."

"They can be where they're assigned and hold that position until they get proper approvals to go elsewhere," Adni said.

"She takes your point, Adni," Hirnu said.

That quieted him a moment. Giovel wished, not for the first time, that Hirnu or Ralden led the Order instead of Adni. Hirnu might be a stubborn old mule, and Ralden might be half-motivated by her guild's profits in everything she did with the Order, but at least they weren't vengeful vipers.

Adni himself reported next. "Optate Olura asked each member of her Council to share, in our circle of confidence, that the Redremel have definitely amassed a new army." He unfolded a map and positioned pebbles along it to show gathering locations in the east. "They've got somewhere between six and eight thousand spears, if the latest scouting report is correct."

They'd all wondered as much, heard a hundred rumors to the same effect. It was almost a relief finally to hear things confirmed.

"Are they moving?" Giovel asked.

"Not yet."

"I doubt they'll try before the spring thaw, despite anything the Vermilion Commander says," Ralden said. "But they probably have as many spies and scouts as we do, so they're bound to know we're vulnerable."

No one spoke for a moment. Probably because none of them knew what to do. It wasn't their place to advise on the war against Redrem, and even it were, they could scarcely hunt witches, train the Grays, and investigate spiritings all at once. There were only seven in the Order now, and rarely more than ten in the past two centuries. Too few to be responsible for so much.

"I'll be meeting with the Optate's Council again tonight, so we'll speak more of the Redremel later," Adni said after a long silence. "Until then, let's hear Giovel's report on the latest spiriting."

What even to say? Not too much, at any rate. "A Candleguard officer discovered another spiriting two nights back. She doesn't speak Medín, and our translator is working on identifying where this spiriting comes from."

Adni stared at him as if expecting more. When Giovel didn't give it, Adni asked, "Why do you think I assigned this spiriting to your care, Giovel?"

Giovel could think of numerous reasons: Because Adni knew it would cause him immediate discomfort. Because it kept Giovel from hunting the witches *behind* the spiritings. Because Adni wanted to punish him for not leaning deep into his games.

Instead of answering honestly, Giovel lied: "I don't presume to read your intentions, Lord Adni."

"That's a jar of spit. I assigned you to investigate her situation because I keep hearing such wondrous reports about your abilities," Adni said. "I expected more than the information we all knew already."

Giovel raised an eyebrow before he thought to stop himself. Did Adni really want him to answer all his questions in the span of time between five consecutively pointless meetings? No, that wasn't it at all. Giovel was willing to bet a cup of his own blood that Adni just wanted to watch him stumble, a reminder that even a Divine Mage like him had to grovel to the Illumined Knight.

"When my other duties allow me, I'll gather more information on this spiriting's situation," Giovel said.

"Good. We need to get to the heart of these spiritings before the Redremel march on us," Adni said. "For all we know, this coalition of witches is connected to the spiritings. These witches of ours might even be Redremel mages hiding in our midst to weaken us before they attack again. I want a greater effort from you all to piece this together. We need to know why these spiritings are happening, how they're doing them, and where the responsible witches are."

Questions worth a crown, as Uri had said. Giovel had asked the same things ten thousand times since finding Iremni. Who did this? How? And most importantly, why? Why spirit Iremni away?

That, though, was a question Giovel could answer. No one had ever been willing to voice the truth in his hearing, but he knew exactly why witches would target his wife. He'd had a clear, reasonable explanation since the day it happened.

Because of me. To get to *me*.

Not because I suddenly found my stride and became Commander of Divnum's Candleguard battalion. But because I became a Divine Mage. Because even a new, untrained, weak member of the Order is worth hurting, and spiriting Iremni was the perfect way to do it. It succeeded completely. How better to weaken and torture me than to take my wife away and send back a mad doll that only looked like her? And what better way to make me despise Yulena in all its forms before I even knew two leaves of magic?

It was why Giovel cursed Yulen every time he saw it floating there in the southern sky. And why, no matter how patient Hirnu was or how much Adni insisted, Giovel knew he'd never give Yulena his all.

If he hadn't awakened as a mage, if he hadn't been pressed into the Order, he'd still have Iremni.

Her spiriting had left their home feeling like an empty walnut shell, all the goodness scraped away. Inorovel was still there, of course. But now there was no one left to guide her to becoming all that Iremni had been. Just an aging man who'd had a dull career. After Giovel's late bloom and rise through the ranks, all within just a few years, he felt too busy and drained from worthless meetings and magic lessons to father Inorovel properly, let alone to provide what Iremni had. So sometimes vengeance felt like all he could give her.

Not quite all, though. They needed answers too, Giovel reminded himself. We might know why they spirited Iremni, but we still don't know why so many other poor fools get the same. And we *will* find out, if I have any say.

"We might have a real lead on the witch coalition," Ralden was saying now, drawing Giovel's attention back to the meeting. "Suresni has been watching a sort of gathering in North Hold that he believes is led by one of these witches."

"What kind of gathering?" Elínla asked.

"Someone's been speaking out against the Order," Ralden said. "Sur thinks they're using it to recruit supporters for something."

"Sounds awfully wilted as far as intelligence goes," Adni said.

"He has heard first-hand accounts of the man behind this meeting demonstrating Yulena to coerce people into attending."

"He threatens them so he can convince them to join him?" Elínla asked. "Any sane person would report him and be done with it."

"I didn't say he was threatening them," Ralden replied. "This witch claims to know a way for others to gain Yulenic power for themselves. He's offering to teach people to have their own awakenings."

A horrifying thought. Awakening to Yulen had terrified Giovel enough that he couldn't imagine others wanting the experience. There was no comfortable place for an awakening, not in Foneth under the Order's watch, not far from it. After all, few people felt truly at peace to be near someone who might slip up and destroy an entire city by mistake. The risks were greater yet for the very people who awakened because they were the ones most likely to die for their Yulena.

No one really knew how many awakenings were hiding throughout Foneth, let alone the larger world. Perhaps two hundred were currently certified, in addition to the sixty or so that made up the Grays and the seven who constituted the Divine Order. Ten, fifteen, sometimes a few score would be found each year, and though few seemed truly malicious in their efforts to hide their power, some did, and those few made everyone suspect now. Despite what any of them might claim, no one really knew how long each awakening had kept quiet—if they'd brought their new power to light immediately or hidden it for years, building spells and endangering everyone around them all the while. Little wonder that even those who openly certified their awakenings and trained to keep their power fully in check were likely to be mistrusted, rejected, or feared at the very least. They might become witches, after all, where others never could.

Giovel had certified his awakening to the Optacracy the very day he recognized it. He was confident, given his position by then, that he'd be welcomed into the Grays if he wanted; he'd even known an assignment to the Divine Order was a possibility for him. Yet other Candles had awakened and been arrested, held by the Grays because everyone had to wonder whether they were truly new to their power or just too tired to hide it any longer.

All that was to say nothing of the other fears awakening heralded. Giovel had worried for weeks that he'd be writing a letter and it would somehow become a glyph, that he'd breathe Yulena into a crack in the floor and suddenly blast his home apart. Even after months under Hirnu's tutelage, now knowing full well how difficult it was to build a spell deliberately, Giovel still sometimes struggled to shed those worries.

He didn't like imagining what sort of person would want that. Then again, Ralden was describing people who still lived in North Hold, people who held very little power of their own. Of course they would latch on to some chance for more of it.

"Sur wants a few hands to investigate," Ralden was saying now. "He has a small contingent of Lances at his command, since it looks like it might be a Redremel-led incursion, but he'd like one of us to go along as well."

"It sounds worth pursuing," Hirnu said.

Adni studied her a moment, then nodded. "Let's send Dlenar, then. He's due back any day now."

"It might be too soon for Dlenar. The supposed gathering is tomorrow night," Ralden said. "Besides, I'd rather we send someone who actually knows how to handle himself if things go sour in there. Infiltrating a gathering of would-be dissidents isn't really Dlenar's sort of game."

"Too recognizable anyway," Hirnu said. "Giovel should go."

His heart almost leaped at that. Another chance to get close to a witch. And this might actually be the one he'd been looking for.

"Giovel's investigating this new spiriting," Adni replied with a scowl. "And I think we should send someone more experienced. Elínla, for instance."

"Elínla's almost as recognizable as Dlenar," Hirnu said. "Not to mention how many people know Suresni's face already. Giovel's the only one who suits."

"Hirnu has a point," Ralden said. "It sounds as if Giovel handled himself well against that witch the other night, not to mention that he probably has more experience working in disguise than the rest of us combined."

"Candleguard aren't the ones they'd send in, disguised, for this kind of investigation," Adni said testily.

"He's not a Candle anymore, and we can't let Suresni investigate alone," Hirnu said. "It's either Giovel or one of us." She motioned between herself, Adni, and Ralden.

Adni looked as if he'd swallowed a bad lump of cheese. Giovel nearly held his breath until Adni said, "Very well. Giovel will accompany Suresni to investigate."

He could hardly believe his fortune. In truth, Adni was right. Giovel's experience as a Candle didn't really equip him for the task at hand, but he was too elated to worry over that. The assignment itself was all he could think about through the remainder of the meeting, even as Ralden instructed him on where and when to meet Sur.

One more chance to find some answers from the only ones who could give them now. And I will find them for you, Iremni. I swear I will.

"Do we adjourn already?" Ralden asked, somehow managing to keep her cloak wrinkle-free as she stretched dramatically. "I have other responsibilities to attend."

"Yes, dismissed," Adni said with a sharp look toward Giovel. "I think we all know our assignments."

Yes, they did.

THE WORDS

My Dearest Golkorun,

First, know that I have not left you to live off Recia's riches. If I ever truly intend to do that, I'll make sure you know it. And, wise sister that she is, Recia would probably tell me to find my own riches anyway.

What has happened is harder to explain. When you hold this note, you won't be able to see the long pauses between me digging for words. Believe me that writing these few lines has been more difficult than anything I've set pen to before.

I am far from our home now. I have no previous knowledge of this place. I don't know which direction it is from Dundal. What little I do know I've learned in another's tongue as I try, like a child, to shape my words and motions for someone who has no sense of what they mean.

It was not by choice that I left home. I'm told that a certain kind of witchcraft has done this to me. That, at least, I've learned to understand in the words they use here, because it hints at how I can come back to you. And I will come back. I only need to find my way.

I can be sure it's a long way. I have no wish to lie about that.

I've asked eight different messengers if they can get this letter to Dundal. No one has an answer yet. Not one I can understand, anyway. None of their maps show anything I recognize. Even without the maps, I knew I was far from you, because the first thing I saw was a sky that is different from ours.

A red moon fills the horizon, day and night alike. I've heard the wise say that the sky changes every mile you step, new stars appearing beyond each hill and mountain. This gives me hope now, because I know I can walk to the next hill and look for stars to find my way back.

Not just walk. I'll run. I'll run to you.

I might be the very one to put this message in your hands. If not, assure the boys of my love. I pray to every god that something in here can assure you as well.

With love,

Your Varan
—The Witherclaw Witch; letter to Golkorun.

BATTLE PLANS

They didn't know what to do with me. So I pieced together how to help myself.
—The Witherclaw Witch; letter to Drova.

Giovel wore old working clothes as he left home that morning. Odd how a uniform felt more comfortable than clothes in colors and cuts he could choose for himself. He put on his sword belt—never mind that he had no sword for the time being—to make the outfit feel more routine. Inorovel was reading by lamp light when he stepped into their Sanctuary. Her eyes narrowed as if she were upset about the words in front of her.

"You'll ruin your sight reading in the darkness like that," Giovel said as he packed dry fruit and hissleaves for the road.

Inorovel mumbled a string of half-words in response without looking up from her book.

"I'll be on assignment again tonight, so I probably won't be home."

More mumbled words.

So Giovel said, "Books are a fixation that distracts you from reality."

"Then why do you buy them?" Inorovel replied.

"Ah. So you were listening. I'm leaving some spans on my table in case I'm not back in time to buy more herbs."

"There won't be any merchants open tomorrow, da. Silence Day."

How could he forget that one? A day of utter stillness for a sept everyone publicly praised but no one could define. "I'll leave it to you to keep our larder stocked for the next few holidays. Don't forget to go to school."

"I'm almost done reading. Anything else I can do to help you on your way?"

He considered it a long moment while mashing grain and grini nuts for breakfast, startled and grateful as always that this child went out of her way to do anything for him. He knew what she really wanted was to help with his work, the real work of finding witches. But that was a danger to everyone involved. Not what he wished on anyone, his daughter least of all. She never begged or whined, though, no matter how much she might have wished to help.

"There is something I've thought of," Giovel said. "It might be dry work, but it's important."

She looked up in interest. "What is it?"

"I want you to search for anything you can find on a place called Dundal. Check maps, ask your tutor, even see if the scholars at the library can tell you anything. It could be nothing, but there's a spiriting who mentioned the place to us."

Inorovel nodded. "Dundal. I'll do my best."

He knew she meant it.

Sometimes saying goodbye to Inorovel was a relief, a cup of clear water in high summer. She neither clung to his arm nor avoided him like some parents said their children did, but leaving her alone at home gave Giovel something to think about other than the empty ache where Iremni had been for so many years. He still felt her absence every time they were together, as Inorovel must too. The stillness of home was a constant reminder that it was only the two of them now. No other voice to reason between them. No translator when they couldn't understand one another. No one else to help bind the family together. Just themselves.

But instead of that, when Giovel said goodbye he could think of *Inorovel*. Instead of obsessing over witches and spiritings and finding the bastards that ruined Iremni's life, he could worry whether Inorovel would forget to study or fall from another tree. Simple worries that somehow pushed heavier ones aside.

Not that it would work today, he thought. Today I might be confronting another witch or two, so the normal worries will be constant.

At least there's a hint of gold in that too. These might be the witches I've been after all along.

Giovel collected Boulder from the Candlespire, saddled the great horse, and rode east for his appointment with Sur. A Tovómil man-at-arms met Giovel outside Divnum's northeast garrison, recognizable by the Silver River emblazoned across his coat. He bowed, took Boulder's reins, and directed Giovel to the northern training yard. So someone had dragged House Tovóm into this little maneuver as well. Possibly Dlenar's idea, somehow keeping family fingers in every operation the Order undertook, even when he himself was on the road from Yeren. Giovel didn't like it. More disparate forces meant more pieces to control, more risk of being detected or of the witches escaping altogether. They'd escaped enough.

As he'd feared, Giovel found ten more Tovómil vassals in the training yard along with twenty Lances and five Candleguard. What an odd war Foneth's was, where battles were fought fifteen or twenty blades at once instead of a hundred or a thousand. It meant all the fighters in every district of the city were spread thinly across a massive space, like Zuris had pointed out yesterday. Three Candles here, a pair of Grays there, mixing lines of duty since they were always on watch for criminals, witches, and Redremel warriors alike. Giovel much preferred the older way of fighting where squads of Lances would raise their pennants and get things over with. This new kind of fight was harder to maintain since an enemy could appear—or vanish—as quickly as someone could cross a road or close a door. It made catching the witches challenging, demoralizing, and confusing because it was impossible to focus on an enemy that blended in with your friends and allies. Hard even to know who your friends and allies were anymore. That was why, in the end, it felt like a war without an enemy, no matter how many skirmishes they had or how many spiritings took place. Even the daunting, endless war with Redrem felt easier. It at least made some kind of morbid sense.

Giovel found Sur inspecting a cart full of weaponry at the end of the training yard. He wore drab working clothes, like something a stable hand or a ferryman might wear, though it would likely do no good. As Optate Olura's nephew, Suresni Medín had one of the most recognized faces in Foneth.

"Giovel," Sur said with a nod. "I see you're matching my repulsively practical garb. Thanks for hurrying over here."

Giovel gave a small bow. "Can you fill me in on our operation?"

"I'll tell you all I know once we're on our way. Our little partnership with the Lances requires us to do an extra count of all the crossbows, wrist-throwers, and swords I've appropriated first, just in case someone robbed me between dawn and now. Typical military dog shit, don't you think?"

"I can't say I'm sure," Giovel said gingerly. "Perhaps you have the advantage of familiarity over me."

"What's that supposed to mean? That I know Lance policy or I know shit? You count the blades. I'll count the bows."

"Isn't there someone under your command who can do that?"

"Not according to Lance codices, but I think they'll make an exception for a member of the Order. Start counting."

Giovel counted.

There were other supplies as well—food, torches, hand lanterns, rope, saddlecloth, and what looked like an immense pack of rustwood. Seeing that almost made Giovel excited about the operation. It looked like enough of the sedative to subdue fifty people.

They took their tally, Sur recorded it, then he whistled to gather his team around as they began shuffling out. The only horses they took were two drafters to pull the wagon, which was now disguised as a sort of junk cart, with odds and ends emerging from under cloth coverings and heaps of dirt thrown across the exterior.

"I take it we're not going into a very refined part of the city?" Giovel asked.

"One of the old estates near Holderím Tower," Sur replied. "We only had to meet here to organize a division of our approach. Olinos and a few more Lances will meet us there, by the way."

Giovel grimaced before he could stop himself. "I'd prefer if we didn't involve Captain Olinos, if it's all the same to you."

"He is a bit of a bonfire waiting for a spark, isn't he? Well, we need someone else who won't be recognized, so we're stuck with an empty bottle like him. Welcome to the Divine Order. You ready to hear the rest of what I know?"

"Please."

"Every five nights there's some sort of gathering led by a suspected witch from Belnum. He doesn't gather his own ears, but someone's doing it. The Cloudblade investigating for me thinks everyone who's responded to his past little meetings has been invited for a larger one tonight. We also think the witch who attacked Ralden on Star Day will be there."

"Two witches, then," Giovel said, feeling his eagerness and nerves expand. Two chances to find Iremni's spiriter.

"Maybe even more of them," Sur said. "We're expecting a few hundred rabble to hear whatever the witches have to say. With a crowd like that, they'd be fools not to take some precautions. Of course, they're all mad to be witches as it is."

Giovel wondered. He'd only really faced the one witch yet since joining the Divine. That witch was fighting a kind of wildness, like all witches were said to, but he had hardly seemed mad. And hadn't they all known dozens of ordinary people who felt the same hunger to use new power? Green captains in the Lances who commanded forcefully, just because they could? Or Optacrats who bent and pressured the laws in their favor? Or even mages who practiced their magic craft a little too diligently, not because they wanted to serve the Optate but because they wanted to stretch their own abilities?

"You're scowling," Sur said with a sidelong glance at Giovel. "Why so glum?"

"My face tends to rest in a scowl," Giovel said. "I'm not sure I agree with your assessment of these witches, though."

"You don't have to agree with me. But agree or not, we'll have our hands full when we arrive. Adni wants us to let them talk as long as we can before we make any move. More insights into what they're about and all that."

"And if they persuade any of these rabble, as you call them, to enlist in their cause? If there really are a few hundred of them, we could easily be outmatched, even with these Lances and Tovómil on our side."

"*They* could be outmatched. I'm not so sure about you and me, Giovel."

Giovel didn't know how to respond. Sur, at least, was a seasoned mage in addition to his background with the Lances before joining the Order. Not like Giovel.

Sur split their little group several ways as they moved toward North Hold. The Tovómil went in two different directions, while the Lances scattered and followed in threes and fours, leaving only Giovel and Sur himself with the supply cart. Even then Sur insisted on varying their route and steering wide around trade streets, thoroughfares, and recognizable crossings. They also took the long, lumbering hill road north of the Divnum walls to avoid crowds gathered for Silence Day.

Unsurprisingly, they passed most of the habitable remains of North Hold and entered the battered, burned-out wreckage along the northeast edge of the district. The war with Redrem had done most of the damage, though people blamed witches for it as well. Whatever the cause, the Optacracy had not yet seen fit to rebuild, so half or more of the district's population had fled to Belnum or Divnum or elsewhere. North Hold wasn't likely to recover. Not before the war ended, anyway. Maybe Zuris was right. Maybe compressing Foneth was the only way to keep this from happening again.

Giovel found another surprise when they reached their gathering point. Not only were a pair of Grays and thirty more Jade Lances assembled and ready, still wearing brazenly green surcoats for all to see, but Olinos Vlada *commanded* them. Oily Olinos, Giovel thought of him. He was a Candleguard, not a Lance at all. Someone must have applied a hefty influence to get him this assignment. Giovel purposefully met Olinos's gaze and gave a slight nod in greeting.

"I understand you two know each other?" Sur asked as he began unloading supplies.

"Lord Giovel and I have had the pleasure of knowing one another for quite some time," Olinos said with a sideways smile.

Not the terms Giovel would use. "We're not here for pleasure now," he said. "Report."

Olinos stiffened and saluted, bringing his left fist to his chest. "Captain Olinos, ready at your word, Lord Giovel."

"How did you come to be in command of these Lances?"

"Special assignment, Lord Giovel."

"Assignment from whom?"

"From Optate Olura."

Not again. It wasn't the first time Olinos had attracted the sponsorship of an exalted official to spread his name and fame. They never quite promoted him simply for being friends with every rich family in Foneth, but they always gave him tasks, duties, and privileges that facilitated ample 'proving' of his capabilities. It was how he'd become Giovel's Banner Captain in the Candleguard four years ago, when Olinos was barely twenty-five. At least so Giovel suspected. It still irked him that he'd never been able to verify that particular suspicion.

In truth, he hadn't found Olinos to be a bad captain. He was competent as a spearman, and his leadership was clear enough to follow without much question. It was just Olinos's obvious taste for praise and position that set Giovel's teeth on edge. A leader who would undercut his friends to elevate himself, who'd endanger his men for the sake of his own reputation.

Not the sort of man Giovel had envisioned following when he first joined the Candles.

Things had changed, of course, when Giovel suddenly began surging through the Candles' ranks—becoming a Banner Captain himself, then Cloudblade and District Commander all within a few years and no thanks to Olinos's leadership. Then he awakened and was nabbed for the Divine Order, and Olinos became greasy and mockingly deferential in a single day.

Well, I may be late in life to bloom, Giovel thought. But I'm your superior now and I won't give you the satisfaction of seeing me treat those under my authority how you treated me.

While Sur's men finished unloading key supplies, Olinos launched into a report. "This meeting will take place at a dilapidated old estate east of here," he said. "The Croen Estate, I believe."

"Yet another thin bloodline that ran out of money," Sur said darkly. "Go on."

"My men and I believe the best way to approach will be to send a few eyes inside the meeting—in disguise, of course—while we surround the estate at a slight distance and prepare to cut off any retreat."

"I take it this estate sits close between some other properties, then?" Giovel asked.

"Of course, Lord Giovel. The streets outside its walls will give ample protection for my Lances, as well as the Tovómil who've accompanied you. I've also found enough hiding places nearby that I believe I can get a score of Lances inside quickly if a disturbance does break out."

"Sounds to me like you've thought out how you think this should happen," Sur said.

It was Olinos's signal. He gave a reticent half-nod. "I've considered it carefully, Lord Suresni."

"Have you, now? Well, I have a different plan," Sur said. He didn't even look at Olinos as he continued. "Here's how this will work. You, Giovel, and two of my men will get inside that meeting. I'll lead the forces outside and wait for a cue. As soon as you signal, we storm from two directions. Just two, mind you."

Olinos shifted in visible discomfort but managed to keep his voice mild as he said, "If I may point out, Lord Sur —"

"Yes, yes, point out what you want."

"The Croen Estate has many possible exits. If we strike from only two directions, the witches' crowd will be free to scatter."

"Exactly," Sur said. "The only ones we need to worry about are ones who will rally around the witches themselves. By all reports there will be far too many angry nobodies for us to apprehend them all. Let them run off to their rat holes. Also, they'll be much weaker fleeing in twos and threes. If we force them to move as one body, we could have a real brawl on our hands. I prefer not to spill too much blood. Not that I care about the bats and beetles living here in North Hold. I've just learned that I have nowhere higher to be promoted for killing innocent fools."

That made Olinos flush a bit. About time, though. Giovel had never worked closely with Sur before, but he found his opinion lifting higher and higher.

"Might I raise one more consideration?" Olinos asked after a moment of silent regrouping.

"There's no need for ceremony," Giovel said. "What is it?"

"You, Lord Giovel. It seems to me that putting you close to these witches might not be wise. The risk of your being recognized and captured before we properly execute our plan seems very high."

"Ah, but you forget," Sur said. "Giovel's not the kind of soldier that drinks fame for tea. Half the city might know his name now, but he still looks just like any other fifty-year-old man to me."

"Forty-six actually," Giovel said.

"There is the matter of combat risk as well," Olinos said. "These witches have killed Grays before, and, forgive me for being blunt, many of these Grays have had more training in magical combat than you do, Lord Giovel. I think we should be cautious in exposing a Mage of the High Optate's Divine Order."

Typical Olinos. Finding a way to praise and to insult in the same breath. Did he even realize he was doing it, or did he think it was all praise and flattery?

"I assure you," Giovel said, fighting to keep his voice free of bitterness. "I may be new to the Order, but I'm prepared to do my duty."

"Of course, Lord Giovel."

Sur took just a few more moments to gather the Tovómil and Lances and to marshal them into ranks for his plan. When the time came, twenty would storm into the estate with Sur at their head, ten more would rally around Olinos, two groups of ten would wait at strategic exit points outside, and the remaining dozen or so fighters and Grays would stand by to move where they were needed. The Lances kept on their green surcoats to distinguish one another if it turned into a throng, while the Candleguard and the Tovómil wore grubby work clothes like Giovel's and Sur's.

"You'll have to go lightly armed," Sur said, handing Giovel a sheathed dirk. "Not that this really counts as going armed at all. I'll bet half our soldiers' members are longer than this knife. How are you with a wrist-thrower?"

"Not so accurate anymore," Giovel admitted. "Lazy wrist after all these years."

"Then you should keep your tablet handy, if you can hide it in your coat or shirt."

Giovel grunted. In spite of his assertions and barbs, Olinos was right about Giovel's lack of ability with Yulena. He'd be lucky to control the few glyphs he knew well. He'd survived his share of fights, to be sure, but not by virtue of Yulena. It hardly seemed worth trying now, especially since he'd like to keep his anonymity if it came to combat. At least until he was face to face with one or two of those witches. After that there'd be no need to hide any weapon he could wield.

I want them to know who I am. I want them to realize what they've taken from me.

The Lances fanned out to hide around the estate walls. The Candleguard and Giovel were just about to move as well when a scuffle broke out behind the supply cart. Giovel followed the sounds to find three men dragging a bedraggled woman between them. She had dark, wild hair like tangles of briars. That made him recognize her. The spiriting, Varan.

"We found this one hiding underneath the cart," a man-at-arms said. "Who are you, woman?"

Varan struggled against their grip, trying to motion with her hands as she spoke in her own tongue. Despite likely not understanding a word of what went on, she seemed oddly unafraid.

"What is this about?" Olinos asked, appearing with Sur and five more Lances. "Where did this woman come from?"

"I think she's a spy for the witches, Captain," the man-at-arms said.

"How did she get here?" Sur asked.

"Tied herself underneath the cart, it seems. She must have joined us before we left the barracks in Belnum."

"Bind her in her same ropes," Olinos said. "If she's a spy then we need to question her thoroughly before our men are in position."

"Hold that command," Giovel said. "She's no spy."

Olinos looked sharply toward him, almost opening his mouth. But he couldn't order Giovel to silence now. He'd have to break himself of that old habit. It might have been easier if he hadn't relished it so much before.

Varan looked his way as well, now speaking more quickly and motioning to him as she seemed to recognize his face. No sign of guilt or alarm at seeing him. Just frustration at not being understood.

"You know her?" Sur asked.

"She was just spirited into Divnum," Giovel said. "Adni assigned me to investigate her appearance." He hadn't thought she'd sneak out, follow him this far from the Candlespire. Then again he hadn't done much of anything to keep her there either.

"What's your name, girl?" Olinos growled.

"She's probably five years your senior and she can't understand a word," Giovel said. "She doesn't speak Medín."

"What? Then where did she come from?" Olinos asked.

Giovel ignored him and waved the men-at-arms back, holding his hands palms upward to show Varan she was in no danger with them. Then he said her name a few times and reminded her of his own, hoping that too might reassure her.

"Can you understand her?" Sur asked.

"No, but I imagine I know why she's here," Giovel said.

He drew a glyph in the dirt and bent his mind the onerous way Hirnu had taught him to infuse the shape with Yulena. Then he gestured between it and Varan. He had no words to share that she might understand, but he hoped his question was clear.

You came for this? You came to find the witches who've suspended your life indefinitely? You came to pursue the people who spirited you from some home so far away our maps can't help you find it? You came so you could force them to undo what they've done to you, if that's possible at all?

Varan's eyes lit up and she gave what seemed to be a nod. More words. A motion back at the same glyph he'd drawn. Yes, she understood. Because she, of all people, shared Giovel's drive to find the witches. She might have even better a reason than he did to hunt them. His reason was dead where hers was not.

"She's wearing a strange insignia," Olinos said. "With respect, Lord Giovel, I doubt whether a random woman would wear livery."

"Your reservation is noted, but that's the last you'll say on the matter," Giovel said. "This woman is here for the same reasons we are, so we'll treat her as an ally and not a prisoner. Do I make myself clear?"

Once again Olinos nearly opened his mouth to protest. But the tables had turned. Giovel leveled his eyes on Olinos a long moment until Olinos bobbed his head and mumbled an acknowledgment.

"I trust your judgment, Giovel," Sur said, giving Varan an appraising look. "If you vouch for her then that settles it for me. I'm impressed that she followed us this far without us detecting her. Underneath the cart, no less. Tough woman."

Giovel agreed. If the victims of all spiritings turned as bravely as she did in the faces of the witches, they might have rounded them up months ago.

"What should we do with her?" Olinos asked coldly.

Giovel met Varan's eyes, signaled toward the soldiers, the glyph, and then the direction of the estate. We're going after them, he meant to say. We're going to find the ones who did this to you. And they can't escape us forever.

More words. Something like a confused shake of the head. No comprehension.

Giovel took the ropes she'd used to hold herself under the cart. He pointed to the glyph, then looped the ropes over his wrists and held them toward Varan. The people who did this? We'll take them and bring them back here.

"You'll have your chance to question them," he said, just hoping his intentions were clear enough to reach her. After a moment she bowed, crossing her arms over her shoulders and falling silent a moment. Acceptance, perhaps? That would have to be enough, whether or not she truly understood any of Giovel's attempted message.

"Two of you," Giovel said to the men-at-arms. "Stay with her. If things take a turn for the worse, lead her back toward Divnum. Until then, treat her as a guest."

"I hope you know what you're doing," Olinos said.

"That sounds a lot like you're chafing at the orders of a Divine Mage," Sur said. "Better to hold your tongue if you want to keep getting promoted past—what was your rank again—Banner Captain?"

"I follow my orders, sir," Olinos said, though his voice had an edge again.

"Good. Get those Lances ready and watch for Giovel's signal. I'd like to bring a witch head or two home with me tonight."

Varan's eyes seemed to brighten at the word 'witch.' So that, at least, she did know.

WITCHES, WIND, AND FLAME

At first I wondered why they mistrusted me, but the answer is actually simple. It's because I speak a different language.
—The Witherclaw Witch; letter to Golkorun.

UNLIKE THE ESTATES in the south of Foneth, North Hold's had never had leeway to grow. They were more like walled-in manors, with great halls and gardens stretching only a bowshot or two from end to end before stout stone walls marked the start of another family's properties. All empty and ruined now.

The Croen Estate was a wolf trap. It looked as if it had been abandoned for thirty years—like much of the area had since the Redremel War began in earnest. Combat and neglect had riddled the estate's main hall with holes, leaving sections of wall sagging ominously into one another. Heaps of rain-washed roof slates lined the edge of the estate. Clumps of golden grass sprouted between the floors and wooden stairs, and rusted tangles of metal stuck out where iron had once reinforced the structure. The place reeked of mildew. Even without the damage, it was big enough and broken enough for there to have been thirty different ways in or out.

There were no visible guards, no lanterns, no indications of any gathering nearby. Giovel found his hands shaking slightly. Fear was good. He knew what to do with it.

He, Olinos, and two disguised Lances spread out to enter at different times. Giovel first. He went through what was left of the main entrance, ducking under hanging beams of wood until he spotted the flicker of candles ahead and found the estate's Sanctuary.

It must have been grand once. An entire goldmaple grew in the center of the room, with moss and grass and rocks, even a tiny creek flowing through the room. A true Sanctuary, a piece of the earth preserved at the heart of the old building.

It was hard to estimate how many women and men already milled around the room, most in clumps of two or four that seemed to know one another. There could have been anywhere from forty to a hundred of them. The dim light, coming only from an old chandelier and piles of guttering candles here and there, made it impossible even to trace the edges of the room accurately. A few groups spoke quietly, but the room was nearly silent.

Giovel's hands shook enough now that he had to press them against his own hips, pretending to be examining the decrepit place rather than fighting to stabilize his breathing. Would the others know he was different? Would they recognize that he wasn't one who'd joined them before?

They had a long wait. A dozen candles sputtered out as everyone stood or whispered together. It seemed the red glow of Yulen through the open ceiling was almost the only light left when a group of five or six figures moved to the center of the room carrying bright hand lanterns. A tall man walked at the front of them. He sat on a rock beside his companions and waved for people to gather closer around the weathered goldmaple.

"No need to be strangers here. We're all the same," he said, and seated himself on the rock. "You can call me Etelier."

Giovel searched his memory for the name. It didn't sound familiar. He felt he would have recalled if he'd met this Etelier before, though. Even seated, Etelier's head rose above the little crowd closing in on him, and he had a deep, powerful voice. While others shuffled toward the warm glow of Etelier's lanterns, Giovel looked sidelong to spot Olinos or either of their Lance comrades. There'd be no turning back now.

"Are you the one with witch friends?" a woman asked near the front of the crowd.

Silence for a moment. The woman's nerve impressed Giovel, but others shifted nervously around her.

After a moment Etelier met the woman's eyes. "We might all have witch friends. The question is whether we know they're witches in secret. I've invited you all here in hopes that it needn't always be that way."

"Your man told some of us you want to change the way of things with the Divine Order," the woman said. "Is that what you wanted to talk to us about?"

"Yes, not to put too fine a point on it," Etelier said. "Gather closer, everyone. I want you to hear me when I say why we ought to change the Divine, maybe even get rid of them."

Now people began to trade looks. If the woman was brave for asking forward questions, Etelier must be equally brave. Or mad. The people around him didn't look like rebels and enemies of the Optate. Just . . . people. There were no voicings of support or agreement. Only confused or worried murmurs.

"Hear me out," Etelier said, standing again. "You've all spoken to my friends before, so you know my frustration with the direction of the war efforts. But I think we should do more than just voice our opinions to the Lances. I think Foneth needs something else to thrive like it did once."

"I've heard enough," someone whispered right behind Giovel, making him jump. It was Olinos.

"Where'd you come from?" Giovel snapped.

"I was checking exits nearby. We've got at least ten to our backs, and so does this Etelier. I suggest we grab him now, before he changes anybody's minds."

"He's not very persuasive," Giovel whispered back.

Etelier was now detailing his take on the state of the war efforts— an exaggerated account of the Lances' failures and the Optacracy's indifference. Still, it was hard to dismiss completely because most of the people listening were likely from nearby sections of North Hold. They'd lost their home to the Redremel. The Optacracy had never adequately shielded them, and there was little recompense for that now.

"Why should we stick our hands in the Order's business?" the first woman asked, cutting Etelier short. "They're not the ones running the war."

"But they're the reason we're not *winning it*," Etelier said.

More murmuring. Giovel looked sideways at a cluster of three men who looked ready to walk out.

"None of you have to listen," Etelier called, eyes narrowing ever so slightly. "If you don't want to talk, leave. But I can give you good reasons for us to get rid of the Order altogether."

Silence once more, the quiet of an ugly curiosity that loves to hear the worst of things. So Etelier went on.

"First, they're keeping plenty of secrets for themselves where Yulena is concerned. Yulena used to do amazing things. We still have the Optate's Citadel and the Divnum walls that were built with Yulena. But now? Nothing new. Just a weapon to clobber the Optacracy's enemies into submission. I wouldn't care so much except that we could win this war with it if they only let awakened mages join the fight instead of executing them and leaving their corpses in our streets."

The Order's detachment from the war with Redrem was a common complaint, one with some merit Giovel knew. Centuries of law forbid them from wielding their power in open war, reserving that sphere for the Lances alone. One or two High Commanders had sussed a way around the restrictions by claiming witches fought among their enemies, but such claims were difficult to prove and easy to dismiss.

Perhaps the war would end sooner if those laws changed. Furthermore, there were many awakened mages who'd likely certify their power and join the Grays if they could. Many did. But others were hunted and locked away without much chance to come to grips with their sudden access to Yulenic power. It was the great balancing act. Should the Order let them choose whether to bury their own magecraft before warning what consequences might follow its use? Or should they step in quickly, before a new awakening became a second Renma unwittingly destroying an entire city, another Gaianu slaughtering her family in her hurry to learn what Yulena really was?

"Another reason," Etelier continued. "The Divine answer to no one. Not even the Optate really tells them what they can or can't do."

Another common criticism, this time glaringly in error. Even the Candleguard had less rules and inspections and suspicious Lawrits peering over them than the Order did.

"There's more, too," Etelier said. "Did you know that the Divine can actually cause awakenings to happen?"

Now the little crowd began to rumble in earnest. And this was not an argument Giovel had heard before.

"It's true," Etelier said. He took a book from a redheaded woman beside him. "My colleagues and I have been observing it for years now. The Divine have a place they take someone they want to awaken. Sometimes they do it subtly, and maybe sometimes they just spirit them there directly. We think this place must be the ruins of Old Vindil, hidden right here in Foneth somehow. In any case, everyone awakens who goes there. As it happens, any of us could really be a mage and simply not know it yet. You there, Hannin. You visited some obscure edge of the Estates on a task for the Lances last week, didn't you?"

The man he'd pointed to frowned. "How did you know that?"

"Your work crew was sent all over the city to collect different materials. Is that right?"

"As it happens, yes," Hannin said. "All normal enough."

"Then you won't mind a little test," said Etelier. "Come over here."

Hannin looked around as if he did mind, maybe trying to find support in the dark waves of faces. No one else said anything, though. So he walked up alone.

The redheaded woman handed Etelier a sheet of parchment.

"A known glyph," Etelier said. "Touch it, Hannin."

Giovel found himself leaning closer, glancing around the head of a man in front for a better view. He couldn't discern the glyph's shape, but it wouldn't matter. Glyph knowledge was still no good to a non-mage. Only someone who'd awakened could connect a glyph to Yulen, and even then the heart-link was often inconsistent without training.

Hannin touched the parchment. The glyph flared red. A flash of something shot from the glowing parchment and up into the air, the unleashing of the newly-formed spell.

Giovel joined others in gasping and swearing while Etelier held up his book, a scorch mark showing where the glyph had been a moment before. They were lucky none of them had been hit, none of them had *died*. Hannin looked most surprised of all—and terrified. A good actor, then. Giovel wondered how the man had ignited the glyph with so little motion. Almost like he had no tell. But no one managed to activate a glyph who couldn't also make one, and no one but a mage could breathe life into a glyph's outline just by touch as Hannin had.

Hundreds, *thousands* of people tried those very methods to see if they might awaken. It never worked.

Either Hannin was the first in history or he was a witch too and simply covered it by cursing with the rest of them and pretending to be scared of his own shadow now.

Whatever Etelier intended from his demonstration, he had people's attention now. There were no more grumbles, just a sort of fearful attentiveness as people pushed forward—or shrank back. They were all witnesses to witchcraft now, one way or another, and any of them could be its victims if someone as seemingly untrained as Hannin decided to try it again.

Etelier raised his voice, making his words carry all through the room. "The Divine have known their awakening technique for years. *They* choose who has Yulena now. And that's not even the last reason to fight them. The fact is, the walls of Divnum are filled with gold."

Giovel was so taken aback he actually laughed at the pathetic argument. No one else did, though. They all pressed in closer, raising their own voices now to ask where and how much and how Etelier knew.

"Adni Aman himself sneaks valuables in and out!" Etelier shouted back. "I've watched him do it. They're storing boulders' weight in gems and metals, and the rest of the city's blind to it."

More men and women voiced their questions now. How much treasure? When do they take it in? Perhaps Etelier should have led out with this nonsense. He had half the people in the room in his hands now, hanging on every word he said.

In his years as a Candle, Giovel had often wondered what would prompt ordinary folk like these to abandon loyalty to the Optate and help cutthroats, liars, or witches. He'd learned soon enough and saw it plainly again now. It wasn't that they hated their city or chafed at the Order's restrictions on Yulena. It was so much simpler. They were *poor,* and Etelier the witch friend had found a way to promise wealth.

This was getting out of hand. Whether these people hated the Order or not, believed Etelier or not, they wouldn't soon forget what they'd heard. Time to shake Etelier's gathering up a bit.

"You have any of this treasure to show us?" Giovel shouted, just managing to find a tiny break in the braying of voices around him. "Seems to me you'd have gone in for some if it was really there."

"You don't have to stay if you don't trust me, friend," Etelier said, now stepping off his rock to walk closer to Giovel. "I'll prove it to anyone who wants, with time, though I can't do that tonight."

"Can't or won't," Giovel said. He shook inwardly to be so close, almost eye to eye with this man now. "Who's to say you haven't stolen all these jewels and now you just want us to go kill some of the Order for you to turn them off your trail?"

Etelier opened his mouth to argue, but he stopped short when a door slammed open against the wooden walls of the Sanctuary.

A man ran in and shouted, "LANCES! THEY'RE HERE!"

Five soldiers in jade surcoats burst in through a hole in the wall, weapons raised. They didn't strike right away, but they may as well have. The entire room erupted in response.

Hellfire. Had someone given the signal? They were far too early.

A score of people from Etelier's crowd ran for the great main doors, shoving and shouting as they went. Five more Lances cut them off, but more of the crowd spilled into hallways and out broken stretches of wall even as the Lances jumped ahead to get control of the huge room. Near the center of the chamber, men and women together seized rocks, wooden beams, clumps of fallen debris, anything that could be used as a weapon, and began striking at the Lances nearest them. It was just as Giovel had feared. Etelier had found yet another way to light a fire of support in these people. There was little Giovel could do to protect them once they attacked.

The crowds would have to wait, though. Giovel fought the surge of bodies to get even closer to Etelier himself. Etelier's height made him visible even as he too retreated toward a hole in the wall and a possible line of refuge. The men who'd come in with him now clustered nearby, shifting to cover his sides as he moved. Giovel doubted he could get through half of them alone.

Four more streams of uniformed Lances burst into the room, securing additional routes of escape but pushing the crowds roughly to one side so that many of them half-tripped, crashing into one another. A row of people toppled then, blocking Giovel's path. He steered around them as quickly as he could, but Etelier had vanished by the time he found his bearings and made it to the back of the room.

"Suresni Medín is outside!" someone began shouting. "The Divine are here!"

Flames on dry straw. The men and women who'd armed themselves charged furiously at the Lances now, hurling bits of broken flooring, or striking with clubs of rotted wood. A wave of others flocked to the front entrance only to be repulsed by more Lances and to double back to the center of the great room.

Then someone started unleashing Yulena.

Flares of white light slashed across the room like lightning. A spell like the Talon hit the ground near Giovel, and another shattered a chunk of wall behind him, showering shards of stone and glass across the room. Giovel spun wildly to spot the witch—or witches; there seemed to be too many spells for one witch alone.

Etelier stood at a stairwell across the room, outlining glyphs with a charcoal pencil and his book he'd held before. So he *was* a witch himself. One of his spells took a Lance in the side of the head, smashing into his ear.

Giovel gritted his teeth and ran at him.

One of Etelier's seeming guards barred the path, raising a handbow from his coat as Giovel approached. Giovel snapped his own hand upward to unleash a dart. Though he'd aimed for the face, his throw took the other man's upraised thumb, earning a yowl of pain. The wounded guard dropped his handbow to clutch his bleeding thumb, and Giovel snatched the weapon midair, loosed a bolt into the guard's thigh from only a hand's breadth away, then rammed his elbow into the man's face to knock him fully out of the way.

Two more guards. One was on Giovel as soon as he rushed by the first, whipping out with one long arm to catch Giovel by the shoulders while he yanked a knife from his belt and thrust at Giovel's heart. Instead of trying to escape the guard's reach, Giovel steered straight between his arms, throwing his weight forward to grapple the man before his knife could connect. Giovel was smaller—and probably fifteen years older—but his aggressive strike caught the guard completely off balance.

Head into the chin. Dirk out, into the guard's gut. Shoulder forward to shove him back. Then Giovel grabbed his opponent by the left arm and swung him like a great shield into the remaining bodyguard. He whipped his dirk away at the same moment he released the first man's arm, letting the spray of blood catch the remaining guard full in the face as his companion toppled over him.

Giovel was through to Etelier, who'd burned through nearly all his parchments in the scant moments since Giovel charged. Etelier's eyes widened. Then he turned and ran for it. Giovel almost hurled his red dirk at Etelier's back. He needed him alive, though, so he sprinted in pursuit, barely glancing to the side to be sure no other bodyguards were near.

Up the stairs. Over a gaping hole in the estate's floor. Down a hall as dark and worn as a rat's lair. Away from the cries and crashes in the old estate's Sanctuary. Etelier was too fast to catch, though Giovel stayed close as the witch raced through another hallway and up yet more stairs to what seemed to be the middle level of the building. Giovel whipped his wrist forward to launch another dart. The motions of his own running sent the shot far to the left.

Etelier turned back briefly, slashing the shape of a glyph across the wall as he did so. It was a shape Giovel knew, one much like Hirnu's method of getting it into his head. A Rod. A blunt bolt of force shot from Etelier's glyph like a brick from a catapult. It was nearly invisible —just a blur of glassy something flying through the air. Giovel skidded onto his knees to duck under it. The wind-battered floor scraped through his clothes, tearing skin and stabbing splinters of dusty wood into his legs. Then the propulsion of his upper body caught up with his knees, which were jarring to a halt, and threw him forward almost flat onto his face.

Etelier leaped on him. Perhaps he relied on his size, large man that he was, but Etelier went for the dirk, fumbling to control Giovel's hands. The motion of a man with little experience hand to hand. While Etelier lunged at the weapon, Giovel whipped his other wrist up twice to throw darts into Etelier's neck. Both connected. Etelier recoiled, clapping a hand to the wounds as if he thought he'd die. Not even a man his height could last long with two pins spreading rustwood through his blood.

Etelier toppled backward, probably more shocked than subdued just yet. Then he tore the darts right from his neck, hurled them aside with a snarl, and ran off again before Giovel could get back to his feet.

Breathing felt like drinking fire. Giovel had to pause to examine himself, looking for new wounds. He couldn't find anything beyond his badly scraped knees, but he felt as if he'd been running for a year without so much as a sip of water. He couldn't do this forever.

The Sanctuary below still echoed with shouts and clangs. Giovel debated furiously whether to run back and help his comrades there or to keep on Etelier.

He was almost ashamed how easy the choice was.

The dark hallway led up several half flights of stairs, circling toward the top of the old estate. Etelier's heavy footsteps thudded ahead, leading Giovel past rows of slim doorways and black corridors. The footsteps stopped when Giovel reached what looked like an immense skybridge from one arm of the building to another. It was a wide room too, like the Sanctuary far below. In fact it looked like another Sanctuary altogether, an open star room, with polished bits of glass or gemstone embedded in narrow metal frames all along the walls, now catching the dim light of the real night sky. Even the floor was part of the illusion, making Giovel feel as if he were stepping out on a body of clear water.

He couldn't see Etelier anywhere. A gentle curve in the walls made it impossible even to see where the skybridge ended. Then a flash of violet lit the room momentarily. A spell ripping across the hallway — from *behind* Giovel.

It looked more like a flare than an attack because it shot wildly to Giovel's side. He spun around, gripping his dirk in his left hand while he readied a dart with his right. Whoever had cast it was shielded from sight below the star room.

Another spell shot past his side a moment later. It crashed into the walls nearby and sent bits of wire frame and crushed glass flying out into the night air. Giovel dove onto his belly to dodge two more spells —one from each direction. So they had him surrounded, *two witches*, both hidden by the mirror-like room.

Giovel didn't know whether to be ecstatic or terrified.

He crawled forward, almost flat on the ground. More spells shot overhead, blasting holes in the Sanctuary, ricocheting off the walls to dissipate against each other or simply misfiring and exploding near the witches themselves. As more bits of constellation broke free from the barrage of Yulena, Giovel's eyes adjusted enough to see the dark outlines of stairwells branching off the star room. He just had to get up one, get behind cover long enough to find another way around.

The spells behind him cut off with a loud scream and a roar of something like a waterfall. Then the ones ahead faltered for a moment, and Giovel saw Etelier's tall figure peering out of yet another stairway. Was this a trap of theirs? Luring him out into the open once again?

There wasn't far to run. Giovel took the chance and raced forward.

Etelier's tell seemed to be a wrenching out of his arms, as if he meant to push a robe off himself. He went through the motion three times, releasing more Rod-like spells and a wave of something like blue fog. Giovel dove aside or into nearby stairways during each motion, dodging handily as he advanced. Then he opened his thrower six times in a row, catching Etelier once each in the knee and ribs. And Etelier was slowing down already, the poison from the first darts catching up to him.

Only ten more paces to go. Giovel shouted, "Hands in front, witch, or I'll throw worse than a dart next time!"

Etelier unleashed another spell. It shot wildly off course, far beyond Giovel's side. Or maybe it wasn't off course. Giovel's eyes turned half to follow it, and he saw another figure sprinting forward through the ruined Sanctuary.

A woman running toward them. *Varan.*

He almost loosed a dart at her reflexively but managed to back into another stairway instead, waiting half a breath to make sure of what he was seeing. Varan didn't run at him. She dashed toward Etelier, somehow ignoring his new sputtering stream of spells in her direction. No, not ignoring them. Waving them off-course, as if the motion of her own arms could steer the spells in a new direction.

Then she threw herself forward on one foot, twirling a hand over her head. It was an odd motion, a distinctive one Giovel knew immediately for a witch's tell.

An immense gust of wind rattled the skybridge just around Etelier, sending an arm of fire roiling up the steps behind him with a bang. Flame encased the stairs before Etelier could even move, and the wind pressed harder, stirring fire behind him in a way that completely cut off that avenue of escape. Giovel just watched in shock and wonder, almost forgetting to breathe.

Varan shouted something in her own language and threw herself forward again. The wind turned fully in the opposite direction. More fire. Another explosion on a staircase behind Etelier. He was fully visible now, outlined by the flame's blue-orange glare. He clutched his bleeding neck with one hand and staggered against the wall. Then he swore and released another spell, smashing a hole in the wall just beside him. He leaped through before the debris cleared the air.

The wind stopped as suddenly as it had come. The fires dropped to little more than flickers on the stairs. Varan hurried to the spot where Etelier had stood, howling out the hole he'd made.

Giovel still stayed rooted in place. He realized now why Varan's show of power had startled him so much. It wasn't that she came after him, attacked Etelier, or even that she'd diverted spells mid-motion and tamed a force like the wind—neither which Giovel had ever seen done before. It was that while Etelier drew glyphs, Varan had been running the whole time, and her powers had manifested near Etelier himself.

No glyphs. Just witchery.

Varan walked back toward Giovel now, a look of dark fury on her face. And this time he felt afraid in a way that was new.

REGROUPING

There are so many people to fear in Foneth—Lances who fight their wars, Candles who watch their streets, and mages whose whole work is to find witches. But I can't tell whether I'm afraid of everyone or whether everyone here is afraid of strangers like me.

—The Witherclaw Witch; letter to Inivar and Sil.

CLARAVENA CHOSE TO abandon caution in favor of speed. Her pattern of retreat usually involved winding wide around her true route, doubling back on her path, pausing frequently to check for tails. This time she took the simplest way she knew to the bolt hole at the far end of Belnum.

It wasn't the Order she worried about following her. It was that demon woman with hair as black as a midnight storm and eyes to match, the witch who'd ambushed her right when she'd caught up to Etelier. There was no sign of her now, no sign of anyone but the occasional Candle on ignorant patrol in the darkness. Claravena still kept a quick pace until she was safe in the southeast bolt hole.

It was a tiny place to meet, a sort of workshop above an old woman's dusty house, filled with unused nails and hammers, files, chisels, rasps, mallets, and rifflers, along with half-finished lumps of oak, maple, and coldwort wood that still smelled green and grainy despite the long abandonment of the place. Tranin was already there, brim with questions and curses when Claravena said they'd been ambushed by the Order.

"They're everywhere, the maggots," Tranin said, now tearing pages from an old book and crumbling them one by one. "Why didn't we have more warning before they hit?"

"I don't know," Claravena replied.

"And who the hell sent these Lances? They must have known about this for days to get that many —"

"I don't *know*."

"What about Etelier? I assume you and he took different routes for safety."

"I DON'T KNOW!" Claravena shouted at last. "Shut your face half a minute while I catch my breath."

Tranin's mouth narrowed to a pouty line. She quickened her destruction of the old book, an even surer sign she felt slighted since she tended to demolish things when she held her words in for half a moment.

"Where's Wurelna?" Claravena asked.

"Am I her mother now? Last time I saw her was Foliage Day."

"You were supposed to meet yesterday."

"She didn't show. So like her, isn't it?"

It was the first thing Tranin had said that Claravena agreed with completely.

What a weak group they were. Angry Tranin whose rage was so hot she couldn't make a plan, lazy Wurelna who didn't finish much of anything, distracted Etelier leading then against the Order when all he really cared about was his daughter. Not that anyone could blame him or the rest of their companions for a lack of focus. They all had their reasons.

Etelier had intimated that Tranin's lover reported her to Dlenar Tovóm for money when she first awakened. Wurelna had once been a Gray, but she left as a discouraged, broken woman. It was the same for the others, too—all deprived of something or someone thanks to the Order's unfettered power. Claravena herself had lost her four sisters to Yulena.

They'd awakened close together, first Lolen and Uro, before Eronea, Alene, and Claravena last of all. Some people said it ran in families. There really was no explanation for why or how Yulena got its claws in someone, though.

After only a few months, Lolen and Alene killed each other experimenting with it. Imbeciles. Adni Aman himself had hunted Uro. After that, Eronea reported to the Grays, not to run from Yulena but to join them. Shit-mouthed traitor.

And yet we're all betraying something. I still love Eronea as much as the others. I just hope to the stars I never see her again. Can't believe we'd both live to remember it.

The bolt hole door rattled open, siphoning a cold gust of air as Etelier limped in. Claravena cursed and tightened her fists to bring her mind back where it should be. There'd be more time to think of her sisters later. All too much of it, as there always was.

"How badly are you hurt?" Claravena asked.

Etelier winced as he dropped to the floor. "Darted. Repeatedly. Some old Candle got me with rustwood, and I had to vomit it off for half an hour before I could even walk."

"What about that fire witch?" Claravena asked. "She was right behind you when I had to cut and run."

"Fire witch?" Tranin asked, finally dropping her book. "What fire witch is this?"

"I saw her," Etelier said. "Almost had me. I only escaped by jumping from the star room."

"That room must have been twenty paces off the ground," Claravena said. "You should be dead."

"Maybe I don't die so easily. I landed in a tree anyway. Just got bumps and bruises and crawled away before the witch could climb down and chase me."

"What witch is this?" Tranin repeated, so Claravena finally began to explain from the beginning of the gathering.

Tranin's interruptions made for a long account, but it gave Claravena a chance to inspect Etelier's ragged dart wounds. None looked bad, though it was amazing that he'd gone ten steps with that much serum in him. The man was hard-willed. She admired that, no matter how poor a leader he'd turned out to be.

"There are really just two questions for us to answer," Etelier said as Claravena finished answering Tranin's interjections. "How did the Divine hit so hard without us knowing? And who is this witch that's helping them?"

"Don't scowl at me for answers," Tranin said. "Wurelna was the one working with the Lance informer. We'll have to ask her why we were in the dark tonight."

"You can be sure I will," he growled. "But what about this witch?"

Claravena found her fists tightening again. "She's dangerous. She hit me with six, maybe ten different spells. She had wind and fire, like she was calling them out of the sky, and something that made me sick up in my throat. I've never seen Yulena like she used."

"Maybe she's not part of the Order," Tranin said. "Ithilo says the Optate has her own secret ring of mages."

Etelier shook his head. "That's goat wallow. Even if the Optate had a hundred secret mages, they'd use Yulena the same ways the Order does."

"This witch was deadly accurate too," Claravena said. "She was running straight at me while she hit me with her spells. I've never seen a Gray sketch glyphs, imbue them, and control the spells that perfectly on the move."

Etelier stood and paced around the tiny workshop for a moment, kicking Tranin's crumpled pages aside. After a moment he said, "We need a closer look at her, whoever she is."

"You make her sound more dangerous than the Divine Order," Tranin said. "How the blazes do you want us to investigate someone like that?"

"Patiently, Tranin. I'll ask Wurelna to figure out how the Lances assembled so quickly. Claravena, I want you to find out who our new witch is."

Of course it fell to her. She was the only one he trusted, wasn't she? The only one he *should* trust, anyway.

There was also something in Etelier's eye that made Claravena suspicious of the assignment. Not that she questioned the threat this new witch posed. What worried Claravena was Etelier's nervous energy, like the jolt of speed he'd summon when they found a fresh lead or got some shaky clue.

That was his fire, wasn't it? He didn't seem to care so much who their enemies were. He just cared about finding new glyphs like the fire witch had used on them. Another direction to try in his dead-end quest to help little Mota. And once again, Claravena couldn't really blame him. Just pity him as she pitied them all.

"I'll find her," Claravena said. "I don't think she saw me close enough to recognize my face."

"Let's hope you're right," Etelier said. "Now scatter. The Candleguard and Lances will be scouring the city for us before dawn."

AFTERMATH

They care so much about Yulena while knowing almost nothing *about it.*
  —The Witherclaw Witch; letter to Golkorun.

Almost as soon as the witches were gone, Varan seemed to deflate before Giovel's eyes like a punctured skin of wine. She sat on the floor of the star room skybridge and lowered her head to her knees. Waves of dark hair obscured her face. No more fury. Just weary defeat, like a child's.

Giovel moved slowly toward her. Three urgent voices fought in his mind: One saying to strike while he could, one to flee from Varan and her glyphless power, and yet another to reach out and comfort her. She looked so helpless. A feeling Giovel thought he might share after his failure to capture not one but two different witches.

A few Lances and Tovómil spread across the battered skybridge just moments later, hesitantly surrounding Varan and taking her hands to bind them. This time Giovel made no move to intercede. She was some kind of witch, after all. Varan, in turn, showed no effort to resist. Just stared dejectedly at the floor as they led her back toward the front of the estate.

There was no sign of any other witches.

The attack had gone badly wrong, more poorly than Giovel had thought. Sur was already gone, being carried to the Belnum barracks with a knife wound gaping across his chest. Several Candles and Lances were dead. Most had fallen to Etelier's spells, nearly all killed in the same way—blunt impact to the side of the head, smashing portions of their faces and tearing whole ears off. Olinos's men had managed to capture thirty of the poor rabble from Etelier's gathering, but the rest were long gone in the night.

So Giovel gathered the remaining fighters, marshalled their ranks to keep the prisoners secure, made assignments to carry their dead companions, and moved them out.

There were no spare hands to send after the escaped witches. If Varan turned her power on them, they might need every fighter left where they were.

They left their prisoners in the Divnum garrison just before dawn. Most would be released within a day, because there was no proof they'd meant to help Etelier. No proof they wanted the Order brought down, either. Just proof that they'd acted like fools for an hour.

Adni was waiting in the Candlespire Sanctuary when Giovel arrived, Olinos tailing him like an obedient servant. Somehow Adni always knew when to be ready to berate someone.

"How many dead, Giovel?" were Adni's first words as Giovel entered the round, grassy room.

Too many.

"Four Lances, two Candleguard, one Tovómil man-at-arms, and five civilians," Giovel said.

"And I've already received word that Sur is badly wounded," Adni said. His voice seemed to quiver as if he were holding his rage in with nothing but the strength of his lips and jaw. "Oh, and a score of senior Lawrits are demanding that Ralden and I explain whether the night's events were even legal, so I want you to explain to me how this asswipe catastrophe happened and just what you plan to do about it."

Giovel had never wished so much that Olinos weren't there, with his greasy cheeks turned down in mock humility, but there was nothing for it now. No explanations or roundabout reports would bring back the fighters who'd died, and they deserved better than that, anyway. So Giovel reported everything he could from the start of the operation to the bloody end.

"It was a faulty plan," Adni said when Giovel finished. "A nearsighted fool's faulty plan that never would have worked with that many moving parts."

Exactly why Tovómil or Lances should never have been involved, Giovel thought. What he said was, "The plan wasn't the problem, Adni. Someone went sour on their assignment. The Lances weren't supposed—"

"I don't want your opinions. I can't go out and tell these men's families that you blame them for their friends sinking in Cold Lake."

"I never said I did. I'm only saying—"

"You're saying nothing now, Giovel, *nothing*. I'm the one who has to go to the Optate and tell her that we got no witches for the lives of five of her best and bravest."

"*Seven* of her best and bravest."

"If I may speak, Lord Adni?" Olinos asked quietly.

Adni looked ready to shout him down, but then he waved his hand and looked away.

"This plan was not Lord Giovel's," Olinos said. "He was simply following orders from Lord Suresni. My original plan was to send more men in at once to ensure no one was injured. However, Lord Suresni took charge and changed our operation at the last minute."

"Don't blame this on Sur's plan," Giovel growled. "His plan was three times safer than yours, and he's the one who's paying for it being botched by your stolen Lances. Something else went wrong. Someone under your command jumped in too early and forced everyone else to respond."

"Enough!" Adni said. "Banner Captain Olinos, thank you for clarifying this matter and cooperating with Order business. You're dismissed."

A flash of irritation crossed Olinos's face, but he bowed before leaving the Candlespire.

"Wait upstairs until the others arrive," Adni said to Giovel, walking out after Olinos. "I need to bat off the Lawrits, the Lances, and any Tovómil who might be waiting for explanations."

Not a task Giovel envied. Perhaps having work like that explained Adni's general bitterness. Or perhaps he was just an acerbic bastard to everyone.

Giovel wondered, not for the first time, what Adni had been like before he led the Order. Maybe he was a paragon of decency and respect when he'd first been taken from the Grays' wing and appointed a Divine Mage. He was young then, with only his reputation as a skilled spellcaster to push him up any higher. Perhaps Adni had played the part of a patient, dutiful follower until he got his try at command, waiting to show what color his blood really ran. Giovel had seen the same thing happen thirty times in the Candleguard. Everyone seemed magnanimous and brave the week before promotions. But the week after, once the new captains had taken a sip of their authority? That was the week to keep your head down and be quick about your work, knowing full well a tyrant or two would brandish their whips no matter how competent you were.

Most officers grew out of it quickly thanks to the disciplining prod of the officers above them. Adni, however, had only Optate Olura to answer to, and even she couldn't override the Order where witches were concerned. So perhaps Adni was Foneth's one exception—a leader who could treat people however he liked because it was so unlikely anything but his own death would ever unseat him.

The rest of the Order filled the upstairs council room perhaps an hour later. Ralden and Hirnu were there first, both looking dour. Then Elínla, who at least had the manners to ask whether Giovel was alright.

"Just bruised," he said.

"Ah. Too bad your wounds aren't more serious," she said then.

Perhaps it wasn't manners after all.

Dlenar Tovóm arrived next, finally back from assignments in Yeren. Dlenar was simultaneously the most and the least like Giovel of anyone in the Order. Near the same age, a widower, and he had a daughter maybe twelve or thirteen years old. On the other hand, he was a Tovóm, so he was wealthy as a Redremel queen and lived on an estate that would have made the Croen's look simple back in its time. It was a mystery to Giovel how Dlenar had ever been appointed to the Order, since he was almost as weak a mage as Giovel, had no military experience or tactical skills, and didn't seem particularly interested in his responsibilities. But having a Tovóm there had its uses. Prices too, like immediate repercussions for the Tovómil men-at-arms who'd just died.

Adni returned last of all and called for a formal meeting with a formal report, because that was how things were done. So Giovel started his account of the disastrous night all over again, trying to address every detail that mattered so this could be the last time he had to speak about it.

"I don't think we should have let Suresni oversee such a large move on the witches," Dlenar said when Giovel concluded. As always, Dlenar spoke so softly Giovel swore he was trying not to be heard. "It sounds like his rubbish plan didn't hold up at all when it counted most."

"Is sticking to the plan all you care about?" Giovel asked. "The plan itself wasn't the issue. It was a matter of execution."

"Then Suresni shouldn't have been allowed to oversee the execution," Dlenar countered.

"Suresni has more experience doing this kind of thing than most of us combined."

"Your report's done, Giovel, so shut up," Adni said. "Anyone have questions?"

"He can't answer questions without violating your order to shut up," Hirnu said, looking at the ceiling as if she saw patterns in the stone.

And as usual, her words shut Adni up.

"Plans go wrong all the time," Elínla said with a hard frown stretching her blue sept tattoo into long slashes across her jaw. "I want to know more about this witch who got spirited to us."

"If she is a witch at all," Ralden said. "Her power sounds like something different. Some kind of other-world power that's not Yulena, I'd say. Maybe she's one of those elemental philosophers who can make explosives by mixing liquids."

"Varan wasn't using explosive liquids," Giovel said. "Her power didn't use glyphs either."

"But she used it as a weapon, unless I failed to follow your report," Dlenar murmured, tapping the side of his face and looking into the distance. "How could she be anything but a witch? And how can we treat her as anything else?"

"It seems she used her power to *fight* witches," Hirnu said, still not looking at anyone.

Dlenar frowned. "So?"

Hirnu shrugged ever so slightly. "I wouldn't call that witchery just yet. We need more information."

"She was spirited here," Giovel reminded the others. "She clearly doesn't have any love for the witches behind her being forcibly brought here from who knows where."

"Are you suggesting we view her as an ally?" Dlenar asked. "Unless I'm mistaken, it's my responsibility to investigate uncertified forms of magic—not yours, Giovel."

As if Dlenar cared three coins about his duties. "We should at least see if it's safe to release her from the custody of the Candleguard," Giovel said. "She doesn't deserve to be held for helping us, and she probably saved my life earlier tonight."

"She still sounds dangerous to me," Elínla said with a scowl. "I don't think we should turn her loose without knowing something about the nature of her powers."

"If she doesn't use Yulena, then she's not legally under our watch to begin with," Giovel said.

"But we don't know yet whether she uses Yulena or not," Hirnu replied. "We should ask her cooperation demonstrating these powers for us to study."

"That sounds reasonable," said Dlenar. "And I don't believe any Lawrit will see studying a glyphless witch as exceeding our mandate."

"You mean like some experiment?" Giovel asked. "She doesn't even speak Medín."

"One doesn't have to be part of our civilization to threaten it," Dlenar said.

Ralden groaned. "This is pointless. I say we find out where she came from and send her back. She probably has a family that's worried sick for her. And if she could have killed Giovel—and didn't— then I don't see any point in being afraid of her. Adni, what do you say?"

All eyes turned to him. Adni paced slowly around the length of the council room table, looking down at each member of the Order as he went by. After a moment, he said, "We have no reason to make an enemy of this Varan person. Whatever else happens, she might be a witch's target now. Hirnu's right that we need to gather more information, and I think it should be done as delicately as possible."

"I completely agree," Giovel said. It was refreshingly reasonable, a glimmer of the leadership he'd always expected from the Order's head.

"I take it that when you say 'delicately' what you mean is slowly?" Ralden asked.

"Cautiously, at least," Adni replied.

"And we should keep this within the Order as much as we can," Giovel said.

Adni gave a slow nod, still walking around the room. "That might help protect her from any witches trying to reach her after her show of power at the Croen Estate. Which means we need a member of the Order to lead out who can devote reasonable effort and energy to her cause."

"I agree again," Giovel said. "Her power is unique enough that we can't just leave her as some afterthought and risk witches getting to her."

Adni took his seat once more. "Dlenar, this sounds like just your sort of task."

"I don't have time for it," Dlenar said.

"We can reallocate some of your responsibilities."

"But doesn't it make more sense to keep Dlenar where he is?" Giovel asked, his hopes rising now. "Having him train one of us on tasks he already does would cost time we might not have." So assign me to find the witches, he wanted to say. Let me get to the bottom of this river.

"There's logic to what you say," Adni acknowledged. "Are you volunteering?"

"I don't have other pressing duties, at least," Giovel said, his hopes surging higher.

Adni nodded. "Very well. I'm assigning you to maintain a personal watch over Varan until we find out where she came from. In line with your suggestions for keeping her as safe as we can, you are to protect her only—not to investigate her spiriting—so we can better shield her from public attention."

Giovel's thin hope shattered. It would take all his time. Keep him from helping with anything else in the Order. And, despite what Giovel himself had said before, it might even be a waste since Varan could clearly look after herself.

The worst part, however, was the way Adni had issued the assignment. He could have simply ordered Giovel to continue watching her at the start of the conversation. Instead, he'd hinted at a larger purpose, let Giovel talk himself into all but asking for the opportunity. Perhaps no one would else would think anything of it, but the satisfied gleam in Adni's eyes made Giovel sure it had just been a trick of power, a game Adni had invited Giovel to play purely for the sport of pushing him into a corner swiftly, effortlessly. Damn him. Then again orders were part of the Divine Order, and Giovel doubted he had any ground left from which to argue.

"I'll do my best to watch over her," he said.

"When she communicates enough to make it clear where she came from, we can revisit the matter," Adni said. "Perhaps we can help each other mutually then."

No one else spoke up about the futility of the task, so the matter was closed.

"At least this report confirms our suspicions about witches working together," Elínla said. "And that they're trying to rally against us."

"Then let's not sit here," Ralden said. "We ought to organize a search for these witches. Maybe post more guards to watch for any Divnum wall gold miners," she added, laughing at the very idea.

"We can discuss more this afternoon," Adni said. "I need to report to the Optate first. Reconvene at four turns—except you, Giovel. I don't want you letting this Varan woman out of your sight."

"Am I dismissed, then?" Giovel asked.

"Yes, you're dismissed," Adni said, somehow managing to sound as if nothing was wrong at all.

Giovel bowed and walked out, trying not to grit his teeth visibly.

As usual, Adni's pettiness would make a slop of everything. He had to know Giovel was better equipped than anyone but Elínla to help find these witches in the first place, and that Giovel itched to do it for more than just a second chance to prove himself. For Iremni. Even for Varan's sake. For anyone like them who'd been spirited and left without an explanation.

Well, pettiness or not, Giovel swore to himself that he wouldn't let Varan's spiriting stay unexplained. If his orders were to guard her until they found out where she came from, then he'd try to find her home as fast as wildfire so he could accept real duties.

He might just get another chance at the witches in the process.

WITHERCLAW

The very way they see knowledge and power is slanted toward their old, pointless wars. Where I see a leaf, they see a claw.

—The Witherclaw Witch; a letter to Recia.

It LOOKED AS if Varan hadn't moved since being locked in the narrow garrison cell. Civilians from last night's gathering shouted in cells on either side, but she just stared at the ground, black eyes round and empty. Giovel wondered whether her apparent calm spoke to self-control or a great despair. He felt no fear of her now as he had before.

"I've come to free you," he said as he opened the heavy door. "You can come with me now, Varan."

He held out one hand, not commandingly, just open for her to see he wouldn't force her. She looked him in the eye a long moment before she stood and followed him out past the lines of other cells and shouting prisoners. There were no crowds to greet them by Cloud Lake today, no nosy Birenlu writing more books on the Order. Just cool sky and yellow leaves and the calm of water and autumn wind.

Giovel led Varan along the shore to Uri's little house. Uri was expecting them, probably tipped off by a Gray or a Candle that they'd be enlisting her services again. She asked no questions about where Varan had been the previous day, why she seemed so dour now, or how it was that Giovel had come straight there in filthy work clothes. Rather, Uri had prepared a light lunch of herb bread and greens with dwallonuts—language anyone could understand.

"I made some for you too, Giovel," she said, seating herself in the grass overlooking the lake.

Giovel accepted, feeling ravenous, exhausted, and grateful all at once.

"I'd like you to meet with Varan daily," he said between crunchy mouthfuls of greens. "The sooner we can help her find her own independence, the sooner we can help her get home where she belongs."

"Seems reasonable. What do you think, Varan? Would you like to learn more of our talk?"

Varan looked up from her food and said, "Talk."

"That's a real word. Not bad, eh, Giovel? And that's with only one afternoon that I had her in my tutelage. She's smart enough that she'd probably speak as well as you can if she had a few months."

Another boon, then. The sooner she could speak, the more likely they were to find her home and end her torture. Getting her home—or tracking down the witches who'd so totally interrupted her life—might also help find the witches who'd ruined his.

Just thinking it evoked a stab of guilt.

Half an hour since I determined to help you, and already I've pieced together exactly how this will help *me*.

"Does she understand enough to answer some questions?" Giovel asked Uri.

"She might just. Try her directly."

He began by drawing a glyph, making the motion slowly so Varan could see what he was doing. He even imbued it with Yulena, unpleasant though the very idea always was. Then he asked, "You don't use these?"

She shook her head, uncomprehending.

"My son-in-law claims she has some kind of magecraft or power," Uri said.

"How did he find out so soon?"

"All the Candleguard in Divnum probably know now, Giovel. Apparently she fought a few witches at once last night."

Giovel almost considered lying, trying to talk it off. But he couldn't well ask Varan about her powers without Uri knowing now, so he just nodded.

"Well then," Uri said. "Let me see if I can help you."

She tried posing Giovel's questions a few different ways. You are a mage? You can make glyphs too? You use Yulena? Uri finally pointed to Yulen itself, which was half covered by clouds today but still clearly visible to the south.

Varan shook her head. "No." A few words of her own tongue. "No Yulen."

"What do you call it, Varan?" Uri asked.

"No Yulen."

"Do you mean . . . your power doesn't need Yulen?"

It wasn't clear whether Varan understood this any better than their earlier questions, but she said yet again, "No Yulen."

A thrill went through Giovel, then a wave of fear as he made sense of what she was saying. Witchery without Yulen, as he'd thought when he first saw her handling raw power with nothing but her odd tell. And if she managed it, others could too. The simple discovery of *one* mage who didn't need Yulen glyphs could change everything the Order fought to regulate and preserve.

Varan wasn't finished, though. Up, she seemed to motion. Up there, somewhere, perhaps the sky. Then she said, "No Yulen."

Uri's eyes widened. She held a hand up, blocking Yulen's girth entirely from where she and Varan sat before asking, "No Yulen in the sky?"

"No Yulen."

Then it dawned on Giovel. "She can't even *see it* where she comes from."

"She'd have to be hundreds of leagues from her home," Uri said, eyes even wider than before. "Maybe thousands not to see Yulen. No wonder our tongues are so different."

"Is there a safe place we can have her stay?"

"You tell me. You're the one with Grays bowing when you call."

"I don't mean like that. I mean somewhere quiet where she won't be noticed."

"I'm not sure I can help you with that. I'm just a translator."

"And as a translator you're one of the only people I trust not to try bending Varan to your own purposes. Uri, as soon as word gets out that she can wield witchery without drawing glyphs, everyone in

Foneth will want to take her under their wings. Witches, nobles, Optacrats, Redremel spies. Anyone you can think of."

"We translators have ambitions too."

"You know what I mean." Giovel turned to face Varan again, who watched them both with interest but no clear comprehension. "I want to find a place she can be comfortable while she's here." If such a place could exist for her.

"You mean like a home," Uri said.

"Exactly."

"And you're asking me to find somewhere, after telling me how dangerous this woman could be to whoever is near her?"

"I don't mean for her to stay there. Just to visit, to give her some sort of calm. If you can't do it, just say so."

Uri lowered her eyes. Then she said, "Kirida and Nomis might be able to watch her some of the time. Not constantly, Giovel. But they'd welcome her and give her latitude to come to terms with everything."

A new wave of guilt hit Giovel as he took in what he'd just asked for. "I don't want to put your family at risk. Isn't Kirida with child again?"

"Yes, and Nomis has assigned more of his squadron to patrol nearby as a result. No one will blink to see extra Candles going in and out of the house—or even a Gray or two."

"I suppose that's one way to hide her in plain sight. But only if Nomis and his wife agree."

"I can't decide that for them, but I'll ask," Uri said. "You truly think she's at risk? People will be looking for her?"

"She was spirited here, probably from hundreds of leagues away. I don't think anyone's safe who's captured witches' interest like she must have."

"Ah, but she's not like others. She can fight the witches off herself from what Nomis heard."

That at least gave Giovel a small measure of comfort as he thought of Varan spending an afternoon with Uri's family. He knew they were kind people, the sort he could only wish every spiriting met. Much like Uri was herself; it was why Iremni had befriended her so easily, years before.

"I'll take her by to meet Kirida and Nomis tomorrow," Uri said.

"Thank you."

"Any more words, Varan?" Uri asked. "I'm sorry we ignored you so much."

Varan seemed to understand the apology, if nothing else. "Talk," she said once more.

"One more question, then," Giovel said, and pointed to the claw emblazoned on her dress. "What is this? What does it mean?"

Uri said a word or two of Varan's own tongue as it sounded. Then Varan stretched her hand out to make the same bent claw shape shown on her dress. She said a short word that sounded like *rith*.

"A claw," Giovel said and made a swiping motion.

"No. *Rith*." Varan again shaped her hand like the emblem then trailed her fingers through the air. She frowned, then plucked a leaf from a nearby tree, holding it against her dress. "*Rith*."

"Not a claw," said Uri. "A leaf."

Giovel laughed. "And here Olinos thought she was wearing some sort of battle livery." He saw it clearly now. While the shape was indeed claw-like, the withered texture of the image was much more like a dried leaf.

"Why?" Uri asked softly. "Why do you wear it? What is it?" She added something in what Giovel hoped was a word or two of Varan's own tongue.

Varan made a few motions with the leaf she'd gathered. Crushing it. Grinding it down as if with a pestle. Spreading it on her arm, wrapping it.

"I think she's some sort of medicine maker," Uri said. "A healer." She matched Varan's motions to show she understood.

Giovel laughed again, though less hopefully this time. However Varan had used her powers before, Foneth would see them in a different light. Knives and glyphs and claws.

But perhaps they could find her home before that mattered.

SCHEMES

Pettiness looks the same no matter what language we speak. I simply can't decide whether that comforts me or not.

—The Witherclaw Witch; letter to Drova.

FOR THE TIME being, Giovel led Varan back to the Candlespire. It was a cold, lonely place to make her stay nowadays, with so much of it empty and unused. People said hundreds of mages had once filled the great tower, with ten unique orders like the Divine and the Grays divided through its many rooms and levels. The deadly realities of awakening to Yulen—or at least admitting to awakening—had trimmed their number generations before Giovel's, leaving dusty chambers and quiet stairs for the mages at work there today. There wasn't much about it to welcome a lost woman like Varan, but there was almost nowhere else Giovel could leave a few Grays without raising unwanted banners for her.

Reds and golds in the trees began to glint as the sun dropped below Divnum's walls. Giovel realized he'd gone another night without sleep. His body would feel the effects soon, no matter how much his mind recoiled at the thought of resting, so he tried to make Varan understand goodbye, instructed two Grays to situate her in a tiny resting room, and hurried off.

Back home to the quiet of the Featherwood, the smell of pear in the wood, the clear calm of Iremni's mirror pond in the Sanctuary. Going home meant shedding the mantle of the Order, finally finding space and time to clean a few bruises and sleep. Varan, Sur's plans, and the witches filled Giovel's mind, but he pushed them all aside as dusk truly settled and he reached his house.

He found Inorovel trying to position an old ink painting of the Muold Mountains on the wall in the Sanctuary.

"Isn't that the same place it was before?" he asked, frowning as he watched her struggle with a copper frame hook.

"Is it? Maybe."

"Who knocked it down, then?"

Inorovel sighed. "I took it down on purpose. I meant to put something else there."

"Ah. And what would that be?"

"It doesn't matter. I'm putting this back now."

Inorovel looked away as she spoke, maybe to focus on the hook which kept sliding below the hole she was trying to reach, or perhaps just to avoid his eyes. Giovel thought for a moment of probing further. But Inorovel wasn't a child anymore. Couldn't be. And he'd been questioned enough in the past day to lose any taste he'd ever had for it.

"Can I help?" was all he asked.

"I can't quite reach the right spot," Inorovel said, handing him her frame hook.

Giovel stretched up and positioned the hook, taking the painting from Inorovel a moment later and clipping the hook under the lip of its old ash frame. Inorovel kept her eyes down as he did so. Yes, he'd been right. Not the time to question her.

"There. Good as ever. Do you want to walk before we make some dinner?"

She nodded mutely.

"You pick the route and I'll get myself a clean coat. I've got criminal blood all over this one."

"Really?"

"Of course. See for yourself."

"That's just spilled goldstem sauce, da. I can still smell it."

He shrugged. "That's lucky. Must be masking all the blood from my day fighting dissidents and witches."

That at least made her almost smile, even if it was more indulgent than heartfelt.

Inorovel picked the winding forest path by old Keep Hatahad for their walk. They'd followed this route a hundred times before, but Giovel still enjoyed it. Hatahad was the third or fourth largest building left from before the Fall of Vindil, a thousand-year-old structure of glossy black stone shaped like the tail of a swallow over the trees below it. The Lawrits used the building now, much as the Order had taken the Candlespire at its founding. Giovel wished not for the first time that Foneth had a few more ancient wonders like this, from an era when mages marshalled Yulena to craft stone and wood and clay, not just to unleash as a weapon.

As always, he pointed out the features he admired most in Hatahad. The structure's sloped roof that slanted out into the air; the polished texture of the stone itself; the tiny specks of glistening color in the rock.

Would Iremni and I still have taken walks like this? We've stared at so many of Foneth's old buildings so many times. Maybe we would have tired of it all eventually.

It was odd, though. Of all the things Giovel remembered most clearly before she died, it was their architecture walks, as she liked to call them. Just idling by the same old lumps of stone and brick and metal and woodwork, pointing out the same things they found impressive over and over again. Perhaps the repetition alone kept them sharp in Giovel's memory now, or maybe the utter *unimportance*. He treasured those memories more perhaps than any others, because there was no fog or worry in them. Just Iremni's green eyes and her hand in his and her voice as clear as sunlit glass.

"Are you thinking of Mother?" Inorovel asked.

Giovel blinked. As when anyone mentioned her, his first impulse was to lie, despite the surge of longing her memory brought him. "Just wondering what mages' lives must have been like back when they made buildings like this."

Inorovel paused, staring not at Keep Hatahad but at her feet. "I'm thinking of her, da. I've been making a painting of her."

"You're painting? When did you take up painting?"

"A few months ago. It was going well, it really was. I think you would have liked it."

"Did something happen to it?"

"I tripped and dropped it in the mirror pond. I was trying to put it in the Sanctuary before you got back. But it's ruined now."

So that was why she'd moved the painting of the Muolds. And once again Giovel felt himself almost overcome at his daughter's way of caring, thinking of him and their home in the hours when he was gone. Did he ever think of her that way, when his mind could wander anywhere he chose? He didn't know.

He smiled, though. "One day I come home to hear that you fell in the lake. Today you're telling me you dropped your Mother in the mirror pond. I suppose it's my turn next, then?"

He wished he could find it in himself not just to smile but to laugh. It might help keep his eyes from watering as he thought of what it would be like to see Iremni's face again or hold her close to him.

When he and Inorovel finished clearing their meal, Giovel lit a few lanterns against the cold dark of his bedroom and started jotting ideas to find Varan's home. Look at older maps, of course. Talk with cartographers. Ask merchants who took the long trade roads west of Yeren, where Foneth's maps were blank. All ideas Uri would have considered and perhaps even tried Varan's first day here. More than that, Giovel couldn't bring himself to focus on any one plan for long.

He sketched a few lines of movement. Part of the previous night's operation at the Croen Estate. *That's* where his mind had tried to return despite its mounting fatigue. Again and again Giovel heard Adni's and Dlenar's criticisms of the plan, and with their words came the unshakable sense that some piece of that plan was invisible.

Maybe he just wanted to prove Adni wrong, wanted it badly enough to search for argument where there was none. Or maybe this feeling of imbalance was one, he knew from experience, he couldn't set aside so easily.

He drew the rough outline of the estate as they'd been able to see from the outside. Then he traced from memory the paths of each group Sur assigned, marking what their signals were to advance. Wait for Olinos here. Hold until anyone exits there. *Had* someone exited? Some listener at Etelier's meeting, perhaps walking out early and kicking the whole plan into motion? But that couldn't be it because the Tovómil were the ones set to move if anyone left, yet it was Lances who'd converged first.

Giovel ran his hands through his hair, stretching to envision everything more precisely. The division of multiple forces made it all the messier, not to mention the muddled hierarchy where neither Tovómil nor Candleguard nor Lances technically outranked one another.

Tangled diagrams floated in and out of his mind as he slept and stayed with him through the following morning. As soon as he'd breakfasted, he went to see Sur about it.

"What do you make of this?" he asked, dropping his sketches on Sur's bed in the Belnum clinic.

Sur stared at the diagram for a moment, then scowled at Giovel. "Just yesterday I got slashed across the chest so deeply I looked like a piece of cored fruit. And this is how you choose to say hello?"

"I know it's rude, but I think we might have been sabotaged."

Sur shifted gingerly. He was bandaged all across his chest in addition to a tight wrapping at the joint of his left shoulder. He didn't have much room to move, either. Just a narrow bed set slightly apart from two more rows of them in the same soap-scented room.

"Let me look more closely," Sur said after a moment. "Am I supposed to be able to read this? It looks like a child-drawn map of the Citadel."

"I had to reconstruct everything from memory. But look at this. We were supposed to have Lances come in only two places—here and there. And they came in at *five* all at nearly the same time. What's the likelihood that they could have arranged themselves to do that in perfect synchronization without someone changing the orders?"

"Maybe I did change the orders. Everything happened quickly, Giovel, and you weren't outside to hear about it. Are you sure you mapped this out accurately?"

"I'm sure. I did this kind of exercise a thousand times as a Candle. Look for a minute and tell me if this matches the orders you gave."

Sur sighed. "You'll have to hold the left side for me. I can't really use that arm for now."

Giovel knelt on the flagstones beside Sur's narrow bed and guided him through the diagram, pointing out the entrances the Lances had filled, the numbers he remembered, and the departures from the original plan. "It's as if they mixed your orders with Olinos's idea— and did it with flawless timing—minus one thing. Neither Olinos nor I ever gave a signal for them to come in."

"Maybe some imbecile thought the situation was getting dire. They told me this Etelier had his wolves ready to storm the Optate herself."

"They exaggerated. And I don't think so little of your Lances as to assume they'd shuffle ranks without a direct command."

Sur's scowl intensified. He offered no argument.

"Tell me this, Sur. Could it have been sabotage?"

"Plans going wrong could *always* be sabotage. But I don't think this was." Sur shifted, wincing in pain as his bandaged arm rubbed against the layers of wrapped cloth covering his chest. "I trust the Lances too. If you're asking my opinion today, the Croen Estate was too complex for my initial plan. The Lances probably had to splinter to adapt."

Giovel folded his diagram and pocketed it for later. "I don't believe they would have bungled things without interference. I'm going to look deeper until this makes more sense."

"Do what you want, but I'm not a Jade officer anymore, and you're not a Cloudblade, I might add. We can't authorize one another to investigate the fighters assigned for the operation. I don't think even Adni could make that happen unless we had a real suspicion that one of them was helping the witches—and then it would be Dlenar and his network of spies investigating this, not you."

"I'm not looking for authorization of anything," Giovel said. "Just trying to understand."

"Understanding can be a dangerous scheme itself. Not really part of an underling's duties, is it?"

"I'm already trying to help Varan find her home," Giovel said. "If I uncover anything amiss—especially that relates to the witches—I'll be fulfilling my duties too."

Sur gave Giovel a measuring look. Then he twitched, winced in pain, cursed, and ordered a nearby healer to bring him some tea.

"You can tell yourself that. And you can tell me what you find too," Sur said. "Just don't come so early next time. I'm supposed to be sleeping like an old grandsire. And watch yourself, Giovel."

On his way out of the clinic, Giovel checked on the four other fighters who'd been seriously wounded alongside Sur. Two were Tovómil and said little to Giovel's inquiries. One was a Lance who'd been cut so badly across his neck that he couldn't speak yet—perhaps not ever again. The last was a young Candleguard woman Giovel knew from three years back, a new recruit when he'd been a lieutenant. What had her name been? He felt too embarrassed to let on that he'd forgotten it.

"How did they get you?" he asked instead.

"One of them hit me in the leg with a glass lamp," the Candle explained, half seated now with her leg wrapped in an enormous sling. "Burned me mostly. It's torture in the meantime, but they say I should be hobbling in a week."

Giovel nodded. "I thought I'd lose my foot once when I was new in the guard. It got smashed by a boulder dropped at a quarry. At least you have a good story to tell for the week you'll be out."

She bowed her head slightly as her confined position allowed. "Thank you for visiting, Lord Giovel."

He glanced sidelong before continuing. Each patient's bed was separated enough to provide some quiet, but the whole clinic was open. The mute Lance lay just twenty paces away.

"Can you tell me something of what happened the other night?" Giovel asked quietly. "When the Lances went in, I mean."

"Not much, sir. I was stationed at the front entrance. Didn't see any action until the bastards started pouring out on us."

"And was that Sur's assignment for you?"

"No, sir. I got moved after you went inside."

Now they were getting somewhere.

"Who gave that order?" Giovel asked, carefully controlling his voice so as not to worry the woman.

"Some Lance who came and moved us. My group of four split in two, and one other group joined ours. They told us we had more blades arriving so we could split more ways."

There it was. A made-up order or a falsified report of reinforcements. "Can you remember which Lance that was?"

The Candle tensed. "We didn't do wrong in following him, did we? The line of authority was all strange last night, sir."

"I only need to clarify the details I can for my report," Giovel lied. "You know how it is."

She slumped backward then. "Of course, sir. I didn't know the Lance, but he's a captain so we marched when he said the word."

"As you should. Can you help me correct my diagram of the operation?"

She digested it more quickly than Sur had, commenting and adding details Giovel hadn't pieced together. Apparently there had been more changes than he'd thought, though every addition was small and made some sort of tactical sense. When the Candle had given all the facts she recalled, Giovel thanked her and went to find Varan.

He'd need more information yet, but he knew now that his experience had led him true. Either some Lance had abandoned Sur's plan, or Sur had directly lied to Giovel about it.

WATCHING

Why must everyone talk about me here?
  —The Witherclaw Witch; letter to Recia.

It took a week for Claravena to find the new witch. Unsurprisingly she was in Divnum, right under the thumb of the Order. No one in the Order was likely to recognize Claravena milling close at hand, thanks to her meticulous patterns of discretion, but Eronea likely worked near here as well, walked near here. They could cross paths unexpectedly, and that would be that. Especially if Eronea caught her spying on the new witch.

Claravena often wondered what her Gray sister was like now. Would she immediately strike if they met? Call for help to bring Claravena in? Was she even still *alive*? They hadn't seen one another in three years.

While there was no sign of Eronea in Divnum, Claravena found no shortage of hints as to the new witch's ways and daily patterns. People talked freely about her in the chilly streets and trade stalls, holiday gatherings, taverns, and guildhalls of the city. It let Claravena keep her distance while learning a great deal. Part of the Divine's game, perhaps—spread stories of their newly acquired weapon to crush the hopes of any who opposed them.

It seemed to be working.

Varan Witherclaw, people called her. Street talk led Claravena to a cluster of gold-leafed trees near the Candlespire, close enough to see the witch for herself. She was a grim-looking woman with waves of black hair folded around her head and eyes just as dark. Little wonder she would be grim, with a Gray or two, if not Giovel Ullin himself, always right at her shoulder like a lead for a hound.

Claravena spent a day loitering at a distance as Giovel and the new witch ventured throughout the city. They went to see merchants, archivists, bards even. Claravena didn't dare get close enough to hear much of any conversation they had, but they were always talking about maps and geographies. Tactics, perhaps? Some move against the Redremel? Or maybe something more, an alliance with the people from whom this Varan witch came?

Their guard often dropped as they talked. Giovel, for all his reputation as a Candle, seemed to forget to look over his own shoulder. Or could be that was part of his training, appearing absent and distracted while somehow keeping a keen eye on everything around him.

Just to get the new witch away from Divnum sooner, Claravena considered spiriting her right under Giovel's watch, taking the risk that she could find this Witherclaw woman again before he did. It wouldn't be hard. She had a clear sight of the Witherclaw ten, twenty times the first day after finding her, and sight was all she needed to do a spiriting reliably. It was just the matter of drawing out the large, complex glyph required without some passerby screaming for Candles to come. She could even spirit Giovel away first and take Varan Witherclaw where she was if it weren't for the powers everyone gossiped about Varan having, powers Claravena knew were real from their brief exchange of spells at the Croen Estate.

When they weren't out in the streets, Giovel often took Varan to a little home northwest of the Candlespire, a translator's house from what Claravena gathered. She'd sit there for hours, puzzling over children's books and speaking with the translator herself, exposed and vulnerable the entire time. One windy day, Giovel left her there without a contingent of Grays, without even a Candle for protection. Alone.

Claravena walked in distant loops around the house, just far enough to keep her face hidden, just close enough to smell woodsmoke from the chimneystack. *I could kill her today,* she thought. *Forget spiriting her out and dragging her to the others. I could walk up* without any preamble, carve a glyph in the dirt at the doorway, and off them both without a motion when one comes to greet me. So much for the Order's new weapon.

Etelier doesn't expect to meet with the others for four days yet. I can have this done before then. Maybe even set a trap for Giovel at the same time. I could bring not one but two enemies' heads back.

But wouldn't that just prove what they say about me? Doesn't that make me the murderous, selfish witch the Order says to expect?

So Claravena knew she wouldn't do it, right from the moment the thought took shape, and shame poured through her like a jolt of cold when the wind picked up.

She'd started out so purposefully, so peacefully even. Not killing Grays or burning supposed Order hideaways. Just talking with Lawrits, sharing concerns with Optacrats, trying to elucidate the dangerous precedent for hunting awakenings who hadn't done anything worth being named *witch*. Something had to cause those awakenings, something far outside any one person's hunger for might and control of the world. They just had to find a way to show it so all Foneth could see, show it so clearly that the Order would stop hunting the fools who never wanted Yulena in the first place.

It had been just Claravena at first. Before she met Etelier, she'd written a hundred letters to influential Medíns and Jadas, met with leaders of a score of septs to try finding safe and peaceful ways to manage awakenings or calm the heart-link to Yulena. When none of that worked, she'd grown bolder. She'd tried finding a Gray who would sympathize with safer regulations for awakenings. She'd sought support from Lances and Candles who'd seen firsthand what so called witches could be—peaceful or otherwise. She'd even spoken with old Sironis Lun when he stepped down from the Divine Order. Couldn't he make a case for trusting awakenings a little more, protecting them, helping them learn to manage the power they'd stumbled into? Couldn't he push for the Order to reveal more of their knowledge of Yulena and encourage more ordinary awakenings practice some productive, useful branch of magic?

Sironis had suspected. He even accused Claravena of being a witch herself, so she had to kill him. Her first time killing anyone.

Still. There *were* other things to try, other methods to employ before waging red war with the Order itself. It was just that Etelier wouldn't wait. He seemed to believe his daughter would get worse if he sat still, that the world itself would collapse on them if he did nothing to stop it. Maybe walking fast helped quiet the voices he must hear. Claravena didn't know. But she cursed Etelier to Cold Lake for dragging her this far, where she'd consider murdering some old translator just for a chance to barb the Order in its side.

Four more days until she'd see Etelier and the others. She could wait that long, keep Varan Witherclaw in her sights and be sure, when the rest of the witches gathered, that they knew what Varan was doing. Then someone else could choose what to do next.

Claravena had made enough decisions to hate herself since her own awakening.

FEAR AND MOURNING

I've made a friend, of sorts.
　—The Witherclaw Witch; letter to Golkorun.

KIRIDA'S FIRST MEETING with the Witherclaw Witch was at mother's
house, a tiny little building near the northern curve of the Divnum
walls. The walk there seemed longer than ever before. Progis pulled on
Kirida's hand most of the way, wanting to run off to chase birds and
ochre leaves caught in the autumn wind. The weight of her unborn
child always seemed to lean in the opposite direction when Progis
tugged at her, threatening to split her open on the grass. Still three
months to go and the baby felt like a teetering barrel of bricks.

Mother came out to greet them and hefted Progis onto her shoulders
to show him her wind charms. Kirida went inside to sit, hoping for a
minute to catch her breath. It already felt like an odd meeting, to be
sure, like a game two parents forced when they wanted their children
to be friends—except instead of another mother it was Giovel Ullin
arranging things. Odd indeed.

The witch was waiting in mother's leafy Sanctuary.

"You must be Varan," Kirida said, and bowed from her neck since a
full waist bow no longer felt feasible. "I'm Uri's daughter."

The witch's appearance was as distinct as she'd heard while also
being almost ordinary. Her hair was like wavy shadow, her eyes too,
but there was no demonic visage like people described. She looked like
any other woman might aside from her unusually stark contrast of

dark eyes and pale skin. She held a child's book when Kirida stepped into the room, mouthing things in a half mumble as she did so.

Seeing that, Kirida's uneasiness began to lift.

Varan stood and bowed as well, though she did it perhaps even more clumsily than Kirida had. "I am Varan. You are Kirida?"

She said Kirida's name with tripped consonants as if they were as foreign to her as everything else. Just what Kirida needed. An adult to teach how to speak, as if a little boy wasn't enough. At least Varan might not run away the moment Kirida said no to anything.

"Do you mind if I sit?" Kirida asked, indicating to the long bench fashioned to look like a fallen log.

"You have child," Varan said, seemingly surprised. "Sit. Sit."

"Can you read the words, Varan?"

Varan held her book up, trying to answer. After a moment she said, "I don't have words."

As she'd expected. As anyone would expect for a spiriting of . . . what? Nine days now? Eight since mother had been introduced to her? Kirida was frankly amazed Varan had learned anything in that time. She was looking at the book again now, with a kind of intense thirst, like she meant to drink the words off the pages. Her eyes drifted every now and then, not to Kirida so much as to her belly.

"I have another child as well," Kirida said, not knowing how much Varan might really understand. "A little boy. Progis is his name. I don't know if he'll be mannered enough to come in and say hello."

Progis's laughter echoed outside, followed by a nervous shout from mother. "Don't touch that! Oh . . . You need to listen to your Old Mother." Varan's eyes seemed to follow the sound. Then they were back to her book.

Mother came in a moment later, carrying Progis over her shoulder like he was a heap of cut grain. "Varan, any water for you? Kirida?"

"Yes please," Kirida said.

Varan looked confused.

"Water," mother repeated, motioning with one hand and almost dropping Progis, who squealed and laughed.

"Yes. Please water," Varan said.

"Down you go, wolfling," mother said, and rolled Progis onto the moss-like rug of her Sanctuary. "I'll be back in a hop."

Now the Witherclaw Witch's eyes were up, her book set aside. She watched, seemingly entranced, as Progis pulled a stick from his hair and tried to scratch a hole in the moss-rug. Ah. So she was a mother too, Kirida thought. Maybe of a child close to Progis's age.

It made her ache for the strange woman. And wonder what *she'd* do if Progis were a spiriting, or if she herself was.

"Come and say hello, Progis," Kirida said.

Varan bowed unsteadily again. "Hello."

Progis mumbled hello back without looking up from the rug. "Old Mother found a dead rat."

"That's disgusting," Kirida said, smiling to match his smile. "Did you poke it?"

"Old Mother said I can't pick it up."

"Old Mother's wise about these things."

Beside her, Varan laughed softly. Kirida turned to face her, wondering if she truly understood what she was hearing. When she met Varan's eyes, though, Varan just said, "He speaks. I don't have words."

Perhaps that was why mother had truly wanted Kirida to meet Varan. Just to give her someone to talk to. It was the first time Kirida had met any spiriting, and she certainly couldn't help translate like mother could. But she could speak and listen.

Varan surprised her by asking a question then. "You are afraid?"

It took Kirida a moment to answer, "I don't know."

"Other people are afraid," Varan said. "I am afraid."

"People might call you something. They might call you 'witch.' But my mother says you aren't like the other witches."

"What is witch?" Varan asked.

What would mother say? "Power. Yulena."

Yulena Varan understood. "I am not Yulena. I am not witch."

Yet that was why mother said people *would* fear her, no matter how she used this power, this witchery without Yulena. But Kirida vowed not to be one of them. She had enough to fear without adding a lost woman, a young mother like herself.

"People with power don't frighten me," Kirida said, meeting Varan's deep eyes. "I'm only afraid of people who *want* power. Do you understand?"

"No," Varan said.

"I'll try to explain. Witches brought you here, yes?"

"Yes." The focus of Varan's gaze said she truly did understand that.

"Witches have power. But others have power too. The Divine Order. Lord Giovel."

Varan nodded. "Giovel has power. Varan has power."

"Giovel is your friend," Kirida said. "Witches are not your friend."

It seemed as if Varan understood this time. She asked, "Giovel wants my power?"

Did he? "I don't know. Giovel might want your help to find the witches. Giovel might ask you to use your power."

"Yes."

"You would help him? You would help them find the witches?"

"Find witches," Varan said with a look as hard as stone in her face now. *That* was a look people could fear. "Witches lost me," she went on. "Witches can find me home."

And once again Kirida found her fears dispelled by what Varan said and did. She couldn't fear someone so far from home, missing her own family and trying to learn a new language so she could find her way back. Kirida mourned for her already. And it was hard to fear when you mourned.

CIRCLES

The person I see most is Giovel. He seems to be my guide, as it were, but his mind is far away.
    —The Witherclaw Witch; letter to Recia.

THREE DAYS AFTER the events at the Croen Estate, Giovel found a note tucked into the crevice beside his front door. Few words, but plenty of substance.

When can we begin testing the witch's powers? We should ascertain their nature soon. Elínla agrees with me.

Dlenar Tovóm

Not an order. Not even a formal request for anything. Just a question that, as far as the Order was concerned, hadn't yet been answered. Giovel threw it in the fire and started preparing breakfast. Varan wouldn't be turned into a caged spectacle while *he* had any responsibility for her.

He found her at the Candlespire that morning, alone in a bare, terraced watch room with a Gray standing guard outside. She jumped when Giovel stepped inside.

"It's just me," he said.

Varan stood quickly, stepping in front of something on a stone shelf by the nearest lookout window. Not quite quick enough to block what it was—a torn piece of parchment marked with shapes. Patterns like Yulen glyphs, too big to be writing in her own language. Lifeless, though, not glowing at all. Little wonder Varan had jumped, the poor woman.

"You didn't clap," she said.

"We only clap outside. Not when coming into a room." Giovel walked closer, eyeing the ink glyphs. "No luck, I suppose? No Yulena?"

With a weary look of acceptance, she showed him her parchment and said, "No Yulena."

Her glyphs didn't correspond to any Giovel knew. He wondered if he should be relieved that she hadn't learned any true patterns or concerned at her willingness to try unknown ones. At any rate, they were nothing but sketches in her hands, lifeless, powerless, unconnected to Yulen itself. Not that Giovel could blame her for trying to craft them.

"Few people can use Yulena," he said. "Less than three hundred in Foneth are authorized, and Dlenar doubts more than one or two thousand in the area could have awakened to it. But until one does, there's no bridge between them and the power. Do you understand?"

Vacant eyes, then a scowl. "I don't understand."

"May I use your pen?"

Vacant again, so Giovel plucked the pen from the shelf, sliding a little cup of ink beside it before he drew a set of circles to one side of the parchment. One large circle for Yulena, five small ones for people.

"Some people awaken. They can use Yulena. They have a connection to it." He drew a line between one small circle and Yulen. "*I* awakened. All of the Order awakened. Witches too. We have the bridge." Another line. "Other people can't touch Yulena. They can see it, and sometimes they can hear its effect—a faint kind of humming noise. But they can't use it. Do you understand?"

She started to nod. "But me. I have power."

For which she had Giovel's deepest pity. "Maybe you can awaken too. Maybe you can have the bridge, the heart-link as some septs call it. Maybe. But if you don't awaken, you can't use it." No backward-crafting the spiriting spell that stranded you so far from your home. It was probably impossible to reverse any such spell in the first place.

Varan's next question surprised Giovel. "Are you angry?"

He thought about it. Dlenar, Hirnu, or Adni might be livid to find her drawing her own glyphs, and he probably should be as well. She'd tried to use a craft forbidden without the careful scrutiny of the Gray Order and a certification steeped in layers of law. She'd tried to do something forbidden by seven centuries of process, the very thing the Divine Order existed to oversee. She'd tried to use a power that destroyed Vindil and broke half the world with it. She'd almost made a witch of herself.

But she didn't know enough to understand why it was forbidden, and what child in Foneth didn't try drawing glyphs? Who wouldn't when they felt powerless and alone?

"I'm not angry," Giovel said, and handed the parchment back to Varan. "I know why you tried."

It was what he would have done. The difference was, when Iremni died, he already knew enough about Yulena to be sure that what Varan wanted was unreachable. Where she had hope, slim though it might be, he had only the sorrowful knowledge that Yulena was only truly good at destroying.

He led Varan out into the crisp fall morning and north toward Uri's for another bout of instruction. As they walked, he tried to assure her, tried talking with her and smiling and setting her at ease, though Dlenar's cold request to study her powers kept a knot of indignation buried in his own mind. That and his muddled musings about ranks of Lances and Candles defying orders to move against the witches.

His diagram of the Croen Estate pressed on his thoughts all through the afternoon. It gave him something to focus on while Adni presented the Optate's displeasure at the recent failure to capture this Etelier witch, and Ralden proposed new plans for collaborating with Lawrits, metallurgy guilds, and even a group of musicians. It was still on his mind afterward when Hirnu pressed Giovel to practice the Gag for an hour without commenting on his pitiful mistakes.

When his meetings ended, he collected Varan again, tried to explain where they were headed, and set out to harvest the seeds he'd been planting through the last few days. He'd called on as many Lances as owed him favor—and several to whom *he* owed help as well. No one could say much about the group assigned the other night, but Banner Captain Ulia had hinted she had a name for him.

They met in The Opal Mare, which was starting to crowd as daylight faded. It was a broad, open food hall near the Citadel, smelling more like wood polish than roasting meals. Most of the clientele were Optacrats and Lawrits—people with money. Giovel picked a narrow table near one corner of the big place, not so much for his own privacy as for Varan, who'd already attracted more than one stare and whispered conversation. He'd hoped he could somehow gather information while she was with Uri or otherwise out of public sight, but the risk couldn't be helped entirely, not unless he dropped his search for the missing Lance. At least no one was likely to bother her while he sat nearby.

"Spiced broth?" Ulia asked, stepping up from another table nearby. She towered over Giovel, already holding two bowls the rich color of maple.

"Try some, Varan," Giovel said, sliding his bowl over. Varan stared at it a moment, then sipped it tentatively. A moment later she was lapping it up as if she hadn't eaten in days. Had she? Giovel couldn't remember whether he was responsible for her meals. His own stomach twisted uncomfortably at the thought of her going hungry no thanks to his negligence.

"I found your man," Ulia said, taking a seat and sipping from her own bowl. "A handsome fool named Riddin. I assigned him to be Sur's right-hand for that move the other night. He's not the smartest by himself, but he's quick on his feet and not afraid to look down the sight of a handbow."

"How much of a strategist is he?" Giovel asked.

Ulia narrowed her eyes. A long scar marked one side of her face—a knife-wound from a training accident, Giovel had heard. Ulia's face looked ready to split open when her eyes slanted like that. "You trying to steal Lances from me?" she asked.

"I wish it was as simple as poaching," Giovel said. "And besides, I seem to recall that they stole you from my battalion in the Candles. Why can't I take a few toughs for future tasks with the Order?"

"I can give you better names than Riddin's if you tell me what sort of soldier you want."

"Sounds like you're volunteering, Ulia."

"You can bet your Divine breech I am. I'd jump ranks today if it meant a promotion somewhere else. No woman besides Jinaten

Teserot has ever risen past Banner Captain without trying something well outside official duties."

It was similar in the Candleguard, Giovel thought ruefully. "I can't offer you anything right now. That's not part of my authority anymore. But I would be grateful if you could help me find this Riddin's current assignment."

"Already done." Ulia passed him a crumpled duty roster with Riddin's name near the top. "Just don't forget your old loyals when you do get more authority."

"I promise I won't."

"Not that I'm volunteering for the kind of duties that get a woman promoted," Ulia added. "Not for you, anyway."

Giovel thanked the stars that he knew Ulia well enough not to wonder if she were joking. Sometimes he wished for someone who'd flirt with him—or more. But Iremni was too easy to remember for him to find real comfort at the thought of another woman's interest or company.

"You learning much from this old tree?" Ulia asked, now turning toward Varan. "He's a decent leader if you forgive his ugly face."

Varan turned toward them but frowned as if she couldn't follow what had been said.

"She's still picking up Medín," Giovel said quietly.

"So she does have her own language. I thought it was all talk."

"There shouldn't be talk like that, not yet. What do people say about her?"

"That she's a witch," said Ulia. "That she can call blizzards from the sky and eat fire."

Giovel raised an eyebrow.

"I've got men who were there with you and swear they saw her do it, Giovel."

Now Varan looked their way. So she could understand, or at least knew they were talking about her like a child who couldn't respond for herself.

"I should get out to find this Riddin fellow," Giovel said, rising to leave. "Let's go, Varan."

Riddin's duty roster showed the last six days of work, plus the following four. He was slated for drill with a group near Hushwater

Lake today. Even with the roster, however, it was hard to find the man. The sun had been gone an hour when Giovel finally navigated to the correct Lance hall in Belnum.

Riddin wasn't there.

"Traded his schedule with me, Lord Divine," a pale-skinned man said. "I'd be proud to serve in his place, if I can."

"How often do roster exchanges get approved?" Giovel asked.

"Not too often, Lord."

Curious. "And did Riddin say why or what he'd do to make it worth your while?"

"Didn't ask. He didn't say."

"Does your hall roster show where I can find him tomorrow?"

"See for yourself, Lord Divine."

The Lance directed him to a charcoal board in a smoky corner beside the hearth. Riddin's name was nowhere to be found on the next three days' duty sheets, despite what was written on the roster Ulia had given Giovel.

Could be he was wounded and his comrade didn't know it. Perhaps he was taking time off to celebrate the two-day Leaf Festival held in the estates. Giovel could imagine any number of explanations. He was getting anxious enough to meet this Riddin, however, not to wait a few duty-free days to do it.

"What are you doing?" Varan asked, peering at the rosters herself as if she meant to untangle the words there.

Giovel sighed inwardly. What to say that she'd understand?

"I'm walking in circles," he said finally.

He probably couldn't ask many more questions among the Lances, not right away at least. Sur had been right—this was veering well outside Giovel's authority, despite that it all pertained to an Order assignment. If he'd intended to follow protocol, he should have gone straight to the legion Commander as soon as he learned which colors Riddin wore and let the Lances pursue their own line of investigation or recourse.

Maybe weeks of meetings or the nearness of Etelier's escape had spoiled his patience. In any case, Giovel decided then and there that he wasn't going to wait for Riddin to show himself. Whether to prove Adni wrong, to vindicate Sur's original plan, or just to shake off the nagging sense that he'd missed something, Giovel meant to talk with Riddin on his own terms.

And if he had to walk in circles to get there, so be it.

MORE SEARCHING

People here talk about awakening to Yulena as if it wasn't there before. Some people report themselves and witness to other witches that they can be trusted with their power. Not many, though. I think they're too ashamed.
—The Witherclaw Witch; letter to Golkorun.

ETELIER WAITED FOR an hour before Wurelna showed herself. The sun was fully down by then, exposing glimmers of fire and lantern light in the scattered houses below. Etelier had to breathe into his hands every few minutes to keep them from stiffening against the bitter air. The pine and spruce trees on Vision Hill did little to block the wind, and the ground was still cold as iron on a mountaintop.

"What took you so long?" he snapped when Wurelna finally arrived.

She sat on the frosted grass nearby, unwrapping a waxed cheese from her cloak. "I didn't mean to be so late. I brought food."

The cheese smelled fabulous—sharp and nutty and fresh—and Etelier hadn't eaten since before his work shift began that day. He'd spent his allotted rest investigating a dead end lead Ithilo gave him for a possible awakening nearby. Now he eyed the cheese hungrily.

"Go on and have some," Wurelna said.

"I'm not a beggar."

"And I'm not a hoarder."

Etelier needed no further persuading. He devoured his portion of the food almost before Wurelna had eaten three bites.

"I'll take your speed as thanks," she said, eyebrows raised. "What did you want me to show you this time?"

"Spellbuilding."

She paused, lowering her food from her mouth and swallowing slowly before she answered. "That's not an art that needs much teaching. If you want to experiment, you can do it on your own."

"Claravena says you're the best at it."

"That's only because I'm the most patient about it. There's really not much to show."

"Then it shouldn't take you long. Just get on with it before we freeze solid up here."

"The Parity Sept has an old shrine on the other side of the hill. We could at least get out of the cold there."

"Here's fine."

Once again Wurelna was silent, and at first Etelier thought she was pouting. He had to remind himself that she wasn't like Tranin or Claravena or Ithilo. Wurelna just watched him instead, gazing as if she meant to read him. Sometimes he thought she could, that she somehow knew how to peer right into his thoughts and voice what was in the far reaches of his mind.

"Alright, then," she said at last, and moved forward onto her knees to begin drawing the outline of a glyph with a stick of juniper. "You know this one?"

"The Nettle."

"And if I elongate this curve a little past the rest of the glyph?" She moved her juniper stick as she spoke, extending the shape on one side.

"It still looks like the Nettle."

"And it essentially still is. But the variation in length of just one prong of the glyph will change the spell's outcome as well, however small the change might be. Now what if I add a tick on another prong?"

It was a tiny indent, barely noticeable in the frost. Etelier doubted he'd be able to see it at all when she imbued the glyph and the glow of Yulen filled its outline.

"Does that little of a move really change it?" he asked.

"The key to spellbuilding is that *every* variation changes things. Whether it's drawing the glyph with different proportions, making one line not quite straight, or just adding a little drag when you lift your finger from the shape, each variation will change the spell's outcome."

He frowned. He knew better than to invent his own glyphs, but he'd never paid close enough attention to consider the effects of such minor alterations. "What patterns can you show me in these changes?"

Wurelna smiled softly, and Etelier thought she was laughing at him. But no, he reminded himself. She wasn't Claravena. Nor Pramél. Wurelna was more like a child than those two, amused for her own sake and not because she looked down at him.

"If I did know many patterns, I think we would have gained more ground against the Order by now," she said. "There are a few, to be sure, like size. A bigger glyph tends to allow a bigger spell. Hence they say Renma's glyph destroyed Vindil not because it was engineered to do so, but because the glyph spanned thirty paces from its center."

"That's fish talk. If it were true then witches would have wrecked the Divine fifty times over."

"Only if they could control spells that size. I'm not saying there aren't other changes that come with size as well—and size alone *will* make any glyph more challenging to tame when it comes to casting the spell. If you don't believe me, try it with something simple like your Hammer glyph."

"Fine. What other patterns do you know?"

Despite her insistence that she didn't know much, Wurelna showed several patterns that were new to Etelier. How horizontal elongation tended to produce spells with more rapid effect. How more detailed variations like ticks and cross-marks and scorings tended to vary things much more than size or proration would, prepending conditions to a contract as Wurelna put it.

"What about patterns that build instead of just blasting things apart?" Etelier asked after nearly half an hour of explanations.

Wurelna stared again, and once more Etelier felt as if she might be reading his thoughts. Was that why she wanted to meet on Vision Hill? So she could look inside his mind and unravel him like a rope?

"There's some debate as to whether Yulena can do anything like what you're describing," she said at last.

"There are records of it, though. And evidence. Look at the Divnum walls and the Candlespire."

"I believe that Yulena *did* help create them, yes. But did a mage use Yulena to plaster carved stones together? Or to imbue the walls with protection against other spells? Or did someone simply use Yulena to cut the stone in patterns that were impossible with hammers and chisels?"

There had to be more to it than that. "What about accounts of ancient mages using Yulena to mend wounds?" Etelier asked.

Her eyes were on him once more. "Is that what you're really looking for, Etelier?"

He didn't answer. It was hard to admit, even in the solitude of Mota's tiny room at home, but it was the only thing he'd ever sought in Yulena.

"Let me share a few more principles," Wurelna said when Etelier didn't respond. "First, the spells you're describing could have been done with Yulena a lot like what we use today. Yes, old books claim Yulena once healed as well as killed. That could mean someone touched a pierced lung and it became whole. Or it could mean that they used Yulena to cauterize an open wound, to cut bad tissue away with greater precision than a knife could, or even to disintegrate bits of debris in a wound. We don't know. Second idea—and this is the most important thing I can add to the rule of variations—we can only really test anything by small increments. I wouldn't know any patterns if I hadn't tried a thousand variations between each version."

"This doesn't answer my question at all, Wurelna."

"I wish I could give you more, but that truly is most of what I can offer. Even if you are looking for spells to heal, you'll have to start from spells that *don't*. That's all anyone has right now."

What she was describing could take more than just months. Decades. Or even centuries. The Divine had been tinkering like this for seven hundred years, hadn't they? And they were still no closer to doing great works of Yulena than they had been after the Queen's War and the dawn of their founding. Just as Pramél so often said. Just as the world accepted now.

No. He couldn't believe that. They *must* be closer. The Divine had just hidden all their findings, buried them. Well, they couldn't keep them hidden forever. Not while Etelier was searching too.

"You and I are done here," he said, standing and beginning to walk down the hill. "Don't be late when we gather tomorrow."

As soon as he set out, he felt guilty for offering no thanks that Wurelna had come at all. Her measured calmness, even kindness, always brought him guilt. It just felt thin next to the ever-present hurt he felt for Mota.

Etelier walked to meet Claravena next, following the twisted maze of hillocks and clustered houses, tiny ponds, and rocky outcroppings that dotted the southeast edge of Belnum. Claravena lived in the heart of the district, one of the most crowded places in all Foneth. It took nearly two hours just to walk that far from Vision Hill. So this might be yet another night without sleep. Not that Etelier managed to sleep much when he was home.

He felt a cough forming in his chest, and his body ached for a pause. The thing was, his mind hadn't found solace in a year. Maybe it never would again.

A pair of lamps lit the window of Claravena's narrow cottage when Etelier arrived. The house thrummed with the residue of old spells, barely perceptible but clear enough to Etelier that he might have worried—if three quarters of Foneth didn't have Yulen's old hum about it now, and if anyone actually paused to notice. It was late enough that he walked in without clapping, as only he or one of their companions would. Claravena was reaching for a knife when he stepped in, but she relaxed visibly when she saw it was him.

"I thought you were coming at sunset," she said.

"So did I. Wurelna was late to meet me."

"I found our mystery witch," Claravena said as she put her knife away. "She's in Divnum, right where the Order can guard her."

"Damn. Is she working with them? Or simply courting them?"

"Not sure yet," Claravena replied. "I couldn't find any evidence that they're ordering her about. Old Giovel hovers near her constantly, so I couldn't get close enough to find out much else. Just that they're calling her Witherclaw."

"Witherclaw?"

"The claw on her dress the night at Croen. And the fact that she's some kind of monster."

"What did you find out about her witchery?" Etelier asked.

"Nothing but rumors. Plenty of Candles are speculating about her."

"Let's hear it."

"It's loafer talk, Etelier."

"*Let's hear it.*"

Claravena smirked. "Fine. They say she can breathe flames. One guard said he saw her split stone with one finger, but he was drunk enough to say Olura Medín eats childflesh for breakfast. There's also a story that her mother bedded a demon and that's where her black eyes come from."

Rubbish, all. It made Etelier want to kick the door he'd just walked through.

He'd find out more if he went himself. Not that he could enter Divnum's walls with any confidence. A dozen or more Candles had to know his face by now, and they'd have him marked to the feature before another week was out.

More importantly, he couldn't get distracted now. Not even at the chance of Yulena as unique as this Witherclaw's. Being different didn't mean her witchery was what Mota needed.

Claravena folded her arms as if to warm herself. "Do I go back? Or can I return to normal work? We're risking a lot to spend time watching this witch."

"And we'll keep risking a lot until we start finding real answers," Etelier said.

"Then let's spirit her out and be done with it. Or you can send someone like Noru for this. I have more important things to do."

"You know precisely where she sleeps, Claravena?"

"No."

"Then unless you've learned to spirit someone you can't find, I need you to get close again."

Even then there was the weighty risk, if they tried spiriting her, that the Witherclaw would turn up somewhere Claravena couldn't reach in time. They couldn't send anyone else to watch, either. Noru was hot-blooded and petty, too quick to cut a Candle's purse just to get back at them. And Ithilo was busy gathering ears for their next meeting. Órkol, Tranin, Piatém, and Raf were too well-known. And Wurelna too, former-Gray that she was. In the end, there was no one ideal for any of the tasks Etelier had given them. Just least suited to get caught.

What a broken group we are.

They were ten strong now, though that might not matter when compared to the Divine, the Grays, and the might of the Optate. Etelier and Claravena had met first, and most of the others joined them soon after. Some had died along the way, as they knew they might. The Grays got some, Candles' handbows got others, and a few just crafted a bad glyph in some moment of abandon; old Furapar had blasted himself open simply trying to teach Etelier a new spell. Etelier had worked tirelessly to find others, like Tranin who had joined the cause most recently, but growth always came slowly.

"I need Noru to keep searching for the ruins of old Vindil," Etelier said after a long moment of thought.

"Noru hasn't found so much as a clue in weeks."

"Let me remind you that all your clues about the Divine's library have been frass too."

"They wouldn't be if you let me go out and look instead of babywatching a witch in the heart of the Order's territory!"

"You spoke up for *me* to lead us, Claravena. Me. If you want to walk that choice back, maybe you should go fight the Order on your own. If not, I suggest you do as I say and watch that witch."

A wild look came into Claravena's eyes. It wasn't the first time Etelier had seen it there. She had it every time they saw a Gray, every time they made a move against the Order.

But now, he thought, it's a wild look because of me, because she despises me like she despises them. I can't care about it, though. If I'm going to lead, I can't care what anyone thinks of me.

"Do I make myself clear?" he asked.

Claravena spat on her own floor. "Clear as drool. Get out of my house so I can go to bed."

"I'll be back tomorrow night. I'm checking another lead on the Divine's library after my work shift."

"You're wasting your time."

He left without another word.

Yes, I am wasting my time. Wasting it on weak witches when I could be with Mota and Pramél instead. I've probably known it all along.

Maybe he would give the hunt up tomorrow. Maybe the next day. He didn't know. For now, at least, he was out and doing, following new leads, searching for something to bring back what he'd lost. So for now he'd keep searching.

RISE

I spend my days in silence. I think I understand now how hard staying quiet is for you.

    —The Witherclaw Witch; letter to Inivar and Sil.

GIOVEL CHECKED ON Riddin's duty roster four consecutive mornings. "Part of the routine," he told Varan, who had started asking more of her own questions as she trailed along with him. He wished, not for the first time, that he'd been in the Cloudblades even a month or two longer, learned a few more investigative skills to help speed up his search. Lower-ranked Candleguard like he'd been for so long only learned to enforce the law, not to find those who dodged it, so now his shapeless investigation felt like searching a lakebed for one particular handful of mud. Disorganized, ineffective. Pointless.

On the fifth day, Giovel found Birenlu waiting when he led Varan from the Candlespire.

"I found your man," she said hurriedly, her breath rising in puffs of mist. "He lives in a quiet little stretch of south Belnum near Vision Hill. I've seen him, too, or a man I assume is Riddin, anyway. No uniform, but he's built like he could use a spear."

At last. Perhaps learning when to beg for a favor was the only skill Giovel needed from his brief time as a Cloudblade. One day since he'd sought Birenlu's help, and she'd accomplished more than he had over nearly a week.

"Well done," he said. "Can you mark his home on my map?"

"And our deal? You'll grant me an uninterrupted interview for my research?"

"Yes, yes, as soon as I can get Riddin in my hands."

He thanked the stars that Birenlu only wanted to talk to him and not Varan. The way she stared at Varan now—who stood aloof a few paces back—Birenlu might have been eying a necklace she wanted to wear.

"One more favor in return?" Giovel asked.

Birenlu charcoaled Riddin's home onto his map. "If it's reasonable."

"Find out if he's gone anywhere in the last few days or if anyone has come to meet him."

"That's not as easy as it might sound. And I'd have to skip a very interesting ceremony Belnum's Storm Sept is putting on for Scholar Day."

"Do it and I'll strong-arm any one of the Spireblades into giving you an hour or two of time as well."

Birenlu's eyes snapped to Varan and then back to Giovel. If she wanted more, she held it in, simply saying, "Done."

She looked happy enough to fly. It was almost how Giovel felt this morning too. The air was fresh and brisk, the leaves were in their last week or so of vibrance, and he'd found his quarry by a means no one was likely to suspect. More than worth letting Birenlu badger him for a few hours about the inner workings of the Order. In fact, he wondered if he might use her services again in the future. She seemed to be uncannily good at finding things—including people who didn't want to be discovered.

Giovel stopped back by the house to see Inorovel off to her lessons. Then he led Varan to Uri's once again, meeting a Gray there as a precaution. Varan started reading before he left, still using a child's book but clearly learning rapidly since she had little else to do outside her visits with Uri's daughter or following him for his errands.

"You know where to find me if you need anything else," Giovel said.

"Not really," Uri mumbled. "I know where you live, but you're not there half the time. Are you sure this isn't a problem, me watching Varan for you?"

"I'm not exactly leaving you defenseless, and I trust you completely."

"It's not your trust I'm worried about. What if Adni finds out you shirked her off onto me?"

"Her studying the language is good for all of us. And I'm not afraid of Adni's displeasure."

"Well *I am*, and I can't afford to have enemies in the Order."

Giovel thought a moment. "I can easily justify it. Learning our language is all furthering the effort to find out where she really comes from. It's all part of helping her."

"Not good enough. Those Grays and I could be flogged for less than this. If Adni really didn't like our arrangement, I could lose the work I do for the Lawrits. And that's not even mentioning the risk of someone else coming for her . . . power."

He knew Uri was right. Knew it and wished he could ignore it. He was just so close to piecing together Riddin's odd orders at the Croen Estate, so close to unwinding the broken chain of events that night. But he couldn't keep risking Uri like this. Or her daughter's family too. Yes, the Grays would protect them from most things—but they wouldn't be enough of a shield to stop Adni's idiotic wrath if word got out that Giovel was entrusting Varan's care to them.

"Has Varan shown any more intimations of her power?" Giovel asked, thinking rapidly now.

"Not a bit."

"Good. She should be safe one more day. After that, I promise I'll take her back under my wing directly and stay with you for any lessons she has."

"I'll hold you to that," Uri said. "And I hope you know I'm not doing this as a favor to you, Giovel."

"Then I'll trust it's for Iremni. For your old friendship."

"You can be such a fool. I'm doing this for Varan herself, so don't come back expecting my help for any other reasons. I've risked as much as I'm willing to for your personal cause."

Giovel looked away quickly. "Understood. I'll collect her tonight and find a new arrangement."

"You talk about her like she's a dog," Uri said, voice rising now. "She's a woman. A mother of two little boys, she tells me. She has a husband who must be faint with worry. You know what that sort of worry is like."

How many hours had he spent with Varan now? Perhaps five dull days' worth? And Uri knew more about her than he did. Yet here he was, chasing Lances who changed their duty rosters when he could be chasing the witches who brought her here. Why? Not because he'd given up. Not because he didn't want to find them. Certainly not because he cared about Adni's orders to avoid such an investigation. So why?

He wasn't sure he could answer himself, so he kept his eyes away from Uri.

"I'll be back before dusk," he said.

"Good enough," Uri grunted. "And by the way, Adni might see things you don't, Giovel. Think about that."

He was already walking on, thinking no such thing.

Lessons with Hirnu were as slow as usual. From the confines of her walled-in yard she had him repeat a glyph called the Illumina thirty times before casting it half as many—mostly losing control of the glyph. The spell opened a sharp flash of light that made Giovel's sight swim when he tried redrawing the complex shape. As always, Hirnu offered neither praise nor complaint for his work. Just a few terse instructions to practice on his own, which he hadn't done in weeks.

Giovel left feeling shamed and sullen. Rather than practicing or figuring out what to do with Varan, he went to see Sur in the Belnum clinic again.

"I've found him," he said upon arriving.

"Riddin? You should have found him days ago," Sur said. "And hello to you too—and I'm healing well so thanks for inquiring about that."

"I couldn't ask more Lances where he was, not without stirring anyone's suspicions. I had to find him on my own."

"Well, I did some checking too. Riddin *has* submitted a request for relief from duty. Just an informal one that Lances have to repeat every day or two, but he's done it. So you could say he's keeping himself in line with the rulebook, even if his quietude is a little suspicious."

"Did he give any reasons for requesting leave?" Giovel asked.

"I'm not going to ask for any inside information I'm not allowed to have. What's your obsession with him, anyway?"

"It's not an obsession. I'm trying to make sure we don't have a traitor changing our plans at the last minute. And Riddin *did* change them without your authorization."

"Everyone changes orders when a move begins. You have to. Circumstances change too fast to do otherwise. You ought to know that as well as anyone."

Giovel looked away. "Am I wrong to be pursuing him?"

"It's not what I'd do. Why are you asking me, anyway? You're old and experienced. You don't need my advice." Sur sighed and scratched at his bandages. "But I'd rather be you, chasing empty news about an inept Lance, than stay tied to a bed here. Everyone else was moved or discharged three days ago. Just me and my ugly scars here now."

There was no word of comfort for that feeling. So Giovel said nothing.

"Why, though?" Sur asked again. "What makes you believe Riddin's gone poison on us?"

The same question he'd asked himself just before lessons with Hirnu. And now an answer came to him, clear and direct as rain on a bright morning.

"I'm tired, Sur," Giovel said. "I want a victory."

Perhaps he wanted it badly enough to go looking where there was no fight in the first place.

He expected Sur to waive his statement off, maybe even to laugh at him. Sur didn't, though. He just nodded silently.

After a moment Sur said, "I've been where you are before. In the Lances and in the Order. Is it Adni wearing you down again? Elínla? She thinks you're vying for command of the Grays, by the way."

"She should know better than that."

"Doesn't, though. She thinks you manipulated her, set her up for trouble on that witch hunt a few weeks back. She also thinks you're skulking around not to find some rogue Lance but to find *witches*. So maybe Dlenar and I need to worry about our seats in the Order too."

Of course Elínla would think something like that. Of course everyone would see Giovel in such a hue, knowing what had happened to Iremni. Little wonder they didn't trust him yet. Just hoisted Varan onto his back, waiting for the witches to find themselves.

"I know I shouldn't care what they think of me," Giovel said slowly. "And sometimes I convince myself that I don't. But when it's all said and done, I'm tired of being the dregs of the Order. I want to rise a little."

"You had a good taste of rising these last few years in the guard."

Yes, he had. And while he hated to see himself like Oily Olinos or even Elínla, it was harder and harder not to be jealous of their ascent through the ranks while he was stuck watching a woman who could hardly speak. They, on the other hand, were off doing work that might turn the leaf of the war over, despite being ten or twenty years younger and greener than Giovel.

"I know that look," Sur said, watching Giovel and scratching at his bandaged side again. "So I was right. They *are* wearing you down."

Giovel gritted his teeth. "Just Adni and his fool orders. Hirnu might make me feel like an idiot sometimes, but at least she doesn't do it in front of anyone else. And it's probably not her fault, anyway. Why Olura Medín picked Adni over her or Ralden I'll never know."

"Picked him as Illumined Knight, you mean?" Sur asked.

"Yes."

"Ah. So you haven't heard how things happened."

"How what things happened?"

"Old Aunty Olura *did* pick Hirnu to lead the Order. Sure, Adni had a reputation already, but Hirnu was most senior, and everyone knew she was the best mage in the Order if not the best alive. She said no."

Of course she would. Giovel found himself revisiting every interaction between Hirnu and Adni, tracing back through her mild reprimands and Adni's stilted deference to her. It made a sour kind of sense, almost explaining why Adni was like a vengeful child so often. He wasn't just proving his authority. Trying to prove that he was *worth it*, rather, knowing all along that someone else was the choice of the Optate.

"Did Hirnu ever explain why she turned it down?" Giovel asked.

"Said she felt her skills were better employed continuing her research instead, and she was probably right about that. Can you imagine Adni taking her place as Observer, experimenting day in and day out? The man would probably have burned the city to the ground five years ago."

Now Giovel wondered that too. He knew as much as most people did about Adni's history with the Grays—how he'd soared into fame after dueling and defeating the Worenthi Witch. Giovel had been one of the Candles who secured the streets after two of the Worenthi's attacks. He'd seen what the witch did to her targets of Optacrats and Lawrits, and he'd seen more than one Gray corpse in the aftermath of those fights. But Adni somehow emerged victorious, bringing the Worenthi witch down by himself after the Order had failed for weeks to do anything about her. He was twenty-four, maybe twenty-five then.

He'd showed so much promise, both in his magecraft and his bravery. Perhaps they would have blossomed into something great if the Order hadn't been gutted soon after he joined it and the Optate hadn't pushed him to take on a mantle he wasn't yet ready for.

"So what are you going to do, now you know where Riddin is?" Sur asked.

Giovel sighed. "For your sake, I'll think on it a little longer."

"Wise choice. I'd hate to see you crack your knees on an unauthorized move and get stuck with another year of pointless duties. Adni *will* give them to you if you provoke him."

And now Giovel was starting to understand why.

UNAUTHORIZED

Until I can learn their language, I'm alone.
  —The Witherclaw Witch; letter to Golkorun.

THE ORDER MET again that afternoon, and Giovel entered the round council room to find Vermilion Commander Zuris Medín there once more next to Ralden, Elínla, Dlenar, Hirnu, and Adni. Zuris had shaved his beard off; it made him look ten years younger than when they'd met a few weeks before. Giovel mumbled a greeting as he took a seat across from Zuris and Dlenar.

"What if we were to allow certain guilds the rights to retain nearby Sanctuaries for a fee?" Ralden was asking. "It would be good for them and might just raise your funds for the destruction of others."

"I'm not suggesting these consolidation efforts to make a profit, Lady Ralden," Zuris said.

"I don't see why that precludes us from making one anyway."

"Perhaps we should backtrack now that Giovel's here," Dlenar said. "That might dam your stream of bad ideas, Ralden."

"I haven't even introduced my *best* ideas yet," Ralden said with a wave of her hand. "What if we hired Yerenel to do the hard labor, for instance? The Redremel couldn't attack us without killing some of them, and that might win us another ally in this war."

"Preposterous," said Dlenar. "Totally immoral. House Tovóm could do the labor for half the price since our vassals wouldn't need to travel a tenth as far."

The meeting went on, mostly wild deliberation. A dozen more ideas from Ralden. Quibbles from Dlenar—not to Zuris's plan so much as to the possibility that Ralden's guild could make money off the efforts. More obstreperous objections from Elínla, sharing complaints from other septs in Foneth in addition to her own. Dlenar finally spoke up in Zuris's favor, stating that the lives of Foneth's people mattered more than trees or grass.

"That's easy for you to say," Elínla snapped. "Your own estate won't be touched!"

"And just because you're an irreligious noble doesn't mean everyone in Foneth is," Ralden added.

"I'd like to hear Lord Giovel's opinion, if I may," Zuris said forcefully.

Lord Giovel. Not Giovel anymore.

Despite thinking about Varan and Riddin and everything else in the world, Giovel had devoted some thought to Zuris's plan. Not much, but it had itched in the back of his mind as he looked over Cloud Lake or walked through the Featherwood. He couldn't imagine filling that quiet forest with homes and streets and sanitization trenches instead. But nor could he imagine defending Foneth against the Redremel forever.

When everyone's eyes fell on him, Giovel simply said, "I need more time to consider this, Zuris. I'm sorry. I can't say more than that today."

He recognized a hint of betrayal in Zuris's close-lipped frown, but Zuris didn't pressure or argue. "Might I ask how the rest of you would vote if it were in your power to enact my plans today?"

Their responses came almost as Giovel now expected. Elínla, Dlenar, and Hirnu voted no. Adni voted yes with the express assurance that Sur did as well. Ralden, along with Giovel, wasn't yet sure, though the staggering financial implications of the project seemed to have eroded her greatest reservations since Zuris's visit. So if Giovel said yes, the majority of the Order would likely fall to Zuris's side.

"May I return in ten days' time for a formal vote—considering the issue once again as if it were in your power to accomplish?" Zuris asked.

"That might not be enough time for Giovel," Adni said. "His duties are very demanding right now."

Elínla snorted, but Zuris didn't seem to catch the jape. He just bowed, asked for a messenger to inform him when they could reconvene, and left.

The rest of the meeting was ominously predictable. More disturbingly unsubstantiated reports of Redremel movements. No witch sightings, though there was another spiriting in the Estates. Sur would normally investigate them alongside Dlenar, but Adni assigned Ralden to accompany him instead. Never mind that her own load of duties was immense, and that Giovel's was the size of a child's hand.

When Adni asked what else there was to report, Giovel stayed silent. No need to mention Riddin until he had the blackguard in hand, confessing to whatever he'd done or denying for whatever he hadn't. Adni wouldn't get the chance to take that responsibility away as well.

Giovel was on his way back to Uri's, supposing he'd better bring Varan home with him, when Birenlu appeared from a crowd of Scholar Day gatherers on the grass below the Candlespire.

"I've been waiting for you," she said with a bright look in her eye. "I have news."

The fatigue of Giovel's meetings seemed to dissolve. "And?"

"A tall gray-eyed man has been visiting your lazy Lance. Three times in the past three days, and again today. I saw him there myself not two hours ago."

Gray-eyed. Giovel immediately thought of Etelier. He was tall, certainly. Possibly with gray-eyes. It had been too dark to be sure that night at the Croen Estate. "No one knows who this man is?"

"He's not from that neighborhood," said Birenlu. "A woman up the street said he was hauling lumber one day, moving tools the next. Maybe a woodworker?"

"Did you hear anything he said?"

"Not clearly. He has a deep, booming voice, though, like an old gong."

That settled it in Giovel's mind. "Well done, Birenlu. Was this man still there with Riddin when you left?"

"As far as I could see, yes."

Then there wasn't much time. "That's just what I needed to know. Come by tomorrow night and I'll give you as much time as you like for our interview."

"And the Spireblades? I'd like to talk with Deleos Tovóm of all of them."

"I'll see to it," Giovel promised.

He doubled back inside to find Elínla. She sat in her tiny office on the Candlespire's third level, reviewing a training regimen for the Grays by the fading light of the autumn sun. She didn't look up when Giovel appeared.

"I have a favor to ask," he said.

Still no response. Elínla crossed out a few names, circled another, added one more.

"Elínla, this can't wait."

"Defending the city against Redrem can, but your badgering me can't?"

"I know where the witch Etelier was a few hours back. He might still be there now."

That made her look up. "You didn't say anything about this to the Order."

"I didn't know then. I do now."

"How's that?"

"We don't have time for this. I want you to come with me to catch him."

"He might be long gone if he was last sighted hours back."

"He was visiting with a *Lance*, Elínla. He's been there three days in a row, talking to the same Lance who switched orders and ruined the raid at the Croen Estate."

Her eyes were wide now. She set down her pen and notes. "Why are you coming to me with this? This should go straight to Adni."

"Maybe. Maybe not. Adni never technically relieved me of my assignment with Sur a few weeks back. You could say this is a continuation of those responsibilities."

"But he assigned you to watch the new witch instead."

"Are you coming or not? I need to know in the next three minutes because that's when I'm leaving, with you or alone."

She almost took a step toward him. "How do I know this isn't a trap? Some hop you've invented to get me in trouble again?"

"You're a smart woman, Elínla. Which means you should realize I'm no halfwit myself. If I wanted to play political games to get ahead of you, don't you think I'd start kissing Adni's ankles by now? If you don't believe me, stay here and write assignments."

She followed as he walked out. "Who else are you bringing?"

"Someone I know I can anticipate completely," Giovel replied. "And maybe a few of his Candles."

"This sounds completely unauthorized, Giovel."

"That's why it's risky. Come on."

RAID

I can't help but feel that someday the Order's methods will demand a heavy recompense. No number of laws could keep their own mages in check.

—The Witherclaw Witch; a letter to Recia.

ALL GIOVEL NEEDED to convince Olinos was to mention Sur's interest in the raid. Olinos brought five Candles with him, meeting Giovel and Elínla at Scout's Bridge hardly twenty minutes later. Teams of workers filled Scout's Bridge already, filing either east or west toward their homes as the last of the day's light receded. A good time to make their move.

"How is our mystery witch, by the way?" Olinos asked as Giovel hooked a borrowed Candleguard sword to his belt.

"We're not here to socialize, Olinos," Elínla said. "Is this everyone?"

"This is all we can afford to take along," Giovel said and motioned for everyone to crowd close as he lowered his voice. "Listen well, because there's not much to say. Olinos. I brought you not because I want your help, but because I know you like to wear accomplishments on your chest. Well, this will be one. We've got a known witch and a conspirator to apprehend."

Olinos managed to look affronted, but Giovel noticed his usual gleam of hunger too. He likely didn't care about Etelier so much as about the honor of stopping him, part of which would be his. It was why Giovel trusted Olinos to play his part precisely until their operation was complete.

"As for the rest of you," Giovel said, turning to face the five Candles, "we don't know whether our traitor and his witch friends will have allies ready to protect them. We're walking in half-blind."

"Is this supposed to inspire them?" Elínla asked.

"It's supposed to inform you all," Giovel said. "No one's obligated to join me. But I welcome you—and there's no reason our enemies should know we're coming."

"Then how soon do we move, Lord Giovel?" Olinos asked, restoring some sense of calm in his face.

"Right now."

They found the house Birenlu had described just as the glimmer of the Dancing Crow constellation peaked overhead. Naked trees framed in the little clump of streets, with Vision Hill looming behind them like a wall. The night air was starting to bite, and gray clouds blocked Yulen in the south. Could be the night of autumn's first snow. A good night to move, to feel blood coursing through feet and fingers.

"Elínla, cover the back," Giovel said, pointing where a narrow lane wound behind the house in question. "Olinos, you're with me. Two of you will follow us after five counts, one will cover Elínla from behind, and the other two will stand ready by the door."

"So now you're giving orders?" Elínla asked. "What if there are a dozen Redremel axes in there?"

Giovel was starting to feel like a dozen axes wouldn't be enough to stop him. "This house is too narrow for more than a few to fight us at once. If they have us outnumbered, we'll withdraw to the doorways so they can only confront us one at a time. Then we light the building on fire. Understood?"

The Candles nodded silently. Olinos donned a pair of leather gloves and lowered his spear. Then they waited on Giovel's word to proceed.

There was only one prick of worry to give Giovel pause now. What if they waited, watched, let more of Etelier's companions gather round Riddin? There was no telling whether more witches would come, but it was easier to observe from a distance than to hunt in the dark. The question was whether to play the patient man's game and make sure Etelier was there, or risk Riddin running before they had a chance to strike?

Giovel forced the worry aside and shouted, "The Divine Order's here!"

He went straight for the door, ramming the handle with the hilt of his sword while he kicked at the center of the wood. It snapped open, exposing a narrow corridor toward firelight.

Inside. Past a tiny Sanctuary of rugged mountain stone. Toward the fire, where someone was standing up. Riddin, still wearing his Jade uniform. And holding a parchment already marked with a glyph. A red, glowing, active glyph.

Giovel loosed two darts, one from each wrist, piercing Riddin's parchment in two places before the startled Lance could react. Then he charged forward and rammed Riddin with his shoulder left, hurling him head-down over a table and chair. Riddin crashed into the far wall with a grunt but rolled right to his feet and dashed into the next corridor.

"Cover that stairwell," Giovel said, waving Olinos toward a tiny passage above the hearth. He ran after Riddin himself.

Riddin tried to surprise him, leaping from a shadowed corner, but Giovel saw his reflection in a tiny windowpane and skidded to a halt, whipping his sword out as he did so. His blade clanged against a short sword in Riddin's hand. Riddin pressed forward, stabbing near Giovel's neck, face, chest, and Giovel battered each attack aside one-handed. Then he loosed another dart with his left, catching Riddin in the belly.

Riddin grunted again, pawing at the tiny wound and trying to get the dart free. He backed past a second stairwell just as someone jumped down, landing squarely in front of Giovel. Not Etelier, not Olinos either. It was a broad-shouldered man Giovel recognized from Etelier's gathering—the very man he'd tripped getting to Etelier that night.

The bigger man wrestled Giovel's sword arm down and yanked a knife from his belt. Then he rammed it forward at Giovel's neck. Giovel abandoned his own sword and wrenched his sheath up, catching the blade of his enemy's knife on the metal clasp near his sheath's mouth. Then he whipped the sheath's point up between his attacker's legs, punched at his throat, and brought his left elbow hard into the other man's eye. Each strike connected cleanly. The other man toppled over onto the floor, groaning and dropping his knife.

"To me, Olinos!" Giovel yelled. He scooped his sword from the ground and ran after Riddin once more.

Riddin was halfway down one more hall overlooking a garden. He turned toward a doorway, slashed the outline of a glyph into the wall with his short sword, and lit the glyph with Yulena. Giovel threw himself to the floor just in time to dodge a flare of ice-blue light. A pair of windows shattered. Wooden splinters showered over Giovel's head. Something cracked where the spell had hit the wall, and stones scraped loose as a wide chunk of wall began to cave inward.

While Giovel tried to get back on his feet, Riddin turned to the garden door and tugged it open. Riddin was starting through when a foot caught him right in the chest. He spun upside down, snapping his head against the floor. Elínla had her sword at his throat a breath later, with her foot on his hand to keep his blade to the ground.

"So you've awakened, Riddin," she said. "Funny. I don't remember you certifying to use those glyphs."

"Well-timed," Giovel said, now panting for breath. "Olinos! Anyone back there?"

"Just a fool clutching his manhood," Olinos called back. "They're checking upstairs now."

"What the hell do you want with me?" Riddin snarled, trying to shift farther away from Elínla's sword point.

Giovel stood. "I want to take you to Jade Commander Teserot's office to see what she'll say about the company you're keeping." He reclaimed his sword, prying Riddin's own weapon away with it. "I want to find out why you've taken so much time off after changing everyone's marching orders at the Croen Estate." He leaned down and tugged his dart from Riddin's belly. "And I want to know where your friend Etelier is."

Two of the Candleguard stepped in beside Giovel. "All clear, Lord Giovel. No one upstairs. No one moving outside, though the others are keeping watch to make sure."

"The back garden's empty too," Elínla said. "I think we've got our catch."

"They know more about you than you think," Riddin suddenly snarled. His eyes were losing focus as the serum from Giovel's dart worked into his blood. "They know where you live, who your families are, what your weaknesses are. They know everything about us."

"The witches?" Giovel asked. "I wager you're right. But thanks to you, we're going to know a little more about them as well."

He hauled Riddin over his shoulder, not even waiting to tie him up. "Let's get back to the garrison and hear what you have to say."

REPERCUSSIONS

They hover over me like I'm a boiling pot of soup. There must be a whole world I'll never see because I'm watched so closely.

—The Witherclaw Witch; letter to Recia.

NO ONE PURSUED them as they hauled the prisoners back toward Divnum. No Etelier, no more witches, just woodsmoke and clouds and a cold breeze over the Iceflow.

Giovel wasn't sure where Riddin's companion ought to be taken. Since Riddin was a witch, he decided to take them straight to the Divnum barracks for the Grays on duty there. "They might both be witches," he said as four Grays secured Riddin and the other man. "I'll be back to question them myself after I tell this one's Commander where he is."

He wondered how long it had been since Riddin's awakening. In his efforts to find the rogue Lance, Giovel had learned enough to know that Riddin had the trust of his colleagues. He needn't have hidden his awakening from them; most would have accepted it if he'd just chosen to come forward and certify. What a waste that he'd gone witch instead.

Giovel, Elínla, and Olinos didn't get far from the barracks. Ralden, Dlenar, and Adni met them in the lamplight barely outside the barracks doorway. Damn.

"I got word from Uri Janata that you didn't show to take the Witherclaw off her hands," Adni said without preamble. "She made it sound as if she's done more than a few hours of child-watching for you in the past week."

"Is anyone hurt?" Ralden cut in. "And what's this the Candles are saying about two witches?"

"Just one witch that we know of," said Elínla. "But we also know Etelier was there a few hours before."

"Where did you get this valuable intelligence?" Adni asked, swiveling between Elínla and Giovel. "And who approved this interference in Lance business? Who failed to invite Dlenar to investigate? And who gave the damn authorization to involve Candles in this?"

"Don't be too stiff on them," Dlenar said. "I don't mind a little breach in decorum if it means we got a witch in Etelier's circle. I say well done to everyone. Have you extracted any information yet?"

Giovel felt his shoulders and fists loosen slightly, realizing just now that he'd tensed all over as Adni spoke. "Thank you, Dlenar. We haven't questioned either man yet."

"I'd like a detailed report to make sure you truly kept to protocol, but I'm with Dlenar," Ralden said. "It was bold to go after any witch—and potentially this Etelier himself—so promptly. No casualties at all on your side?"

"A slight singe of my hair from a spell Riddin built," Giovel said. "Otherwise, nothing to report."

"It was an excellently planned operation," Olinos said softly. "I feel honored to have been included under the leadership of Lady Elínla and Lord Giovel."

"You're dismissed, Olinos," Adni said.

"You can't dismiss Olinos from a conversation in the open streets," Giovel said, tensing in his shoulders all over again.

"Then we'll move into the Candlespire, Giovel. You were supposed to be *watching the Witherclaw*, and I've already received a complaint from Azure Commander Telen about you interfering in Lance business. He's furious. Livid. He told me he might go straight to Optate Olura to make sure the Order doesn't cross such boundaries again."

That was it. "I don't care what you think about the operation, Adni," Giovel said. "We did it, and it worked. It wasn't Lance business because *Etelier* was there hours before, and Riddin's a witch himself. So let Ralden look at our report and confirm that it's our business, done according to our protocol, not Telen's."

"So if I interview these Candles you somehow requisitioned, they'll admit that you posed this strike as official, sanctioned Order business?" Adni asked, voice rising perhaps to make sure Olinos and the other Candleguard heard what he was saying.

It was a question Giovel hoped dearly he wouldn't have to answer, so he ignored it and struck back where he could. "Telen isn't even Riddin's Commander. He's in the Jade Army, not the Azure."

"It's still the Lances' concern."

"I don't believe you about Telen anyway," Giovel snapped, voice rising to match Adni's. "You're making this whole sideways story up as you go."

"How *dare you?*"

"Ind Telen and I might not be the closest friends, but I know that if he had an issue with how I handled this affair he'd say it to my face and not crawl to you in the middle of the night to share a grievance. If you care so much about process and protocol, you'll let Ralden figure out whether I need to be censured or not."

Before Adni could even respond, Giovel turned and began walking away.

Silence first. Then Adni called out, "I've had enough of your belligerence. You will confine yourself only to duties guarding the Witherclaw until we find where she came from."

"Acknowledged," Giovel replied, still walking. "Oh, and your shit order means I'm forbidden from attending your shit meetings. Unless you care to reword it, you won't be seeing much of me for a while."

He didn't look back to see what Adni thought of that.

Frost crunched under Giovel's feet as he cut across the grass by Cloud Lake. He felt flushed and sweaty, though. Defeated, too, no matter how he'd worked to catch Riddin.

I should be firmer than Adni. One of the level-headed ones. And here I am playing his games perfectly, bending rank, dodging orders, and giving him new reasons to push me around. I could have stirred up all kinds of trouble for Ralden and Dlenar, could have been wrong about Riddin, could have broken into an innocent man's house tonight and brought doubt and mistrust over the whole Order.

But I didn't, did I?

Elínla caught up with him a moment later, and Dlenar's and Ralden's voices echoed over the grass, arguing loudly with Adni as they walked off in another direction.

"You were right about one thing," Elínla said as she fell into step beside Giovel.

"And what's that?"

"You're not going to climb fast in the Order. Not the way you're going."

"I have a lot of pointless guard duty to get back to, so is there something else I can do for you?"

"I won't let Adni ruin your operation," Elínla said. "I think you were right to go after that Lance."

He was surprised how gratifying it was to hear. "So we're all agreed on this except Adni."

"I need to get back to the Grays to discuss interrogation. But I'm glad you trusted me to join you on the move."

"Maybe you shouldn't feel grateful. You'll probably get to taste the weight of Adni's displeasure next."

"I'm starting to think it's worth it. I'll let you know as soon as we get anything from Riddin."

Elínla hurried back toward the barracks. Ralden's voice was still audible in the distance, now shouting outright at something Adni was saying.

Let them argue. Giovel had done his part tonight and wouldn't gain anything from regretting it now. If it helped them catch Etelier, it would be worth whatever punishment Adni might summon up yet.

But perhaps that was what had made Giovel feel defeated. Not the reprimand, not the punishment, not Adni's bald lie about Ind Telen. But that he'd left Uri with Varan, despite promising otherwise. She was one of the few people who still treated him as she had before, back when Iremni was alive. And he'd done her wrong enough that she reported him to Adni, probably knowing well their distaste for one another.

Giovel thought for a moment about going to Uri's to apologize, to take Varan back to his own home instead. It was late now, probably nearing midnight, and Uri and Varan were likely sound asleep. Since it wasn't worth waking them to apologize for being late, Giovel walked back home, hoping he could believe Elínla's words. That their actions tonight were worth the outcomes.

PERCEPTION DAY

Mother once told me beauty had its price. She said someone with a beautiful face can never be sure if they're loved for their beauty or for their own sake. She probably meant it to cheer me up when I felt ugly or plain, so I of course didn't believe her—then.

—The Witherclaw Witch; letter to Recia.

GIOVEL WOKE TO the low sound of trinireeds playing outside, like a thousand ducks attempting to sing together. He groaned and tried to block the sound with his blanket, but the trinireeds were moving closer. That must mean it was Perception Day, the start of the Sept of Blue Heaven's winter festival. Which took place along Cloud Lake, almost right outside Giovel's house.

He sighed, rolled over, and got out of bed.

Snow covered the ground outside his little window, an ankle-deep spread just from during the night. Undeterred by the snow, what looked like hundreds of festival-goers had already congregated around Cloud Lake and parts of the Featherwood. Scores of food carts and stalls stood along the lakeshore, and the smells of smoke and spices reached Giovel even from the distance. A massive raven-black dome tent marked the center of the festivities. And of course the music, dolorous, low, steady, and almost devoid of melody, flooded everywhere nearby.

After a light breakfast, Giovel said goodbye to Inorovel, who was meeting a group of Tovómil friends to attend the festival, donned his long boots, and trudged through the snow to Uri's house while rehearsing his apologies. No excuses, though. There weren't many people whose friendship he'd rather keep than Uri's.

He found Varan outside with Progis, Uri's little grandson, teaching him how to pack the snow into little shapes. Progis laughed as one of his buildings fell apart in his hands, and Varan laughed with him. It was the first time Giovel thought he'd seen her smile, let alone heard her laugh. Her smile alone made a different person of her.

"She's good with the boy," Uri said, walking around the side of her house with an armful of firewood from her shed. "She and Kirida have formed something of a friendship too."

A puddle of good news before the storm of disappointment.

"Can I help you with the wood?" Giovel asked.

"This is the last I'll need until tonight. I hope you don't have cause to come by then."

"I won't leave Varan another day, if that's what you mean." Giovel bowed low. "I was wrong not to come yesterday."

"And I was wrong ever to let you talk me into helping beyond my official duties of translation. Now you've gone and made me like Varan—made her like us too. It'll be all the harder to send her off when we figure out where she comes from."

Giovel pulled Uri's front door open for her, letting her walk in with her armful of wood. She grunted and jerked her head for him to follow her. "You probably know by now that I sang on you to the rest of the Order."

"So Adni told me, though I wasn't fully sure what to believe at the time."

"Angry that you shouldered her on me, was he? It's only to be expected. He's even more used to being obeyed than you are."

"I really am sorry, Uri."

"Save your words. I don't need your apology."

"I've come to take her now."

"No need anymore, is there? I've found her some work nearby, with a little corner for her to sleep in. She's going to help old woman Garathina with odd tasks before winter really hits us. Garathina needs a strong back, and Varan's willing. She stayed there last night, in fact. Just came back here to see Progis for a bit."

Uri's voice was calm and even as ever, but there was something to the set of her eyes that showed her anger. As perhaps they should, much as Giovel himself resented everything about Varan's situation.

"You must feel so used," he said quietly.

"Don't try to tell me what I feel, Giovel. That's my business, and I don't expect your understanding. I just expect you to show yourself when you say you will."

Which he'd failed to do. Thanks to another unauthorized operation.

"Don't eat that," someone said just outside. Varan.

"She's speaking more and more," Giovel said. "Her accent isn't too odd either."

"Varan's done nothing but practice and read—yes, she taught herself something of how to read Medín—except when she's visiting with Kirida or the boy. It's amazing how easy learning a language can be when you have no other choice."

"Is she still looking over maps as well?"

"She's given up on that for the time being. I think it's obvious we can't point her in the right direction."

"So she's stuck here."

"Unless she goes off beyond where our maps mark," Uri said. "Which she might just do. She's no coward, if I can read anything about her."

"You're right about that," Giovel said, thinking back to Varan racing after witches at the Croen Estate. "I'll take her off your hands now. And I swear I'll try to make this up to you."

"Do what you think is best. But don't make me any more promises. You haven't kept many before."

Uri's grandson hurled a handful of snow into the air as Giovel stepped back outside. He laughed as if he'd done the funniest thing imaginable. Varan laughed the same way as the snow settled again.

"I see you have a new friend," Giovel said.

Varan's smile was gone almost as soon as she noticed him. "Do you have news?"

"Send the boy inside. I'll tell you as we walk."

"Walk?"

Giovel motioned away. "Just around the lake. I do have news for you, as it happens."

Varan said goodbye to little Progis and helped him inside with her promise to come tomorrow. Then she wrapped a green shawl tighter around her neck and followed Giovel into the wind.

"What news?" Varan asked almost at once.

"You know the word witch by now? Witch?"

"I know witch," Varan said eagerly. "You found the witch?"

"We found one of the witch's friends. But there are always more witches. Many witches. Do you understand me?"

"I understand many witches. You are looking for witches?"

He nodded. "I think we'll find them soon. Now we know who their friends are. But we don't know if the witches . . . we can't be sure . . ." He broke off, trying to decide whether to say what he truly feared.

We don't even know whether Etelier and his lot spirited you. We don't know who did. We know so little about *any* of them, let alone why this has happened.

"I met a witch," Giovel finally said. "Caught him. We have him. I hope he can tell us about the others, but maybe there are more witches out there. There could be hundreds of them."

Varan watched as he spoke, her dark eyes locked on him. Whether she followed or not, he couldn't be sure this time.

He continued. "I've been looking for witches for a long time now. You see, you're not the first one to come here. Do you know what spiriting means?"

"Spiriting. Like me."

"Yes. Just like you. Lots of spiritings, though. And we don't know who the witches are, the ones that did this. But the thing is, I've wanted to find them for months. Ever since my own wife was spirited. That was half a year ago. We still don't know who did it."

If she understood any more of this, she gave no indication. Just stared as if she meant to absorb his words through the force of her gaze. As well she might, since Giovel didn't even know what he meant to say. Just trying to come to some understanding of my own experience, he thought. Trying to be sure I haven't squandered my time looking for witches who don't have answers in the first place. I have to believe the ones behind Iremni's spiriting are out there, still spiriting others like Varan herself, that helping her will lead toward the same witches I've hoped to find all along.

"What is wife?" Varan asked.

Giovel smiled. "You know Kirida?"

"Yes. My friend."

"And Nomis? Have you met Nomis?"

"With Kirida."

"Yes. Kirida is his wife. Mother to Progis, and their new baby soon. Together. Wife and husband, Kirida and Nomis. Understand?"

Varan frowned and said, "I'm a wife."

"You have children too, don't you? Two little boys?"

"Two boys." Her face softened. "My boys."

Without thinking of it, Giovel had led them toward the Perception Day festival, close enough now to hear the crackle in firepits and the bubbling of broth pots by food sellers' tents. The gathering had grown since he awoke. It looked like a few thousand people had come from across Foneth for the Sept of Blue Heaven's big occasion.

"Do you want to come explore?" Giovel asked. "See things?"

Varan gave a tentative nod and followed him closer.

There was no shortage of spectacles. The Sept of Blue Heaven was one of the quieter, more contemplative septs from what little Giovel knew of them, but Perception Day had never been a quiet holiday. There was dancing in the snow, a score of little groups competing with different styles of music, haggling and bartering of cloth, woodwork, jewelry, clay, leather, and dried foods that would keep for winter. Smells of stewing onions and tubers wafted over every row of stalls, enriched with the pungent scents of herbs like millowik, chase, rue, hotwort, and mint. Many people wandering in the crowds bore the angular face tattoos of the Sept of Blue Heaven, like Elínla did, but more than half of those gathered were just coming to enjoy the festivities. After a moment walking among them, Giovel almost felt ready to enjoy things himself.

Maybe watching Varan would be a relief after all. Maybe he was ready for some time away from the Candlespire and schemes and witches. She asked questions as they walked, pressing him to test her speaking skills and help her learn more, but she also seemed content as he was to see and smell and listen.

Eyes followed them where they walked, though. Most of Divnum knew who Giovel was now, maybe even most of Foneth, and many people seemed to recognize Varan as well. She wore her leaf-marked dress today, only half-obscured by her shawl. People peered at her dress almost as much as they looked at her face, and sometimes Giovel caught whispers of 'Witherclaw' and 'witch' nearby. He thought, from the slight turn of Varan's head sometimes, that she did too.

"Kirida," she said suddenly, pointing ahead.

Kirida waved from beside a bread stall. "Come and order Nomis to hurry up, Lord Giovel." Nomis stood nearby, pondering a tray of samples with total focus.

"Those look good," Giovel said. "I can't order Candles around anymore, but I suppose I can claim them myself and make your decision easier, Nomis."

"I was here first," Nomis said. "You can go find your own."

"Ignore his rudeness, Varan," Kirida said. "Nomis and Giovel are friends."

"Friends might not be the right word," Giovel said. "I seem to recall you being an impious new Candle when I was your Lieutenant."

"That's not how I remember it at all," Nomis said without taking his eyes from the tray of bread.

While Nomis pondered the various bakes available to him, Kirida found a tree to lean against and talked idly with Varan. Their conversations were simple, given Varan's grip of the language, but they seemed earnest and genuine. Friends, as Varan had said.

"A lot of people have taken an interest in helping Varan," Kirida said when Nomis and Giovel joined them, Nomis juggling six different steaming, fist-sized loaves. "One of our neighbors does grain trade in Lacia, and he said he'll check his old maps of their region to see if they have any landmarks she might know. A woman we'd never met came by yesterday, asking whether she could help teach Varan Medín. Kind people," she added when Varan seemed not to grasp what she was saying.

Giovel frowned. He hoped it were so. "Between the few of us, how many people likely know she'll be helping Garathina for the next stretch?"

"No one we've told," said Kirida. "We know better than that. But people talk."

"And people watch," Nomis said.

Yes, they did. And here Giovel was, letting hundreds of them watch at once. He'd known for days now that he couldn't keep her secret, but he felt suddenly vulnerable to have so many eyes watching nearby.

"I'm sorry I've involved your family," he said. "Truly, I didn't mean to put any of you at risk."

Once more Varan looked between them as if waiting for more explanation. Kirida smiled and said, "We wish we could help you more, Varan."

Giovel and Varan stayed with Kirida and Nomis as the procession of trinireed-playing sept members returned, now walking in unison between the makeshift rows of stalls, the little gathering fires, the clumps of festival goers, and the winding lanes where snow had been shoved aside or packed into a hard walkway. They talked for a while of nothing important at all—Varan's new tasks with Garathina, Nomis's duties with the Candleguard, Deleos Tovóm's new marriage prospects. Then they listened as members of the Sept of Blue Heaven went by, speaking of the mysteries they espoused—how to empty their consciousness until only a few pricks of starlight remained, all the easier to see for the blank night sky around them, all the easier to discern with other voices being poured away like water from a bowl.

It was nearly midday when Kirida and Nomis took their leave to fetch Progis and send Nomis off for his shift in Belnum. Giovel had no sooner waved them off then he realized that Varan was gone too.

He swiveled around to spot her, but she was nowhere in sight. Had someone grabbed her, kidnapped her under his own nose? He'd only just started *trying* to do his assigned duty here and she was already missing.

Think. She wouldn't be so easy to subdue and sweep away. The people who know about her likely wouldn't try here, where all it took was a scream to draw a crowd. So perhaps she went off on her own, gave him the slip while he was distracted saying goodbye. But why would she do that?

Maybe to take her fate into her own hands, to look for witches herself.

That thought sent a wave of excitement through Giovel's body. He'd have no choice but to go along.

He began turning around again, tuning out as many voices as he could to focus on what he saw before him. She'd stood to his right, so she couldn't have gone the direction Nomis and Kirida went. He'd have seen her walking toward the lake as well, where there was no barrier to conceal her. Just two directions she could have gone, then. Giovel picked the more crowded one at his left, following a line of Blue Heaven initiates toward the heart of the festival itself.

There was something wildly appealing about trailing someone. Giovel often missed it from his years in the guard—never mind that he'd had to do it recently for the Order too. He was good at it too, measuring where people could or couldn't, would or wouldn't go.

He measured well. After just a minute or two he spotted Varan walking quickly through a crowd of youth just now joining the festival. She'd covered her head and her Witherclaw dress with her shawl, so not even her hair was visible. A good precaution, but not varied enough to disguise her from Giovel.

Once he had her in his sights, it was easy to follow her. What confused Giovel was that she seemed to know exactly where she was going. She walked outside the festival, which now spilled right into the streets by Scout's Bridge, then south beyond the giant bridge and down a few winding rows of homes and craft halls. She often glanced back as if she expected to be followed, but Giovel doubted she'd notice him lurking at corners or in narrow indents between buildings.

She led to an empty alleyway behind a guild hall. The sounds of the festival didn't reach this far, so the street was silent beyond the faint humming of the Iceflow perhaps five hundred paces to the east. Varan waited there until someone emerged at the alley's far end. Giovel prepared to loose a dart. Then he saw that the figure approaching was Olinos.

Olinos carried a handful of flowers. Giovel didn't want to imagine what they must have cost on the first day of snowfall. If he was confused, Varan looked to be even more so.

"Hello, Varan," Olinos said with a smile. "I brought you these."

She took them with an agitated look that almost wilted his smile. "Why?"

"I thought you might like them. That's all. Do you care to walk with me by Scout's Bridge? There's a beautiful view of the district from there."

Varan didn't move. "Do you have news?"

"What kind of news?"

"Witches!"

"Oh, yes. I can't share anything officially, but there's a rumor that the Order captured two witches last night. I could probably get a conversation between you, if you'd like."

"Giovel's witches?"

Olinos's smile wilted again. "Yes, Lord Giovel helped capture them. From what I hear."

"You have more news?"

"Not right now, Varan. I can find out more about the witches, though, if that's really what you want."

"Why did you make me here if you don't have news?"

"What?"

"Why did you make me here?" Varan asked, voice rising.

"I wanted to get to know you a bit," Olinos said, smile returning. "I just wanted to spend some time with you."

Whether or not Varan understood what he was really saying, her voice continued to rise as she said, "I thought you had news!"

"Calm down. What if I walk you to the barracks where the witches are being held?"

"Why . . . these?" Varan asked, holding the flowers back out as if she wanted him to take them from her.

"As I said, I thought you'd like them. I just wanted to show some care, to make you feel welcome."

"I am a mother. I am a wife."

"Of course. Of course," Olinos said, wincing ever so slightly behind his smile. "I'm not . . . I just want to help you find your place here."

Varan recoiled.

"Please don't misunderstand me," Olinos said quickly. "I don't mean anything."

But you *do* mean something, Giovel thought, gritting his teeth, and Varan reads it too. Giovel almost ran out to tell him so, to bat him away. But he could tell from the set of Varan's shoulders that she wasn't flinching back in fear.

"Language is so tricky, isn't it?" Olinos asked, trying to chuckle. "Varan, I doubt that your family would want you to be lonely here. I'm just trying to make sure you know you have people here who are ready to help you or listen to you."

She dropped the bright, costly flowers in the snow. "I need news. Witches."

"It will take time. That's all. Give yourself that."

"What's time?" Varan growled.

"How to explain . . . I hate to be the one to say this, but you don't know what your family will do with you gone. If they've never seen spiritings before, they might not believe you're still out here, trying to get back to them. They might not even think you're *alive* anymore." Olinos reached out as if to touch her shoulder, though she looked up with a hard glare that gave him pause. Then he added, "It could be months. Years. That's what time is. What if your husband has to marry again, to find someone else to care for your children?"

Varan yelled something then, her own language perhaps. Then her arms spun forward, hair whipping out behind her. Olinos jerked in place as if he'd been hit with a pail of cold river water. He coughed, gagged. Then he tripped and stumbled several paces back in the snow.

Her power. Her witchery.

Once again Giovel almost loosed a dart—at her this time—but whatever she was doing, her glyphless magic was transfixing. The spell didn't last long. Olinos seemed to recover himself within ten breaths. Then he yelped like a puppy, rolled to his feet, and ran back the way he'd come.

Giovel let out a pent up breath from his hiding place. No need to save Oily Olinos today. The bastard deserved more of a scare than what he'd got, luring Varan here as if he had information when he just fancied her. Now Giovel just had to puzzle out how to make the incident known to Olinos's men without incriminating Varan for what might not be a legal use of her powers—Yulena or not.

He paused, though, when Varan dropped to her knees in the snow, covering her face in her hands.

She just shook in place for a long moment. Then she pulled her hands back, wet with tears, and moved closer to a little melt puddle by the wall of the guild hall, perhaps close enough to absorb some heat from a fire inside. She stared at the puddle. At her reflection, maybe? Then she wept again.

Damn Olinos and everyone who tried taking advantage of spiritings. *I suppose that means damn me too, hoping Varan had run off to help me in my own hunt.*

Giovel wondered, though, if her family *would* wait for her, *could* wait. He'd waited. It had been less than a week that he didn't know Iremni's whereabouts, and torture though it was, he hadn't given up on her, not even when she came back haunted and hurt and broken inside.

So I swear I won't give up on Varan's family either, he thought. I swear I won't let her be left waiting like I was, or her husband be left with an empty husk of her when this is over.

Then again, I've already broken one promise to help her. Maybe Uri and Adni are right about me. As soon as I saw her I could understand some measure of her pain, but I went to chase Riddin instead of helping Varan. Damn me all over again, because Olinos and I are no different in that sense.

One thing was sure, though. It wasn't Giovel or Olinos or Varan herself who was most responsible for her lonely tears by a puddle. It was the witches. And when Giovel swore to make them pay, he felt sure it was a promise he would keep.

ALARM

Sometimes these people try earnestly to help me. I wish I could thank them.
  —The Witherclaw Witch; letter to Golkorun.

Giovel waited nearly half an hour outside the alley, listening for the crunch of snow to know when Varan moved. When he was sure she'd had time to compose herself, he got a running start and sprinted into the alley, huffing as if he'd raced the whole way there.

"Varan! Where have you been? I was worried sick I'd lost you in the festival."

He bent over, still panting. Would that he didn't take the game so far she saw through it.

Varan was dry-eyed now, composed as ever. "You watch me," she said. "Like a child. I am not safe."

It took him a moment to decide she meant it as a question. Then he said, "I got punished for not watching you more closely last week. And I deserved it. I don't want to make that mistake again."

"Like a child," she repeated.

What to say to that? Here he was, pretending he hadn't observed her every move, ready to beat a fool suitor away. So he couldn't deny it without lying to himself as well.

"I wish I didn't have to treat you like this. I wish I could let you be. But I have my orders." He tried to let his face soften. "I know you can look after yourself, Varan. I'm sorry if you don't feel that. But I know you could."

"When will you go to the witches?" she asked with a brittle edge in her voice and eyes now, like when she'd spoken to Olinos.

"I'm not sure. It's not my place to be looking for them now, actually. I'm just supposed to help you."

She said nothing, but her face seemed to show what she thought. You can't help me. Not in any way that matters. That made Giovel feel for her more than anything else yet.

"Has Uri shown you the Divnum Library?" he asked.

Varan frowned. "What's library?"

"It's full of scrolls, books, old charts. Maps, too."

Maps she knew. "I've seen maps."

"Uri told me you didn't recognize anything on the maps she'd shown you. But the library has other maps, many so big that they can't be moved from it. Maybe there's something on one of them that you'll know. You understand me?"

"No."

"Then trust me a moment. Let me show you the library."

She sighed and relented.

Giovel led Varan northeast over Scout's Bridge, the widest bridge in all Foneth. A spear-like tower marked each end of the bridge, seven levels high to afford a view in every direction. Crowds of festival-goers moved opposite Giovel and Varan, filling the great bridge almost to capacity. It looked as if all of Divnum would throng around Cloud Lake before the afternoon was over.

The Divnum Library itself was like a bubble of pale green stone rising from the ground. It was nearly as tall as the towers flanking Scout's Bridge, and half the great structure rested below the earth itself. The roads were empty nearby, the snow untouched in most places. Only a few archivists seemed to be there when Giovel and Varan stamped their feet clean at the entrance and walked into the still darkness of the round building. The interior of the library was largely open, with a high ceiling and tall shelves towering upward before an immense balcony marked the beginning of the next level. The openness of the entrance exposed even another level of broad walkways twining up and down the inside walls of the dome.

"Mages built this place almost a thousand years ago," Giovel said. "Even the Optate's Citadel isn't as old."

Whether or not she understood him, Varan seemed impressed as she took in the lattice of open walkways and the quiet grandeur of the place.

Giovel led her up a twisted stairwell to the higher tiers, through the massive star room that was the library's Sanctuary, coming finally to the smallest, highest level of the building, where great windows looked out across Foneth in all directions. A single map filled nearly thirty paces of wall between the northern windows, showing all the world known to Divnum's archivists—and long stretches of unknown, empty lands.

"This map doesn't stretch any farther than most others, but it might include more details than Uri's maps could," Giovel said, and pointed.

Varan went right to it. She sounded out the names of Lacia, Yeren, Redrem, the Moulds, everywhere she'd learned so far, testing them against whatever land lore she brought with her. Then she traced the outlines of rivers and mountains and forests as if to recall her own maps and compare them side by side. After a few minutes she seemed to realize Giovel was still there and said, "Thank you."

He nodded and stepped away to let her be.

"I didn't expect to see you here today," Ralden called, emerging from a row of shelves by the west wall. She carried a dusty pile of volumes, though her hair, dress, and cowl seemed as perfectly tidy as ever. "Not that you're the kind of person I'd expect to attend a festival."

"Ralden," Giovel said with a nod. "I won't pretend to know what you mean by that."

"I take it she's our Witherclaw Witch?" Ralden asked. "Different from what I'd imagined. With everything people are saying, I expected her to look a little wilder."

"She's just an ordinary person." In most ways. "What brings you to the library?"

"I'm looking into some pointlessly unjust laws over where entities can and cannot sell during war time."

"Why are you looking up laws in the map room?"

"Because half our laws were created based on then-current maps of Divnum and Belnum streets. If our friend Zuris gets his way, it might just be possible to get around the restrictions without appealing to the Lawrits themselves."

"I should have known you'd be digging escape tunnels. No wonder you're taking Zuris's idea seriously."

"No need to take that condescending tone of voice with me," Ralden said. "I'm willing to bet cold coins that I've given Zuris's proposal more careful thought than you have."

It was almost certainly true. No matter her faults or selfish aims, Ralden worked unflaggingly. In fact, Giovel almost found himself more impressed than disgusted this time.

"Has Adni given you his next round of punishments yet?" Ralden asked, now following Varan with her eyes.

Something seemed to bob painfully in Giovel's stomach. "I haven't spoken to him today."

"Well you can be sure you'll hear from him soon. Right or not, you were rude last night, and he's farsighted enough to discipline you more than just by confining you to your work with the Witherclaw. Poor girl. Has she found anything to occupy herself?"

"Yes, as it happens," Giovel said, trying to banish Adni from his mind. "An old woman near the Candlespire has brought her on to help with her housework."

"Pity. I would have tried her at the guild if she weren't spoken for. Who authorized you to bring her up here, anyway?"

Giovel stiffened. "I wasn't aware that bringing a guest into the maps room needed any authorization."

"Well then you didn't ask. The archivists have decided that any maps showing lands beyond Redrem should be kept from the eye of the public until we're more sure what *they* know about us. Tactical advantage and all that."

"I saw three of them on the way, and no one stopped us from coming."

"You're a Divine Mage now, Giovel. You have to stop acting like you're nobody and assume that others will defer to you. You could take berries from a baby and half the city would say you were under orders from the Optate, and never mind that my entire job is to make sure we don't flaunt our authority like that."

He bit his lip. He really hadn't thought about it like that before, and he felt suddenly self-conscious, floating back through everything he recalled doing in the last few days. Right down to convincing Olinos and his Candles to help him with his unsanctioned raid. Could they say no to a Divine Mage? Could he have, back when he was in their position?

"By the way, do you know that dotard Luciron Inian?" Ralden asked.

"Luciron is no dotard," Giovel snapped. "And yes, I know him. He's a friend, so I don't appreciate hearing you insult him."

Ralden went on as if his rebuke meant nothing. "I'm preparing a proposal for him, and it might come better from someone he knows. Someone like you."

Damn this woman. "What kind of proposal is this?"

"Luciron manages all the contracts for Candleguard uniforms, if you didn't know. Capes, cloaks, tabards, britches, emblazoned gloves for the Spireblades, everything. There's quite a bit of money in it, and I'd like a cut of it for my guild."

Giovel felt as if his mouth should be hanging open. "You just told me to beware how I use my influence as a Divine Mage. And now you want me to use my friendship with Luciron—even my influence as a member of the Order—so you can get a deal to *sell clothes*?"

"More or less, yes."

"I can't believe this. I knew even the Order would have its sinkholes, but how can you be so brazen about it?"

"How can *you* be so close-minded?" Ralden asked. "Walk back half a pace with me. I can negotiate a deal to save the Candleguard a few pennants per uniform. At just three uniforms per man or woman, that's a whole day's wage every year at least. Think of what the Candleguard could do if I open up that much funding. Think about the extra tools and supplies that money could pay for, or the new training and new hands they could hire. Better yet, consider the funds they could devote to widows and widowers who lose a Candle. We're talking about a hundred thousand pennants of compensation for things like that. Wouldn't that kind of support be worth you having one simple conversation with Luciron?"

That left Giovel silent, though he found his fists tight and blood pounding in his ears.

"I mean it, Giovel. *Think about it.* Yes, my guild will pocket some extra coins. That doesn't mean I'm not helping Foneth itself in the process."

He was just starting to frame his response when a rhythmic pounding sounded somewhere outside. One, two, three, four, five, on and on. The alarm drums at the Candlespire. The beat drove Ralden's argument right from Giovel's mind.

Ralden met his eyes, dropping her maps.

It was the signal for a Redremel attack.

WOUNDS

RALDEN HADN'T HEARD that drum pattern in over a year. It wasn't one she could forget, though.

The alarms came from more than just the Candlespire by the time she cleared the library's doorway and blinked at the glare on the snowy hills. Drums sounded from the walls to the southeast, from Scout's Bridge nearby, and from somewhere else near Bone Hill. Attacks in all directions. Or one fractured attack. It was impossible to discern the signals anymore, though not all were sounding the same rhythm as the first.

Giovel and the Witherclaw Witch emerged right behind Ralden. "I'll go toward the Candlespire," he said.

"Not yet," Ralden replied. "Stay with me until we know more."

With that she began running toward Scout's Bridge, the nearest watch station sounding the alarm. Giovel ran right behind her.

A wave of Candles emerged from the streets by the river just as they reached the east tower of the massive bridge. A wide-eyed lieutenant was shouting orders there, trying to divide her fifteen or so guard in a way that made sense.

"What can you tell us?" Ralden called, silencing the guard nearby.

The lieutenant's eyes widened even farther. "Lady Ralden! And Lord Giovel!" She tried to bow.

"What can you tell us?" Ralden repeated.

"Attacks on the Divnum walls and the Candlespire. It looks like someone attacked a crowd at the festival too."

Ralden thought for a moment. The walls and Candlespire would have their own guard. The festival wouldn't.

"You should send all but three of your guard to Cloud Lake," she said, already walking on. "Keep those three here to run messages at a moment's notice."

"Where do we go, Ralden?" Giovel asked.

"Get the Witherclaw somewhere safe," Ralden said. "I'm going to the walls."

Just as Ralden passed the watch station, a stream of shouting civilians converged from both sides of the bridge, cutting off access in any direction. It seemed as if five hundred people were coming from the east and another five from the west, all colliding there at once and fighting to flee the other way. Ralden thought for a moment of shouting for order and questioning anyone who'd seen an attack, but the throng was too frantic already. Most had children with them.

She'd thought the Redremel were months away from any attack.

Ralden whipped her tablet from her tabard and made a quick Illumina. She loosed it into the air, half-blinding the scores of people nearest her, but catching their attention and clearing a pathway through.

"Let me through!" she shouted. "The Redremel might be coming, but they have a member of the Order to reckon with today."

The crowd stayed parted until Ralden passed by.

She wished, not for the first time, that Foneth's laws would let her part the Redremel like that.

When Ralden finally cleared the crowded bridge, raced southward, and reached the walls, she found a battle underway. Thirty or forty Lances held the wall top itself, defending two long staircases as men and women rushed at them from below. From *inside* the walls. A slash of amber light cut through one of the Lances, shattering his shield and ripping his body apart as if it was scrap cloth. Yulena.

It meant the law was on her side today.

Ralden spotted the witch at once, a long-faced woman holding a genuine sand tablet, identical to Ralden's own. She used it well, drawing glyph after glyph and firing them precisely at the Lances above her. They were retreating now, cowering behind the walls for protection from the onslaught of Yulena. Ralden roared and drew a Vice. She released it and caught the witch in the left hand, crushing the witch's thumb so she lost hold of her tablet.

"Rally to me, Lances!" Ralden called.

There were perhaps fifty enemy fighters between them—far closer to herself than to the Lances now—but she sent them scattering with two quick Flails and a Talon that slashed one through the leg. Then there was just the long-faced witch, who'd recovered her tablet and was drawing another glyph even now.

And a second witch activating a glyph she didn't know from the trees nearby.

Ralden dove to the ground as the spell shot past. She spun around and drew a counter glyph to loose back, but the second witch withdrew behind the trees for a moment. His long-faced companion took advantage of Ralden's distraction and released another two spells immediately, blasting chunks of earth apart and showering Ralden in snow, rock, and dirt.

A cloud of debris obscured the way as she struck back. More blasts. More clumps of grass and mud flying up in front of her. And the Redremel swordsmen couldn't be far off now, if they meant to overtake her.

Ralden began backing away, prepping an Illumina on her tablet to cover a dash out of range. Then the Witherclaw was at her side, her hair whipping behind her as she threw her hands forward in some kind of spell. Nettles and Rods from the two witches ricocheted like pebbles off a wall, jetting backward from Varan's position and forcing the Redremel swordsmen together in a jumble. It gave Ralden just enough time to get properly to her feet and to finish her own glyph.

The second witch was out beside the first now, also holding a stolen tablet. He was huge, probably two full heads taller than Ralden herself was.

"Etelier!" Giovel shouted, appearing at Ralden's side with a handbow in one fist and a drawn sword in the other.

Ralden hurled her Illumina at Etelier, who was now running toward them. He staggered at the blinding flash and tripped in the snow. Then the long-faced witch began another stream of glyphs—

Tremors, Gags, and other spells Ralden couldn't recognize. She was fast, whoever she was. Her spells came so quickly Ralden barely had time to finish two for every third the witch completed. The low hum of Yulena resounded under the din of feet on stone and spells erupting.

Even as the spells pelted past them, several swordsmen rushed at Ralden as well, shouting wildly like a pack of dogs. Giovel shouted back and loosed both his handbow rounds before running to meet them with his own blade upraised.

Fire and wind from the Witherclaw. More glyphs, some misfiring and hitting the witches' own fighters. More bursts of snow and dirt. Steel on steel. Cries as Lances left the walls to help Giovel and a second wave of swordsmen rushed the stairs to intercept the Lances. Ralden realized she'd been standing a long moment, somehow still as a tree despite the chaos around her. She felt so stupid not to be moving, running one way or another or building new glyphs to help Giovel. But she also felt so drained all at once, like all the life in her had been sucked out through a leak in her head.

The Witherclaw saved her again, pushing her toward the stairs and the Lances as swordsmen tried circling around her. The witches' glyphs had stalled for a moment, maybe just so they wouldn't kill their own fighters while striking at her or Giovel. Before Ralden recovered herself, she was halfway up the steps, with Lances flanking her and loosing handbows down at their attackers. But the long-faced witch was on the great Divnum wall as well, pushing those same Lances back with more spells, ripping them apart with great gouts of Yulena.

Ralden came to herself and drew a Flail to hurl at the witch.

Her spell missed, ramming a Lance across the shoulder. While the Lance shook in place and dropped his own weapon, the long-faced witch spun toward Ralden, kicked the Lance in the groin, and loosed two rapid Talons. Both hit Ralden near her waist. She slid back against the crenelation, blood pouring from her sides.

The wounds didn't hurt. Shouldn't they be agony?

Dlenar leaped over her and ran at the witch. When had he come? He was halfway to the witch before she had a new glyph ready this time, and his tablet was full already. Dlenar hit her with a Tremor, and her whole body jerked sideways, tablet tumbling to the ground. Dlenar kept running, pausing only to draw one more glyph.

Then the witch Etelier hit him from the ground with a spell like a fist of glass. It caught Dlenar right in the side of the head, throwing him so hard off balance that he fell back against the crenelation and dropped off the wall. Ralden screamed out and tried to run to him, but she hadn't even stood before he was gone, falling the long way down to the rocky ditch outside.

Giovel shouted in rage from nearby and ran toward the long-faced witch. She had her tablet again and started to draw, but Giovel curled his arm back and launched his entire sword at her. It glittered over the snow as it spun upward. Then the blade smashed through the witch's tablet and cut her across the arm. Giovel's throw was so forceful that the blade continued flying past the witch, trailing blood and magnetic sand from the shattered tablet behind it.

A wave of pain hit Ralden then, as if her twin wounds had finally told her mind they were there, bleeding out on the stones of the Divnum walls. She screamed again and fell backward.

More Lances. More spells from somewhere. Steel on steel again, smoke from somewhere below. Giovel reached Ralden and pushed something hard against her sides, staunching the bleeding a bit.

"Can you hear me?" he shouted. "Can you move?"

She nodded mutely and tried to push his hands away. Her sides burned and ached and felt like they'd tear open all over again if he didn't get his hands away. He kept hold of her, though, shouting for help as he did so.

More hands. Cloth tearing, wrapping tight over her. Someone hauling her upward.

Ralden saw a brief glimpse of fires below, trees burning. Then the long-faced witch hobbling away with a cluster of swordsmen around her, launching darts at a few half-hearted Lances. More Lances, face down in the snow. The taller witch Etelier running into the trees that looked black as the sun sank, with someone breaking from the Lances to pursue him. No sight of Dlenar, though, because the witches had blasted him out of sight. Ralden yelled for whoever was carrying her to take her back where she could see him, just to be sure he was dead. He might not be, after all. Shouldn't be.

The next thing Ralden knew, she was in a snow-drift, landing with a soft crunch. The men who'd been carrying her were ahead, drawing weapons as more fighters ran at them. Too many more. They were outnumbered somehow, outnumbered by Redremel who never should have found a way into Divnum in the first place.

"Don't move, Ralden," Giovel said nearby, and sprinted past her toward the fighters.

I can't move, she wanted to say. I can't do anything. I could hardly move since the battle began.

DUEL

I'll have a good scar or two when I return.
  —The Witherclaw Witch; letter to Inivar and Sil.

ETELIER HADN'T COUNTED on finding the Witherclaw Witch as part of the attack. Here he'd thought their strike was over, broken by Giovel Ullin and the Lances, that the whole angry ploy was for nothing. But the Witherclaw didn't seem to care how the battle went elsewhere. When Etelier ran into the nearby forest, she followed. It was like the stars had brought her right where he needed.

His long legs made it easy to outdistance her when they broke from the others. He could have left her lost in late-afternoon gloom and the dark cluster of trees, circled back behind her, and struck once to remove her from the Order's control for good. He didn't, though. He slowed enough to let her know he wasn't trying to escape. He even peered back, waiting for her occasionally.

"The Order has tried to stop us from finding you," he called across the snow. "But I only want to talk."

A burst of air hit the tree beside Etelier, knocking loose bark, needles, and a shower of white powder. Etelier scrambled back for cover as another wave of air struck nearby.

So she wanted more than just a conversation.

More air swirled wildly and buffeted the trees on either side of Etelier. He darted forward to roll behind a tall drift of snow before the Witherclaw could close the distance between them. There she was in sight now, spinning her hands as if she meant to spur the wind forward by the force of her own motion. But maybe that was her tell, her strange power at work."

She moved the wrong direction, blasting snow, dried leaves, and fallen pine needles into the sky every few moments as she searched for Etelier. Whatever glyphs she made, she made them quickly in the snow itself, too fast for Etelier to discern. He started to circle wide through the dark trees.

"I have an offer for you," he called. His voice echoed oddly in the woods, hopefully masking his location. The Witherclaw spun around to search with her eyes, but she stopped short of spotting him where he crouched fifty paces away.

"Send me to my home," she called back.

Her arms stopped spinning. Now she made a different motion, pushing her hands toward the ground as if she had to fight to keep herself balanced on her feet. Something rumbled beneath the coat of snow. Wood began to crack in a tree near her. A row of icicles shattered and fell into drifts below. Then a flood of cold hit Etelier like a river. His nostrils began to freeze. His throat seemed to tighten as if he were choking.

Her witchery could control the cold, too. Fire, wind, winter, was there anything she couldn't manipulate?

The shrill cold bit so hard Etelier knew he needed to move. Still crouched low, he started around again. "We didn't strike today to fight you," he called. "I want your help with something, Witherclaw."

The Witherclaw turned in search of his voice once more. "Send me to my home!"

She broke from her balancing motion and the cold began to lessen. Etelier shuddered as the sudden change in temperature overtook him again. What sort of power would she show next?

"There are rumors that your witchery can heal people. They say you can mend wounds and speed a recovery from illness."

More air this time, blasting a tree near Etelier. He dropped to the ground and held still until the Witherclaw turned another direction. She was closer now, barely thirty paces off through the brush.

Etelier slid through the snow to the cover of a giant beech tree. "I want you to look at someone. See if you can tend an old hurt that never healed well. That's all."

The wind picked up—not the Witherclaw's but a sharp winter wind from the west. The Witherclaw made a third tell motion, fists forward, shoulders low, teeth bared as if she were silently howling. Then the wind turned on itself, swirling in a violent spiral. Heaps of snow flew free from the trees. Dried branches snapped loose and showered the ground. A rotted trunk buckled and collapsed near Etelier. He jumped for new protection when the beech in front of him started to crack. And there, peering past bare trees, the Witherclaw's eyes met his. She snarled and began twirling her hands again.

Something hit Etelier in the side. He swore, flew off balance, and collapsed in a heap of scratching branches.

Footsteps. She was running at him through the dark trees, coming for him.

Etelier climbed upright and sprinted farther into the woods, sketching a single Hammer in the snow to fire back as a distraction. He aimed wide. The glyph succeeded in waving the Witherclaw off for a moment and stopping the mad, directionless wind until Etelier found an immense stump to shield him.

"Wait, Witherclaw! Wait! I don't want to hurt you!"

She shouted words he didn't know. Now, after running for cover, Etelier realized he couldn't see her. She'd turned his own game against him. Had she noticed where *he* was, though? She could be close enough to leap on him now, and he'd never see her in time.

"All I want is your help to heal *one person*!" Etelier shouted, risking exposing his location yet again. "Please, just come with me and see if you can do it! I'll do whatever I can to help you find your home."

Something shuffled in the snow to his right. Or to his left? He couldn't tell, damn it, couldn't see anything but swaying trees and a few flurries of snow from the wind. He drew another Hammer, just to be sure she didn't take him off guard.

"I won't heal for you," the Witherclaw called, her voice so close Etelier thought she must be right beside him.

Another wash of cold came over him, making him gasp and stumble with shock. He leaped out to see where the Witherclaw was. As soon his head rose above the stump, a barrage of wind struck at him, flinging branches, pebbles, and shards of ice at his bare face.

The attack stung and cut at his skin, but all Etelier could think of was her words.

I won't heal for you.

Poor Mota.

Perhaps he should say it was for a child, a girl whose life was ruined if he couldn't find a solution for her ears. Perhaps even say outright that Mota was *his* girl, his child. People said the Witherclaw had children of her own. She understood his words, clearly. She might understand his desperation too.

But if the Witherclaw meant what she'd said just now, she was useless to him. Just another weapon for the Divine as they closed in. Rage like a waterfall coursed through Etelier's chest, almost hot enough to fight the buffeting waves of wind. Etelier roared into the air and unleashed his Hammer, finally spotting the Witherclaw twirling her hands half behind a fir tree. She was only ten paces off.

The Hammer flew true, humming as audibly as any spell Etelier had ever cast. It hit the Witherclaw's left ear, spraying bright blood onto the snow and hurling her completely upside down. Her head slapped back into a pile of snow, hair splayed out over her. Her hands didn't cease spinning, though, and a plume of yellow flame erupted from the air, lashing back at Etelier's exposed face. He tried to duck but light and heat caught the side of his jaw before he could escape.

An explosion of pain in his skull, his cheek, his ear. Hard impact as he tumbled over. Cold on one side, stabbing fire on the other. He still heard the hum of his own Hammer. Or was it something else ringing?

Then Etelier thought he must be dead, it burned so hot and stung so hard.

There was frost beneath his hands, something wet on his knees. Blood in his mouth. Must have bit his own tongue?

He was crawling through the snow, trying to regain his footing. He tripped twice, too blind from the flare of fire to see where he was going. Branches and roots clawed at him, and the snow brought no relief when his burned face hit it. Just cold that felt like hot metal all over again.

He found a break in the wall of trees. Clear air. His eyes were starting to adjust again, showing him a way forward, away from the Witherclaw. Clutching his face with his left hand, Etelier stumbled out and ran toward the lights of some part of the city.

He didn't look back to see whether the Witherclaw followed.

TRAILS THROUGH THE TREES

I thought I was so close to answers.
  —The Witherclaw Witch; letter to Recia.

GIOVEL USED A dead man's spear to fight his way through the press of bodies. The Lances' Wall Captain was done for—a spell to the head from Etelier—and the band of attacking swordsmen seemed to be scattering as well, leaderless now that both witches had run for it. Giovel would have been glad to stay and take command, to rout or capture or kill the rest of them if he had to. But not while Etelier and his witch friend were on the run.

Etelier had been the first to flee. He'd broken from his position below the wall almost as soon as he hit Dlenar. At the time when he might have won the battle, he'd escaped instead, vanishing into the twilit trees. His path was clear in the snow now, easy to follow despite the rapid darkening of the sky. Another pair of footprints followed Etelier's, though.

Are they both here, two witches combining to ambush me? Giovel wondered. He couldn't delay to find out, not with attacks elsewhere, alarms ringing from the Candlespire and Scout's Bridge. He had to catch up and bring them down while he had half a chance.

His darts were all gone. He'd dropped his sand tablet somewhere, little use it would be anyway, and he'd abandoned his handbow after the first rounds he launched. So he held someone else's spear in front of him and ran on with just that to fight two witches.

The forest blocked out many of the sounds of the clash behind him. It was thicker and more enclosed than the Featherwood, more like a Yeren jungle, with swaths of dried vines, gray brambles, and bushes thick with whipping branches. Few trees had leaves any more, but the last daylight was gone almost as soon as Giovel ran into the brush. He just had pale, reflected snow light to guide him now.

The forest was a mess, too. Chunks of powder were missing, burst aside as if by a windstorm. Scorch blackened the bark of many of the trees. Etelier's trail wound in a wild river-like course, dodging back and forth on itself, turning behind one tree and then in front again almost as random. When Giovel realized how the other pair of tracks veered apart, doing the same thing, he knew it wasn't the second witch who'd followed Etelier. It was Varan.

Her footprints were smaller and closer together. And the trees weren't burned where she'd run. Just near Etelier's trail. What was she thinking, chasing after him alone?

With a curse, Giovel abandoned Etelier's trail to follow hers directly.

It looked as if she'd steered west, hiding behind trees herself. Near the north end of the little woods, Giovel found the trail again. Blood dripped across the footprints.

He spotted Varan herself collapsed just outside the trees. When he saw her, he dropped his spear and ran to her as fast as his tired legs could take him. Both her hands held her left ear, which had been crushed by something. Her skin looked gray and sickly, but she heaved rapid, shallow breaths. Alive.

"I'm here, Varan," Giovel said, pulling her hands back gently to examine her wound. "I'm here."

He couldn't find any other traces of injury, so he bent forward, groaned, and scooped her from the ground. Another trail caught his eye nearby, also marked with blood. Etelier's. Giovel forced himself to look away, to turn around and try to find his bearings. He knew the southern gates should be close, but he didn't know this corner of Divnum well, didn't know where the safest place was to take Varan now. He already felt too winded to carry her far, and he couldn't run after the bastard who'd hurt Varan without putting her down first.

"Can you walk?" he asked, trying to determine how to wrap her open wound.

Silence.

"Varan, I need to go after Etelier! Can you keep upright if I leave you here—just for a moment?"

Silence again, other than Varan's unsteady breathing and the occasional grunt of pain.

But, of course, I can't leave her like this. Can't chase Etelier. Can't go back to help Ralden. Can't do half of the things I'm *needed* for right now. All I can do is follow my fool orders from Adni and get you to safety. If I can even do that.

He turned toward the Candlespire, knowing he'd find the Iceflow soon enough. He could take one step, and then another, despite the aching weariness in his back and legs and arms and neck.

He hoped to the stars that the fighting had ended in that direction.

FATHER AND DAUGHTER

I miss your voices.
—The Witherclaw Witch; letter to Golkorun, Inivar, and Sil.

ETELIER WAS VAGUELY aware of the sounds of another clash nearby, but he ignored them. He just clutched his wounded ear and limped toward Belnum and quiet and safety. He wouldn't regroup with the others. Not tonight. Any hope he'd had at the start of their attacks was gone now, burned out during his fight with the Witherclaw. It had felt so perfect at first, especially when he found his chance to confront her, but there was *nothing* to show for it but a burn on his jaw and a ruined left ear like what he'd given her. An utter waste.

Candles, Lances, and even Tovómil men-at-arms filled the streets, running in little groups to search this part of the city, to check that street, to reinforce somewhere. Etelier had to pause four times before he reached the cheap, drunken stitcher Piatém had once tipped him off about. True to form, the stitcher asked no questions but whether Etelier had coin. Etelier dropped a few silvers and the stitcher started to work.

He tied Etelier to a table shaped like a feather. Then he used a set of thick belts to strap Etelier down, binding his head back at a steep angle.

"This will burn," he said quietly. He shoved a piece of wood into Etelier's mouth without asking permission, then he poured something hot and fiery all over Etelier's face. Etelier bit so hard his jaw hurt. He tried to howl in pain, but all he was aware of was the sharp taste of the wood and explosive pain across his face.

Needle and thread came next. Etelier screamed even more. He couldn't writhe away, couldn't get free. All he could do was bite his wooden tongue guard and wonder whether it was sweat, tears, or alcohol pouring down his face and stinging into the searing blister that had once been his ear.

He felt feverish and half-numb by the time the stitcher finished. He couldn't hear anything on one side, and it was hard to balance, as if his eye, not his ear, had lost its sense. The stitcher wrapped the closed wound with a bandage that smelled like rue, then waved Etelier away without any more instruction.

"Do I have to take these stitches out at some point?" Etelier managed to ask.

"If you want. It's another silver to do that."

Etelier couldn't think clearly enough now to say anything else, to know what to say or plan or expect. So he just grunted and left the stitcher's workshop, following dark streets farther east toward home and ducking into the shadows whenever he heard sounds that might be a patrol.

Pramél was waiting for him by the door, as always. She began to ask what had happened, what the alarms meant, before she saw his bandage and screamed.

"What happened to you, Etelier? Are you hurt anywhere else?"

He ignored her, kicked off his boots, and walked through the Sanctuary to get to Mota's room.

"Are you alright, Etelier?"

"Leave me alone," he snapped. He shut the door to Mota's tiny room behind him, partially cutting off Pramél's shouts.

Mota stirred in her little bed. She couldn't hear much, but she'd surely heard Pramél's outcry and the sounds of the door. Etelier took one of her little hands and counted the fingers out one by one. It was their ritual, how she recognized him even in the dark, since she couldn't discern his voice well anymore.

"I'm here, Mota," he said, coming close. "I'm here."

Pramél said something loud and angry outside. He couldn't tell what it was. Couldn't hear so well either.

"Look at me, Mota," Etelier said, turning his head. He peeled off his bandage to show her his bad ear. "Look at your old father. I'm just like you now. See? I have a hurt ear too. No need to be sad about it. We can help each other, we can understand each other like no one else. I know what it must feel like now."

Pramél screamed again, now standing behind Etelier and seeing his red, ruined, badly mended ear. The light from the candles outside the room crossed his face, and then Mota's eyes went wide with horror too. Her scream was clear to him where Pramél's was not, shrill and cold and pure as an icicle. She thrashed backward and tried to get away from him, turning her eyes from his horrible wound.

"You don't have to be afraid of me, Mota!" Etelier said again. "It's just like your ear now, so much the same."

"Leave her alone, you bastard!" Pramél shouted, pulling at his arms. "Can't you see you're terrifying her?"

He pushed Pramél back and leaned forward to hold Mota in his arms. She struggled and flailed, but he held her tight.

"I still love you, Mota, and I'm learning to understand you. Don't you see? Please stay close. Please don't leave me, little girl."

Mota shrieked and fought to get away. Then Pramél hit Etelier in the head with something and he grunted, dropping Mota on the bed to clutch the point where he'd been struck. Pramél snatched Mota, who leaned close to her chest, and carried her out into their room, locking the door behind her.

Alone again, Etelier thought.

Mota can't hear me. Because we aren't the same yet. Both her ears are bad, and she's too young to realize how alike we are. My poor beautiful girl, robbed of half her life before her life was half-started. And now she's been robbed of half what little she had left, because now I've made her scared of *me*. So maybe Pramél's right to carry her away. Maybe I have nothing else to give. I can't find a cure, can't find the Divine's library, can't find anything but blood and waste and empty glyphs that burn things to the ground instead of fixing them.

The sounds were muffled, but he heard both his wife and daughter weeping in the other room, sobbing into each other.

He wept too as he unlatched the front door and walked back into the cold night.

AFTER

They try to console me, sometimes. And sometimes I feel like I need to console them.

—The Witherclaw Witch; letter to Golkorun.

THERE WAS FAR too much to do as the sun dropped from the sky. Giovel left Varan with a healer near Scout's Bridge and rushed back to the walls, worried the fighting might not be over there. He found the Lances scattered. Of the fifty wall guard for that section of the city, only twenty remained on their feet. They'd killed at least as many of their attackers, though more seemed to have fled.

"Where's Lady Ralden?" Giovel asked when he found the Lance in charge—an unranked Azure who'd more or less assumed command in the absence of an officer.

"I haven't seen her, Lord Giovel," the Lance stammered. "I thought she left with you two hours ago."

"She was bleeding out, soldier!"

The Lance swore and shouted for someone to help him search.

Giovel found her himself, right where he'd left her, almost covered in snow. She looked like a corpse, but she still breathed, and the deep cuts on her sides seemed to have slowed thanks to the tight bandaging they'd applied before Giovel pursued Etelier. But damn every Lance in the world for leaving her like this, freezing and bleeding her way to Cold Lake behind a heap of muddy slush.

It made him wonder if they'd even gone looking for Dlenar yet.

"He's dead," the same Lance said when Giovel asked. "He fell from the wall."

"Have you seen the body yourself?" Giovel demanded.

"Yes, Lord Giovel. We carried him from the ditch almost as soon as we routed the last of the Redremel."

Then they'd at least done something as they should. Focus on that and you won't have to think about Dlenar's fate.

"Are they Redremel, though?" Giovel asked. "What markers do they carry?"

The Lance faltered. "They attacked us without a warning, sir. I don't know that we found any markers to show them as such, but—"

"Then we don't know who they are. Make no assumptions or reports about who they are until we have more information."

"But who else could they be, sir?"

Giovel had some ideas after attending Etelier's little gathering a few weeks back.

"Ralden, can you speak?" he asked softly as he and two more Lances gently picked her up.

Her teeth chattered audibly against one another, but she nodded. "I think so."

"Get us a carrier for her!" Giovel called. "I'm taking you to be treated. Try to stay awake until we get there."

Even when the Lances found a canvas carrier and placed her delicately into it, the journey to a healer felt like a long one, and all the way Giovel thought not of her or of Varan and their wounds, not about Dlenar's recklessly brave end and how *he* could just as easily be next, not of the attacks elsewhere and the many more who could be dead or dying. Just of Etelier, walking free after all this.

The only two healers by Scout's Bridge were working far beyond their capacities as it was, so they rushed Ralden all the way to the clinic near the Candlespire. Things weren't much better off there—ten Candleguard, a dozen civilians, and several more Lances wounded badly—but Divnum's clinic had more hands to devote and immediately took Ralden under their care.

Giovel was getting shaky with weariness, but he jogged back to find Varan before anything else, just to be sure she was in no more danger for the moment. The snow made for a bright night. Still, every shadow in the trees and hills and streets seemed like it could hide another enemy. Giovel found himself swiveling around on edge until he saw Varan with his own eyes, her ear bandaged, face and hands washed clean. She sat in a quiet corner of the first healer's hall where he'd left her, while a score more patients kept the healers occupied.

"Can I take her with me now?" he called to a healer who was scrubbing blood from her hands in another corner.

"If it pleases you," the healer said dourly. "There's nothing more we can do for that one."

"Let's go to Kirida's," Giovel said, and offered Varan his hand.

She still said nothing, but her eyes seemed to move when he said Kirida's name and she stood to follow him a moment later. Giovel gave her his coat, though it was ragged and dirty after the day's events. Her Witherclaw dress was gone, probably burned already, and all she had to wear now was her shoes and a plain gray robe the healers had given her. She took the coat without looking at it.

Walking again, back across Divnum through deep snow and growing cold, with neither of them now dressed fit for the night. Giovel felt so exhausted he could have slept on the floor at the healers'. If there weren't other places to check, questions to ask, reports to share, and two hundred more things to do before the night ended.

After a long, silent time, Giovel asked, "Did you hurt Etelier?"

The question seemed to surprise Varan. "Yes."

It couldn't be enough to pay for the beating the Order had taken that day, but hearing it gave Giovel a jolt of fierce satisfaction.

"It was very brave of you to follow him," he said. "Brave of you to come with me at all when the fighting started."

"He wanted me to follow."

Giovel frowned. "Me? Or Etelier?"

"Him. Etelier. He wanted me to follow."

"...Why?"

"He tried to talk to me."

"Stars. What did he say to you, Varan? Please, tell me anything you can remember about it."

"He wanted healing. I used to heal people. He wanted that. But I said no. He hurt me with Yulen." She pointed to the waves of dark hair covering her left ear. "I hurt him. The same hurt."

Ice and fire, this could be what these witches were after from the start. "Did he say who he wanted to heal? What of?" Giovel asked, halting to face her. "And how did he know you used to heal people? Did he say anything about that?"

"I don't understand."

"Did he say he's the one who spirited you?" Giovel went on, ignoring his other questions.

"He didn't say spiriting. He wanted me to heal."

Still. The implications were staggering as it was. If they could find out who it was Etelier was working for, who craved Varan's power so much—and if they could finally learn for sure who'd spirited her to begin with—they'd be only a step away from both sending her back and cutting off the spiritings for good. And now, if they wanted her this badly, if Etelier had truly lured her away as Varan seemed to think...

"They all want my power here," Varan said, interrupting Giovel's line of thought. "Everyone wants my power. I'm not a person here. I'm a child. Or I'm a power. I'm a tool. Do you understand me, Giovel?"

Shame flooded through him as if he'd drunk it from a bowl. He couldn't meet Varan's eyes just then. Yes, he understood.

What you say stings inside because in the very moment you said it, I was viewing you the same way, as a bridge to my plans and hopes. A thing to be wielded. In this regard I'm no better than the witches, am I? Only a few months hunting them, and already I'm *like* them.

After a long moment, Giovel put a hand on Varan's shoulder then began to walk again. He didn't know what he could say that wasn't an outright lie.

Was that why they'd spirited her to begin with? For her unique power? To recruit her, like they'd been recruiting at the Croen Estate? And what about other spiritings? Was it part of how they forced anyone to join their cause—spiriting people from so far away they'd have no hope of returning without the witches' help?

Yet more questions Giovel couldn't answer right now. But he swore he'd investigate it no matter where Adni ordered him to stand. And even more, he swore he'd see Varan as herself and not just a weapon.

She of all people deserved that much.

* * *

Nomis hadn't been hurt in the fighting, though blood flecked his uniform when Giovel found him at his home. He called for Kirida and the two of them took Varan inside to feed and comfort and watch her for the time.

"I'll get more Grays to you," Giovel assured Nomis. "Candles too, if I can get it approved. Whoever I send will answer to you until I come back to relieve them personally."

Nomis's eyes widened. "Was Varan a target of these attacks today?"

"Possibly. That's all I can say."

Nomis nodded. "I'll keep close watch until the others get here."

"Don't tell Kirida, if you can avoid it."

"Shit. She's my wife, Giovel."

"Don't tell *anyone* until I'm back here with more arms."

Giovel had to backtrack to the barracks to find men and women who weren't already on patrol. Then it was back to the Candlespire itself, where hundreds more Lances, men-at-arms, Candles, Grays, and even volunteers were receiving assignments. Adni seemed to have taken direct control of them all, given the presence of witches in the attack.

"There were witches in other strikes too," Elínla explained as she and Giovel waited for a chance to speak to Adni themselves.

"How many?" Giovel asked.

She shook her head. "At least five. A group attacked the festival. I was there, fortunately, and half a dozen Grays with me. Another group hit the Candlespire, though they didn't get far, and two more groups went toward the north edge of the city before Hirnu and a hundred Citadel Guard cut them off."

"They were going after the Optate?"

"Could be. No one knows. But there were witches at all five places, Giovel. All attacking at precisely the same time."

Five witches. No, *more* than five since there'd been two at the south end of the wall. And here we are, limping along, Giovel thought. Dlenar dead, Ralden badly wounded, and Sur still weeks from walking free. They've chopped us apart like a carrot for stewing.

"Giovel, Elínla," someone called, pushing through the crowd of bodies. Hirnu, face hard as a mountain. "Are you hurt?"

"Just shaken," Elínla said. "You?"

Hirnu ignored the question. "Adni and I are making assignments with the Jade and Azure Commanders next. Report back here in an hour for us to talk properly."

"Waiting an hour will be like sitting on thorns," Giovel said. "Is there something we can do in the meantime?"

"I suggest you check on your own homes, if you haven't yet."

Inorovel. How had he *forgotten* to go looking for her first?

Giovel raced back toward the Featherwood.

He realized just twenty paces from the Candlespire that he should have called a few arms to come with him. Too late now. He'd have to bring Inorovel back with him instead, curse him for a careless father. A blind fool who hadn't even *thought* to check on home while he checked ten other places. How could he ever do this without Iremni?

Inorovel stood by the window, watching for him when he arrived. Her eyes were red. She cried again when he appeared, running to meet him and throwing her arms around his neck.

"I'm here," he whispered, squeezing her shoulders. "I'm here, Inorovel. I'm sorry it took me so long."

"People at the festival said two of the Order died fighting by the wall," Inorovel sobbed. "They said that's where the Witherclaw was. I thought one of them had been you."

"I'm here," he repeated, and found himself weeping too.

He held Inorovel for a long time.

My last and most important piece of Iremni, and I didn't even think to come until Hirnu suggested it. Is that how much or how little I value her? Is that how much I value the Order and Foneth itself in Inorovel's place?

He sniffed, wiped his face, and asked, "When did you come back home?"

"In the middle of the attack," Inorovel said, wiping her own face as well. "Da, come inside properly and sit by the fire. You're frozen."

He followed her in, throwing on another cloak despite the much greater warmth in the Sanctuary. "I can't stay long—and you'll need to come with me when I leave—but tell me what happened."

There wasn't much for Inorovel to recount, thank every sacred thing in the world. She said she'd been at the south end of the Perception Day festival when a witch attacked near the north edge of the crowd. Plenty of warning for her to flee before the fighting drew nearer.

"You did the right thing to come back here," Giovel said, squeezing her hand by the fire. "Tomorrow we'll make a plan for if this ever happens again, so you have an even safer place to wait until I can come."

And tomorrow and every day after, I'll come here faster, sooner.

"Where are you going now?" Inorovel asked. "It's almost midnight."

"I need to meet with the Order." What was left of it at least. "You can stay outside our council room at the Candlespire while I do."

She nodded mutely and went to get her own cloak, boots, and scarf. While she did, Giovel refilled his dart quiver, grabbed two folding handbows, and went for his sword. But there was no sword. He still hadn't replaced the one he broke hunting the witch with Elínla, and he'd hurled away the borrowed blade he'd worn earlier. He sighed, rubbed his face to try waking his mind up more, and took a rope knife instead.

The walk back to the Candlespire led them right past the site of the festival. It was too dark to see much of it, even with the snow light and Yulen's faint reflection in Cloud Lake, but it looked as if many of the stalls, carts, and displays had been burned or smashed in the commotion. A small group of Lances scouted around it now. Looking for bodies hidden in the wreckage and the snow.

Adni, Hirnu, and Elínla were waiting when Giovel left Inorovel outside the council chamber. All of them looked just as tired as he felt. Hirnu's hair was half loose from a fighter's tail. Elínla had mud nearly to her waist, as if she'd had to wade across a creek since their last conversation. Adni just held his face in his hands, shaking his hair as if pulling it would help him stay calm.

"Reports," he said in a dull voice.

It was almost the same from all three of them. Two witches had gone north toward the citadel with a band of non-uniformed fighters around them. Hirnu insisted that they weren't looking for the Optate. Just looking for a dark-haired woman. They'd found five who might be called dark-haired, killing two of them before Hirnu rallied the Citadel Guard and fought them off.

"And the witches?" Adni asked.

"I killed one," Hirnu said. "The other ran free."

Elínla's report was similar, though she'd seen only one witch at the festival. With the help of several Grays, she'd run him off quickly. The witches had fighters there too, killing six Candleguard before disbanding to flee as well.

"We captured nine of them," Elínla said. "Killed maybe thirty."

Only Adni hadn't fought then, and he'd been trying to marshal forces near the Candlespire, where yet another attack took place. After hearing Giovel's report, Adni asked simply, "Is there any evidence whether the Redremel were involved?"

"Can we worry about the Redremel another day, Adni?" Elínla asked. "It's the witches that bother me. *Seven* of them at least, and all working together."

"And all looking for Varan, by the sounds of things," Giovel said gravely.

"Not only the Witherclaw," Hirnu said. "They killed your two prisoners."

"Riddin?"

"Yes."

All that work to find the Lances' leak, and now he was dead along with his companion within a single day.

It was just as Giovel had feared the previous night; he should have waited, should have watched until Etelier went back to Riddin and they could cut the head from the witch's pack in one clean motion. But Giovel had overridden patience and his own experience for the flush of a small win—now made pointless by the witch's swift counterattack.

"But Giovel's right," Adni was saying now. "They were looking for the Witherclaw Witch. And they almost got her, despite whatever you did to guard her."

Giovel twitched. "Do you have a complaint about how I've fulfilled my duties?"

"Yes, as a matter of fact. You should have taken her far from the fighting the moment you heard the alarms. You should have holed up somewhere until it was safe and let the Lances and Candleguard do their work."

"Varan saved Ralden's life today," Giovel said, voice rising more than he'd meant it to. "And I probably saved hers as well. If we hadn't gone to the walls—"

"Then Varan wouldn't have got her face split open by a witch's spell."

Elínla leaped to her feet. "At least Giovel did something during the attacks! Dlenar *gave his life today*, Ralden almost gave hers, and we all risked our heads without a second thought. But you were nowhere near the fighting!"

"I was close enough to spit at the men attacking the Candlespire!" Adni yelled back.

"And yet you're the only one who never stepped in, you gutless scarecrow cocker."

Adni jerked back silently as if he'd been stabbed through a lung.

"Enough of this," Hirnu said.

"Enough of all of you," Adni said, taking another step back. "Hirnu and Elínla, you're dismissed."

"We need to talk about how to allocate the Grays," Elínla started to say, but Adni waved her silent.

"You're *dismissed*," he said again.

"Why? So you can berate Giovel without embarrassing yourself to anyone else?" Elínla asked.

"*Enough*," Hirnu said, now pulling Elínla by the arm. "We're leaving."

Giovel felt cold dread go through him. Elínla might have pushed Adni too far. There was an almost mad look in his eye now, a hunger Giovel hadn't seen there before. And Adni wanted Giovel to stay behind, him alone.

"You need a new sword," Adni said.

Not what Giovel had expected. "I'll go to the Belnum Iron Guild tomorrow to select one."

"Get one from the barracks now. We're going out."

"Now?"

"Yes, now." Adni tightened the clasp on his white cape, walking out of the room. He swept past where Inorovel sat, then right by Hirnu and Elínla who were huddled in conference with each other. Giovel hurried to catch up. He had just enough time to wave for Inorovel to stay put.

"It's halfway to dawn, Adni. Where are we going?"

"Witch hunting."

The dread in Giovel's stomach expanded. For the first time he could recall, he'd rather be anywhere else than hunting a witch.

SISTER AND SISTER

The way they think of their families here is so much like how I think of you.
—The Witherclaw Witch; letter to Recia.

THERE WOULD BE no quiet corner in Foneth tonight. Patrols of Lances brought in from the edge of the city scoured corners of the streets and waved bright blue lamps in crevices throughout North Hold and Belnum. The Candles, despite their losses today, were out in force as well. Other fighters took to the streets too—the Shields of the Citadel, taking charge of various guild halls owned by Optacrats or rich friends of those appointed to lead, or men-at-arms and sellswords serving contracts for families like the Jada or the Tovómil. Scores of Grays would be out too, so Claravena took her time crossing streets, snow-blanketed hills, and stretches of icy forest.

She didn't know how things had gone for the other groups. After helping Raf get into the Candlespire, she alone had watched from a distance, marshalling their messengers to be sure no Divnum trap took them all at once. It was probably foolish of Etelier to give her that duty when she had so much to offer with Yulena. But maybe it was wise to wait and play the long game she'd always played, sliding one step closer to changing the way of things.

A throng of Azures searched around the Voiceless Meadows when Claravena neared it, so she steered around to try the west bolt hole instead. Hopefully someone would come there. If anyone could make it past so many patrols.

Etelier had found this one, an old serum-refiner's den turned meeting room. It was little more than a cellar, really, with one-third windows peeking above the ground but not clearing the snow now. There was no chimney, no possibility for fire without leaving the doorway open to the cold in the first place, so Claravena filched an oil lantern from a street over, checked to be sure no one saw her slip inside, and shut the ivy-covered latch behind.

She found Wurelna inside, covered in blood and clutching one arm.

Wurelna had a glyph outline on the table before Claravena could raise the lamp to show herself properly.

"I thought you were one of the Sept of Blue Heaven," Wurelna sighed, wincing as she abandoned her glyph and clutched her arm again.

Claravena brought the light close to inspect Wurelna's wound, fighting the hard lump in her stomach. Blood had puddled on the broken worktable. So much of it. It was hard not to be dizzy.

"Did you come back alone?" she finally asked, gritting her teeth and holding the light out to block Wurelna's wound from her own vision.

"Etelier ran another way before I left," said Wurelna. "I don't know if he made it."

A flicker of hope went through Claravena. Not that he *had*. That they wouldn't see him again, wouldn't need to follow his dangerous leadership. She cursed herself for even thinking it, though.

"You need stitches. Will you be alright waiting for me here?"

"I think so. I can wrap it for the moment."

Strong woman, Wurelna. She seemed almost as calm as ever, despite peering over her own gashed, bleeding arm and hearing that she'd need treatment that would hurt like the cut itself.

"I'll hurry back," Claravena said.

"Do you know someone we can trust to do it?"

"I know *me*. As soon as I can find a proper needle and strong thread, I'll come back for you. Do you have anything to clean it?"

"I have some alcohol."

"That'll hurt."

"It hurts now. I'll live."

It didn't take long for Claravena to find the supplies she'd need. She simply ran to a big house with a lamp still on, pounded on the door, and cried out that a Candle was bleeding in the street. An old woman came to the door, heard Claravena out, and returned a moment later with everything she'd need to tend her wounded companion. Now she just had to hope no Candle walked by as she raced back to Wurelna. If one did, she might have to make her story a reality.

Wurelna had her wound wrapped tight when Claravena returned. The moments that taxed Claravena most were looking at the wound again, as Wurelna unwrapped it, and beginning the first stitch once the cut was clean. Once she began, she felt a rhythm forming quickly.

I've done this before. Done it twenty times now. I can do it once more, and maybe twenty times yet if that's what it takes.

Wurelna took nothing for the pain, did nothing Claravena could see to restrain herself, and said nothing until the stitches were complete.

Then she said, "Claravena. I saw your sister at the walls."

All this time Claravena had kept from shaking, vomiting, passing out. Now she dropped the red needle and had to lean on the rotting edge of the table to stay upright. All she could think for a moment was that it was wise of Wurelna not to speak sooner.

I couldn't have helped her if I knew this before.

She steadied herself for a silent moment. Wurelna began washing her hands with the alcohol she'd brought, not expounding any more until Claravena brought herself to ask, "Where was she?"

"She came from the south gates. My guess is she was assigned in Tovómil. I don't think she saw me. She fought Etelier while I was running for it."

So Eronea was alive after all, still a Gray. Still an *enemy*. Claravena had almost hoped she was dead. Better that than to meet her, Gray and witch, and have no chance for peace between them. There was so much more to discuss about the attack, so much information Claravena lacked. So much she lacked about Eronea too, and this one little piece made all those missing ones stab more acutely.

"I'm sorry," Wurelna said, wiping her hands dry on her dirty cloak.

"It's not your place to be sorry for me."

"I'll be sorry for myself, then. I knew her too when I was a Gray myself. I suppose you could even say we were friends, of a fashion."

Friends. But not sisters. So there was little chance Wurelna felt the uprooting rush of betrayal like Claravena did.

She'd always wondered, a little. Yes, Eronea left to certify her own awakening, to join the Grays, to *fight* witches on behalf of the Optate and the Order and all they stood for. But what did that really mean? Was she playing them? Was she infiltrating their sacred rank to someday bring them down for what they'd let Adni do to Uro? What they'd driven Lolen and Alene to do to one another?

It was a hopeful thought some days, because having a sister alive at all meant Claravena wasn't so alone. Having a sister as a Gray, though? That made her isolation all the surer.

I can fight myself or I can fight you. I don't know how to live with any other path.

Claravena's dizziness receded. Her hands stopped shaking. She realized she hadn't felt cold since Wurelna first spoke up. Perhaps because she knew now, knew clear as starlight, what they had to do.

Etelier was right, in his own pathetic way. We have to move. We can't delay. There isn't room for one more winter with the Order ruling Yulena and hunting witches.

"I'm going to try to regroup with the others," Wurelna said, half-shaking Claravena from her thoughts.

Claravena nodded. "I'm coming. We'll talk as we go."

"I can tell you what happened with our attack, at least."

And Claravena could tell her what needed to happen next, what had to change about how they managed their little band of rebels. She already knew the first step ahead.

It was time her fellow witches had a new leader.

LEADERSHIP

There is no rest for these people.
　—The Witherclaw Witch; letter to Recia.

THEY TOOK HORSES from the Candlespire stables. The animals were almost never used for official business—just exercised well by their grooms in case the Order ever deigned to ride. Giovel was immensely grateful to have them tonight.

Adni led all the way past the east end of Belnum, finally dismounting in a sort of quiet village east of Vision Hill. It was a beautiful little place, clean and isolated. Just the sort of spot the Redremel would raze if Foneth didn't implement Zuris's plan and flatten it first.

Adni instructed Giovel to tie their horses at the south end of a narrow back street, while he pulled an annotated list of names from his tabard and consulted it by the light of Yulen.

"What's this?" Giovel asked.

"Awakenings," Adni said.

"You have a list of them? Of known ones?"

"Of course I do, Giovel. My duties as Illumined Knight include guarding Foneth against the dangers they all pose to themselves and the people around them. So yes, I have a very thorough list. We're paying a visit to one of them."

The existence of such a list was staggering enough. Giovel had thought Grays and the Order went promptly after unregistered awakenings one-by-one, all by individual reports Dlenar and his workers painstakingly verified. Not by some thorough, detailed list Adni kept to himself.

"These people should have been brought in as soon as someone identified them," Giovel said. "Why are they left running loose?"

"You think I'm shirking my duties? The written law is only to bring in anyone who practices uncertified Yulena. There's an unwritten law too, which allows us to show them a little mercy if they're benign."

So Adni's unwritten law meant he, perhaps alone, judged who was a witch and who was just an awakening with their powers in check for the time. "Who else knows about this list?" Giovel asked.

"Keep up. I'll just say that there's plenty *you* don't know because you don't need to."

All the way there he'd held his tongue, waited for the stroke of Adni's anger to fall. Now, though, Giovel decided to speak up. "You're not a good leader, Adni."

"I'm glad you finally conjured the stomach to say that to me."

"Did you expect me to let you keep pissing on the rest of us?"

"I knew you'd share your opinion eventually. You've got that kind of arrogance that demands to be heard. But you might be wrong about me."

Giovel grabbed him by the shoulder now, stopping him. "Then tell me what in Cold Lake we're doing, chasing some awakening now of all times. Tell me *anything*, Adni!"

Adni didn't resist Giovel's grip. He just turned slowly to face him, folding his list and putting it back into his tabard. "So I'm a bad leader because I don't tell you things. Is that right?"

"The way you head the Order is a trough of shit."

"It's good to hear you say that out loud too. While you're feeling bold with your words, tell me this. What makes a decent leader of anyone, Giovel?"

Giovel clenched his mouth shut. He was too angry and tired and confused to have a ready answer.

"No wisdom for me?" Adni asked.

"Hiding things from your people or pushing them into the ground just because you feel unsteady in your own boots isn't what I call leadership."

"That wasn't so hard to explain. So you think it's all sharing information or persuading people to like you. Is that it?"

Giovel hesitated. He'd never seen Adni quite like this, quite so open in his desire to spar with his words. Usually he just stabbed at the target he wanted to hurt, and he never conceded an argument. Not to Giovel, anyway.

"No words still?" Adni asked. "Well then. Let me tell you what I've learned in my years in the Order—and the same with the Grays before that. There might be hundreds of skills of value, but there's only one that any leader really needs. It's choosing the people that surround you. Picking those who are better or different or willing to speak up or act on their own. And I picked you, didn't I?"

"Choosing me from a handful of recommended awakenings couldn't have been hard," Giovel said.

"There are no recommendations. Just a choice. That's my single greatest duty as Illumined Knight—not to watch or lord over you. To *choose* you. To hand-pick the rest of the Order to do the real work. When Hirnu refused to lead the Order and I was selected, there were only three of us left, all junior members of the Order with five years or less of experience. The Redremel had killed the rest of us in barely a week. And suddenly I was tasked to choose five new mages in the Order as soon as I could. As more have died, I've had to choose again and again, which is a damned hard task when everyone knows a Divine Mage is likely to die within a decade.

"So whom did I choose, Giovel? I could have picked bowing fools who would have worshiped and obeyed me without question. But look at the Order. I chose Dlenar, who was too weak to help other than by his influence, and Ralden, who uses the Order to put gold in her pockets. I chose a Lance who hated our Order to begin with. I could have filled the Order with Grays who think like me and listen to what I say, but the only one I've ever selected is someone too interested in her own excellence to ever stay under my thumb. And then there's you, who I knew would despise me from the start. But I still settled on you. So you might not like all my decisions, but when you complain about my leadership you're also complaining about yourself."

"Choosing people like me doesn't matter if you insist on holding us down or pinning us with responsibilities that don't matter," Giovel growled, now shaking with rage at Adni's idiotic defense.

"You live to see yourself as the helpless underling, don't you?" Adni asked, smirking. "I'd bet my own head that you do better work when you assume everyone above you is a fool. It's why you took so long to reach the vine as a Candleguard, also why so many lowly Candles respect you. As long as I can coax results from your own sense of victimhood, I'll keep doing it."

"What results? All you want me to do is play handler for a woman who doesn't need any help protecting herself!"

"Five different groups of witches tried to capture that woman today, so you can swallow that pathetic argument. The Witherclaw needs protecting, and you're the best situated to give it because you're the one who hates the witches most out of all the Order."

Adni walked on, not waiting for Giovel to respond. It took all the strength Giovel could muster not to launch a dart at his back. It would be so easy just to kill the swaggering vulture out here, far from watching eyes. And no matter what Adni said, no matter what sick logic there was in his words, Giovel wished he were dead and burned and out of his life for good.

"Keep up," Adni said, waving for Giovel to follow.

Should I? Or should I stick you with my rope knife and leave you here to think about how your leadership has shaped me?

But he's almost right, Giovel thought. What he says about me, at least, is the truth. I've *always* thought my superiors were fools and worked the harder for it. And the others—all so different from Adni— aren't the kind of Order someone else would have built. The shape of the Optacracy is proof enough of that.

Most of all, Giovel thought of the witches. He knew he'd never turn on Adni now, not because the man wasn't cruel and cold and paltry. But because the witches were still out there, and Adni had come to hunt one.

"Who is this we're going to find?" Giovel asked, hurrying to catch up.

"Lower your voice. We're looking for a man named Kanis. He's an unregistered awakening with an unusual amount of Yulenic control."

"Why now, though? If you thought he was one of the witches behind the attacks, why didn't you go after him sooner?"

"I don't think he was part of anything. We're here because I want him in the Order."

"You're fooling."

"No. You're just not listening. We've been fighting these witches with Grays and Lances and Candleguard. I think what we need now is our own witch, someone who can think more like they would."

Adni took another step, then paused and turned back to face Giovel.

"It's *choosing* our allies that matters, Giovel. If you could see a tenth of what I see, you wouldn't ask me to explain myself again."

Adni led to the end of the street, slowing almost to a halt as he crossed slick patches of ice where the snow had been tramped down already. A tiny house fit snugly between the street's final shop and a sort of grain barn at the corner. There were no lights, no sounds from inside.

"Stay behind me and don't leave the street open," Adni whispered.

Giovel was just opening his mouth to ask what Adni's plan was, when Adni clapped, shouted, "The Divine are here!" and opened the back door.

The house was tiny inside. Just a half-Sanctuary of mossy stone adjoined to the hearth wall, with one little bedroom behind it where a young man was removing blankets and cursing. Their witch, Kanis.

Adni walked to the edge of the bed and kicked Kanis in the chest. The witch cried out and rolled backward, collapsing onto the floor with one leg still tangled in his own blankets. Before Kanis could recover himself, Adni leaped over his bed and struck him hard in the jaw. Then again. Then on the left knee, sending the witch toppling over again as he tried to get his feet under him.

"He's beat, Adni!" Giovel said and tried to grab Adni's arm.

Kanis wasn't beat, though. He had a glyph forming in the dust by his bed, the individual points joining now during Adni's momentary distraction.

Without a pause, Adni slid forward and ran his foot through the glyph, breaking it apart as it began to glow. Then he kneed Kanis in the ribs and hit his face with an open-palmed strike that sounded like a splash. Kanis spun sideways from the strike and collapsed in the corner of his tiny room, weeping and bleeding and holding his hands over his face like a child.

And he *was* a child. He couldn't be twenty. Maybe only sixteen. He was dirty, ill-dressed against the cold, and looked too skinny to have eaten properly in weeks. Despite the witch's attempted glyph, Giovel felt an immense wave of pity for him.

"Still not broken, are you?" Adni asked, kicking at Kanis's bare toes. Kanis flinched and rolled into a ball.

"He's practically helpless, Adni! Tie his arms if you want to keep him from fighting back!"

Adni kicked him again. And again, before Giovel swore and grabbed him by the shoulder.

"What do you want with me?" the witch yelled, uncovering his battered face for half a moment before he cowered back again, sniffing and crying as blood poured from his nose.

"Not to tie you up, Kanis Delirot," Adni said.

"Who the hell are you?" Kanis growled. "I haven't done anything to you!"

"But you've done something to that poor girl. What was her name? Trilien?"

Kanis's weeping paused amid what might have been a gasp or a new cry of pain.

"I know what happened to her," Adni said. "And I know who did it. And I know what you were *trying* to do when you showed her your power. She was unlucky to be your friend, and you were a fool to experiment with Yulena instead of coming to the Grays when you first awakened."

Kanis's eyes were wide behind his eyes. He made no denials, just heaved in place, trying to staunch the flow from his nose with half a blanket. Giovel wanted to look away.

"Ah, and I also know how your power first manifested," Adni continued. "I know what your mother said when you told her, and what you did to her. What your father said he'd do *to you* if you ever showed your face again after hurting your own mother like that."

"Damn you!" Kanis shouted. "Who are you?"

"I'm Adni Aman, Councilor to the Optate and Illumined Knight of the Divine Order. And I'm here to warn you that using Yulena has consequences, no matter how innocently it all might have started."

Kanis went rigid now, only his mouth moving, trembling with fear. He looked toward Giovel a moment later, as if seeking help and mercy. But then his eyes moved over Giovel's gray cowl.

So he sees me as he sees Adni, Giovel thought. As a monstrous power coming to punish him for being young and a fool. When Adni's dead and I have some sway with the Order, I swear we'll never hunt witches like he does.

But am I lying to myself? This is just how I hunted Riddin, and now he's dead. Just like I hunted Londir with Elínla. So what can I promise? I'm not just like Olinos and the witches—I'm like Adni too. Maybe his methods of leadership really do work; he's made me into what he wanted, after all. Into another one of him.

"What consequences?" Kanis asked, lowering his blanket at last.

"I'm not here to deliver those," Adni said. "Not yet, anyway."

Then he turned and started walking out, leaving both Kanis and Giovel wide-eyed.

Giovel glanced back at the dirty wretch that was their witch. Then he looked away, too ashamed to stay, and followed Adni out.

"Oh, and don't try running," Adni called back as he began closing the door. "I know this isn't your real home anyway, and I'll find you wherever you go next just as easily as I found you here. Expect me at dusk tomorrow night. You can decide what sort of meeting it will be."

Giovel stepped out. Adni pulled the door shut gently, as if he was saying goodnight to an old uncle. Then he walked off into the snow.

And Giovel followed, hating everything about the Order and himself as he did so.

They were half back to Divnum before either of them spoke. It was Adni who broke the silence saying, "He's going to join us, Giovel. He's going to become a member of the Order."

"...Why?"

"Because he's strong and he wants to survive."

"That's not what I meant. Why did you attack him like that?'"

"Too much for your self-righteous sense of decorum? I showed him a clemency you'll never understand because you grew up half-worth respecting. His only chance at that now is to grow up as one of us. Are you going to chastise me for making that clear?"

Giovel thought about it. He also thought once more about waiting for Adni's back to be fully turned, then testing the edge of his rope knife against Adni's spine.

But no. He was in too deep with Adni's poisonous swill as it was.

"I want a copy of that list," Giovel said.

Adni raised his eyebrows. "My list of awakenings?"

"Yes. I want one."

"And how will that help you fulfill your duties to guard the Witherclaw Witch?"

"I'll be able to get familiar with who's out there, who's a possible enemy. I also want to study it against what we know of the witches we're already facing and see if any of them overlap."

He fully expected Adni to refuse. Instead, Adni opened his tabard and pulled the parchment out, handing it to Giovel without a word before he rode away.

Giovel waited until he was sure Adni had moved on before continuing toward the Candlespire to collect Inorovel. Only a few hours of nightfall remained, and Giovel knew he'd find no rest during them.

MASTER OF THE STARLIT ORDER

Why do they want me here?
—The Witherclaw Witch; letter to Golkorun.

No one used the old Belnum Echo Hall anymore. It had once housed a moderately popular sept, but Etelier doubted anyone so much as visited now. Rats and spiders filled the corners, and the roof had rotted through in places. The Sanctuary was still intact, though, a star room wide enough it could have sheltered Etelier's entire house.

He often found himself sitting in that star room, gazing at the lines between constellations. They weren't particularly accurate—probably the case of an artist only working during the day, too lazy to look outside when the allotted hours of labor were past. Still beautiful, though. Bits of glass marking each star made the room look almost like a real sky when dusk came, so Etelier shivered and sat and stared and breathed into his hands and looked up until nightfall, finding some sense of peace for the time he could see a sky that wasn't his own.

After the sun vanished, the third day since the attacks, Etelier left the Echo Hall and headed toward Wurelna's bolt hole to face the aftermath. He felt sure it would be an angry, defeated meeting. For him, at least, it was hard to care as he had before. Maybe he'd had one day too many, one measure of fatigue more than he could truly carry by himself. A new despair weighed on him now. It was almost a firm belief he'd never find what he'd sought from the start. The ache and bite in his face every time he moved his mouth didn't help either.

Wurelna's hideaway overlooked the south end of the Voiceless Meadows, one of the few parts of Belnum populated enough that its patrols hadn't changed that week. Only she and Claravena were there yet. Wurelna was trying to cook something without moving her wounded arm. Claravena just glowered at the fire or the empty chairs spread in a ring nearby. Neither spoke as Etelier arrived and started warming himself.

"Any word from the others?" he asked. "I thought more of us would be here by now."

"Noru wanted to check something by Bone Hill before coming," Wurelna said.

"Still looking for Vindil's ruins?"

She mumbled something back that he couldn't quite hear. Or spoke clearly, and his hearing was just too hampered thanks to the Witherclaw ruining his left ear.

Life would be different now.

In any case, Noru's was another search helplessly bound to fail. People had looked before, for hundreds of years now. Etelier was starting to think old Vindil had never existed to begin with. Or that all of Foneth *was* the bones of old Vindil. Nothing remained that showed the truth either way. No treasure for that search.

"What about Raf?" Etelier asked.

"He died at the Candlespire," Claravena said.

"I see. Órkol?"

"She died too. Hirnu Pala killed her."

Had someone told him they'd died earlier? Had he just forgotten it? The last three days were empty in his mind. He didn't even know whether he should grieve now or if that was what he'd been doing all along.

"Piatém?" he asked dully.

"Barely alive," said Claravena. "He took a rusty sword to the gut, and the wound is festering. He'll be lucky to make it three more nights. Or maybe he'll be lucky if he dies sooner. You don't walk away from a wound like that."

"So we're as broken as the Order," Etelier said, smiling for some reason he couldn't fathom. "Maybe that's proof enough that they can be toppled too."

"If you say so," Wurelna replied. She and Claravena met each other's eyes then looked away when they noticed Etelier watching them.

He wondered half a moment what they were plotting now. As it happened, he didn't really care about that either, so he just leaned closer to rub his hands by the fire.

Tranin, Ithilo, and Noru arrived soon thereafter, each coming from a different direction. Noru had a bad bruise beneath his eye, but he was the only other one hurt from the attacks. They all sat by themselves along the edges of Wurelna's hearth room, though several still shivered since the fire's heat likely didn't reach them meaningfully.

"I suppose we can get started now," Etelier said. "Reports."

"There's another item of business first," Wurelna said, not looking toward him. "We've decided that it's time for a change in our direction."

Etelier stared dumbly at her. "Who's we?"

"All of us," Ithilo mumbled. "Everyone but you, Etelier."

Claravena and Wurelna were glancing toward each other again. Noru too, blinking rapidly as if his eye were watering. No one gazed in Etelier's direction, so he realized soon what they meant.

"You want me to leave."

"No," Wurelna said. "We want you to *follow*."

"I vote that Etelier step down for a new leader," Ithilo said.

The others mumbled agreement. A wave of dizziness almost toppled Etelier into the flames.

I should have seen this coming. I know they've all been unhappy with me. I know they've been dubious about my decisions. So here we are, drinking what I poured. For the best, perhaps.

Wurelna stood. "I vote that we name Claravena as Guiding Knight, Master of the Starlit Order."

No mumbles this time. They all said yes or aye or agreed loud enough for Etelier to tell even with his ruined left ear.

"I made us what we are," he stammered. "You're all here because of *me*."

"We're here because Yulen made witches of us," Claravena said. "What is your vote, Etelier?"

His face spasmed with pain as he found himself trying to scowl. He might still be able to persuade some of them, to talk a few back to his side. But what was it worth? What difference would it truly make?

"The vote carries with or without Etelier," Wurelna said, still standing.

And just like that Etelier's resolve to fight buckled within him. "And so it is. I didn't know any of you wanted titles or a name for our 'order' as you call it."

"There are plenty of things you didn't know," Claravena said. She stood too, finally meeting his eyes before looking around. "I accept your vote of trust in me. And as Guiding Knight and Master of the Starlit Order, I pledge not just my leadership but my service to you all."

It was done so quickly. Like cleaning blood from a knife blade when the wound is fresh enough to be spilling.

"What is the grand purpose of this new Starlit Order?" Etelier asked.

"I'll address that when it's time," Claravena said. "First, reports."

There was one more moment of furtive glances and hesitant silence between the others. Then they seemed to realize Etelier wasn't arguing, wasn't denying the situation. Ithilo and Tranin relaxed visibly, and Wurelna resumed her attempt at one-armed cooking. They all began their reports with ease after that. Etelier wondered idly if one in five hundred usurpers got as civilized a response as his.

The attacks had fared poorly, despite their small victories. Noru had succeeded in finding Riddin and Girt, though he'd made the decision to kill them both rather than try releasing them. He claimed it was because half a dozen Grays jumped them. Etelier doubted it but said nothing.

Órkol and Tranin had tried unsuccessfully to find and capture Riddin's contacts at the Perception Day festival, eventually engaging with more Grays and Elínla herself. Little wonder they lost most of their fighters and Órkol died. Piatém had raided near Ola's Gate as a distraction, successfully pulling several hundred Candleguard and Lances there from the Divnum barracks and garrison, but it hadn't been enough to keep more of them from gathering at the walls, where Wurelna led a search for Adni's stash of treasure. She reported on their clash with the Divine there as well.

"We did find the Witherclaw," she said, "but Etelier was unable to apprehend her."

I never even tried, he thought. I never wanted to apprehend anyone.

"Etelier wasn't supposed to be there," Claravena said with a stab to her voice. "I seem to recall you saying you were going to search inside Keep Hatahad for their hidden library."

"My plans changed," he said simply.

"We did disable Ralden and kill Dlenar," Wurelna added. "So at least our attack wasn't a total waste."

"The word is you wounded the Witherclaw pretty badly too," Noru said darkly. "Maybe enough that she'll die with Piatém."

Etelier shook his head. "Rumors. She's no worse off than I am."

"Is that all you have to report for yourself?" Claravena asked. "I'd like a little more explanation."

"There's not much to say. I asked her if she could heal someone, and she made it clear she couldn't. Or wouldn't. She doesn't speak much Medín. She was only interested in finding her way home. That's all."

"In that case," Claravena said, pursing her lips between her words, "we're going to alter our plans. There's no point capturing her if she views us as enemies—which she surely will now. Perhaps we should just spirit her again and kill her."

"That's idiotic," Tranin said. "Completely foolish. What makes you think we could find her in time after we do a spiriting? And who *did* spirit her in the first place?"

Silence.

"It might have been me," Etelier said after a moment.

"What do you mean, it might have been?" Claravena asked.

"I can't remember."

"Why would you spirit someone with so little thought that it wasn't worth remembering? *That's* what's idiotic."

"Do you remember everyone you've spirited?" Etelier asked quietly.

Claravena couldn't respond. Just bristle a little and look away, because they all knew she'd spirited the most of any of them. Far more than you could recall, Etelier thought, far more than we could ever find afterward. Maybe you brought her here and forgot all about it— unlikely that it was, since no one seemed to know where she'd come from in the first place.

"It doesn't matter, anyway," Etelier said when no response was forthcoming. "The Witherclaw won't be keen to join us now. Probably never was. The Divine had her poisoned against us from the day she arrived."

"We'll deal with her later," Claravena said sullenly. "Let's continue our reports."

There wasn't much more to say. Ithilo gave a short account of striking west of the citadel, where there were still too many Lances for the attack to make any real difference. Then Claravena herself reported on her infiltration of the Candlespire with Raf.

"I didn't stay there long, but we did obtain some reports that looked very much like intelligence. Namely, we copied a list of assignments the Order has made to Grays—watch positions, patrols, the like."

She said it as if it was nothing, but Ithilo let out a laugh. "We could remove a score of them overnight with information like that."

"And we *will*," Claravena said. "But that's not all we found. We also stole a long list of known, unregistered awakenings."

If they were impressed before, they were shocked now. Noru dropped something. Wurelna tripped on her own floor. Etelier just found himself tightening his grip on his chair. They'd looked a long time for something like this, something to elevate their odds against the Order. A list of known awakenings might do it nicely.

"How big is this list?" Tranin was asking now. "And how do they compile it?"

"And more importantly, are any of us on it?" Noru cut in.

"Be patient and I might let each of you look it over," Claravena said. "The important thing is that the Order kept it a secret. They watch these people like they were infants, which means these awakenings aren't likely to feel much love for the Optacracy, especially when we show how pockets of Grays are stationed near almost every one of them, waiting to apprehend them at the slightest hint of Yulena. The Divine are probably stretched too thin to realize that we have this list just yet, so we have a little time to act."

More questions. What do we do first? How do we keep them from discovering what we know? What's your plan, Claravena?

"We have two main ways to proceed," she said. "First, we combine the information on Gray locations and attack them in rapid coordination, like we struck a few days ago. As Ithilo said, we could remove many of them at once. If we plan carefully, we might truly be able to kill *half* of them in one night."

She let her words sink in before she went on.

"Another approach would be simply to start spiriting these awakenings out from under their noses. Now that we know who and where they are, we could do it. We might not be able to find all of them again, but I think we should focus our recruiting efforts here."

"Spiriting doesn't usually make them eager to join us," Wurelna said.

"No, but finding out the Order watches their every move might. We just have to make sure they know this—even show them the list we stole. They'll see, sooner or later, that for people like us there's no escaping. Just changing the odds against the Divine Order—which is the great purpose of our own order, Etelier, as it always has been."

"And if they still refuse to help us?" Etelier asked.

"Then they can't walk free again."

This time there were no questions, no eager interjections, no statement of great purpose. Just silence like snow falling at midnight.

After a long moment, Etelier said, "We swore we wouldn't let our own power make us like them. We can't just kidnap and kill every awakening in Foneth."

"You're in no position to tell any of us what we can't do," Claravena said.

"But he's right," Wurelna mumbled. "We'd be no better than the Cloudblades and the Order itself if we're so indiscriminate with these awakenings. I won't just call them and kill them."

Claravena stared hard at Wurelna for a moment. Then she gave a stiff nod. "You're right. I'm sorry. I lost myself for a moment."

They'd all lost themselves in this race against time and the tug of Yulena. And we will all lose ourselves a hundred times more, Etelier thought. Unless *we* die first.

"We can't leave these awakenings to the Order," Claravena went on. "They need to be shown that they're under watch. If, after that, they still choose not to join us, so be it."

"So you still mean to spirit them out from under the Grays' noses?" Tranin asked.

"Sounds a little hasty," said Noru.

"We don't have time for your indulgent walk through the city," Claravena said. "We've tried it for almost a year without a bowlful of results. If we want to make any change before the Redremel arrive to kill us all, we need a new way to proceed."

Silence again. Etelier wondered if anyone else would argue. He could think of plenty more to say. The plan is too reckless, for example. You'll make as many enemies as you'll find allies. The Divine will realize we have their list if we target only known awakenings, and so on. In fact, he found Claravena's change of temperament even more unsettling than her move to unseat him. The truth was, his care for those things had drained out with his own blood when the Witherclaw smashed his ear. Even more so when Mota was too afraid of his face to want to see him.

But he *did* care about unseating the Divine, and this would help them do it.

"Any other ideas, then?" Claravena asked. When none were coming, she said, "We have three, maybe four months to do this."

"Why so little time?" Noru asked. "I've been searching for Vindil's ruins since spring without any success. I don't think I can hasten my search much."

"You'll have to. I'm planning another city-wide attack before spring returns and brings the Redremel with it, so a few months is all the time we can spare anymore."

Then Claravena gave them assignments, divvied the work of ambushing Grays, and sent them back out into the cold. Etelier accepted his tasks wordlessly and, for the first time in weeks, went immediately home to apologize to Pramél and try to sleep.

ZURIS'S PLAN

The people here care as much about forest and grass and water as they care about the cities they've built. I hope I can bring this care back with me.

—The Witherclaw Witch; letter to Recia.

NEW ROUTINES. WHERE he'd gone to meetings and listened to reports before, now Giovel spent his mornings with Varan. They stayed in the Candlespire for the most part, with her installed in a small room off the second level for her own safety, so while he saw the other members of the Order coming and going, meeting and working, his labor was not like theirs.

Most of Giovel's energy went to talking, trying somehow to encourage Varan, or trying just to help her master Medín more quickly yet. He told her everything he could think to say, babbling about what it was like to be in the Candleguard, buildings he admired, how he'd loved climbing as a boy. Nothing seemed to reach Varan. Though she still studied, mouthing, chanting, and writing the words over and over to learn them, there was a new heaviness in her that hadn't been evident before. She stayed mostly in her bed, sometimes running a hand over the bandages on her ear. She'd still show something like a smile when Uri, Kirida, or little Progis came to visit, but otherwise she kept almost totally to herself in spite of Giovel's best efforts to gain her trust.

After the first week of it, Giovel nearly begged Adni for more duties. There were new ones to fill, after all. Someone had to take over intelligence and investigations for Dlenar. Elínla had been given twice her normal workload—now shouldering Sur's responsibilities to try finding the witches on top of her own duties marshalling the Gray Order. Hirnu seemed to be doing more too, likely working with the Candles to identify the fighters who'd helped the witches on Perception Day, not to mention carrying Ralden's responsibilities for compliance and certification. Giovel knew he was getting desperate for work when even those tasks sounded appealing to him.

Still. He couldn't bring himself to ask Adni for anything. And Adni might be right that Varan needed him.

Two weeks after the attacks, Varan's healer recommended Giovel take her out for some exercise. She resisted glumly but finally followed Giovel out to Lilywater Lake at the edge of North Hold, the farthest she'd gone from Divnum since being spirited. Giovel only wished it were for a better cause.

More than three hundred men and women labored in a trench not far from the lake, preparing to flood the old stretch of village once ravaged by the Redremel. They had first cleared hard-packed snow where traders and farmers and workers walked between their homes and the rest of Foneth. Then they'd started removing trees, digging up brush, clearing boulders, and now hacking into the frozen ground while people evacuated the homes nearby and looked for new ones in Divnum.

Was this the first lake Inorovel had played in, back when she was young, when Giovel and Iremni were poor, and they'd lived in a crowded corner by the Great Holderim? Giovel couldn't remember now. Vague images crossed through his mind, though. A tiny golden-haired girl kicking in the water. Iremni watching from the grassy shore, radiant in a pale dress that seemed to mirror the sky as her bronze skin matched the warm earth along the water's edge. Now the place those memories belonged—or at least where Giovel thought they should—would be transformed in a way he couldn't reconcile.

Zuris had spent five months of unfruitful effort trying to get his consolidation plan approved. But the first day after the witch attacks, he'd managed to get support from the Lawrits, two large labor guilds, and Optate Olura herself. Now Giovel wondered whether he should have spoken against it when he had the chance, because whether or not Lilywater Lake was truly that same one he'd once visited, whether or not his memory or Iremni and Inorovel was even real, he risked losing it to the scarring change of the landscape.

He was surprised to see Elínla there as well, despite her busyness and opposition to Zuris's newly approved plan. She stood by the edge of the trees, watching with a few others Giovel didn't know. They nearly blended in with the bare trees because of the gray and brown they wore. They all bore the same blue tattoos marking patterns beneath their eyes. Members of her sept, here together to see what was happening to the city's Sanctuaries.

"Let's go over there a moment," Giovel said, and began walking before he was sure Varan even heard him.

Elínla's companions turned to give stiff bows as he approached. She stared out over the lake, only glancing in Giovel's direction for a moment as he came nearer.

"I'm sorry you have to see this," he said.

"You could have recommended something else. Zuris respects your opinion, so the other Commanders should too. They might have listened."

"His plan is the best I've heard. I think it would have been wrong to propose something else."

Elínla made a sort of snickering sound. "Wrong for whom? For the people who now have to uproot their homes? For the hundreds of Optacrats who'll spend the next decade sorting through the logistics of this project? Or just wrong for you?"

Her question gave him pause. "I didn't come to try to persuade you. I'm sorry if I gave that impression."

"You sometimes do."

Perhaps it was best left at that, then. Giovel hesitated, though, and asked, "Did Lilywater Lake mean something specific to you or your sept?"

"Why does that matter?"

"I'm just trying to understand."

Elínla gave him a hard, measuring look. "You can say that, but I'm not sure you will. You always talk about what's right or wrong for Foneth like a Candle does—what's defensible, or what's orderly. What gives us a tactical advantage. There are other things to think about, though. Our sept tries to consider some of those things, like tranquility, or beauty, or all the lives that are part of this lake already. There's no Lance or Divine Mage speaking up for them."

"Is that why you're here, then?" Giovel asked.

"That's only the smallest part. Zuris sees this as a potential floodplain. But we try to see it as other people have for generations—a sacred place kept free from the touch of artifice. The Sept of Blue Heaven teaches us to ask what's good for other forms of life because it's *also* good for us. That's the difference between the Lances' plan and what we'd hoped to preserve here."

"I admire the sentiment," Giovel said after a moment of consideration. "But I don't think that's the way of things."

"It could be. We live in a day when the works of Yulena are obvious to everyone. You can look any direction and see the craftsmanship Yulena once made possible. If we hadn't lost so much knowledge about it, we could have a way of life that benefits all others. Not just some."

It was a thought Giovel had weighed before, more than once prior to his own awakening and countless times since his induction into the Order. As before, he couldn't see any clear path for what Elínla or the Sept of Blue Heaven or anyone else wanted from Yulena. Unless they wanted the same things witches wanted, or Adni wanted. What Giovel assumed *everyone* wanted who pursued Yulen's power willfully.

"You see all that in a lake being dammed?" he asked.

"What else is there to see?"

"I see the end of a place I once brought my family. I didn't want this to be necessary either."

Elínla turned away, staring once more over the lake and the trench reaching toward it. "There you go again, Giovel. Talking about what's necessary. Well, if we shift the 'way of things,' as you call it, we can change what's necessary or not. You might think I'm in the Order to pull my way to the top, to build alliances and catch the Optate's favor. That's not it at all. I'm in the Order so I can alter what Yulena is."

"Not even Adni can do that."

"That's why it's not Adni's seat I want. It's Hirnu's, researching what Yulena could really be if we built new spells again. That's why I spend so many hours trying to dodge Adni's hoops and fighting to get half a grain of recognition. If Hirnu gave her sphere the effort I'm willing to give mine, she would've found scores of forgotten glyphs by now. But she only experiments for the sake of safety. I have a better reason to do it."

Giovel didn't know what to say. Only that he *had* judged as she said and seen Elínla only for her will to climb higher. He'd never paused to ask why, let alone to question whether he might agree with her way of thinking.

"Why are they digging holes?" Varan asked, stepping up from the windbreak of a spiderbark tree. They were her first voluntary words to Giovel in four days.

"It's too big for our men to surround. They're trying to protect the city," Elínla said simply. She turned to walk away without another word.

And she was right. They would build defenses of flood plains and rivers by flattening Foneth's Sanctuaries, pushing its boundaries inward, toppling homes, moving people by the thousands, felling what was beautiful about it to begin with. It was to be a sixteen-year undertaking, according to Zuris's plans. A staggering amount of effort, longer than Inorovel's life so far, and the only hope to pause it was if the war with Redrem ended long before the effort did. Giovel didn't believe it would.

"Are you ready to walk back?" he asked, turning to Varan.

She didn't respond, perhaps because her bad ear was toward him and she hadn't realized he was speaking to her, or just because she didn't want to. He gave her another moment before tapping her hand and guiding her back, away from the sight.

FONETH

My dearest Golkorun,

Forgive my shaky hand. I've been practicing letters in the language they use here. I'm surprised how quickly my grip tires from writing, even when I do it slowly like I must with letters and words I don't know well.

The snow is deep here already. I don't mind. Giovel takes me out to try meeting and talking with people—presumably people who might help find my way home. Otherwise I mostly stay inside, letting winter pass me by across the window. I had a small injury a few weeks back, and I feel as if part of my will to move and explore is buried under the bandages. Age getting to me, perhaps?

My friend Kirida will have her baby soon. I pray it will come without event. She has lost two children before, and she wants the new child badly. Kirida and Nomis remind me of us in some ways. That's the one difficult thing about seeing them and the little boy they do have.

Enough of my news, thin as it is. If I could truly send this letter, knowing it had a chance to reach you, I'd ask what you're feeding the boys, how your winter woodpile is coming along, what you're shaping in that dirty workshop—assuming you still haven't made progress on clearing things up?

Of course, I wouldn't much care what you wrote back as long as your words could reach me. I think your scratchy letters would still bring your voice to my mind, and I'd treasure that on long, dark afternoons like this one. I miss your voice, and your touch and closeness.

I'll keep writing while I try to find my way back to you.

Your Varan
    —The Witherclaw Witch; letter to Golkorun.

SECRETS

I learn words but I don't learn what I want.
  —The Witherclaw Witch; letter to Drova.

THE FOLLOWING TWO weeks stretched Giovel's patience so far he thought he'd shatter. First there was Adni, who treated him differently since their visit to the young witch called Kanis. He was almost respectful now, which made Giovel more nervous than ever before. Then there was Varan and the daunting task of guarding and helping her. Giovel gently led her to meet with a cartographer from west of Yeren, a bard who swore he'd traveled so far the land ran out and there was nothing but water left, even a horse master who ran his animals with wild herds on the great Red Plains north of Lacia. All three had ideas for where Varan might go—other lands with other languages and peoples that might be hers. Varan only ever asked one question.

"Do they have Yulen?"

"She means to ask whether they can see Yulen there," Giovel explained.

The answer was always the same. Of course. Yulena is everywhere. And after that Varan would fall silent again, no longer interested in anything but returning to her tiny room in the Candlespire.

"It'll be easier to search once your ear heals," Giovel said as they walked back from seeing a salt road merchant.

No answer. No acknowledgment that he'd said or done anything for Varan. So Giovel swallowed his impatience as best he could, reminding himself that Adni had tried him more than this quiet woman could. Yet.

She was probably lonelier than ever. Kirida and Nomis continued to visit, though, and Uri too. Ralden sent her a wildly expensive set of dresses, all patterned with Varan's Witherclaw, as thanks for Varan leaping to her aid on Perception Day. Even Elínla visited once to try cheering her up, dour as that conversation was. Varan remained despondent and reserved, so Giovel had little he could do but talk one-sidedly to her, suggest new ideas, walk her outside like a pack animal, and wait while she worked through her own recovery.

The one benefit of the assignment was the time it gave Giovel to study Adni's list of awakenings, looking for patterns or insights that might help thwart the witches. The list was more substantial than he'd expected—hundreds of individuals identified only by vague information on their whereabouts and tiny briefs of intelligence on their awakenings, presumably provided by Dlenar's network of allies. When Varan studied or rested, Giovel sat outside her room and compared Adni's list to maps, certification records, reports of witch activity, and anything else he could think to use. Slow work, like much that he'd done his first few years as a Candle. Just the relief he needed now.

Maybe we can finally come to some sense of *why* the awakenings happen, he thought. Maybe that will help ensure people like Kanis or me are never forced into the Order in the future.

He knew the Order was flooded with work, like Elínla's frantic efforts to marshal the more senior Grays throughout Foneth. Adni, meanwhile, was training their new Divine Mage in secret, readying him for the work before even the Grays knew who he was. How Adni had persuaded Kanis to join them, Giovel would never know. How he trusted Kanis not to murder them all was another question altogether, but Kanis seemed serious and responsible so far, from what Elínla and Hirnu reported. Granted, Adni hadn't told them how he'd coerced Kanis into joining up. Only Giovel knew that.

Does that make *me* more of an enemy to him?

He didn't know. Couldn't afford to care about it.

Despite his still-serious wounds, Sur had been tasked in Hirnu's place to coordinate a wide investigation of the many fighters who supported the witches on Perception Day. Not many had been captured, but getting information from them proved much easier than identifying the many more who'd died. Some confessed that they were helping the witches. Others didn't talk at all. The evidence pointed equally to Redremel spies, seditious Optacrats who wanted Olura's seat, and simply poor workers who were hired to do a bloody job.

There was talk that the witches were performing more spiritings too. Giovel didn't know whether it was true or not; he wasn't privy to any official reports on it now, because his duties kept him right at Varan's side, far from any witches or investigations but his own trail of notes and guesswork.

Three weeks after the attack, Giovel's lessons with Hirnu went worse than usual. Hirnu wanted him to cast the Illumina over and over again, and his sight started swimming and blotting black before he'd done it ten times. He was getting better at activating his completed glyphs—taming the heart-link, as Hirnu sometimes called it. Every time he lost control of the spell, though, or introduced a slight blemish in the glyph, she'd have him start his count over.

"Twenty times without errors. Then you can trust you'll make no errors when you need it."

"I don't intend to need it," Giovel growled, dropping his borrowed sand tablet; he still hadn't replaced the one he'd lost on Perception Day.

Hirnu leveled her eyes on him like a hunting bird sighting fish in the water. "That's the attitude of an impatient child. Yulen will be your primary tool if you want to make any change as a member of the Order. Unless I'm mistaken, you haven't even tried to practice since we last met."

"I haven't. I hate Yulena."

"And you'll hate it the rest of your life, one way or another," Hirnu said, raising her voice perhaps for the first time Giovel had ever heard.

That made him pause and look in her eye as she went on.

"You'll never be rid of this," she went on. "You're a mage now. And while you're part of the Order, there's no outdistancing Yulena. You can run from using it, run toward it, or you can run from those who will use it against you. In any case, it *will* follow wherever you try to go, Giovel, just like age, or responsibility, or whatever else you might actually care about."

"You talk as if I didn't care at all."

"Today I'm not sure you do."

And maybe she was right.

"Form the Illumina again," Hirnu said, turning away and calming her voice as if she only had to breathe to push any anger away.

"Why did you let Adni take charge of the Order instead of you?" Giovel asked.

"I said form the Illumina again."

"I want an answer to my question. I'm beginning to think you're the one I ought to blame for Adni's rot-hearted decisions."

"I didn't say no on as flimsy an excuse as yours for not learning Yulena."

"I'm not sure I believe you."

"Whom you believe is your decision to make. But how you use my time is not. If you won't form the Illumina now, then leave. I have work to do that you won't understand until you're willing to admit that you are and will be a mage for the rest of your life. If I can't teach you anything, I'll return to that work."

So that was it. Her work. Her study of Yulena. And she thought *that* was more important than the good she might have done as Illumined Knight? She was more selfish than Giovel had thought.

But for whatever reason, the will to fight had gone out of him almost as quickly as it flared. It happened often lately. He retrieved the borrowed sand tablet, cleared it with a swipe of the leveler, and drew the Illumina again. Five times before he miscast it and almost blinded himself. Twelve more and he smudged a line while withdrawing his finger. Then twenty times sequentially at a level that satisfied even Hirnu.

When Giovel finished, Hirnu said, "If you have questions you really want me to answer, come back when neither of us has duties."

"What's wrong with now?" Giovel asked. "My so-called duties will wait."

"Mine won't."

Hirnu walked off without seeing him out of her secluded training yard, disappearing into the little stone house she'd occupied for years untold. Giovel almost followed her, but once again his steam had faded, so he left the borrowed tablet where she'd showed him it belonged, slipped out a gate at the back, and resumed his tedious study of the awakenings list as he walked back toward the Candlespire.

Birenlu was waiting for him when he arrived to sit outside Varan's room again.

"Good afternoon, Lord Giovel," she said with a bow. "A moment of your time?"

"What now?"

"I have information I think you might like to hear."

He raised an eyebrow. "Is it something you've written for your book on the Order? I don't really care to talk now, if it's all the same to you."

"It has to do with someone who helped organize the attacks a few weeks ago," Birenlu said.

Giovel's resentment melted like shadows from a lamp. He began to walk down the hallway, looking sidelong to be sure no one was near enough to listen. "I need some cool air."

Birenlu followed him outside. When they were a few dozen paces from the Candlespire, she said, "The Candleguard have already determined that most of the attackers were locals. But a few were not."

"What are you saying?"

"Some of them *were* Redremel. And they weren't just refugees or independent actors. They were sent to work with those witches by a ring of Redremel scouts right here in Foneth."

Giovel's first thought was to laugh, to wave it away. Then a hot surge of excitement went through him. "How big is this scouting ring?"

"I don't know yet. But I do know that seven of them leave their houses at the same time every night, disappearing somewhere in Belnum. Their number includes two from the attack on the walls, one from the attack by Cloud Lake, and one who helped organize the strikes near the Citadel."

At last. A direction to push, a crack in the wall of secrets. "You know where they start from each night?"

Birenlu pulled a small map from her cloak and unrolled it to point near the Whisperwood, The Eelwell, Rich Woman's Hill, and four other spots. "I can't prove it yet, but I think they're gathering in one of these places each time."

Giovel had nothing to write with so he took the time to commit all her information to memory. It was hard not to think a few leaps forward, to how he should proceed. The official channel of response would be to inform the Lances. But then again, if these Redremel were involved with witches, the hierarchy of responsibility was harder to define.

"How do you know this?" Giovel asked, pausing now to look Birenlu hard in the eye, measuring her response.

"I can't tell you that."

"It's a matter of our security, Birenlu. If you said that to anyone else, they might accuse you of being a Redremel sympathizer at best if not a spy yourself."

"Of course. That's why I came to you. You know what I want and what I don't want."

He also knew she'd lost her husband and her only daughter—both Candles—during the Battle of Holderim ten years ago. Was that why he still trusted her instead of questioning her ravenous hunger for information? Just because he'd trusted her daughter when they served together? It felt like a shallow reason for faith in anyone nowadays.

"We need to find out where they're going," Giovel said. "And who else might also be there. How can I compensate you for your help this time?"

"I'd like a look at the Divine's secret library."

"We don't have any secret library."

"Of course you do. Everyone knows it, and I'd like to see it."

"What do you mean, everyone knows? If there were to be a secret library, even I've never been told about it."

"Maybe the Order knew you were prone to tell someone like me," Birenlu said, shrugging. "But I assure you, there *is* a library. The histories of Yulena are all the proof we need that your Order has records not available to the Lawrits, the Optacracy, the Tovómil, anyone else. And I'd like to see it."

He almost believed her. After all, he was now carrying around a secret list of awakenings. He wouldn't have believed Adni had that until a few weeks ago. Furthermore, if anyone could sniff out Order secrets, he'd wager it was Birenlu. The hunger in her eyes was real enough to be sure that she believed it, no matter what Giovel said.

"What do you want from this library?" he asked slowly. "If it does exist, which I still don't accept, I might be able to get something specific from it. But I'm certain I couldn't get you into it."

She smiled. "You know I want to write a history of the Order. I don't need *all* that history. Just two or three little gemstones of insight no one else in the world has ever written. If I can get verifiable evidence of just a few small discoveries, my book will get me a position of scholarship anywhere in the known world."

"That's what this is about for you? Getting some kind of work? I thought you tutored for the Medíns."

"And I can do a lot more than read the history books to them," Birenlu said, her face contorting in a sudden jolt of anger. "I'm a scholar, Giovel. Not a servant. It's time I get the respect of one, and you can help me do that."

He scratched his chin, wondering how he'd even go about finding some secret records of the Order. Hirnu would know about them, to be sure. But she'd never liked him, had she? And he hadn't helped that just now. The thing was, Birenlu *had* helped him, and he'd likely need that help again.

"I'll find a way to get your records," he said. "*If* they exist in the first place."

"That's the other reason I come to you and not to them," Birenlu said. "You could have taken the information and walked away. But you're smart enough to know better."

"You think the rest of the Order aren't?"

"There are some lessons you only learn with time, aren't there? Let me know when you have what I want, and I'll find out where our Redremel are going each night."

He mumbled a response and walked back toward the Candlespire, thinking about how to proceed. He'd worry about it more later, though. First, he needed to investigate this Redremel scouting ring for himself.

THE WOMAN FATHER VISITS

Every time I feel out of place, I learn more how much alike these people and I really are.
—The Witherclaw Witch; letter to Golkorun.

INOROVEL HAD AN easy time finding the woman they called the Witherclaw Witch. She hadn't been to the Candlespire many times, but she knew that Candleguard weren't typically stationed there. The Divine didn't need them. They always had a few Grays watching the big tower, but that was it. Now the Candleguard were like a trail of spilled cream leading right to the Witherclaw's room near the southeast end of the tower's second level, though none of them made a motion to stop Inorovel from passing by. Perhaps that was a benefit of having a father every Candle knew. Since father was out at lessons for the moment, there was no one to stop Inorovel from visiting the Witherclaw.

She was alone when Inorovel inched her door open and said hello. Her room was small and round with a single window looking out over snow-covered trees. There wasn't much in it, either, just the bed where she sat, a small side chair, a little table, and what looked like an untouched stack of extravagantly fine dresses. Dark, wavy hair covered most of the Witherclaw's face but not enough to conceal the thick bandages over her left ear. She didn't look up as Inorovel entered the little room.

"I'm Inorovel. Giovel's daughter."

No response from the woman. She reached over to the side of the bed she sat in and pulled a pen toward her. Then she started writing on a long sheet of paper.

"Do you have a few minutes that I can talk to you?" Inorovel asked. She was already starting to feel like a fool for coming, a fool for her curiosity about this strange woman.

When the Witherclaw still didn't respond, Inorovel asked, "Can you understand me?"

The woman twitched that time and turned to face her, dark eyes wide. Then she sighed. "Who are you?"

She couldn't hear me before, Inorovel thought. Stupid that I didn't realize it.

Inorovel repeated her introduction. "I'm sorry to be a bother. Am I interrupting you?"

The Witherclaw looked hard at her, maybe processing her words. "I'm called Varan. Hello, Inorovel."

"What are you writing?" Inorovel asked. From where she stood she peered over the paper, not recognizing the figures on Varan's page.

"I'm writing messages. To my family," Varan said. She spoke slowly and with an odd accent. "I have many messages now."

Varan motioned to a small table beside her. She had a stack of pages there, all filled with inky lines and dried. But nowhere to send them, from what father said. So she wrote to her family but they couldn't write back, like Varan was really just writing to herself. It reminded Inorovel of the messages she and father had penned just after mother died, messages perhaps never even meant to be read by someone else. Just written and remembered.

"What do you want?" Varan asked after a moment of silence. It might have sounded rude from anyone else, but the unique lilt to Varan's voice made Inorovel think it was simply a question.

"I wanted to meet you," Inorovel said. "People have been talking about you." And I need to know if what they say is true.

"Why?"

This time her question did sound as rude as it might from anyone else. Inorovel looked away. But she'd come to see who this woman was and she wouldn't leave without trying.

"You're the woman my father comes to see," she said.

How would the Witherclaw respond? Not in the defensive, worried way Inorovel expected. Instead, Varan just blinked and said, "Yes."

"But he comes every day. For so many hours every day."

Now Varan frowned, bandages stretching across her face. "You think Giovel comes because he . . . I don't have the words . . . because he likes to see me?"

The woman was smart, as Inorovel had heard. "Isn't that why? He hasn't said anything to me about it, but you're the only woman he sees this much. Not even Lady Hirnu or Ralden."

"Giovel said your mother was a spiriting."

"Yes."

"That's why he sees me."

Because mother's gone? Because he's looking for someone else now?

Varan went on, though. "I'm a spiriting. Like your mother."

Da had never once mentioned that. Likewise, Inorovel had never heard this detail in others' talk about the Witherclaw—and nearly everyone had something to say about her origin or her ferocity or her power. But a spiriting? At last the answers to Inorovel's questions were appearing.

She was surprised how much of a relief it was. Guiltily so. A person shouldn't be glad to find out another had been snatched from their home, should they? Yet even that tiny glimpse into why father would come, why he spent so much time with this woman, diminished the weight that had pressed through Inorovel's mind and body.

It's not that he's looking for someone else to replace mother. Just looking to help someone like us.

"Are you going to stop the spiritings?" Inorovel asked. "Stop the witches from spiriting more of you, I mean."

Varan looked down, not responding. She understood, though, didn't she? Just didn't know what to say, it would seem.

"Stopping the spiritings used to be all my father wanted," Inorovel added. "We don't know what happened to my mother when witches spirited her, or why they did it. But she went mad as a blind bird after. She stopped eating. I think she even tried to kill me once. My father stopped her, but she just sort of faded away after that."

And once more Varan looked away a long moment before saying quietly, "I don't know words to say. Your father visits me, maybe, because we understand each other. We both have lost something because of witches."

"Are you going to find the witches who did this?"

"I don't know words to say."

Which meant that when Inorovel asked da, he wouldn't either, so she mumbled her thanks to Varan and left.

ANOTHER VISITOR

The history of Foneth is strange to me. It's not just that I'm learning now what a child here has known for years. It's that it feels so short. Before the Divine Order came along, they seem to have no history at all.

—The Witherclaw Witch; a letter to Golkorun.

THE DAY AFTER Giovel's daughter came, Varan had another visitor. She knew him by sight. Gray-haired, forty or fifty years old by appearances, it was the Illumined Knight Adni Aman. He stood in the doorway and waited until Varan motioned for him to come in. The pale light from her little window almost made Adni glow, wearing clean gray himself. Giovel had stepped out to find something to eat, so no one else was nearby just then.

"They say your skill with the language is improving," Adni said as he walked into Varan's little room.

She set aside a book she'd been studying. "I practice."

"If only we could get our fighters and Lawrits to work as hard as you do."

There was nothing else for her to do, was there? Varan almost said as much, but she didn't feel like saying anything at all. When Adni was silent himself, she resumed reading her book.

The Illumined Knight sat in the chair Giovel often occupied, just watching her as she read. It made her realize that he didn't truly fit what she heard Giovel and others say about him. They called him a fool, an animal. He looked calm, though, almost the most at peace of anyone Varan knew in Foneth. Odd that anyone with so much responsibility could know any modicum of comfort.

"What do you want?" Varan finally asked.

"I want to understand a few things about your power. I hear Etelier himself asked you to heal someone, and while it's clear you didn't help him, I have to wonder whether you could have."

"I don't know. He didn't say what kind of healing."

"Well then, perhaps you can tell me what sorts you could offer."

And there it was, open as anything. He'd come to learn about her power, not to see her at all. So Giovel was right about him.

"I know about herbs," Varan said. "All kinds of herbs. I know how to make medicines with them and how to give the right mixture."

"They say you also enhance them with your magecraft. Is this true?"

"No."

"What, then?"

Varan frowned, once more setting her book aside. "Why are you asking me? Giovel never asks me."

"Giovel isn't tasked to ask questions, and even if he was, I doubt you could have answered much before. Now that you can speak and understand, it's time you do."

There was something like stone in Adni's voice, something that expected not to be moved or diverted aside. That, too, Giovel had spoken of, likely when he thought Varan wasn't listening. Well, she was listening closely to everything Adni said now, feeling her shoulders and neck grow tense as the conversation drew closer to the nature of her powers.

She knew this man could mark her for a witch. He had the power to do more than just scar her. He could have her killed today without a question or kept locked away the rest of her life. Giovel also said he was distractable, though. So there was hope to steer the conversation away yet. And if Adni had power to break her, he had power to help as well.

"I don't have words," Varan said.

"Of course. Our language is not an easy one for anyone to learn. Tell me this, if you can," Adni said. "Are there others with power like yours?"

"Many others use herbs and make medicines."

"And your magecraft? Can others do . . . what you do?"

"Yes. Better than I can, often."

"I see. Such as making fire, summoning storm winds?"

Was that truly all he understood of any magic that wasn't Yulena? "People at my home can do other things too," Varan said. "They can help the medicines we make. They can Temper and Enervate in someone's body while people heal."

"Yes, I see," Adni said. If he was excited at what she said, he concealed it well. "Tell me this, though. How does one come to learn these powers and skills you use, Tempering and Enervation?"

"Practice. I studied many years to become *Ilod*—Witherclaw as you say it."

Now his eyes lit up. "Study, of course. And before that. Did you . . . how did you first begin this process?"

The awakenings, Varan thought. He means to ask how we awaken to power, like how Yulena sparks in people here without warning.

"Anyone can do it," she said simply. It was like walking, speaking, even singing. Some did it faster or more ably, but anyone could learn given time. Not like here, where Yulen seemed to choose whom to empower and whom to leave powerless.

"Then the real question is whether you can teach these same skills to another," Adni said. "You see, Varan, there is no one in Foneth with powers like yours. None of us know how to do what you can do. We're all reliant on old glyphs we've passed forward for generations."

"You want me to teach your people?"

"No, actually. What I want is for my people to learn better ways to use our own powers—Yulena—with you showing us a new way to *think* it through. We've always done it the same way because there is no safe path to learn it. Maybe you can change that for us."

Varan shook her head. "I don't understand you."

"Let me try explaining myself again, then. Do you grow fruit orchards where you come from? I hear it's a place called Dundal."

It felt so long since she had even heard the word. "Yes. We grow fruit in Dundal."

"So consider. Some fruit trees last longer than a man's life, bearing new fruit every year for generations. We tend the same way our fathers and mothers did before us, because that's what we know to keep them alive and well. But what if someone could show us a better way to keep these trees? What if we could increase our yields by changing our pruning, moving the soil, watering less? See, Yulena is like these old trees only more dangerous. If we fail to harvest, we can forage somewhere else. But if we fail to use Yulena, we end up dead at the hands of spellbuilders—witches. One mage in our history destroyed a great city by trying new Yulena."

"Renma," Varan said, though she wasn't sure she followed Adni's words. "I read about Renma in one of your books."

"Renma had no guide when he formed new glyphs," Adni said. "I have to wonder if *you* could guide us, in a way. I know your power and ours are different, yet I think your ways might help us."

Varan paused, reviewing his words to be sure she understood. She found her hand fingering her bad ear. It wasn't the first time she'd caught herself doing this, idling away a moment of energy without thinking of it.

Could she be any use, as Adni seemed to think? More importantly, she wondered, do I dare try to teach this people what I know?

It was easy to answer.

"I can't help understand Yulena," Varan said.

And I won't, even if I come to know how.

Adni's face showed no glimmer of surprise or disappointment. He simply said, "I know I'm asking you to approach something new and complicated. Will you do this for me? Just think on it over the next few days. Think on any case where you might help us. The Optate's Divine Order of Mages has tried for hundreds of years to protect this land, and we still do it poorly now. So please think on it."

She had, many times before Adni cared enough to talk to her himself.

"I have duties to address," he said, standing suddenly. "Thank you for speaking with me."

He left her in silence. A new coat of snow had started to fall outside the little window, piling powder on the stone rim outside the glass. Varan peered beyond it to where the sky bled into a clouded Yulen. She thought once more about Adni's idea. Then she went back to her book, because there was nothing else to consider.

EXHILARATION

There are so many secrets in this city.
  —The Witherclaw Witch; letter to Inivar and Sil.

WHEREVER GIOVEL TOOK her, whomever they prodded for information, Varan's question was always the same. Is Yulena there? Since everyone said yes, she closed each conversation at that point. After trying the twentieth time, Giovel abandoned the tactic.

"We're going to see the city for its own sake now," he said, bundling himself in a thick scarf and handing Varan her own coat and cowl. "Let's go."

She followed.

They walked out through fresh snow to see the wind-scarred stones near the Blue Tree—the oldest remaining structures known to be made with Yulena. Then to the south reaches of the wall, where rumors spoke of hidden gates only a mage could open, and the library, Keep Hatahad, and anywhere else Giovel could admire master craftsmanship. Whether it prodded Varan's slow recovery, he couldn't tell. But it gave him space to think, and though it would never be the same as those walks had been before, with his own family beside him, it still brought a measure of solace now.

Almost six weeks since Perception Day, Elínla came to the hall outside Varan's room and dropped into a chair next to Giovel's, slumping into it with her feet on the seat like a child might. It was probably the first time she'd come out of her way to see him alone since their unauthorized witch hunt months before.

"Are you alright?" Giovel asked.

"I was about to ask the same thing. You've been stuck here a long time now. No change, I take it."

"Not really."

"The Witherclaw ought to be healed by now."

"She probably is. At least her ear," Giovel said. There were other wounds, to be sure. Wounds that didn't mend just with time like cuts and abrasions might.

"There's something I think you should know," Elínla said.

"What is it?"

"Hirnu and I figured out how the spiritings are up so much—and how the witches have spirited away so many people we've specifically been watching."

Giovel thought he knew before she said it. "The list. *This* list."

"Someone stole a copy from the Candlespire, likely the same time that they killed Riddin and his companion. Apparently there were just three copies in all, and Adni had them all scattered in the same room. But he swears only one is left now."

"And I've got the second," Giovel mumbled in new horror. "So they know where he's sent Grays, whom he's been observing, everything."

"Twelve names from your list are dead now. Almost a score more are missing, just within the last week. The witches are targeting them. Maybe trying to recruit them, maybe just removing them one by one. Every awakening we know of is in danger now."

Giovel swore and buried his head in his hands. He'd wondered a hundred times what might happen if he accidentally dropped it, if he'd ever let his copious notes on it leave his sight. So he never took them from Varan's room or his seat outside, where they'd always be guarded. Truthfully, he'd protected those notes with more care than he gave Varan herself.

To no avail, because Adni had another copy he hadn't accounted for until now, when it was too late to save the ones the witches had seized.

"What are you doing about the rest of the awakenings?" Giovel asked.

"Trying to move them. The problem is most don't know they've been watched, so there's a danger to even approaching them. We don't have enough Grays to do it safely, and Hirnu and I are stretched thin as hair."

Giovel knew at least a partial solution, though. *He* could help. He could take a third of the work they carried, maybe more. He could save some of those awakenings who truly hadn't wronged anyone.

He phrased his response cautiously. "Are you here to ask me for something?"

"Not really," Elínla said. "But Hirnu and I did ask Adni whether we could leave the Witherclaw under someone else's watch for a few weeks, even just with the Lances, so you could shoulder some of my work with the Grays."

"Hirnu asked that? She hasn't made it any secret that she thinks I'm worthless."

"Maybe as a mage, but we all know you can make things happen. That's why I came to see you now. Just to let you know."

Giovel's breath almost caught. "Adni said yes?"

"He's thinking it over. He's obsessed with the Witherclaw, though. Seems to think she needs more protection than our own families do. But maybe that's why he assigned you to do it." Elínla almost sounded impressed.

"Thank you for telling me," Giovel said, and bowed his head a moment. "And for asking Adni anything on my behalf. I want to help."

"Hirnu and I might not like you, but I'm starting to trust you at least."

"I suppose that means more in a time like this than usual."

"Maybe so."

"Can I ask you something about the list of awakenings?"

She nodded, leaning back in her chair. "I don't know much, though. I'd never actually seen it until Hirnu pieced together that these most recent spiritings were all of people on it."

"So she knew before. She'd seen the list."

"Right. I think only she, Adni, and Ralden were allowed to before."

"Then who populates it?" Giovel asked. "Is it just scattered bits of information from the Grays or the Candleguard? I'd assumed Dlenar must be the one behind it."

"If Dlenar did it, he kept it quiet. Which sounds like something he would do, unfortunately. We don't really have records to access his intelligence rings."

"And if not Dlenar, then who?"

"My guess is the Optate's own mages do it."

"You believe she has her own ring of mages hidden somewhere?"

"You can be sure she has some secrets even the Illumined Knight doesn't get. Why not her own mages?"

Giovel had wondered before, especially when so few of the best Grays were chosen for the Order. Was it simply because the Optate pressured the Order not to take them? As part of some game to appease other parties, let them share a finger width of influence? Or because the Optacracy had other, less public uses for the best mages in Foneth? Optates five or six hundred years back had often employed squads of trained mages as guards, especially back when the Candlespire was filled with likely candidates. After a few Optates died from miscast spells or poorly drawn glyphs, however, the Lawrit-turned Optate Kraza Legosi had seen to it that such uses of magic were outlawed. It was hard to believe an Optate like Olura could hide an illegal cell of mages now, especially while her own nephew was tasked to hunt anyone operating outside Yulenic law.

Elínla was right about one thing, though. Other than Dlenar himself, there were few who could have created their list of awakenings.

"I have something you should know as well," Giovel said. "I'm closing in on what looks like a Redremel scouting ring."

"*What?*"

"Keep your voice down. I'll need help capturing the leaders. And I have evidence they were involved in the attacks with the witches, so we wouldn't be crossing ranks to go after them."

Elínla scanned the hallway, making sure no one was near, perhaps. "Where the hell did you get this evidence from? I thought you were just guarding the Witherclaw and breaking your mind on that list."

Giovel ignored her question. "The evidence is good. Good enough that I'll move on them soon."

"You haven't told anyone else about this?" Elínla asked.

"Not yet."

"I thought Adni might petition the Optate herself to have you stripped of your position after we went for Riddin. Do you really want to try the same thing again?"

"If I were to try it again, I think Ralden would stand up for me like she did before," he said. "And you too, I seem to remember. Adni's wrong to be using me like a bodyguard, and I need to prove it clearly enough that he gives me the freedom I deserve."

Elínla frowned, sept tattoo twisting around her nose. "I don't know about this. I'd rather report it to the whole Order and let Adni make the decision himself."

"That's why I haven't told you where my evidence came from or what it is."

He almost thought she'd argue with him, that she'd leave and go straight to Adni now. It might be the perfect prize to tug herself upward in the ranks—not that anyone needed it now, with Ralden and Sur too hurt to work, Dlenar dead, and the rest of them trying to shoulder ten mages' worth of work.

In the end Elínla just sighed. "Tell me when you're ready to move. I'll come. I was beginning to think you were just a stuffed collar who didn't care what happens in this war."

Giovel laughed for the first time in what felt like a year. "That's almost exactly what my first Banner Captain said about me."

"Maybe it's true, then. Or maybe you're just slipping after staring at this list for a month. Have you found anything, anyway?"

"Nothing yet. There's something familiar about the list, though. I think it must be some pattern I'm close to breaking."

"All the luck to you, then."

He stared at the list for a few hours after Elínla left. Yes, he'd need a little luck yet.

Another curtain of snow covered Foneth the next morning. Giovel suggested Varan come out and walk with him, snow or not, and she accepted his offer wordlessly. It was early enough that Divnum was quiet. Just the cold, untouched blue of snowfall, the blinding glare of Cloud Lake's icy crust, and the thin trail of smoke here and there where someone stoked a night's fire. Giovel smiled to himself as he breathed the cold air in. He felt more energized than he had in days.

As he had the last few times he'd managed to get Varan out, he tried talking to her. Asking about winter in her home or about her work. Asking if she'd learned much in her slow language study. She rarely answered anything now.

Like a latch clicking open, Giovel recognized something in her. It was almost just how Iremni had responded after her spiriting.

He found himself stopping in the snow, feet suddenly cold. How hadn't he thought of it earlier? How had he not looked at Varan and seen the same exhausted wildness he'd seen in his wife almost a year before?

Maybe because he was looking at something else. Maybe because he tried so hard *not* to see Varan, not even to think of her, so as not to remember. It was just as Adni had hinted when he first assigned Giovel two months before: Giovel could never watch another spiriting without recalling Iremni.

"It's cold. Let's keep walking," Varan said and pushed past Giovel without pause.

She was ten paces away before he realized what she'd said and jogged to catch up, nearly tripping in the deep snow with each pace.

He knew when the change had taken place, with both of them. For Iremni it was immediate, as soon as they'd found her and brought her home. With Varan it was Perception Day, when she'd faced Etelier and nearly lost her ear to him. She'd never said much about it, though. Just that he'd wanted her to heal someone, that she'd refused, and that he'd hit her with a spell after that. Nothing else about what he might have done, though the wound alone was something.

As always, thoughts like that sent Giovel into mazes of wondering what they'd done to his Iremni to break her so completely. Was it rape? Some other, subtler violence? Brainwashing? Even a slow-moving toxin that stole away her appetite for any aspect of life? Iremni had never said a word about it, and now Varan was silent on the matter too.

One more branch on the fire. One more reason to find the witches who did this to her, if only the others would let him.

Giovel wondered, also for the hundredth time at least, whether he should encourage Varan to bait the witches herself. They must hate and fear her now, even if they hadn't before, but it was so risky even to suggest the idea. Giovel knew he'd never have risked Iremni like that. And somewhere far away, Varan also had a husband and children who must miss her with all the desperation Giovel still felt toward Iremni.

He pushed the notion deep into his mind as he walked, wishing he could repel such thoughts soundly enough not to think them again. Was there anywhere that far within him?

A sharp wind stirred as the city began waking, lifting powder into the air and cutting through Giovel's cloak, scarf, and gloves. The path back to the Candlespire was longer than he'd meant it to be—they'd walked almost to Hushwater Lake. So Giovel led Varan in a detour to find some warmth and dry their feet before they headed back. He clapped outside Sur's house by the Trade Road and only had to wait a short moment before a Candleguard woman opened the door to let them in.

"Where is this?" Varan asked.

Giovel stamped snow from his feet by the lintel. "A friend's house. You've met him once, actually."

She showed no sign of recognition but followed Giovel in, clearing snow off her boots. The Candleguard ushered them through a little Sanctuary of river rocks to a narrow hallway darkened by snow on the windowsills.

"Visitors, Lord Sur," the Candle called upstairs.

"Send them away."

She looked askance at Giovel. "But Lord Sur, it's—"

"I don't feel like seeing anyone, and I don't care if it's dear old aunty Optate herself. Send them away."

"It's Lord Giovel."

"Who? Oh. Let him in."

"You can wait in the Sanctuary if you want," Giovel said to Varan. She nodded as he climbed upstairs to Sur's room.

There wasn't much space. A small bed, a few paces of scarred wooden floor, and a chair by a tall window that overlooked the Trade Road, where Sur sat. He looked a mess, with his hair sticking out wildly in all directions, his beard untrimmed, and his clothes smelling like last week's food and sweat.

"I'm glad to know that somewhere in Foneth my standing can top even the Optate's," Giovel said.

Sur grunted. "She got where she is by having an old bloodline, a pretty face, and loads of money. You at least had to do something to earn your position."

Giovel stumbled on a warped board in the floor. "Why do you live in a tiny house like this when you're part of that same rich family?"

"Frugality. Self-interest, too. The best food stalls in Foneth are on the Trade Road, and no one bothers me here except you, I see. And the Witherclaw?"

"In your Sanctuary."

"So you're still playing hand-holder for her. I thought Adni was warming to you."

"He has a funny way of showing it," Giovel said.

"Here, sit." Sur offered the chair by the window, moving to his bed. "Or stand. I don't care either way."

"I only meant to stop in to get warm for a minute. I don't really want to be a bother, especially now that you're finally free of the old clinic."

"Sit or I'll throw my bandages at you. I haven't had a decent visitor in three weeks."

"I'm sorry for that. I meant to come sooner."

"Sure you did. Too busy with critical duties, is that it?"

It stung a little. But maybe it should. "I've been trying to find a pattern in a list of awakenings. I suppose it's occupied me a little more than I thought."

"A list of them, eh? Sounds more interesting than watching the Witherclaw. Tell me what you've found and I'll get you something warm to drink before you leave."

Sur's hospitality consisted of him yelling at the Candleguard posted to his house, along with another officer who apparently was posted at the side door. "He makes better teas," Sur said. "He's just lazy as a lark."

It surprised Giovel how genuinely glad Sur seemed to be for his visit, though. He looked starved for a conversation. Lonely. Like I am, Giovel thought—both of us isolated by our duties and left to sit them out. I should have come back to see him sooner.

He and Sur spent nearly an hour trading thoughts on Zuris's plans, Adni's mismanagement of the Order, possible tactics to watch for the witches, and fearful thoughts about the stolen awakenings list. And for once Giovel felt like he was talking not to a power-clawing rival but an ally, to someone who saw things with a paradigm like his own.

"How is your recovery, by the way?" he asked when they ran out of ideas about the witches.

Sur stretched in his bed. "Hellish. Have you ever been cut open like a pear? It's not something a man sleeps off. My healer says I'll likely be bedridden another two months. I tell him he's a damn liar every day, trying to keep me here so he can squeeze more coin from Order coffers."

"Careful. He might stretch your recovery out even more if he thinks you don't like him."

"He already *knows* I don't like him. But I can walk and I can even leave the house a little—if it's not icy out, which it always is now. I can send written orders to marshal hands for the Order, so that's something. I hope to be able to stand long enough to spit on Dlenar's grave when they bury him next month."

"He died bravely, Sur."

"Lived cowardly, though."

Giovel wasn't sure what to say to that. He shifted in his chair, looking away for a moment. Then he turned back to face Sur, lowering his voice just to be sure no one could hear them.

"I want to ask you something. In confidence."

"Ask away."

"Do you think the Order can beat the witches as we are now?"

"Well, Dlenar was a weakling, so we're probably no worse off without him than we were before."

"I'm not fooling. I want to know what you think."

Maybe because Giovel was beginning to doubt their strength. Or maybe because he'd doubted since witches stole Iremni. *One glyph* was all it took to break him. Why not break the rest of the Order as easily?

Sur rubbed his chin and looked out the window for a long moment. Finally he said, "There's a key that hasn't fully turned yet."

"What key?"

"It's something Adni knows about, and Hirnu as well. Maybe even Ralden. But I don't think Dlenar ever did, and somehow Elínla's missed it too. I'm not sure it will ever turn for you. But if it does, if everyone knew it and saw it clearly, we'd be ready to match them move for move. See, the witches *have* turned that key. All of them. It's part of them. But it's never been part of the Order in the same way. By design after all."

He couldn't mean what Giovel thought. "What are you saying?" Spellbuilding?

"I wish I could describe it clearly, but it's hard to put in any words," Sur mumbled. "I think it's like the skills you learned when you were a Candle—not the laws you had to study or policies we all have to memorize to keep the Optacracy off our heels. More like the things you learn patrolling a street for a year or fighting shield to shield with someone. It's experience, I suppose. Just a specific experience."

"I don't follow."

"That's the whole point, Giovel. *No one* follows until they've got it for themselves."

Giovel frowned. "What makes you so sure witches have this . . . experience?"

"Remember, I've seen some of them up close. Lots of them since being assigned to lead the hunts."

Sur's eyes were wide and somber now, staring hard beyond the window as if he was looking for something out there. The road was empty, though. Just clouds filling the sky. Snow on the streets. Blinding white everywhere. Sur kept staring, now turning in his bed as if shifting his position might show what he wanted to see.

Then he went on as if he'd never paused. "I'm not just talking about these new witches either. I've seen it in others too. It's like hunger and thirst and knowing how to handle them. It's like perfecting the ability to hit a berry with a wrist-thrower. I'd tell you more if I knew how to. Just believe me when I say it could change our order. There's a danger, though. See, I'm *glad* Elínla and you don't know what this is like yet. I'm glad you're free."

"What the hell are you talking about? You make it sound like she and I are some naive children compared to the rest of you."

Sur shrugged. "You'd know more about that than I do. Do you want your daughter to be anything but a child? Do you want her to grow up and lose someone like you lost Iremni?"

"She's *already* lost Iremni too. Sur, I don't feel any closer to understanding you now than before."

"I'm sorry. Truly. Let me try one more time," Sur said. "Yulen is part of this key, see? It's like the exhilaration of a craft you've honed. And the witches have that. Or else they'd just be awakenings on that list someone illegally compiled. But we can have it too. It doesn't need new glyphs or new training or new teaching at all. It's just something Yulena changes in us, maybe, or something you learn to notice eventually. Almost like a second awakening."

"Elínla's been using Yulena since she was fourteen," Giovel said. "And you think Ralden might not have this experience either? She's been in the Order twice as long as you have."

"True. But she has her guild, like a family to her. And Elínla has her sept—not to mention how she worships herself. You have to get past all of that just to see Yulena for what it is." He turned sharply all of a sudden, facing Giovel with an intensity like a pouncing spider's. "Forget I said anything. It's all a mound of shit. I hope you never understand a single thing I've said. Wish no one ever had to, because you can't go back."

He fell silent again, and Giovel pressed no farther. He felt too angrily puzzled to try now, like he was talking to a drunk old man who couldn't remember his way home. A moment later Giovel made an excuse about leaving Varan with nothing to do and excused himself.

"Come back again," Sur said. "Please."

Giovel nodded. "I'll be here sooner next time."

Varan followed him wordlessly when he left the little hallway. She seemed completely unperturbed by the length of their stay or the boredom she must feel. She can handle it, anyway, Giovel thought. She's put me through plenty of it. Her turn for a taste.

His mind was no longer on her or Iremni, or even the awakenings list, though. He thought as they stepped out that he might know what Sur was looking for, that moment at the window, because he realized now that Sur's window faced south. Toward Yulen.

BIRTH AND REBIRTH

My friend is having another child. I'm so happy for her.
  —The Witherclaw Witch; letter to Inivar and Sil.

Ice and snow, shorter days, pages of letters for Golkorun and Inivar and Sil, never to be sent. A slow change in her ear, and the bandages finally coming off. The first sight of it in the mirror, "mended" as the healer woman said with a smile when the wound was clean. But it would never mend, so Varan parted her hair to the side to cover it.

If it can't heal, let me at least forget about it.

More ice. More snow. Feather Day, Lance Day, River Day, Truth Day, was there a holiday every day here?

All through it Varan tried to shake one question from her mind. She'd found herself puzzling over it when she should be sleeping, revisiting it when Nomis and Kirida sat with her and little Progis played with her hands.

What did Inorovel really want from me? Why did she come that day? She had never come back afterward. Varan just couldn't shake the question, perhaps because she couldn't answer what Inorovel had asked her in turn.

Are you going to find the witches who did this?

I did find them, didn't I? And all I got for it was a smashed ear. No road home. No clarity. Not even vengeance. I know more how to ask now, more Medín words to tell those bastards what they've put me through. Maybe my will to chase them has dried up.

So she sat and read and learned more words, wrote more words for her family, and had no answers. She looked half a moment at the beautiful clothes Ralden sent her as thanks for nothing two months ago. She smiled in genuine warmth each time Uri's family visited, and they seemed to smile back with the same sincerity. But timid warmth was all Varan had now. Not fire like she'd need to face a witch again or push for her way home.

It felt like one of those sleeps that only got heavier the longer it went on. Varan supposed she might stay like that a full year, or forever.

Then Kirida's baby came.

Nomis was the first one to tell Varan it was happening. He looked desperate because Uri was out on assignments for the Order, trying to help another spiriting they'd found somewhere outside the city, and there was no one near enough to help as Kirida fought to get the new child out. Giovel understood immediately when Varan told him she had to go, looking relieved to have Nomis with her for a moment. Varan donned a scarf and her heavy snow boots, wrapped a cloak over her shoulder, and followed Nomis out along the lakeshore.

Kirida was well into the labor by the time they arrived. The child would come today; that was certain.

"What should I do?" Varan asked.

"I was hoping you'd tell me that," Nomis said, looking as glum as if he'd just swallowed needles. Then he laughed as Kirida kicked him in the leg. "Just a little joke. I've done this plenty of times."

"So have I," Kirida grunted. "Varan, will you watch Progis?"

She was glad to. "Call for me if you need."

Nomis and Kirida were right, though. They'd done this before, more than once as Varan had learned. Progis had an older brother who'd drowned the year he was born. And a younger sister who died from a fever they called flowerflame. They were incredibly brave to have a child again, Varan thought. But more children with parents like them might make their world a little better. They were better at loving their one son left than most people Varan knew. Had to be.

It made Varan eager to love their little boy the same way while Nomis helped Kirida and they waited for Uri to return or the new baby to break free. They played in the snow until the afternoon darkened, then sat by the fire and sipped a broth Nomis had left out ready for warming.

Their new son came just as the night turned silver and blue, coats of cloud blocking Yulen from sight. Nomis laughed again, and Kirida joined him.

"That's a baby?" Progis asked from the front room.

"Your sister or brother," Varan said, nodding. Then she held Progis close to her until he arched his back and wandered away to look at the fire again.

Progis looked like Sil. Walked like him too. Or at least how Sil had walked last time Varan saw him. But he was three months older now, a large measure of his little life. A child changed so much in that many months, and she would never have them with him.

A wild, wicked plan came to her mind. She could walk out the door of Kirida's and Nomis's home right now, out into the snow while they fawned over their new child, and she could take Progis with her. He was so young. He'd never quite remember his real mother as more than a happy dream, some woman who was kind to him before he knew anything but kindness. And Progis loved her too, didn't he? Trusted her like she needed him?

She ached so badly for Gokorun's arms and Inovar's laughter and Sil's round eyes that she considered the plan a minute, a few minutes together. She thought through how she'd leave Foneth, how she'd take Progis with her to search for Dundal. On a dark night like this, no one would be able to follow. And if she waited for the right moment, no one would miss them for hours, long enough she could get past the walls and be gone.

What a state I'm in. Damn me forever that I'd even think to take a woman's child from her. Damn me most that I'd think to rob people who've been kind to me, who treat me like one of their own.

I could never have done it anyway. Not knowing some fraction of the pain they feel. After all, they've lost two children and so have I. Their wounds are longer, because they've spent years without each of them, but mine are deeper because they know their son and daughter are dead. I don't. There's no telling whether I'll ever see their faces or hear their voices again.

So maybe I'm wrong. Maybe I *could* have done it, crippled with pain as I am in this place.

"Baby's crying," Progis said as his little sibling wailed behind the door to the back room.

Varan realized suddenly that she was too. Tears flooded over her cheeks, salty across her dry lips. She wasn't sure if it was joy or shame that made her cry. Because she *did* feel joy, didn't she? Joy for two parents who wanted another child so badly, so courageously after losing as many before, and shame because she didn't know if she could love in return as they loved her—not while she felt so jealous and angry at what they had and she did not.

Then, as suddenly as her tears had come, she had her answer to Inorovel's question.

She wiped her face, played with Progis a little while longer, then held him up when Nomis invited her back to meet his brother.

"What should we call him, Progis?" Nomis asked.

"Rabbit."

"We're not naming your brother rabbit," Kirida said. "His name is Dalenchivor."

"But we'll call him Chivi," Nomis assured Progis.

He was asleep now, resting on Kirida's chest with one fist—still gray from birth—curled next to her neck. His face was like hers, with eyes shaped like almonds and a tiny chin tucked beneath his mouth. They hadn't yet washed the crown of his head. Varan wished they'd never have to, that Dalenchivor's little island of calm could stay with them until winter broke. She almost wept again just to see him.

Kirida's free hand took Varan's as she stood there. "Thank you for coming, Varan. I think Progis behaves better for you than he does for any of us. I'm glad you were here."

Varan tried to smile back at Kirida. "You always come for me." Of course she'd try to do the same when asked.

She stayed only a little while after that, watching how Progis tried to pat his little brother and laughing as he tried to tell Chivi about their house. Uri arrived soon after, escorted by several of Nomis's friends in the Candleguard.

"They all stink like horse, but they said you invited them," Uri mumbled before her face flared to life at the sight of her new grandson.

The Candleguard took over watching Progis, their new trainee as they called him, and Varan slipped out alone. Maybe Giovel or Nomis wouldn't like that, but she didn't have time to care anymore. She had work that had waited long enough.

She'd decided she *would* find the witches. And that through them she *would* find a way back home.

QUARRELS, OIL, AND FIRE

I'm trying to be patient. I'm also trying not to miss a chance to get away.
—The Witherclaw Witch; letter to Golkorun.

It didn't take Birenlu long to pinpoint the Redremels' location. She came to Giovel's house three nights after Truth Day with a tiny scrap of parchment.

"Our deal?" she asked, holding it back from him in the doorway.

"I'm looking," he said. "It will take me time."

"I only need your word."

"You had it already."

"Hearing it again will make this dangerous piece of intelligence more palatable," Birenlu said. "Humor a woman who's spent her life gathering information."

Was his word worth so little? "I promise I'll share what I find on the Order—at least to the extent you asked me before if not far beyond it."

She smiled and handed him her parchment. "Be careful with them. There are seven or eight in that house, bunkered together like badgers waiting for spring."

Giovel smiled back. Seven or eight Redremel he could handle. The very prospect felt easier than anything he'd done for the Order in months.

There wasn't much to plan, but Giovel took his time, making sure each piece he could control rested where he wanted before he set out. A few hours before dawn the next day, he woke Inorovel to tell her he was leaving on assignment. Then he walked the snow-packed path to Scout's Bridge, where he met twenty Candleguard he'd previously commanded. Elínla was there too, as she'd promised, with five Grays behind her.

"We look like we're off to take a whole city," she said. "Are you sure there are enough of us?"

"I could go wake Olinos Vlada if you'd feel safer with more hands."

"Give us a little faith," one of the Grays said. "We can take these Redremel by ourselves."

"That's easy to say when you've got a score of Candles backing you up," one of Giovel's old lieutenants mumbled.

Giovel almost hushed them but thought better of it. In his mind a little jostling and bragging beforehand meant they felt confident. And that was how he wanted them to be today—fearless, unworried, convinced the Redremel could crawl back to their own city and leave Foneth alone. Maybe someday Foneth would invite them back in peace, but on new terms then and not for grievances with people dead a hundred years before Giovel was born.

His group split to approach their destination in six clusters small enough to be night patrols. They didn't have too far to go, since Birenlu's note said the Redremel hideout was a little house with a cart stable almost right on the Trade Road where Belnum ended and Tovómil began. Even moving on foot with roundabout approaches, it only took an hour to gather there.

The plan was simple. The Grays and most of the Candleguard would spread around the house, handbows and glyphs at the ready, while a few more secured the stable and Giovel and Elínla went right to the door to announce themselves. Yes, there was a chance that a witch or two might be waiting inside, and yes, the Redremel would almost certainly have projectiles of their own, plus cover from which to strike. But they were cut off completely. They'd either surrender or be smoked out to fight four times their number.

"Ready?" Giovel asked Elínla as they faced the house in question. It was a tall, three-level building nearly as old and weatherworn as Divnum's walls.

"There's no being ready for this kind of thing," she said, and signaled to her Grays to advance around the building. "Just ready for it to end."

Giovel had once felt the same way, that you could never truly prepare yourself for an event like this. He'd been wrong, though. He *was* ready. Years of practice, repetition, and patience had equipped him for it. He might be less than half a mage—and getting stiffer and older by the month—but he was finally putting his skills to use for the Order.

He clapped and shouted, "The Divine Order want to come in. Anyone awake?"

There was a muffled sound inside. Then footsteps hammering over the floor. Giovel prodded the door and found it unlocked. He swung it open and leaned back to wait for any surprises in the entrance hallway. Nothing.

A moment later a barrel flew out of one of the upper windows. It landed in the street, splattering the snow with something rust-colored. A lit lantern followed it too quickly for Giovel to shout out what he was piecing together. Explosive oil.

The lantern hit right in the center of the oil, as if it was part of a practiced routine. Giovel heard half the shattering sound of the glass, then an immense concussion as a wave of heat and air shot through the night. The window above shattered, followed by crashes throughout the street and a chorus of startled cries from the Candleguard and whoever lived nearby. A portion of the street was ablaze already, and Giovel was willing to bet half his hair that the explosive oil wasn't the only exit strategy these Redremel had on hand.

"Stick to the plans!" Giovel shouted and ran into the dark hallway of the house.

They'd plotted every step. Wait to withdraw our own wounded until we make sure they can't hurt us anymore. Take the lower levels first so escape is harder. Cut off the stairwells and bring in more fighters to cover us if they show additional tricks.

No one downstairs that he could see. Just an empty kitchen, and a sort of converted workshop, now filled with maps, scrolls, books, notes, perhaps a treasure horde of information. "Get two Grays in here to protect this room!" Giovel called back to Elínla as he raced ahead again.

There was no Sanctuary. It had been torn apart, whatever it once was, leaving an empty husk of a room like the cracked bits of shell when a bird left its egg behind. It made Giovel tighten his fists and speed to the back of the house, where a steep set of stairs climbed upward.

Two heavy quarrels hit the floor by the stairs as he approached. Not just bowguns, then. Redremel springbows. Giovel leaned back for cover and waited as footsteps shuffled over the floor above him—at least three pairs, maybe more. Elínla didn't wait, though. She crouched over the quarrels, held her tablet out, and roared as an Illumina flooded up the stairs. The Redremel cried out in response.

"Now's our chance," she said, clambering upward.

They cleared the stairs before anyone could recover properly from Elínla's blinding spell, but the Redremel weren't unprepared. They'd already scattered backward, leaving the landing empty. Except for another barrel like the one they'd hurled through the windows. Giovel felt his eyes widen. Then Elínla tackled him, smashing his shoulder into the stairs and pulling them both down hard. The pommel of Giovel's own sword hit his ankle, sending waves of pain to his teeth. He banged both sides of his face directly as Elínla yanked him down the rough wooden stairs. He finally hit the ground with an arm beneath him, fearing for an excruciating moment that he'd snapped his bones before he realized it was just the springbow quarrels he'd broken beneath him. Elínla toppled over his shoulder, one of her feet catching him in the gut as she landed hard.

Then the floor above them exploded with a concussion even louder than the first had been.

The entire building shook. More glass rattled and broke. Heat like boiling blood flowed down the remains of the stairwell. Then debris. Chunks of wood, clay, stone, and broken brick flew wide into the sky, which was fully exposed now. Giovel saw with horror that the Redremel hadn't just blasted the second level open—they'd blown the top *two* stories apart with that last explosion.

He and Elínla tried simultaneously to find cover, rolling toward a little table by the wall as mountains of rubble pounded over the stairs. A piece of the roof slammed into the wall near them and shattered, flinging more debris across the room. A brick as large as Giovel's head hit him in the shoulder. He swore and hit the ground, flattened by the force of the blow and nearly biting his own tongue as he crashed down.

Just when he'd felt so ready.

Another set of quarrels jetted through the dust and smoke, striking near Giovel's head. Through the haze and the glint of three small fires, he saw a pair of men reloading springbows down the hall. Either he'd walked right past them or they'd dropped downstairs a secret way. One of Elínla's Grays was wrestling with another behind them. Blades clanged together in the streets outside.

Elínla was on her feet ahead of Giovel, sprinting through the smoke to help her Gray as she unleashed a pair of Talons at the men with springbows. Giovel ran after her and opened his wrist-thrower on them. Then three more fighters dropped down almost right around him, as if they'd unfolded themselves from the walls. How many places could they hide in this old house?

Two went for his sides with knives before he could even halt. Giovel caught one wrist, wrenching it out of its path, but the other knife clipped behind him and cut through his cloak, tabard, skin. A foot caught him in the legs before the pain from the knife registered. Then all three Redremel were on him like birds on a crust of bread, striking and pulling him to his knees with their combined weight, pressing him into the rubble-strewn floor. He breathed a mouthful of smoke and gagged. He only managed to veer the first attacker's knife aside before he flattened on the ground.

More fire. Roiling heat, and light like the sun. Then six Candleguard were there, prying the Redremel off Giovel and binding their hands behind them. Elínla and several Grays pushed past, their tablets bloodred with active glyphs. Flames flared through the narrow rooms like a stray breeze, but only the heat touched anyone this time.

"Get them out of here!" Elínla shouted. "And empty that room! I want every scrap of evidence moved before this place is ash!"

Giovel vomited, covering his own hands with his sick. Two Candleguard helped him up, guiding him hurriedly through the smoke and dirt to snow and blissfully cool air outside. The Candles out there had three more Redremel in their hands. It looked as if these three had leaped from the second or even third story before the explosion, trusting the drifts of powder to cushion their falls. For some reason the very thought made Giovel vomit again.

It took the Grays less than a hundred count to empty the room they'd claimed inside. By then eight Redremel were lined up in the snow, searched and bound, gagged, captive. Scores of onlookers surrounded the area now, but Giovel's contingent of Candleguard had quieted the disturbance almost as quickly as it started, leading everyone away while the remains of the spy house took fire.

Elínla handed Giovel a skin of water, which he used to rinse the burning taste from his mouth. He remembered all of a sudden that a knife had cut him in the back. Somehow the flavor of his own sick was much worse than the stinging from his cut.

"Am I bleeding out?" he asked, trying to turn and wincing in wrenching pain. His shoulder where the brick hit didn't seem to like moving anymore.

"Let me see. Barely a scratch. You got lucky."

"Lucky *you* and your Grays were close by," he mumbled before taking another swish of water and wincing again because spitting felt like getting kicked by a mule.

"I think we won," Elínla said with a gleam in her eye.

Giovel managed a weak smile, despite the pain running through his body. "It looks like it."

The sun began to rise behind them.

THE AWAKENING BY THE FEATHERWOOD

I can't help them and they can't help me.
—The Witherclaw Witch; letter to Recia.

FOUR CANDLES INSISTED Giovel see a field medic before he left Belnum. Pain from debris hitting him lanced from his shoulder blade through his ribs, blocking out even the sting of his shallow cut, so he didn't argue. He just sat there as the medic prodded and measured and examined him by the faint light of a hand lantern.

"Is this really thorough enough for you to see anything worthwhile?" Giovel asked.

The medic ignored his question. "I'll give you something for the pain if you want, but this will all mend itself in a few days."

"I can live with the pain."

"Maybe now, while your blood's still pumping fast. You might not feel so confident when you wake up later this morning."

But I won't wake up because I won't sleep, Giovel thought. I finally have something to do, something to chase other than a list of old awakenings.

Elínla had almost finished gathering everything from the burned wreckage when the medic let Giovel rejoin her. She had the eight Redremel ready to walk, their reports folded in a dirty satchel at her side, and the Grays and Candles quietly dispersing the gathered crowds of onlookers and hurling snow on flames that escaped the old building.

"How are they all?" Giovel asked.

"Scared, but probably relieved we didn't butcher them."

"I meant the Candles. Casualties?"

"A few burns. Nothing worse than what you got, actually."

A wave of relief went through him then. And here he'd wondered whether half their fighters got blasted apart. He should have trusted them more. It made him proud to have been one of them once, proud they'd follow him. His pain doubled as his worries subsided, though, making him grunt and grimace and grab his throbbing side.

"Do you need a walking stick, old man?" Elínla asked.

"I might need a horse and cart after all that. Let's get back to the Candlespire before it's full morning."

They sent three Grays ahead to prepare places for the prisoners. At Elínla's suggestion, they'd agreed to split them apart this time, sending two to the nearby Belnum barracks, one to the Lances' garrison by North Hold, and one more all the way to the Citadel, with just four coming to Divnum directly. No witch strikes would take these prisoners all at once. Not again.

"I'll draft the report, if you'd like," Elínla offered as they put Belnum behind them.

Giovel thanked her. "I suppose having it all documented will give Adni one less thing to scream about before he punishes us in person."

"I'm going to make sure Hirnu knows before he does. Just in case we need support in there."

So, contrary to what he'd told himself when the medic attended him, Giovel left her to it and went home to bed.

For the first time in weeks, his dreams were more than just the awakenings list running through his mind again and again. Now he saw a decoded report of Redremel supply lines and a detailed chart of their armaments. He saw Lances surrounding hidden patrols in the hills, Optate Olura announcing the dismantling of a secret Redremel forward force.

Pain in Giovel's back woke him sometime after sunrise. For a moment he thought he couldn't move, couldn't turn to push himself out of bed. All his bones seemed to have swollen up, pushing his muscles aside and locking him into position. Then he managed to adjust one leg and twisted upright with a wrenching ache in his side.

Only for the flush of victory would I rise feeling like this.

He found a bowl of nuts and grain mash beside his bed. Inorovel must have brought it in before leaving for school. It was cold now but better than what he would have prepared for himself after sleeping in. He wolfed it all down, washed timidly so as not to stretch his bruised muscles more than he had to, and dressed as quickly as he could. Time to see what would come of last night's venture.

The only formal meeting he knew of that day was between the Order and the Lawrits' High Recorder in the afternoon, but Giovel went straight to the Candlespire. He found an arguing bunch of Lances, Grays, and Candleguard outside, all talking about Redremel scouts. It made him whistle to himself with satisfaction. He found Elínla and Ralden—bandaged across her torso and sitting in some sort of palanquin—arguing in the Sanctuary.

"It could be one big fabrication," Ralden was saying. "It sounds as if they were very prepared for you to come. Doesn't that make you wonder whether they might have planted falsified reports as a ruse?"

"They wouldn't risk blasting their own hands off just to give us made-up evidence," Elínla said heatedly. "They could have done that any number of easier ways."

"None of which would have been so convincing. Giovel, talk some reason to her. You don't seriously believe the Redremel let you get a hundred pages of intelligence with that little resistance?"

Giovel grimaced. "Perhaps your interpretation of 'little resistance' is different from mine."

"They wouldn't have coded everything so securely if they wanted us to take fake reports," Elínla said. "A baby could glean more from those papers than we can without some real time and the expertise to decipher them."

"But they would have tried *destroying* them if they really mattered," Ralden replied. "Their throwing one little jug of lamp oil out the window is hardly enough evidence to convince me otherwise."

"Is that the story they're telling now?" Giovel asked. "It was a lot worse than lamp oil. In fact I'm surprised you heard about it so quickly, despite being fully relieved from duty for the time, Ralden."

"How could I not hear? Everyone's talking," Ralden said. "Which is precisely what I'd want if I were a Redremel scout."

"We'll need more time to be sure of anything," Giovel said. Though he had to admit he understood Ralden's reserve about celebrating. Things *had* gone surprisingly well. No deaths on either side, no one even hurt worse than Giovel himself and one Redremel who broke an ankle leaping into a snowdrift that was shallower than it appeared. They'd have to take Ralden's concerns seriously to get to the bottom of this well before any other Redremel spies could respond.

"I take it the rest of the Order knows too, then?" Giovel asked.

"I'm expecting them any time," Elínla said. "Do you need to bring the Witherclaw here so you can stay until they arrive? I can send some Grays for her."

"She's with one of my old men in the guard. She'll be fine."

"Adni might not think so," Ralden said.

"If he complains about me breaking ranks, I'll point a finger at you," Giovel said. "I thought you were forbidden to leave home until the snows melt. They say you nearly got cut in half."

"Would have been, if not for the Witherclaw," Ralden answered. "But that's beside the point. Is Sur coming too?"

"He's probably obediently recovering," Elínla said. "Although I'm sure he's heard the news too."

Giovel hoped so. Lonely as Sur had seemed in their last visit, it was possible he simply didn't see much of anyone lately. Ralden, at least, had hundreds of guild workers still visiting her for her opinions and approvals, so she probably couldn't be lonely if she wanted.

"There they are," Elínla said, turning as both Hirnu and Adni entered the Candlespire together, Kanis trailing behind like a servant. Giovel tensed just to see Adni. They hadn't spoken in weeks.

Elínla put a hand on Giovel's shoulder as the others approached. "Stay at your post. I'll take the meeting."

"You shouldn't have to take the blame in my place."

"Trust me," she said quietly. "It will be better for all of us if you don't violate another direct command from Adni."

Or would it just be better for her ascension in the ranks, another chance for her to raise herself? Giovel pushed the thought aside and nodded. "Let me know how this plays out."

Then he climbed upstairs to sit outside Varan's room while the others withdrew into the council chamber.

The wait felt interminable. With Varan still at Nomis's, all Giovel had to do was stare at his well-worn list while he waited. That and wonder what new form of punishment Adni might conjure after this.

When the council chamber emptied, Ralden's voice echoed in the hallway, still arguing about verifying whether any intelligence was faked. Hirnu floated off by herself, followed soon by Kanis and Adni, who didn't even glance in Giovel's direction. Elínla emerged last, wide-eyed but smiling tentatively.

"Either Adni's sprouted a heart," she said, "or making sure Olura knew first was enough to stuff his mouth shut."

"You let the word slip to the Optate?"

"She would have found out anyway. I just made sure she knew before Adni could complain. She sent a formal commendation for both of us."

Giovel grinned.

"There wasn't much to it, actually," Elínla went on. "The Lances have agreed to help question our prisoners and break their codes, Hirnu and Ralden are happy, and Olura apparently loved that Grays and Candles helped with the move. It sounds like this will restore some much needed trust in their protection. I don't know that anything will change right away for you, but Adni can't complain without making himself look like an imbecile."

"I'll have to remember this for next time I need to get on his good side," Giovel said, still smiling and wide-eyed as Elínla.

"There's bad news too. Apparently the witches did six spiritings from Medínoth last night alone."

"*Six* in one night? Have any of them been found yet?"

"My Grays found three of them already. Dead. I need to get out there to investigate more. I'll let you know if I find anything."

It was the first time Giovel could remember her volunteering information from her work with the Grays. He nodded in thanks and wished her luck. "Can't I help with something? Even from here?"

"There is one thing. You know that list, the awakenings? All six of these names were on it. I have Grays watching some that are left, but we can be sure the witches will come after more of them. Maybe even everyone on the list. Could you check by a few that are in Divnum?"

"I can get Varan to come that far with me," Giovel said. "I'll start on it today."

Elínla turned to go. She paused by the stairs and said, "I think Adni will give you more duties soon."

She seemed to mean it. What it said to Giovel, though, was not that Adni might finally trust him but that she would.

He went directly toward Nomis's house to collect Varan, consulting his list as he walked. There were four names in Divnum, including three on this side of Cloud Lake. He could check them all. In fact he'd probably seen one or two of these people in his many walks by the lake or in the Featherwood. Maybe that was why the list felt familiar to him. Not that he'd learned it so well in his hours of study, but because he might actually know the faces of a person or two on it.

Varan wasn't at Nomis's when Giovel arrived, though Uri said she'd been there earlier to help with their boy while Kirida birthed the new child. Giovel tried to smile when Uri said this, thinking back to the son and daughter they'd already lost. Perhaps that was why Varan liked them so much. They'd *all* lost family in one way or another.

He was so close now to one of the descriptions that he decided to scout the location out before finding Varan. "The awakening by the Featherwood" as the list called it. The notes were harder to follow by foot than they seemed in his mind, like they'd been written from a reversed description someone else imparted. Around the blue-roofed house by the lake. Across the fence by old woman Garathina's gardens. Back through that narrow little patch of forest before the marshy path. Giovel had to retrace his steps five times before he was confident he even walked in the right direction. He almost gave it up for later, but it seemed such a shame to waste this effort now when he had only five or six instructions left.

He found his pulse quickening when he realized he'd come almost all the way back home. This awakening lived near him, so near he *must* have seen them and likely knew them by name. What must someone think, living that near to him while clutching a secret like this?

The last line of notes said to follow the stone path to a narrow house near some pear trees. Giovel froze. The only house there was his.

Most descriptions of the people listed were sparse, but Giovel knew them by heart. A woman. Golden-haired. *Inorovel?* But no. The list said she was older, maybe thirty-five or forty years all told. The list was months old now at least, and there were hundreds of women like that in Foneth—but only one who had lived here. Not Inorovel.

Iremni.

And all at once Giovel knew why witches had spirited her.

THE WEAKEST

This winter might be long.
—The Witherclaw Witch; letter to Inivar and Sil.

THE COLD WAS worse by the lakes. Claravena waited as long as she could in the snow, staring over the Hushwater and listening to the faint hum from the spells she'd been practicing, but her promised informant wasn't coming. It was a bright night thanks to the lake's white reflection and Yulen, clear enough to be certain no one moved within bowshot in any direction.

Another lead that didn't come. Another effort pointing to a wall.

Once she decided she'd waited long enough, Claravena trudged uphill to The Blushwater. Not the fanciest tavern in Belnum, but it would be warm, and people would talk there. Listening to gossip was half as useful as meeting coin-leeching informants, like the one who'd promised to show herself tonight. Sure enough, fires burned at both ends of the room when Claravena entered, and smaller orb lamps warmed the score of tables still occupied at this hour. Smells of butter and spiced broth wafted from the kitchens. Claravena spotted at least seven Candleguard scattered through the room. Maybe more wrapped under snow cloaks. She called for a hot bowl of pepperleaf soup and warmed herself alone at a table behind four of them.

The failed meeting was more disappointing than Claravena had expected. Noru had arranged it, convinced his informant knew something of the whereabouts of old Vindil. While Claravena had never shared his enthusiasm for that particular search, she was ready to try anything now. So many of her best plans had tripped on tree roots as soon as she attempted them. Of course she'd seen plans fail long before she took over the newly reformed Starlit Order, but now she had to take responsibility in a way she hadn't before, and it never left her mind.

They'd tried getting Ithilo into the Lances, but no, we have enough recruits and you're too old. They'd tried extorting Deleos Tovóm with news about his new mistress, but no, everyone knew that already and no one cared what Deleos did because he was young and would never lead House Tovóm anyway. They'd risked an open fight by getting close enough to spirit a few Grays from their posts, hoping to kill them one by one. The complexity of the spiriting glyph—which was too large to do on a sand tablet or ordinary sheet of parchment—already made this challenging, and the Grays were too clever to catch in batches; they almost always fled before Claravena could close in, preparing traps of their own in return. She and the others had increased their other spiritings tenfold instead, snatching everyone they could from under the Divine's claws, rushing to find as many as they could, and showing them exactly how closely the Order had watched them. No one wanted to join. A few ran for it, but Tranin just ended up slitting most of their throats and leaving them to bleed in the streets, often done with them in less than thirty minutes.

That alone pushed Claravena to hunt for other plans. It was killing the very people she'd always intended to help. No matter how much she hated it, Claravena couldn't banish that truth from her mind.

Maybe we should capture them and play a more patient game again. Maybe we need to somehow reach them while the Grays are still there, *show* them the eyes closing in before we pull them away. Or could be we need to abandon all spiritings and focus on recruiting those without Yulena, like Etelier had done. But if we never find old Vindil and unlock the secret to awakenings, what good will that really do? Claravena was almost ready to give her fellow witches free reign and let them do whatever came into their heads. Freedom was half of what they fought for in the first place.

Just not *all*.

The one idea she'd managed to quell was the old, dangerous game of building new spells specifically to fight the Order. Perhaps seeing a few of your friends die in one day reminded them that they could be next. Etelier was useless now—half-deaf and totally unmotivated. Wurelna was too timid to be great, despite her evident skill as a spellbuilder, and Tranin was too wild to be reliable for anything but spiriting after spiriting.

So here we are, Claravena thought dourly, risking frostbite while we wait for *rumored* informants who *might* just know *something* about a place that *could be* involved in awakening people like us. It's like gambling that a litter of dogs will be born with the same pattern of spots on each, and the burden is firmly on my back now. I was right to out Etelier and turn us somewhere new. But I was also a fool for thinking I could do what no witches have ever done. Maybe we're all fools to try like we do.

Eronea had found another way. Why couldn't Claravena too?

She drained her soup bowl, tried to shake the last bits of cold from her boots, and walked back to the lakeshore to wait a little longer. No one ever came. All Claravena saw was the slow motion of the stars and the sky's oblong reflection off the Hushwater.

Back to The Blushwater with more soup and a cup of something sour and numbing. Only three Candleguard and a few other locals were left then.

"He never uses Yulena, though," one of them was saying now. That made Claravena look away from her drink, turning her head slowly to avoid drawing the Candles' attention.

"Doesn't need it, does he?" a woman with a lieutenant's collar said. "He's taken down more witches without than some others can with their magery."

"What others? You mean weaklings like dead Dlenar?"

"Watch what you say about him, idiot."

"Why? Because he's got rich relatives who might come spank me with a piece of sweetbread?"

"I'm not saying he wasn't a bastard, just that people liked him. And it's not respectful. Not to mention he had a thousand fools working for him in secret."

"Now you're talking out of your hair. I'll say what I want about Dlenar, and I say Giovel's twice the Divine Mage he ever was."

"I thought you said he never uses Yulena," the lieutenant replied.

"Sure, and it was you as said he doesn't need it. I've seen him drop three men at once using just a knife. A *knife*. And even the Optacrats like him. Maybe because he's old like them."

Claravena's chair creaked, making her jump slightly. The Candleguard paid her no mind. The loud one just went on as if haranguing a dead Tovómil was the most noble thing he could do with his stinking breath.

They seemed to be moving on from their conversation, curse them. Just say a few more words about this, Claravena thought. Make me sure you know what you're talking about and not that you're slobbering fools skipping their shift to look for someone to fancy.

Perhaps they wouldn't voice what she needed to hear without prodding. And prodding was all she could do anymore, even as Master of the Starlit Order.

Claravena cleared her throat just loudly enough to get the attention of all three Candles. Then she said, "Don't talk like that about the Divine." The Candleguard turned to face Claravena, and she didn't have to feign being afraid.

"Talk like what?" the loud one asked.

Prod again. "Saying bad things about Lord Dlenar. It's not right. You'll bring misfortune on everyone here if you do it."

"Keep your face out of it. I wasn't saying anything bad except to say good things about someone else."

By now Claravena's heart felt like the pool beneath a waterfall—heaving and shifting without pause for a breath. But she pushed herself to speak once more. "All I heard was bad talk about the dead, and I don't like it."

"Then you can leave and go to sleep like anyone should."

"Shut up and leave her alone," the lieutenant said, shoving her unruly guard back when he tried to stand up. "The woman's right that you should put a halter on your fat tongue."

"Halter my tongue and I can't say anything good about old Giovel either. What do you want from me? No words at all?"

"That would be a gift," the other guard said.

"Why you—"

"I could use some good talk now," Claravena said quickly. "Anyone could."

"I told you to keep your face out of it."

"And I told *you* to shut up!" the lieutenant snapped. "I'll have you put on double-watch if you keep ignoring me."

"Please tell me he was lying about Lord Giovel not having the gift of Yulena," Claravena said, now looking to the other two. "I didn't vote for Olura Medín so she could try to fight the witches with people who don't have the power to do it."

"Ignore this fool," the lieutenant replied. "Giovel's as much a mage as anyone. He just doesn't need Yulena like most of them do."

"He made a vow or something when his wife died," the loud one was saying now. He seemed to have forgotten being angry. "Said he wouldn't turn a glyph until he killed the witches that murdered her."

And once more Claravena found herself looking up, hoping no contradiction came from the others. None did. The other man even nodded as if he'd heard the same thing, like it was common knowledge among them. She knew Candles tended to worship Giovel due to his past among them—unremarkable though it was. If anyone was likely to know the old man well, it was their circle. Well. It was all news to Claravena, news to every witch in Foneth, she'd wager.

It rang true, though. She'd seen Giovel that night that they nearly killed Suresni Medín. Giovel had never once drawn a glyph, not even when Etelier faced him down with ten of them. She'd heard about his fight at the walls, too. Wurelna had said Giovel nearly killed her not with magic but by hurling his sword right through a sand tablet. Maybe this drunk Candle's story was true. Maybe Giovel was a Divine Mage with no Yulenic fangs behind his lips.

Then there was the part about his wife. Claravena knew that witches had *not* in fact murdered her. She was there when they let Iremni Ullin go; she was there when they first found her, disoriented from the spiriting. In fact, that might have been Claravena's first spiriting after Etelier taught her the spell to do it. When these Candles talked about finding the witches who'd put an end to Iremni's life, they probably meant *her.*

Still, even with this error in their account, it felt close enough to be true. Just bent from the full truth, like a piece of jewelry that didn't come out quite right. Close enough to look at, to be worth something.

The Candles called for more food to shut their companion up, and Claravena wrapped her cowl tight and walked back into the snow. It was late now, closer to dawn than to sundown, but she felt more awake than she had the whole evening.

For months she'd thought Giovel was the toughest, the most dangerous of the Order. Now she wondered if he might be the weakest of all—a selfish old man who put his lust for revenge ahead of his duties to Foneth. Just the vulnerable stretch of rope she and her own Order could cut.

There was work to do, of course, stories to check against history. Still, it left Claravena with the beginnings of a plan that didn't require killing fool awakenings or hunting for Vindil's ruins. Just the sort of plan they could actually try.

QUESTIONS

They're so casually familiar with Yulen yet so suspicious of Yulena.
   —The Witherclaw Witch; letter to Golkorun.

Answers only brought Giovel more questions. Who'd made this list of awakenings? Who'd watched Iremni from a distance, *spied* on her, known her secrets better even than I did? And when did this all happen? Did no one ever think to check, to see whose wife she was? Did no one realize it? Or did they simply withhold it from me, even after I was appointed to the Order?

Questions brought some answers too. No wonder Adni kept his awakenings list from the Order, for instance, practicing his unwritten rule of clemency as he'd called it the night they found Kanis. He had something to gain from letting milder awakenings wander free. Like a farmer keeping grain for seed just in case the harvest didn't yield what it should. Adni had already shown his willingness to replenish the Order from his hidden list. Perhaps he'd intended other awakenings for such ends as well.

But then came more questions. *When* had Iremni awakened? How long had she lied to keep it from Giovel? How had she manifested her power such that a spying Gray or some hidden hand for the Optate could *notice* her awakening?

Did she ever think to tell us, Giovel wondered. Or even more chilling, had she endangered me or Inorovel with purposeful spellbuilding? That alone would explain why she'd never said a thing about awakening, so that, most of all, was a question Giovel couldn't shake away.

Perhaps Iremni was a witch all along.

Giovel's mind gathered explanations, answers he could see that made him consider any premise of betrayal on Iremni's part. And maybe that was the worst of it. Despite all his questions and presumed answers, there really was no wondering why she'd never said anything to him, why she'd kept her own awakening—or even witchcraft—hidden even from him.

She had to do it. Not because of my position in the Order, not because I was a rising leader in the Candleguard even before that. But because of *me*, Giovel, the man who told her his mind and walked with her every evening and slept beside her, whose suspicion and fear of witches was as deep as the roots of a mountain and as plain to her as a cloud at noon.

Perhaps it's not her fault that she never spoke up. More likely it's all mine.

It was a thought he couldn't banish from his mind. He abandoned any more attempts to find awakenings on the list, walked the rest of the way home, tried to sleep to find some relief. His body still ached and begged for rest after last night, and he found himself drifting into a doze almost as soon as he lay down. He was vaguely aware of Inorovel calling for him, realizing where he was, bringing him another blanket because it was cold as the bottom of a lakebed, but he didn't really sleep again and he knew there'd be no rest in sleep anyway.

Adni knew. He had to. He'd kept that list for some time, clearly, maybe for years. Must have, Giovel thought—since Iremni's been gone a year already. Did I miss the day she died, the one-year marker? Damn every duty that pushed that away from my mind and damn me for caring. *How* did I forget? And Inorovel never said a thing. She must have marked it in her own ways. What else does she have to remember alone because I'm pouring over a list of descriptions so feverishly I never notice who's on it?

Which means maybe Adni didn't know. Maybe he only saw "The awakening by the Featherwood" as I did, never thought twice. He's never even met Iremni. Few did even before I joined the Order, because we swore we wouldn't let them, for her own safety.

But witches knew, witches found out, somehow, witches stole her. And now it's all so clear why. I thought so much of myself before, that my position in the Order was the center of the map, so vital for them to attack that they took my own wife to hurt me before I came for them. And there's another great irony. Witches probably spirited her just to recruit her, or to remove her from the consideration of the Grays and the Order. It's how they spirit and murder awakenings now, moving so wild and fast that our lists are worthless and our plans never work.

Giovel couldn't fathom how the witches had known either who or what Iremni was, though. He didn't have the reserves to care now.

"I'm going to walk," he shouted louder than he needed and threw off his blankets.

It was snowing again. A little after dusk; nightfall came so early now. But the snow made it easy enough to see the thorny edge of the Featherwood where naked fingers of bark reached in every direction and trunks creaked with the wind. It was too dark for a proper view of any of the sites Giovel and Iremni had once walked together—the library, Scout's Bridge, the walls, the Citadel, any of the architecture they'd admired. Then again Giovel had seen them all enough times not to need his eyes. Just memories.

He'd expected to find some solace, but he realized after just a few hundred paces along the Divnum walls that there would never be solace in these walks now. He remembered *too much* of Iremni, too many things she'd said, too many instances of her quiet company, too many moments now that could have been her trying to speak her hidden truth or to mask it all the more.

That time she mentioned being angry—when Suresni's plans for witch-hunting sanctions were voted down by the Optate's Council—was she angry because she was afraid? Because she knew someday I'd have to turn on her like a snake trailing a rat? Or the time two years ago she'd seemed so reserved, weeks on end, like she wanted to say something but didn't dare. Was it Yulena she wanted to talk about?

Giovel now saw a coat of poison on every past expression because he couldn't even guess when her awakening had begun. He heard deception in every sentence. Their moments alone that he'd once remembered with warmth and passion now felt made up. Or worse yet, he thought, painted over.

Memory's odd like that, isn't it? We recall more good than we know there was and more bad than we believe our imaginations could invent. But half of it *is* invention under some screen that gets thicker with time to the point that there's no piling the inventions on one side and the truths on the other anymore. Just shuffling them together and guessing which is which.

I used to tell myself I'd only grown to hate Yulen when the witches stole you away, Iremni. Now I can remember clear as water that I hated it long before. I learned to hate it as a young Candle when a witch killed Banner Captain Gameldisar and I was left without direction in the middle of the night, lost in North Hold and terrified that the same witch was waiting behind every shadow for me. So though I say it's only after you died that this hatred started to build, some part of me must have known better.

That's what forbade you from speaking, that tiny breach that rewrote our home as a place where no one could confess to awakening. I wonder if I'd laugh at my future self now, looking forward.

After all, *I* awakened too.

The cold silence of Giovel's walk didn't help. Despite every effort of his mind to turn somewhere else, he found himself studying the awakenings list again the next morning. Now he just sat by Iremni's mirror pond in their Sanctuary instead of outside Varan's room. Let Adni guard her himself, he thought. I probably couldn't stop a witch from seizing her now. I might even welcome one who came.

Inorovel walked in every few hours to ask if he needed more soup, something to drink. Talking about something while his mind said other words. She must have been angry with him for being so silent. He couldn't bear to look at her now, though. Where she'd once been his reminder of Iremni's beauty and goodness, now he was afraid it would be different. Afraid he'd look at his daughter and see a lying vulture instead.

How long did Iremni hide it, he asked for the hundredth time. Just weeks? They say proximity to another awakening might cause one, and she held my hand a thousand times as I faced my own. Or was it months? Or maybe our whole married life? She concealed it so well.

Giovel wished to the stars he could ask her, no matter how cheated he felt now. Or how I've cheated myself, he thought bitterly. I promised to hold you close when you needed me. Instead, I built a wall with no gate and never once thought to tell you how to clamber over it. Can't unbuild that now.

There was nothing in the awakenings list but more questions. Who else's husband or wife is alone without knowing it? After staring at it almost two days, Giovel dropped the parchment in the mirror pond and tried walking again.

When walking failed to bring him any calm, he sat outside and built glyphs as Hirnu had told him to practice. This almost brought some measure of peace since it almost brought control. Then he miscast a Rod and hit himself hard in the shin, so he abandoned practice and tried sleeping again.

More questions from Inorovel. You haven't eaten anything, she said. Do you need a healer? He carefully avoided looking in her direction or answering her a word. Messengers came next. Where is the Witherclaw? Why didn't you come to the Candlespire? Giovel met them with silence too, and after a few minutes they always went away. Before he knew it, he'd come to the realization that even hunting the witches felt empty now. Their crimes felt shallow in comparison to Iremni's.

Giovel tore down the wall of everything he recalled, hoping to see which stones he couldn't push away. There were patches of grass between those rocks if he looked far enough back. Moments before Inorovel was born, when Iremni smiled with so much fire it must have been real. Yes, she had to have loved him, hadn't she? That was a stone he could stand on.

She had love in her, yes, but was it for you? Or did she only love Yulen?

Giovel would have said it was a fool's question before. Now he didn't know if there was such a thing as foolishness. Doesn't it defeat the term itself if we're *all* fools? And he'd never felt so welcomed in the number of fools as now.

He wasn't sure how many hours or days had passed when he walked into his study and smashed his sand tablet over his chair. He struck it again and again, trying to turn the frame itself into dust like the clumps of magnetic sand that dropped from its breaks. Then he seized a pile of books and hurled them into the fire. Notes next, notes from Order business, notes on the list he'd dropped days before, it was all the same. Into the fire because they were more useful as heat than as pretended wisdom.

He woke up. He smelled like piss and his legs were cold. Inorovel knelt at his side, crying.

He shouted something and pulled his sword out, not to point at her but to hack at the table. There was no more wood in the house because he hadn't chopped any for days and the winter was cold. The table could burn, though, if he chopped it small enough. So he swung and swung, finally denting enough to snap one leg off. The rest toppled into him and he cried out, trapped under it for a moment before he heaved and pushed himself free.

Inorovel was gone from the room. Maybe she'd truly left. Good for her.

Giovel threw the broken table leg onto the fire, curled up beside it, wept to himself, and slept again.

Even in his sleep there were questions.

CALCULATIONS

There are some things we have to do for ourselves, not because other people won't try to help, but because sometimes they simply can't.
    —The Witherclaw Witch; letter to Inivar and Sil.

VARAN DECIDED NOT to leave Divnum too quickly when she first ran away from the Candlespire. Word would get around that the Order was looking for her, and there were only so many ways in and out of Divnum's walls. Varan covered her hair with one of the coppery wraps the Sun Sept wore, hoping it was bright enough to make her eyes look like everyone else's. Then she sold the Witherclaw dresses Ralden had gifted her to a black-market clothier—earning what she could only assume was an unfairly low number of spans—and took a room at an inn near the Citadel. Right where Candles and Lances would be most in force. Where they'd last think to look, with any luck.

It would mean a few days shut in, just to be safe, but that would also give her time to gather her thoughts on how to find the witches.

Although she had no shortage of ideas, two things were clear to Varan. First, she'd need help from *someone*. Second, she'd need to try things the Divine hadn't or couldn't. After all, they'd been searching for months, searching diligently. She'd seen Elínla and her Grays at it and heard Giovel discuss a score of plans and schemes to help. If none of those had worked, Varan would need a different kind of plan. So she sat in a tiny room with a frosted slit of a window no wider than her face and used her time in hiding to prepare.

She had charcoal, pen and ink, three different maps of the city she'd carried almost since arriving, and copies of every note Giovel had foolishly left in her Candlespire guestroom. It had been so easy to replicate his documents the night she gathered her things and left. Giovel wasn't even there to pretend to watch her.

Thanks to Giovel's negligence, Varan's stack of papers included patrol charts from Elínla, daily reports from Candles hunting for the witches, and, most interestingly, a convoluted chart of where and when spiritings had occurred across the past year. When pieced together, Varan wagered she could at least find a few clear patterns in where the witches were or were not active.

With her mess of intelligence spread out across her bed, Varan began to notate.

Spiriting here. Guard station there. An awakening's home. Grays watching here. Another spiriting. Another patrol. Another awakening's tiny home. The site of a raid by the Grays. The Lance's Belnum garrison. One more spiriting yet.

Almost none of it was mapped out for her. Most was written in instructional language, probably created for someone who knew each district of Foneth as well as their own Sanctuary. Reading the Medín reports was tortuously difficult for Varan, especially since most used terms and descriptions she hadn't learned in conversation. Varan also had to pause often to review letters that weren't marked clearly. As a result, it took almost three full days to transfer the information from the written reports onto her maps of Foneth.

Would three days in hiding be enough to loosen any hunt for her? She didn't know. At least the Order had more important worries about where to devote their time and resources. With that small comfort, Varan slipped out of the inn to find an ally.

Her first thoughts had been of Kirida, Uri, and Nomis, of course, but she loathed the idea of bringing any new trouble to them on her own behalf. As far as she could tell, that meant she had to go to Olinos Vlada instead.

Finding his home wasn't particularly hard, because finding *him* was so easy. Varan simply asked a street guard which Banner Captain was in charge, demanding an audience with Olinos. The flustered Candle let on that Olinos's Banner covered south Divnum, and Varan left, changed her clothes to be sure no one remembered her, and went to the Divnum's southern barracks to wait. She spotted Olinos inspecting something by the walls before the day was over and followed him to his house that night.

It was a large house for just one person, built of earth-colored stone with a high-peaked roof over it. Varan clapped outside the door and waited for a response.

Olinos's eyes widened as soon as he opened the door. "Varan?"

"Hello, Olinos," she said. "I'm cold. May I come inside?"

She'd caught him completely off guard. Olinos stammered something she couldn't understand then stepped out past her, looking around as if he was afraid she'd be seen. It was dark out now, and his house stood apart from the others in the west end of Foneth.

"What are you doing here?" he asked. "The Grays and Divine are looking everywhere for you."

"May I come inside?" she repeated. "No one followed me here."

More mumbles. Then Olinos sighed and pulled the door wide for her, still glancing around as if he expected to see Giovel or another mage watching from behind the leafless trees.

His door opened right into the Sanctuary, a tall, tiered room with five little pools of clear water feeding one another highest to lowest. Water-smoothed stones surrounded the pools for a pace or so, some with soft blue moss and wet earth still on them, even in the winter.

"Why are you hiding from the Order?" Olinos asked as he shut the door behind him. "There are all kinds of rumors that the witches are looking for you too. Especially after what happened a few months ago."

"The Order can't find the witches," Varan said simply.

"No one can find them yet. The arms of the Optacracy have been searching for almost a year and we're no closer now than we were when we started."

"But they know you're looking for them."

Olinos's eyes widened a little more. After a silent moment he said, "Maybe you should come sit down."

"We can talk here."

"Ah. Of course. I can get you something warm to drink, though?"

"No." Especially not if he was afraid to be seen with her. "I've been gathering information. I think I need a little more. Can you help me?"

"Don't tell me you think *you* can find them," Olinos said. "Varan, we've tried everything you can imagine. Do you really think we haven't gone witch-hunting outside of uniform before?"

"I haven't even said what information I need."

"And I don't need to know that. Whatever it is, I can't help you. I should probably turn you in just for coming here."

"Look at this first," Varan said, pulling out her set of maps. She unfolded the largest one on which she'd marked everything she could deduce from Elínla's written reports and Giovel's erratic notes.

The map made Olinos's eyes widen. He looked over it, turning to follow the many lines, shapes, and colors she'd used. She had a rich red for locations of spiritings and a midnight blue for their points of origin—in cases where the Divine knew them, anyway; nearly a quarter of the spiritings noted had been killed before the Order knew a thing about them, and half of those had never even been identified. The map also showed Elínla's latest information on Candle and Lance patrol routes, watch stations for the Grays, locations raided in the hunt for the witches' bolt holes, and the home of every spiriting left on Giovel's list.

"Where did you get this?" Olinos asked. "Varan, did you ... did you *steal* this from the Candlespire?" More mumbles, more words she didn't know. "Is this why they're looking for you?"

Varan withdrew her map and folded it halfway to cover everything significant. "I made it myself. Will you help me finish it?"

He ran a hand through his hair, but Varan could see schemes forming behind his eyes now. She knew from more than just how people talked that Olinos was climbing through the ranks, always watching for occasions to prove his mettle. And she presented one. On one hand he could help her piece things together to find the witches. And if not, he could try bringing her back to the Order himself.

The real question was not whether he'd try to help but whether he could stop her from leaving when she wanted to.

"Why did you come to me?" Olinos asked.

"I told you. I need information. I can't say what information unless you promise you'll help me."

He breathed out as if fighting down his temper. "I can't do that without you trusting me enough to tell me more. Please, be understanding here. I have my duties to the Candleguard to consider."

Of course. Duty and reputation. She did understand.

"I do want to help you," he said a moment later.

He almost looked as if he meant it. There was something else in his eyes with the devious workings of his mind. Maybe it was regret? Or actual concern? Maybe his confessed feelings for her now months before were still there, real enough to stick even when she'd refused his interest. She didn't know how they could be, given how little he truly knew her.

And I can't count on it, she told herself, no matter what he might say or seem to mean.

"If you can't help me, I'll leave," she announced and turned to go.

"Wait, wait. Just give me some clue of what you even need, Varan. Please."

"Give me your word you won't tell anyone else what I'm asking."

"Fine. I swear I won't tell anyone what you're looking for."

She'd left an opening on purpose, though, for him to promise not to reveal their meeting. He hadn't given that promise. Perhaps she'd made a mistake even trying to come here. But who else could help her now?

"If we do find the witches, I'll let you take whatever praise for it you want," she said slowly.

He had the presence of mind to look stunned at least. "This isn't about who gets the glory. These witches are heartless murderers who endanger the whole city. They killed Dlenar Tovóm, and they'd probably kill every member of the Order if they could."

"You could be the one who finds them, if you help me."

He paused longer this time before speaking. Once again there was that strange look in his eyes, almost sincere, almost selfless. Perhaps even strong enough to overpower whatever lust for power he'd nurtured so long already.

"Show me the map again and I'll try to help you with it."

He pulled a small table into the Sanctuary, offering Varan a stool beside it as he took one himself. Varan chose to stand, keeping the table between him and herself on the side nearest his doorway.

"There are patterns," Varan said, pointing from spiriting to spiriting to awakenings and patrol routes. "All the spiritings are in Belnum and North Hold."

"Not all. Here's one that appeared in Divnum," Olinos said. "Though I can't see where this one came from."

"That one's me." And nothing about her own spiriting seemed to be ordinary, since every other known spiriting came from somewhere on the maps at hand and usually close by.

"Maybe they're trying to create a false pattern," Olinos said. "Hide themselves by bringing spiritings to other places. They could be hiding in Divnum itself, right under our watch."

Just like I have, Varan thought with a lurch in her stomach. "They always get to the spiritings quickly. Elínla says they can't control where the spiritings arrive exactly, but they're always nearby."

Olinos nodded, eyes moving across the map once more. "So either they have hideaways near all of these places, they're very good at spreading out and blending in, or they're deliberately keeping the spiritings to Belnum and North Hold. Staying farther from the Order's seat of power would make sense."

"But they could be hiding somewhere else," Varan said, now pointing to Tovómil, the other estates, and Divnum itself again. "They attacked all over Divnum on Perception Day. All at once."

"There are plenty of other blind spots, though. Half of Belnum's still unmarked, if you divide your map up. And plenty of these empty patches would be easy places to hide a few witches."

"That's why I need to know patrol routes."

"You've got patrol routes marked on here, haven't you?"

"Those are old. I know your Candles always make new patrols after a spiriting. I need to know those patrols before the spiritings happen."

"That's not going to be easy information to get, Varan. And even if I could get it, I can't just ink it all onto your maps." Olinos looked up, eyes softening. "This is all secret information, really. And even if I could show you every patrol for the Candles, the Lances have some too, and the Grays."

And not even that intelligence would show where the witches truly were, Varan knew. Just a few less places they were likely to hide. If they hid *anywhere* more than once to begin with.

"Help me find them," Varan said.

"You make this sound like some child's game," Olinos replied, sighing and leaning forward over his little table. "Fine. There's one more pattern you haven't mentioned. You say these patrols covering sites of spiritings are all new since those spiritings occurred?"

Varan nodded. "They added these after each spiriting on the map."

"That tells me the witches are spiriting people into places *without* patrols. Even if they can't control it completely, they clearly can control some of the process, *and* they know enough about patrol patterns to avoid them."

"So they plan the spiritings carefully," Varan said.

"Clearly. But Candles all across Foneth shift their patrol routes every few days at most, which means the witches can't just sit and watch and anticipate where Candles will be. They almost definitely know, in advance, where each patrol will be sent."

A wave of cold seemed to pulse through Varan. She'd thought the witches must have friends in the Candleguard, or in the Optacracy at the very least, feeding them key information to keep their spiritings from the Candles' immediate reach. Olinos's words convinced her now.

"Here's another pattern," Olinos added. "The spiritings have accelerated the last few months, maybe just since their attack on Perception Day."

"Lots of people know that."

"True, but the pattern doesn't stop there. Most of these new spiritings are targeting awakenings specifically. Your older spiritings here didn't show that."

Varan had noticed it as well, though she hadn't wanted to consider it seriously. Did it mean the witches *only* summoned awakened mages to them? Did it mean they knew every awakening the Order did, maybe even more? And what had changed after Perception Day to prompt their acceleration?

"One last pattern," Olinos went on. "Even if the spiritings appear mostly in Belnum and North Hold, they're coming *from* all over. Even outside Foneth itself. There's no place out of the witches' reach, it would seem."

And that too Varan had known already, because even *she* was in their reach. She lived so far away no map showed any point she knew, so distant that Yulen was invisible in her sky—and in every sky she'd ever heard of. But the witches could reach even there.

And now I need them to get myself back.

Olinos stood, turning the map around a few different ways as if looking for other clues not visible so easily. After a moment he pushed it back toward Varan with a grunt.

"That's all I can say clearly. Maybe a logistician would see something else, though. I can take you to one I trust."

Varan began rolling the map to store in her coat again. "No one else can know about this."

"Be reasonable. We would have the witches licking mud off our walls by now if finding them was as simple as looking at a map and finding empty spots. And besides, even if I could show you where they were, I couldn't move on them without communicating with the Order, and I can't do that without telling them you came to me."

So his help extended to pointing at the map and confirming what she'd already considered. No farther.

"I'm sorry," Olinos mumbled.

Varan had heard enough. She walked back toward the door.

Olinos reached for her arm, his grip tightening on her wrist. "Wait."

No. No more waiting, no more playing prisoner when she should be getting home. Varan spun her free hand and Quickened a reaction between Olinos's tongue and his pharynx. He gagged, released her, and threw up, reaching for his throat. It might leave him coughing for hours. Maybe even too hurt to speak for a few days. Varan didn't really care.

She was gone before Olinos could recover himself enough even to follow her to the door.

EMPTY

Recia was right when she said having my own children would turn my mind over on itself. Being away from them feels like just as big a change.
—The Witherclaw Witch; letter to Golkorun.

THE LANCES' NEW efforts to consolidate Foneth made unskilled laborers like Etelier highly useful all of a sudden. Within the first month of work, Etelier helped dig trenches to drain Lilywater Lake, fell trees along Rich Woman's Hill, and loot empty houses by what was once the Great Holderim Market. His wages were better now than when he'd worked in Tovómil, and being in the Optacracy's employ meant he could only work so many hours without breaks for food or rest, so his days were shorter too.

Despite little encouragement from Claravena and the others, Etelier used his new free time to search the last few places he could imagine the Divine had hidden their library. Time was running out, to be sure. Everyone knew the Order had opposed the Lances' plans to shrink Foneth. People assumed it was because of the costs or the spiritual implications of cutting so many Sanctuaries from the city. Etelier saw more likely reasons, too: That a consolidated city would make the Order's brutality more visible, forcing them to bend more to the Candles and the Lances alike; that mass relocations would make it easier for awakenings and other enemies of the Order to vanish from their sights and to hide in the throngs of other citizens; that removal of Sanctuaries so long protected by the Optacracy would likely force the Order to move many secrets of their own. Etelier was willing to bet his raised wages that their library and Vindil's ruins were among these secrets.

Still, his own efforts ended up being halfhearted at best. The past six months or so had stifled his faith that he'd find anything to heal Mota. It was as Pramél had told him so many times. A fruitless hunt. He supposed his own ruined ear should motivate him all the more. After all, he had two people to care about healing now. But if anything, Mota's terror at his new scars sapped the last conviction he had for the hunt. Now it was just a means to stave Claravena's criticisms away.

He began abandoning his search earlier after the work day, returning home sooner to try playing with Mota or talking with Pramél about something other than the Divine. Never mind that it had only been a year and a month since his search really began. The icy distance between him and his family had stretched much wider than he'd ever thought it could grow.

Bit by bit he tried to thaw that cold gulf.

He skipped meetings to fetch things for Pramél. He took Mota to the tranquil, reserved celebrations of Deepwinter Day. Instead of paying rats to look for hideaways, Etelier entrusted his increased wages to Pramél; he knew she'd been saving for something for months as it was. A few weeks later Etelier realized that he hadn't drawn a glyph since he faced the Witherclaw. It should bother him, shouldn't it? He should have been practicing his spellbuilding as Wurelna coached him to do. The thing was, he didn't miss it.

More hours at home. Fewer hours awake. The deep cough that had rattled his ribs for two months finally broke. The cloudy shadows beneath his eyes receded. The snapping shutter Pramél had pestered him about got fixed.

It only took a few weeks of change. Somewhere in those weeks Etelier came to a memory, a hint of what his mind and body and home could feel like now, so much like how he'd lived months before. It was a quality of stillness he'd only known when there was no heavy cowl from Mota's sickness or his own awakening. Somehow he'd never believed any semblance of calm or harmony would return, even in the slow, raw, stitched-up way he now experienced it. But it was *peace* of a sort, and any sort felt new to him now.

Etelier doubted it could stay forever. Claravena would have more duties for him soon. She was working everyone in the Starlit Order like draft horses, pushing them to their limits. Spirit another ten people. Reveal another three spying Grays. Spread rumors about another illegal intersection of power between the Lawrits and the Order or the Candles and the Tovómil. While Etelier paused to breathe, she was willing to try any road, regardless of the risks or their efforts' empty returns.

She'll have to wait, Etelier thought. I'm tired from a day spent knocking down walls of abandoned homes beside the Mushroom Shroud. I want another taste of calm before the witchery resumes.

Rather than search or scheme or hunt, he headed home to eat before reporting to Claravena. He almost laughed when he realized how fully he and she had traded places.

When Etelier arrived, he found his house dark and cold inside. No fire. No lamp in the Sanctuary. His bad ear made it hard to tell, but he thought the house was quieter than normal too.

"Mota? Pramél?"

No answers he could hear. As quick as that, his peace was gone.

He ran in, mind flying through all that might have happened during just that one day of work. The Order could have come, could have finally tracked him here. He'd been working for the stars-damned Lances for two months now, hadn't he? He'd never really thought they could identify him that way, but what if they had?

Mota's room was empty. Her bed was stripped of everything but the tattered mattress Pramél's mother had given them when she was old enough to sleep on her own. Her little clothes box was nearly bare too, as if someone had plundered the entire house and stolen her away. Etelier swore and ran into the next door. His own room was less bare, but Pramél's things were almost all gone as well.

Then it came to him. The house hadn't been robbed, his family taken. It had been emptied systematically. Door locked. Lanterns dimmed purposefully.

They'd left. Pramél and Mota had walked away while he was breaking his back to bring home rice and grain and onions.

He supposed he should have known they would.

A cursory search of the little kitchen made him sure. Nothing else was gone except a few dried ingredients from the tiny larder, and though there was no note to tell him what had happened, no true indicator, the house had a tidiness that felt like Pramél herself. For the first time in months, Etelier ached not for his daughter, not for his own grief, but for his wife's. Months too late, then.

I tried, Pramél. At least, I *began* to try. Couldn't you have given me another few weeks to mend what I've been neglecting?

The thing was, he couldn't even feel surprised now. He'd gone mad with sorrow since Mota's sickness and loss of hearing. Withdrawn himself from any deep connection with anyone—even his wife. Buried himself in the work of the witches when he should have been there beside Pramél instead.

But I never even thought about it. I just pushed ahead on my own. And now I'm *truly* on my own. I worked so hard to find a salve for cuts and sicknesses that I forgot there are other wounds too, ones that can't be tended with spells or medicines.

It was only an hour past dusk. Etelier looked out at the streets and thought long and hard about setting out again, trying to follow his wife and child. He was sure he could find them. He knew more than forty different informants in Belnum alone, plus the many who watched comings and goings in the outer districts of Foneth. Not to mention that he knew the streets themselves almost as well as anyone.

He stared out the open doorway for a long time, running plans and ideas through his mind.

What good would following do, though? Because even if I find them, I don't know how to change anything. Maybe I thought I did in these last few weeks—maybe I found how to change things for *me*. I suppose my changes didn't work for them the way I'd thought they should.

So he didn't follow. He just removed his boots, started a new fire, and cooked a pan of tubers and spices. He didn't taste much, didn't hear much, didn't care much at the moment because the emptiness in his home sapped his will completely.

Maybe it wasn't all that new anymore. Maybe home had been empty for a long time.

AWAKE

Sometimes the people who seem like strangers are the people who are kindest to us.
—The Witherclaw Witch; letter to Inivar and Sil.

MORE DAYS MUST have passed, because Giovel found the food in his larder going bad. He went out every now and then to collect wood from the shed once he realized the table wasn't going to cut much more, but that too was running low. Other than those markers, he wasn't sure how to tell what day it was, how long he'd stayed inside alone. The brief, white days of snow all looked the same. Giovel didn't even have Inorovel there any more to say good night and remind him to try sleeping. All the better for her, though. It was safer not to be near people who could kill you with an unintended glyph.

Adni came several times. He was sharp and demeaning during his first attempt, but all he did was demand Giovel get hold of himself. Then he left. The next few times, Adni was soft-spoken, almost nervous about something. Distracted too, perhaps as much as Giovel was. He never stayed long. Just mumbled things about more spiritings and asked Giovel to report to the Candlespire that afternoon. Giovel never did.

Elínla came too, and Giovel wondered if Inorovel might have sent for her or other members of the Order. She was cold as the snow piling outside. She said little, just glowered and demanded explanations, then left again as quickly as she'd arrived. After a few such visits she began reasoning more, explaining all the ways in which the Order needed Giovel's help: Searching for the Witherclaw, who'd apparently vanished a week before; helping her try to protect more of the endangered awakenings; even helping coordinate with the Candleguard as they made a newly concerted hunt for the witches' hideaway. Giovel rejected every argument she made without a thought. She came again, two days later, with some story about Optate Olura threatening the very existence of the Order because they were performing so poorly. Giovel missed most of what she'd said, and she left soon afterward.

Even Ralden came once, carried in by four of her guild workers as if she were a queen. Where Elínla had tried reason, Ralden tried shame, insulting Giovel in the very ways Adni once had. Giovel didn't care, and Ralden gave up even more easily than Adni had.

He wondered idly if Sur would come, hoping so in a way, but his next visitor was Kanis, the new mage. He looked incredibly young, more so in the light of day than he had when Adni burst into his home and beat him. Seemed calm and confident too. The very image of what a member of the Optate's Order of Divine Mages should be. Only when Giovel refused to converse did Kanis lose any semblance of control.

"I know the witches spirited your wife," he said coldly. "'Aren't you going to find them and make them pay for that? Or at least make sure they don't do the same to anyone else?"

Giovel sat in a corner by the fire. "Not anymore," he said.

"This is pathetic. The whole city knows you hate them for what they did!"

Ah, but did the whole city know he hated Iremni's long deception just as much, even as he loved her and ached to see her once again? Giovel doubted it.

Others came too. Frenico, one of the Cloudblades Giovel had served alongside two years before, arrived and tried to persuade him to leave the Order and rejoin the Candles. Little chance of that. The Optate rarely let anyone leave the Order once they joined. Other Candles came too, though. Birenlu came to demand the favors Giovel had promised. She seemed for once not to have heard what was happening, not to know Giovel was useless now. Either that or she just pretended to try to make him at ease. She was too smart for Giovel to be sure.

Giovel sometimes wished Inorovel would visit, just once, to tell him where she was staying. He wasn't worried about her, he realized. He simply thought about it with an idle curiosity, like he sometimes wondered what Boulder was thinking during a ride or where Zuris Medín would destroy next. Inorovel didn't come, though.

Hirnu appeared last of the Order. She didn't clap outside, didn't call for him. He just found her sitting in the Sanctuary one morning, looking at the mirror pond. She nodded when Giovel looked her way and she said nothing. So he walked by to get more wood and ignored her again on his way back.

She sat there all day, as quietly as he sat in his study and stared out the window.

When the sky darkened outside, Giovel heard sounds from the kitchen. Apparently Hirnu was doing his housework now, cleaning dishes left scattered on the floor, throwing out rotted peppers and bread as hard as iron, scrubbing spills and abandoned meals Giovel had left wherever he wanted in the past days or weeks. She still said nothing. Just cleaned.

"This isn't your house," Giovel called from the doorway to his study. "Leave everything alone."

"I'm beginning to think it's not your house either," she called back.

"What's that supposed to mean?"

Giovel didn't wait for an answer, though. He went upstairs to try to sleep. See if her patience extended into the night, if she'd wait there for him in the dark.

He didn't sleep long. Maybe an hour or two he guessed based on the sky outside. Then he walked downstairs to find something to drink. Hirnu was still there, still cleaning. She'd moved on to the hearth in the Sanctuary now, scraping out heaps of ashes to throw in the gardens.

"Did Adni send you here?" Giovel asked.

"No one sent me. I came on my own."

"Then you can leave on your own too."

"I will, soon enough," Hirnu said. "But I'll be back by dawn."

"You're supposed to be helping the Grays and Elínla."

"Right now the Order's too weak to properly punish you for ignoring orders. Why would they punish me either?"

Giovel grunted and walked upstairs again. He stayed in the slim stairwell until he heard the front door squeak open and click closed.

True to her word, Hirnu was back again the next morning. Giovel woke to the smell of fresh bread. She must have been baking for hours already. She had nuts and cream, a spiced broth of some kind, butter, honey, hot grain mash, enough food for five people. She didn't offer it to Giovel, though. She just finished preparing it and then began eating herself as if it was her own home. Giovel grabbed some to spite her and took it into his study.

He found a stack of books there, books that weren't his. He'd burned all of his, he recalled now, when he'd run out of firewood. These ones looked like volumes he'd never read. *A History of the Candlespire, Order and Disorder, Optacracy and Yulen*. All books about the Divine and their place in the way of things. So maybe Hirnu's methods were no subtler than Ralden's had been. Giovel ignored them and returned to his window to watch the snow.

His mind wandered to Hirnu every few minutes, though. How dare she invade his home like this, make herself welcome. He only had two reasons he didn't try throwing her out himself. First, because that was obviously what she wanted—to get some sort of response from him. And second, because he realized he was still afraid of her.

Giovel only left his study a few times that day. Hirnu always sat in the Sanctuary, reading or drawing the same glyph on her sand tablet over and over again. Late in the afternoon it sounded as if she'd cleaned a few more things, some upstairs as well. Then she brought in more wood from outside and called goodnight.

"There's fresh rice in your kitchen, Giovel," she added.

He waited until she left before eating it. He spilled half on the floor and left it there while he went back to his window.

Hirnu came four, five, maybe eight days without a break in her rhythm. She didn't speak much. Just read, drew glyphs, made food, dressed the fire. On the third day she said almost absentmindedly that Inorovel was staying with her niece Aried. Then she was quiet again. Giovel matched her silence with his own, though he found it harder and harder not to shout for her to leave.

Home felt different with someone else watching. No matter how little judgment Hirnu actually spoke, Giovel found himself slowly losing his will to argue, losing his fuel to leave a mess for her to clean when he went off alone. He even sat with her sometimes, staring at the mirror pond or watching her draw glyphs again and again on her tablet. His mind wandered to Iremni every day, every hour, sometimes every few waking minutes. But his wanderings were different now. They'd first left him feeling as if he were swimming in a black current on a starless night, with only Yulen glimmering for him to follow. Now it was more like struggling through an overgrown forest, with flashes of sunlight breaking through the leaves, vines, and brambles every score of steps he advanced.

One morning he found himself awake before Hirnu had arrived, and he prepared food for himself. And then he found his mind turning to Inorovel voluntarily, wondering with worry, not just questions, as to how she must feel today and all the dark days since he'd followed the awakenings list home.

She, at least, could feel just like I do, he thought. She at least could share this with me, if I let her.

When Hirnu arrived, Giovel offered her the food he'd made and cleared the dishes as soon as she was done eating. When he was finished, he said, "I think I understand why you of all the Order were entrusted with studying Yulena. Thank you for waiting with me."

Hirnu gave a tiny nod. She walked from the kitchen back into the Sanctuary, taking one of her usual spots beside the mirror pond. Giovel sat across from her, trying to think what else he could say, knowing he needed to say more.

In the end, all he thought to mumble was, "I'm sorry. I hate how I've acted these past . . . however many days."

Another nod. Then, "There are things we all hate about ourselves, aren't there? Did you know my son was a witch too?"

"No—I didn't know that," Giovel said. She'd spoken with such unassuming certainty, as if Iremni's secret awakening and witchcraft itself were one and the same. And maybe they were, for all it mattered.

"It was before your time in the Order," Hirnu said. "It felt early in mine, though the deaths of other members had already pushed myself and Adni to seniority. Adni ordered Suresni to hunt him, to bring him in. I suppose he thought it would be more merciful to have someone else do it."

". . . What happened?"

"I asked Suresni to defer to me. Not so Joruni could escape—my son. So I could hunt him myself and come face to face with him."

Giovel had never heard any of this. He'd never even known Hirnu had family. "Why?"

"I wanted to see what Joruni would do once I knew his secret. He'd hidden Yulena his whole life as far as I knew, and I wanted to find out for sure. In the end, he tried to kill me, so I killed him first."

She stopped, turning to look Giovel right in the eyes. He thought that might be the first time she'd ever looked at him so deliberately, and he found himself mesmerized.

"That's what I hate about myself," she said.

A moment later Hirnu stood, took her snow cowl from the wall, and left wordlessly. Giovel stayed rooted where she'd left him.

What would he have done if Adni asked *him* to hunt Iremni, or if he'd mustered the courage to beg the assignment from someone else instead?

It sounded far beyond his strength. There was no anger in him hot enough to push him after Iremni, knowing what she was. Not even his own self-loathing felt deep enough to make him hurt her as she'd hurt him already, perhaps because it would have been more than just Iremni who felt the weight of any harm he could have done her.

She was part of me. *Is* part still. And Inorovel is part of her too, not to mention part of me. I would have to push the lance through all of us at once to hunt her, and that wound would spill onto others too, people like Hirnu and Ralden and Uri and Birenlu and Frenico and Zuris and on and on and on. Maybe all wounds are like that—cutting openings into everyone connected close or far.

The only thing Giovel felt sure of was that he was *awake* after a paralyzing sleep. Somehow Hirnu's quiet, non-condemning companionship had helped spark a candle to life in the cold fog. It didn't dispel any betrayal. For all Giovel knew, it hadn't even brought him warmth. Just enough flickering direction for him to see a few steps forward and behind.

As he watched Hirnu go, he found there was some piece missing from her words; there usually was when she spoke. She'd never said *why* her son turned on her rather than certifying his awakening, *why* he'd given himself to spellbuilding, *why* anything. Maybe she simply didn't know. Or maybe to her, as to so many, awakening and being a witch were one and the same. It meant a life subjected to the Order in any case, didn't it? If you awakened and certified, you'd be watched carefully until you were recruited—or died. If you went witch and used Yulena, you'd spend your life locked away instead. Little wonder anyone tried to hide their awakening to power.

Riddles and guesswork and questions as to what was in another's mind. Giovel supposed he didn't truly know anything of what Iremni had gone through except in awakening. But the witches who spirited her would know.

Perhaps only they can give the answers I need now.

Giovel climbed his stairs to change. It seemed Hirnu had washed his clothes sometime this week. He felt a wave of shame and gratitude all at once, wondering what had brought her to do it. Was it care for him? Or just longing for her son? He vowed to find a way to thank her, and two thoughts came immediately as he donned his Order uniform.

First, he'd find the witches plaguing Foneth now. There was nothing that could bring Joruni back, or Iremni, but those witches must have families too, mothers like Hirnu or spouses like Giovel. He'd do it for them. It might let them find some sort of end to the hell Yulena had handed them.

Second, he vowed for her own sake that he would not be like Hirnu hunting her own blood, no matter what it cost him in his search for answers. The haze was too thick to find his way out again. Too heavy to lift off if he fell under it once more.

So for your sake, Hirnu, I'll *stay* awake this time.

DEPOSITION

 —The Witherclaw Witch; letter to Golkorun.

THE FIRST THING Giovel did was send a message to Inorovel. He was afraid to see her face, but it didn't take half a moment's thought to be sure she was the one he'd wronged most in his weeks of collapse.

The next thing he did was report to the Candlespire.

A score of Candleguard and Grays watched him walk through the main doorway, across the Sanctuary, and upstairs toward the Order's council chamber. Most tried to look away, though a few mumbled greetings as if they weren't sure whether to congratulate him or laugh. He'd lost weight and muscle. He'd cut himself shaving this morning and he'd wrapped it poorly in his hurry to recover lost time. The many sets of eyes behind him felt heavy enough to make him break into a run on the stairs, but he was too weak to run long, so he forced himself to keep an even rhythm.

He'd been slow to come into his own before. He could do it again.

He was the second to arrive for the morning meeting. Only Elínla was there already, pacing nervously with her back to the door.

"Is this still the normal time?" Giovel asked as he took a seat.

Elínla stopped mid-step. Her mouth hung slightly open a moment before she managed to click her teeth together. "Just what the hell are you doing here?"

It took an internal breath of air not to recoil. "I'm here to report."

"And what makes you think you can walk in and pick things up after leaving us short-handed—not to mention scared you'd turned witch on us—for the last four weeks?"

Four weeks? It couldn't have been that long.

"Did you really think I'd decided to join the witches?" Giovel asked.

"We didn't know what to think!" Elínla said, now pacing rapidly around the table again. "You treated us all like crows when we came to check on you."

"I'm not here to make excuses for myself."

"You hypocrite. I've noticed that when you mumble about not making excuses what you really mean is you're not willing to make a damn apology."

Steady. He'd known this was coming. And Elínla's words gave Giovel real pause. ". . . Maybe you're right. I didn't realize that before. And I *am* sorry."

"I don't have to believe a word you say now. You should haul yourself out of here before the rest of the Order arrives. You've undercut us more than you could know."

Giovel avoided her gaze, feeling blood rise in his neck and warm his face. What to say, though? Elínla was right. He *had* been missing when the Order needed his help. And she was right about his words too, that he'd somehow been framing his lack of excuses as an excuse in itself at times when he went wrong.

So I was a fool even before these last four weeks, he thought.

Kanis walked in before Giovel thought of anything to say. Like Elínla he looked shocked, though he regained himself quickly and offered a slight bow. "Lord Giovel."

"Don't Lord Giovel this pile of frass," Elínla said.

Hirnu walked in next, bowing to each in turn. "Lord Kanis. Lady Elínla. Lord Giovel."

"Did he tell you he was coming today?" Elínla demanded. "I know you went to his house recently."

Hirnu took her chair without meeting Elínla's eyes, or anyone else's. "It's not my place to assume anyone will attend our meetings."

"How is Ralden?" Giovel asked.

"On the mend, but still mostly bedridden," Kanis said.

"And Sur?"

"Don't tell him anything!" Elínla snapped. "As far as we know, Giovel's just here to spy and sell whatever information we share. He can go back and buy more beer for his wallow hole for all I care."

"Who's here to buy beer?" Adni asked, walking in just then.

He looked the most surprised of all when Giovel turned toward him. His eyes narrowed and one corner of his mouth curled like a caterpillar trying to climb a tree. Then he looked as if he might be sick.

"I believe we're all present now," Hirnu said.

Giovel took a long breath. "Then may I speak for a moment?"

Elínla swore and took her seat again, turning so she faced the wall. Adni just stood still as a mountain in the doorway.

"It won't take long," Giovel added.

Adni gave a sort of laugh, like a child's squeal coming from a grown man's voice. He walked slowly to his own seat near the north-facing window. "I'm of half a mind to depose you from the Order, Giovel."

It took all his strength not to say that only the Optate could do that. Instead Giovel said, "I understand. This is why I'd like to speak, just briefly, before the rest of the meeting is underway."

"So speak. But be quick. The rest of us are fighting a pair of wars."

And I could have been with you, Giovel thought.

He stood and opened his mouth.

"I can't take back the weeks I've wasted, and I am sincerely thankful each of you came to see me during this time. All I can say is that I'm sorry for failing in my responsibilities." He paused, unsure what else even to add. He was so unused to saying anything about himself. It was hard to be sure where to step, when to stop. The words that came next were not the apology he'd meant to give now. "Did any of you know Iremni had awakened?"

Silence across the table. Kanis just frowned, while Elínla looked shocked all over again. Hirnu *had* known, as she'd said already. Adni, though. Adni gave a small nod.

"I knew."

"Why didn't you tell me when I joined the Order?"

"You should ask why *she* didn't tell you," Adni said.

"I'm asking why you didn't."

Now the others' eyes were on Adni. Even Hirnu seemed to be looking in his direction.

Adni lifted his shoulders an inch. "I don't know, actually. Maybe it's because I've never liked you, or maybe I just felt sorry for you."

"...That's it?"

"Yes, that's it. Do you want me to guess about a choice I made almost a year-and-a-half ago? I don't have an answer for that."

Not that Adni intended to wait for her power to develop, bring her into the Grays? Not that he meant to situate Giovel for failure with a possible witch in his own home? Giovel wanted to burn with anger, to carve a glyph on the table and strike Adni with it in front of everyone. But there was no anger left, not even for this. And, oddly enough, he found himself believing Adni, so he just went on with his apology.

"*I* didn't know she'd awakened. Not until I started helping Elínla safeguard the spiritings on your list. I know this shouldn't have kept me from my duties in the Order, especially in a time like this. I truly am sorry."

He took his chair again. As soon as he found it, he realized he was shaking all over. His sight rippled before him as if he'd run five leagues. He had to hold on to the table to keep from toppling forward.

Brace for Adni's anger. Put up shields against Elínla too. I've said all I can, and now they can strike where I'm weakest because I've told them exactly where that is, as if they didn't know already.

Instead, though, he found Kanis saying quietly, "Iremni was your wife? The one the witches spirited before?"

He nodded.

"I'm sorry to hear that."

"We'll say nothing else about this," Adni announced.

"Giovel's torched the whole Order with his—" Elínla began.

"Yes, Giovel's dug a shit hole for us all, but we can't change it now so we'll say nothing else about this," Adni repeated. "Reports."

Giovel's sight still swirled and his legs felt like leaves, but the meeting was underway like it should have been, with Adni asking for reports. Nothing more to say. They all had to know what Giovel's failures had cost them in the past weeks, Adni most of all, yet there were no immediate punishments, no vengeful diatribe. Just the normalcy of Elínla's and Hirnu's voices describing plans for the Grays.

It was clean lake water on a sticky hand, and Giovel found his body calming before the reports were done.

Everything Giovel heard was news after his long absence. It sounded like many Grays had fallen, ambushed while trying to guard awakenings on Adni's list or to find the witches' hideaways. Hirnu and Elínla had tried to rush to the locations of new spiritings themselves, and to take their own part in guarding the exposed awakenings whom they hadn't been able to secure elsewhere. There were too many, and the witches vanished too quickly after each strike.

"We do know the witches are looking for something else as well," Elínla said.

"Something else as in another person?" Adni asked. "The Witherclaw is still missing."

"It doesn't seem to be a person," Hirnu said. "They've been digging up ruined buildings and demanding information from architects and archivists. It sounds like it's a location they want to find."

"Could this be the location Etelier mentioned at the Croen Estate?" Giovel asked. His voice felt raw and dry already.

"What location is that?" Hirnu asked with a frown.

"They said the Order had a secret place," Giovel replied. "A spot we take people to awaken them. They made it sound like some sort of mystical rite, as if anyone who even walked there would awaken."

"What rubbish," Elínla mumbled.

"To us perhaps," Hirnu said.

"Maybe we can use this to decoy them into the open," Giovel said, thinking through a scenario as he spoke. "We could *make* a site like this. We could actually take a hundred, two hundred, even a thousand Lances there and let the word out that they've all awakened now. We could let the whole city know exactly where this site is."

"And how are we supposed to do that without showing our flag?" Adni asked. "Unless you have some secret messenger who can carry a letter to them."

Giovel met Adni's gaze. "They have spies everywhere."

"We don't know that either," Hirnu said. "And it would be unbelievably heavy-handed of us to make any sort of public statement in hopes that they'll hear it."

"I understand that you want to find the witches," Elínla said, turning once more to scowl toward Giovel. "But we'll need a much better plan than this to do it."

"I have more ideas," Giovel said quickly.

"Shut up until reports are over," Adni said.

Normalcy. Giovel found himself feeling all the better for it and thinking more clearly as he waited his turn to speak.

Kanis's report was brief. He was working secretly with the Lances now to help guard many of the relocation efforts. Zuris was worried, as it sounded, that witches would use the relocation efforts to strike exposed groups that might be cut off during the massive undertaking. Every Gray in Foneth was hunting for the witches or trying to watch for spiritings now, so Kanis was all the Order could send.

Adni's report was brief as well. "Optate Olura is considering stepping down," he said.

"What? Why?" Elínla asked. "We need her now more than ever."

"There's pressure for her to do more here and less there, as always. Not to mention extra griping from the Lawrits to replace—or simply disband—the Order so someone else can take over hunting witches."

"But her reelection is only next year," Elínla said.

"If Redremel or witches don't kill us all first," Adni said. "Suffice it to say she isn't listening to me or the others on her council where this matter's concerned."

"Then there's nothing we can do about it," Giovel said. "Can we talk about this some other time and get back to Order business?"

"I'm not done reporting," Adni said. "The Witherclaw was spotted last night. A Candle saw her near the southwest walls."

"Did this Candle approach her?" Giovel asked. "Try to take her in?"

"Some Candles don't violate their orders, Giovel."

"What orders? Varan isn't our enemy."

"Isn't she?" Elínla asked. "She fled in the dark of night. The Candleguard have been ordered not to engage her alone, Lances too. For all we know, she's one of the witches now."

"And for all we know she's just looking for her home," Hirnu said. "Is the report trustworthy, Adni?"

"Olinos Vlada vouched for it. I've already dispatched a few Grays to look for her near where she was seen. So now we wait."

Giovel did wait, expecting to be sent himself to pick up where his duties had ended. When Adni looked his way, though, it was just to say, "So. You had more thoughts on finding the witches, did you?"

"Why wasn't I consulted about these Grays being diverted?" Elínla cut in.

"Look what you've done now, Giovel," Adni said. "You've made Elínla so angry she speaks her mind in our meetings."

Elínla's scowl deepened. "I've always spoken my mind when I wanted to."

"You speak your mind because Giovel showed that you could. And as for the Grays, I didn't have time to consult you. I'm sure you can appreciate the urgency to follow any lead that might get the Witherclaw out of the witches' grasp, since you can be sure they'll hear where she was as well. Now. Back to Giovel's ideas."

This was the oddest Order meeting Giovel thought he'd ever attended. Still. He cleared his throat, mustered his thoughts together, and started putting them forward.

"Kanis hasn't been announced."

"Announced at what? Are we at a social function now?" Adni asked.

Giovel turned toward Kanis. "Only the Order and a few Grays know who you are, don't they? I can't volunteer you, but if you approached the witches somehow, made as if we were hunting you, you might just be able to get into their circle."

"That's not the worst idea I've heard," Adni said.

"We still don't know how *anyone* can approach their circle because we don't know where they are," Hirnu said. "We don't know that the witches actually want new allies, either."

"They're spiriting awakenings, aren't they?" Adni asked. "Of course they want to recruit them."

"They spirit them and they murder them," said Elínla. "How does that constitute recruiting?"

"The chance that Kanis could even find them in the first place is also impossibly slim—even if we made a show of hunting him," Hirnu said gravely. "The witches don't seem to seek out every awakening, after all."

"I'm willing to try it, though," Kanis mumbled.

"He could offer another gem as well," Giovel said. "The Witherclaw."

Elínla groaned. "That's an even weaker idea. The witches know she left us."

"The witches *probably* know she *appears* to be gone," Giovel replied. "What if that's all there is to it? Kanis could tell them it's some gambit and say he knows where she's really hiding."

"Then they'd torture him to get the answer," Elínla snapped. "Giovel, these ideas are worthless. I've been bleeding my feet dry for months on the witch hunt, and I haven't come any closer to finding them. You talk as if this is some game of leaves and pebbles." Her eyes narrowed across the table. "Maybe this would work if you'd kept the Witherclaw under your palm like you were ordered to."

Her words hit him like a whip. He flinched back in his seat and found his sight fading again. What shook him most was knowing what Elínla said was correct. If anyone was to blame for Varan's disappearance, it was him. And if ever there was a time that his help mattered most, it was the last few weeks in which he hadn't been present to offer it.

Stars help me make it up to them.

"Any more ideas to propose?" Adni asked as calmly as if Elínla hadn't spoken at all. Still no fury. Even his disdain seemed to be waning today. Hirnu must have threatened to cut Adni's ears off before they all arrived.

Clearing his throat, Giovel added, "If you deposed me, that might just shock them out."

"Only the Optate can depose someone from the Order," Elínla groaned. "Can we end this meeting so I can get on with the real work?"

"I like this scheme, actually," Hirnu said. "But it would be better to depose me."

That made even Elínla close her mouth a minute. So much for her worries about heavy-handedness.

"Go on," Adni said slowly.

"Mind you, this is only worth trying if we're confident we can crush the witches when they do emerge," Hirnu said, looking engrossed in her own thoughts. "But what if the Order announced publicly that I was being stripped of my position? Not killed. Just ejected. It would give me a reason to hate the rest of you. Maybe even enough reason to want help from a witch."

"Are you volunteering?" Adni asked. "You almost sound as if you relish your chance to leave."

"It could work," Hirnu said. "Say you announced that I'd been spellbuilding in wildly dangerous ways? You could claim I was trying to rebuild Renma's lost glyph."

Kanis shuddered. Giovel found himself nodding, though. "That would catch my interest if I were a witch."

"Your reputation would never recover from us announcing something like that," Elínla said, looking half impressed and half horrified. "No matter what happened afterward, people might never trust you again."

Hirnu shrugged. "I'm old enough to know that reputation doesn't matter when no one ever sees you except those who truly *do* know you. And that's the people who gather in this room."

Maybe not even us, Giovel thought. But he was getting more and more curious to know the rest of who Hirnu was.

"It's as risky as Giovel's idiot plans," Elínla said.

"But we can be sure the witches *will* hear of it, and I won't be defenseless," Hirnu said. "So depose me. Publicly. Let me break out and run for it. The witches might come looking, either for me or for the rest of you, once they hear why you had to push out the longest-seated member of the Order."

She smiled like a patient child who was finally getting the sweetbread she'd been promised for sitting through a gathering of guests.

As usual, Adni seemed unable to tell her no. He just said, "We can try this idea. So how do we trap these witches when they come?"

EXCHANGE

I will come back a different woman. It's not just my bad ear or the new language I'm learning. I've become too much like these people for my own satisfaction.
 —The Witherclaw Witch; letter to Golkorun.

VARAN FELT LIKE a fool when she left Olinos's extravagant home. She spent the next day close to the Candlespire, staying in a windowless room at the back of the cheapest inn she could find. It somehow smelled like both smoke and mildew at once, and the floor creaked with every shift of Varan's weight, but at least no one would see her.

Perhaps it was a given that the Order would scour the streets near Olinos's house for her, or perhaps not. Could be Olinos would keep quiet about her visit. Either way, Varan's funds from selling Ralden's dresses were halfway gone, and she still lacked key information just to complete her charts, let alone to start searching.

Not for the first time, she found her mind losing focus as she had for long hours before Kirida's baby came. After an empty moment staring at a rotted section of the wall, she realized she was stroking around her ruined left ear again. Another growing habit since her encounter with Etelier. She was starting to think she'd made a mistake in trying this alone. But hadn't she been alone since she came here?

So she went back to her notes and diagrams and charts and maps and plans, isolated in a cell of her choosing.

Ideas still came to her mind, of course, but with every thought she put weight on, Varan felt more and more that her odds were just too unbalanced. Finding the witches would do no good if they simply captured her on sight. *She* had to catch them, rather, force them to send her home or at least to tell her where home even was.

She'd need another ally, then. And her list of possibilities was slimmer now than ever before.

Three days after her visit to Olinos, Varan slipped out of her tiny room and walked to the northeast end of Bone Hill. She'd only been here once before, trailing Giovel perhaps three months before. Snow made everything look different now, so it took her a few hours to find anything she recognized and retrace the steps she'd once taken. At last she spotted the home of the odd scholar woman called Birenlu. The one person who'd known how to find the Redremel spies aiding the witches' attack.

It was a solitary house with a roof of brilliantly orange tiles. It looked like some sort of flower sprouting out of a heap of mud-tinged snow beside the road to the river. No one else was around. Varan clapped and waited.

It was a long time before anyone answered. Varan took it to mean Birenlu was appropriately cautious. When she did open the door, the woman held one hand out of sight as if she was ready to brandish a knife. Her eyes softened, though, when she saw who Varan was.

"Well. Hello, Witherclaw."

So much for her thin disguise. Varan thought for a desperate moment of threatening Birenlu, compelling her to silence. Then she remembered how Giovel had coaxed help from the old woman.

"Can I talk to you?" Varan asked. "I can give you information."

It was like blood for a hungry fox. "Come in. Quickly. Did anyone see you coming here?"

Varan shook her head as she stepped inside.

The house was just one wide room downstairs, a sort of half-kitchen half-Sanctuary, with various kinds of branches folded to cover one wall in a net of dried leaves and wood. Birenlu's fireplace was burning something that hadn't cured properly, sending tendrils of greenwood smoke out into the room as often as they went up the narrow chimney.

"I didn't expect you'd show your face while the Divine are looking for you," Birenlu said, eying her as if she was a fish for sale. "Do you want something warm to drink? I have several different kinds of tea."

Perhaps she had one or two that were especially good at relaxing people she talked with, loosening their hold on secrecy. Varan shook her head again.

"Fine, fine. I'll make some in case you change your mind. Where'd you come from, anyway? I'm amazed you've stayed hidden this long with eyes like yours."

"Foneth is big," Varan said simply.

"True enough. Are you from a small place yourself? Ah, forget that question. I should mind my manners. You're not among enemies here, Witherclaw. Sit if you like and make yourself comfortable."

Birenlu poured two cups of steaming liquid, placing one on a tiny table beside Varan while she sipped the other herself. Her eyes still trailed Varan over the rim of her cup.

"So you came with information. You probably think I'm some sort of street watcher like the other people Lord Giovel employs."

"No. I know you're a scholar."

"Ah. You just don't know what I do with the things I know, is that it?" Birenlu set her own cup aside a moment. "What sort of information have you brought me?"

"I can tell you lots of things," Varan said. "But I need your help."

"Of course. Of course. Forgive me, but I still want to know more specifically what you think you could offer. Then we can worry whether or not I can help you in return."

"I can tell you about my home. There's nothing in your libraries about it yet. I'm sure."

"Can you even read Medín? Anyone who writes about your home could just as easily make things up. While it's intriguing to consider, it doesn't interest me enough to be worth an exchange."

"You don't know what I want yet."

"I can guess, can't I? What else do you have to offer me?"

Varan had to step carefully now. It had occurred to her that Birenlu might refuse the first offer, but she didn't have much else to share.

"I could tell you about my witchery," she said after a moment.

"Everyone in Foneth already spills about that."

It stung. "They all tell lies about me."

"I didn't say talk was the truth, but there *is* plenty of talk. In fact you might learn something from the stories they tell. How your demon father bestowed his black eyes to you, how you stole the voice of another witch and that's why you can't speak, how you massacred a score of witch followers in Tovómil the night you first were spirited. All sorts of tales."

"Those aren't true."

"And most people probably know that. But they're not more likely to believe me. Anyone already talking about you can say *they've* talked with you as well, so there's not much advantage of me sharing things about you, even if they are the truth."

There had to be something she could offer. Some pearl of insight or rumor or . . . Her mind cycled back to the Candlespire. "What if I tell you more about Giovel?"

Birenlu's mouth was hidden behind her cup just now, but she couldn't quite hide her interest even as she said, "I can ask Giovel himself."

"He doesn't talk. He doesn't talk to anyone."

"Then why would he talk to you?"

"He stayed close to me for days," Varan said. "I learned things about him that he wouldn't say."

"Prove it. Tell me something no one else could know. Or at least tell me the nature of your information."

Where to begin? "I know what he eats. I know what he does every day. I know he never uses Yulena."

"That's common knowledge."

"No," Varan said. "People don't know that. They think he's like the other mages, or like a witch. He's not."

If this interested her, Birenlu managed to conceal it this time. She set her cup aside, though, licking her lips and considering. "Just what do you want me to exchange for you to talk so much about Giovel?"

"You said you knew what I wanted."

"I said I could guess. You want me to help you find wherever it is you came from, is that it? Extract some old map that leads you so far away that you can't see Yulen?"

Did everyone in Foneth know she couldn't see Yulen in Dundal? "I'm not trying to find a map. I'm trying to find the witches."

"Interesting. You do realize, don't you, that I've been aiding the Divine Order for months through Giovel. I'm practically a spy for the

Optacracy now. Wouldn't I have told then if I knew how to find any witches?"

"It only helps *you* to keep quiet now," Varan said.

"I don't follow."

"If the Order doesn't find the witches, they *need* your help. It helps you *not* to help them, but only now. Someday it won't help any more, if the Order can't beat the witches."

Birenlu looked truly surprised for the first time since Varan had arrived. An almost feral look crossed her face, her gray eyebrows twisting inward while her jaw went stiff and her cheeks pressed inward like a bellows being closed.

"Just what do you mean by that?" she asked. "Do you mean to say I'm helping the witches as much as I help Giovel?"

Varan met her gaze. "I mean you don't tell Giovel everything."

But Varan knew enough to gamble on how it all worked. She could see Birenlu gaining from both sides, even if she only wanted to help one. If Birenlu told the Order nothing, she'd gain nothing back, and if she told them everything she knew, there'd be nothing left to hold in reserve, no space for profit since the Order would no longer need her services. They'd drop her by the road like a pile of weeds. So she pretended to help Giovel while withholding information that could well save his life.

If I had the Medín words to say what I see, Varan thought, I'd make this woman cower in shame before I was done.

After a quiet moment, Birenlu reclaimed her cup. The way she moved it to her mouth made Varan think it must be empty, just a nervous cover now.

"I don't know what you think I could tell you, but I assure you," Birenlu began slowly, "I'm an asset to the Divine. I don't know anything about the witches but what's common knowledge already."

"That means it wouldn't hurt you if I tell Lady Ralden where Giovel gets his information."

Another pause. "I don't see why not."

"I saved her life from witches. She'll believe me when I tell her you're keeping secrets from them."

Perhaps she should have used Ralden's name earlier. Birenlu looked jumpy as a cornered spider now. When she managed to speak, all she said was, "Maybe the rumors about your skills are truer than I thought. They say you can read people's thoughts because you feed on them."

It was more absurd than Varan had even imagined. But she *was* good at reading people. About time it came in use in this godless place.

"What will you tell me?" Varan asked.

"I'll give you a name and directions to find someone," Birenlu said, her voice very high all of a sudden. "He won't know it was me who sent you, probably won't even know who I am, but he has had contact with the witches in the past. He might even be able to arrange a meeting for you."

Varan gave a single long nod, somewhat like how people bowed here. "I will exchange everything I know about Giovel."

"Just leave me. I don't want it now."

"You don't have to accept what I offer," Varan said.

Just accept my warning, she thought.

Birenlu looked away as she told Varan how to find this man. Varan took careful note, drawing a few more lines on her convoluted map as Birenlu explained.

"His name's Penaren. He's part of the Optacracy, but he won't hesitate to turn you over to the witches as soon as he sees you. It'll probably just come down to who's offered him more to find you."

"I'll have to make my own offer." Varan turned to leave, then paused to say, "If you tell the Order I was here, I'll explain why. And Ralden *will* believe me."

"I keep my word," Birenlu growled.

Varan considered seriously that Birenlu might simply seek out Penaren herself before she could. If Birenlu knew where he'd be during the day, and told him Varan was coming, she could easily turn Varan over to whichever side of the hunt she wanted. To be sure this didn't happen, Varan walked just out of sight of Birenlu's house, doubled back through the trees, and watched until dusk settled and she was sure she'd find this Penaren herself before Birenlu could. Only then did she follow the old scholar's directions.

Penaren the Optacrat lived near the Citadel, so close Varan thought he could probably hear people talking from inside the immense walls of pale green stone. His own house was neat and tidy, tucked between a massive stairwell to an upper trade street and part of a bridge over the Iceflow. Lights shone in two windows of nearly flawless glass when Varan arrived.

She tested a wrist-thrower she'd collected before visiting Birenlu. She wasn't all that good with it yet, but she doubted it mattered. It was probably better to Temper or Quicken something if he resisted, let him know exactly who she was. As she had at Birenlu's, she clapped. This time she pulled her head wrap off first, showing her face and hair clearly.

A gaunt, amber-skinned man opened the door, smiling even before he did so. His face fell when he saw her. Ah. So Penaren knew who she was.

"I want you to take me to the witches," Varan said without waiting for him to recover himself.

He slammed the door in her face. His footsteps echoed inside, retreating.

Varan spun her hands a few times and Quickened an oxidation in the mechanism of the door, reducing the latch to a heap of rust as she pushed it open and ran after Penaren. His house was lavishly bright inside, with blue lanterns lining the walls through a pristine Sanctuary painted with clouds in a bright sky. Penaren's footsteps made an easy trail down the hall, around a corner, over a few back steps and out another door into an enclosed garden. He was just trying to climb a wall not quite adjoining to the Citadel's when Varan Enervated his own breath, stopping him short as a puff of air released through his nostrils. He fell backward into grass that must have been painstakingly cleared of snow for weeks. His face shook as he tried unsuccessfully to breathe. Varan put a foot on his stomach before releasing her Enervation.

"I want you to take me to the witches," she said again.

"You'll burn for this!" Penaren hissed when he realized he could breathe. "You witched me just now!"

"You help witches, don't you? If I'm a witch, you should help me."

Penaren tried to grab her leg and throw her off. He was too breathless and weak to shift her foot, so he ended up just whimpering and sputtering for a moment before throwing his head back again. His eyes darted toward the Citadel and he opened his mouth as if to scream. Varan Enervated his breath again, idly wondering whether this fool was being brave or cowardly to try calling for help.

She yanked a fistful of his own collar into his mouth before she let him breathe again. "No one's coming to help you until you help me. You know who I am. You know what I want. Just take me to the witches."

While Penaren coughed into his collar and gasped for more breath, Varan dragged him into his opulent house where she could mask his sounds more easily. She wondered whose name from the Order would inspire the most fear. Adni, perhaps, since Adni worked most closely with the Optacrats? Or Elínla and her Grays?

"Do you know how I found you?" she asked when she had Penaren backed against an immense hearth near the center of the house.

"I don't care how you found me or who you think I am! I don't know where any witches are!"

"Then you wouldn't have run from me. I know you can find them, because Lord Giovel told me so."

"Giovel's mad. Everyone knows he's been sick and cracked in half for weeks."

Varan pushed her bluff a little harder. "Do you believe that? That sounds like a good story for why no one has seen him. He *has* seen you. He watches you every day. Sometimes you lose him when you go out to see the witches. But he says you'll lead him there soon."

She'd picked a good name, apparently, because Penaren all but squealed with horror now. It made her feel sick about herself, furious she had to push this wretch of a man at all. She was done waiting, though. She'd waited for months, just hoping her family would wait too.

"I don't believe you," Penaren managed to say. "Giovel would have come himself. I know what he does to his enemies. You're just trying to scare me into blabbing over something I didn't do."

"I am trying to scare you," Varan said with a nod. "And Giovel *will* come. I just got tired of waiting for him. I'll make you an exchange. I'll let you leave before he gets here if you tell me everything I ask about the witches first. And show me where they are."

His eyes looked wide enough to push his own lids inside out. He lurched forward once more, trying to run for it somehow. Varan easily shoved him back into the corner.

"This is completely illegal," Penaren stammered. "I'll have Lawrits all over you for this. All over Giovel too."

Maybe he was more than just afraid—clever enough to see how ashamed Varan felt to be threatening him. She didn't let up, though, because Foneth's laws had never been her laws.

"Is it a fair exchange?" she asked.

Penaren swallowed. Then he started talking.

A NEW PLAN

I write and write, but I'm still lonely because I can never be sure you're writing back.

—The Witherclaw Witch; letter to Recia.

CLARAVENA PEERED THROUGH a dirty, frost-touched window as starlit clouds tilted high over the Whisperwood. The fire beside her was falling to dim coals. Beyond its smoky crackle the attic was quiet, the other witches keeping to their own thoughts for the moment just as Claravena did.

Etelier was late. Again. He'd become even more useless since Pramél had left with their daughter. Claravena hadn't exactly expected him to brighten when it happened, to regain the spark he once helped light under the others. Nor had she counted on it hitting him so hard.

It made her wonder whether she should have intervened on his behalf, rather than encouraging Pramél to put Foneth behind her for good. But no. She was right to do it. Not because it taught Etelier a lesson, sorely as he might need it. It was right for *Pramél*, and Mota too. No one deserved to be wed to a witch. Being married to a mad one was twice as much to shoulder.

Despite Etelier's steely focus back then, his family had welcomed Claravena when her own dissolved. She found trust and warmth, shelter and belonging from Pramél, and even little Mota had grown friendly over the weeks and months they'd known one another. So it was more than spite, what she'd done in bidding Pramél to leave.

I cared for them like he did, she said to herself. Not the same way, of course, but filling the same empty aches we've all felt since awakening. And now they're safe, away from him, away from me too. Maybe they can reunite when all this is over, if we ever do find the magic cure Etelier wants or the secret to the awakenings I'm after.

Probably not before.

"Are we going to wait all night or get on with this?" Tranin asked from a shadowed corner of the attic. "I have bread rising that I want to bake tonight."

"I didn't know you could bake," Noru said. "Or is that just a phrase for something else?"

"We'll begin," Claravena said, standing to stretch and clear her mind. "Wurelna, tell everyone what you've confirmed about Giovel."

Before Wurelna began, Etelier walked in. He looked to be in no hurry and his face was even as a tabletop as he said, "Hirnu has been deposed for spellbuilding. The Divine are in uproar."

A breath later the Starlit Order was too. Wurelna seemed to be choking on a walnut while Tranin cursed, Ithilo laughed, and Noru hurled questions at Etelier. Claravena just found herself bristling. How dare Etelier walk in with news like that. He should have run his feet red to tell them this.

"How do you know this isn't just tavern talk?" Claravena yelled, pushing Noru aside to get face to face with Etelier.

"I was in Divnum when they announced it. Yilitha Dar of the Grays was reading it in the streets."

"But why?" Noru asked. "What are they getting rid of her for? She's allowed to spellbuild."

"Who cares why they're doing it?" Ithilo asked, still practically clucking with glee. "She was one of the last who posed a real threat."

"Which is why I want to be sure this is more than some angry Candle's rumor," Claravena said. "Everyone shut up except Etelier. I want to hear what they're saying about Hirnu."

Etelier still looked Sanctuary-calm as he recounted it. "They said that Adni himself found her at it. Apparently she was trying to rebuild Renma's spell, of all things. I wouldn't have be—"

"That's got to be horseshit," Noru said.

"Shut your maggot trap until he's done," Claravena growled.

She felt cold, though, despite the embers in Wurelna's attic hearth. *No one* would try rebuilding Renma's spell on a whim. If this was true —which she doubted—Hirnu must have been working at it a long, long time. They said she was as patient as Cold Lake itself. Maybe this was why she had stayed in solitude so much in the years as the Order's Observer.

"Four Grays were with him," Etelier said. "They signed their names that they'd seen it. The *actual* rumor is all four of them are in line to be raised, fill all those empty seats in the Order."

"Forget the rumors for now. Just tell us what Yilitha Dar said out loud."

"Not much more. Just that Hirnu has been deposed and that she's at large somewhere, hiding from the whole Optacracy. They say a Gray died trying to take her."

Ithilo's laugh turned wild and Wurelna seemed to choke all over again. Before the others could leap in with more questions and exclamations, Claravena gave a shrill whistle that silenced them all.

"This might be just the timing we need. So I want you all to keep your thoughts to yourself unless you can share in an organized way. We won't have much time to move."

"Do we try finding Hirnu first?" Tranin blurted out. "Find what she'd made? Or even recruit her? She must hate the Order if she was really trying to rebuild Renma's spell."

"Forget Hirnu," Claravena snapped. "She's gone. And she's still probably the most dangerous mage alive. *And* in case you'd forgotten, none of us are all that good at finding missing people." She surveyed them all but Wurelna, thinking of tasks they'd all failed in the past months. "As I was about to explain before Etelier decided to show himself, I have a plan already."

"You mean we just ignore this?" Noru asked.

"Yes. Just like we ignore that Tranin has totally failed to find the Witherclaw. We're not going after them. We're going after Sur, Ralden, and Giovel."

That made them quiet down. Tranin began ripping scraps from a piece of cloth on the chair she occupied. "Why Sur and Ralden and not these four new Grays?"

"Because appointing *anyone* to the Order takes weeks, you flathead. Wurelna offed Dlenar way back at the start of winter and there's still no replacement for him. Also, there's too much politicking for the Optate to ever appoint four Grays to the Order at once—even during a war. So yes, we move on Sur and Ralden, who are both still wounded but who won't be so tightly guarded now that the Divine have a new witch hunt to take eyes off us."

"What about Giovel?" Tranin asked coldly. "He's not wounded. And he's not a weakling either."

"Actually, he might be the most vulnerable of all, in some ways," Wurelna said.

"What do you mean?" Etelier asked. He actually looked interested, which was something of a first given the past few weeks of sulking.

"Wurelna, tell them what you've been doing," Claravena said.

"Claravena heard some things about Giovel recently, so I went to confirm," Wurelna began. "It turns out he hasn't been on duty in more than a month. He's just been at his house. He barely leaves it. Most of the Order has visited him, apparently, but a few Candles assigned to watch the house say that he's sick or something, maybe even that he's crazy."

"Since when?" Etelier asked. "He almost killed me at the Croen Estate."

"Weeks at least," Wurelna said.

"Since about the time you became pointless yourself," Claravena snapped. "And that's not all. See, Giovel has plenty of weaknesses to prod. First, he's newer to the Order than anyone else, so he's less experienced with Yulena to begin with. Second, Wurelna confirmed that he's very *against* Yulena, so he's an easier target already. Third, he has a daughter, unlike the others, so there are more ways to bend him where we want than there are for lonely stair climbers like Adni or Elínla. Fourth, I happen to know exactly where he lives, so spiriting him out—if needed—is possible. And fifth, Giovel has told more than one Candle that he's hunting us because he wants answers about his wife, who happened to be one of our spiritings from the early days, which will motivate him to try taking us alive. Like Wurelna said, he's probably an even easier target than the other two.

"So. While the Divine are reeling about that cow Hirnu, all we need is a small decoy to get a few more Lances and Candles away from those three. Then we can bring them all down at once, crippling the Order to just *two* mages."

"There are barely enough of us to take them if they're unguarded," Tranin said. "Besides, they'll be sure to have Grays around all the same."

"There are only so many Grays to go around," Etelier said, still calm as anything. "I think this plan is a good one."

"But which of us is going to handle this decoy?" Ithilo asked.

"We're going to use one of Etelier's old ploys," said Claravena. "One that doesn't need witches or that broken Redremel spy ring to run."

"And what is that?" Tranin asked.

"We're going to find gold in Divnum's walls, and we'll tell a few hundred underpaid ditch-diggers in North Hold exactly where there's more."

Now Claravena had their ears. She pulled her city map out and began to draw directions for each of them to follow.

Etelier might be listless. Tranin might be rabid. Wurelna might be timid. But Claravena had spent half her life trying to shift power away from the Order. Now, at last, she felt like the last few branches were brittle enough for her to snap.

THE PARADOX OF WAITING

Our vow day has come and gone. I counted it and thought about you. I believe you did the same for me.

—The Witherclaw Witch; letter to Golkorun.

THE LOST WEEKS seemed shorter in memory than Giovel thought they should, and he felt their effect as he resumed any kind of duties. There was no shortage of work for him now. He was meeting with Lances, directing twenty of the Grays at Elínla's request, and trying desperately to train Kanis as much as possible. Like a real member of the Order. His absence left him disoriented and weak, though, like a boot turned so hard with dried mud that it couldn't fit again, a harp string left stretched so long it couldn't vibrate in tune.

I can only walk in one direction, he'd told himself each of the last three mornings. Either I walk on or I walk back.

His house was wrecked in many ways, even after Hirnu's help cleaning it over her last few visits. Giovel had no more winter wood stocked up, nothing left in his larder, no ink, no rope for some reason, not even a table since he'd hacked his own into chunks. Oh, and his sword needed sharpening since he'd dulled it doing that. If it even was his sword. He couldn't remember if he'd borrowed or requisitioned it after losing his own last autumn. There was little he recollected clearly now, so he tried to finish things one task at a time, sharpening the sword, buying grain and rice and dried peppers, rolling an old barrel into the house to substitute for the table he'd demolished.

Kanis watched impatiently during most of this. They always had to stick together now, either two of the Order or one with a few Grays. Part of Adni's amendments to Hirnu's wild plan.

"Your house will still be there when this is over," Kanis said. "Why don't you just leave it?"

"What do you mean, when this is over?" Giovel asked. "You make it sound as if we'll have some holiday to loaf around."

"I mean when the witches are gone."

"There will be more witches. There always are."

"There will be more winters too, and more swords to sharpen."

Giovel met his eyes, trying not for the first time to puzzle out this new, hidden member of the Order. Kanis still dressed like a civilian and carried no visible weapons since his sand tablet stayed hidden in his coat. Giovel had to remind himself he couldn't afford discomfort with Kanis beside him. He just couldn't find it in him to be at ease either, not after the dark way Adni had pressed him into service, the shaming weakness Giovel had shown not to stop the whole thing.

What had the world come to?

"We'll get back to the Candlespire soon," Giovel said, pausing just long enough to write a note to Inorovel.

He still hadn't seen her. Just sent her notes through Hirnu. He didn't even know where exactly Hirnu's niece lived, where Inorovel was staying. Just that she hadn't responded to his messages.

It was hard to blame her.

I probably would have run away myself, Giovel thought. All I can hope now is that I'm writing soon enough and often enough and openly enough that you'll come back in time. Because your mother *isn't* coming. If you don't either, it'll be just me with this newly-filled larder and a barrel for my dinner plate.

Back to more duties. Though still confined to his own home, Sur had apparently applied his influence over both the Azure and Jade battalions, getting almost a thousand Lances relocated from scouting, perimeter, and supply chain positions outside the city. Now they met with Candles and Grays in bunches of ten and twelve at a time, all dressed to hide as Kanis was. Ralden—also ordered to stay home while she recovered—had helped orchestrate a wide distribution of the Lances' equipment, forming stockpiles, hideaways, armament caches, and defensible bolt holes all throughout Divnum, Belnum, North Hold, and even the Estates. No one really knew what to expect, but they would be prepared to mobilize when it came.

After that came the waiting, while Grays read proclamations on Hirnu's betrayal and squads were sent out in mock pursuit. The Order sheltered back at the Candlespire for the most part, taking reports and sending out messengers in hopes the witches made a move soon.

"The most important element is that we stay together," Adni said the third day since Hirnu's deposition. "They would have killed more than just Dlenar if we'd all been alone on Perception Day."

"Who's watching Hirnu, though?" Elínla asked.

"She has to stay alone for this plan to work," Adni said.

"So she might be the next to die for the cause."

"I thought the Sept of Blue Heaven believed in the value of individual risk."

"We believe in the value of individual actions, Adni. Not just risks."

"Then worry about your own part and let Hirnu do hers, unless you're jealous that it couldn't be you gaining the attention of everyone in the known world."

Elínla glowered and turned to one of the wide windows overlooking the north half of Divnum. "How did I get stuck with Adni when you got the new boy?" she muttered to Giovel.

"You haven't exactly indicated that you'd rather work with me either," Giovel said quietly.

"You haven't indicated that you wanted to work *at all*. I wish Sur or Ralden was here. And when are we going to get more replacements?"

Giovel felt uneasy too, of course—the eagerness to start, the itch to have the witches show themselves at last. Odd that he still felt anything beyond the jumpiness that preceded running a race or giving a speech, but there was an allure to Hirnu's plan.

It's wrong, isn't it? Feeling eager to draw my sword and chase someone who wants us dead. It's one of the only things that still interests me, strange and wrong though it might be. And it keeps me from thinking of *her*.

That was the paradox of waiting. As long as the witches delayed, Giovel could wonder if he'd been wrong about Iremni, if he'd just missed something, if his whole funk over her had sprouted from misunderstanding. And therein lay yet another source of excitement.

While I wait I can wonder if I was wrong, but when the waiting ends I might finally find answers of one sort or another. I just don't know which I'd rather have anymore.

A bearded Gray stepped into the council chamber a moment later with a message signed "The Old One."

"It's Hirnu," Adni said after the Gray was dismissed.

The message was short.

There's a disturbance near the north walls. At least five hundred people, all trying to get inside the walls themselves, for whatever reason. I can't say, but this might be the turn we've been waiting for.

Giovel's excitement surged upward like a bucket overflowing at the well.

"Giovel and Elínla, you two will get close enough to investigate," Adni said. "Kanis, you're with me."

Giovel didn't question that order.

HIDDEN IN THE STARS

Who would ever leave home without some plan to come back?
 —The Witherclaw Witch; letter to Golkorun.

THE CHOICE TO put Foneth behind was surprisingly easy. Never mind that Etelier hadn't lived anywhere else, didn't know where to turn, didn't even know how he'd make his way in the bleak remainder of winter. Direction wasn't what he wanted now. Just change. If he wandered on roads he didn't know, by mountains and lakes he hadn't seen before, he wouldn't have to remember scouting them out for secret libraries or ruins of an old half-legendary city.

It was hard to say when he'd really decided to go. It felt like the stars cresting a hill—one of those choices that came so gently you didn't notice before it was right beside you, bright and silver and cold as a cap of ice. It felt like a fitting time. And who knew? Maybe he'd find answers wherever he went, if he still wanted to look at all.

I will be leaving some things undone, he thought with more than a little regret. Then again, if I hadn't left the most important things undone, I wouldn't have much reason to leave at all. Pramél wouldn't have had so many reasons either.

He decided his last stop would be the Belnum Echo Hall. Where home felt like Pramél's haven, the Echo Hall still felt like his. He'd never brought anyone but Mota here. Maybe he'd just needed something to call his alone, some space where it was only him and the glint of the stars. It had been a place of solace after long hours digging and deforesting for the Lances. The only sound was the faint hum still lingering from old spells—spells likely worked five hundred years ago and fully forgotten now. A fitting way to begin the journey.

Etelier had wanted to build a star room Sanctuary when he and Pramél bought their own house. She liked the idea too. Because there was never money for it, they settled for rock and moss. Star rooms weren't so uncommon, though, not so extravagant now glass was easy to make. The stars themselves were common too, weren't they? Shared by thousands of thousands far beyond Foneth alone. And still they felt like a shield for Etelier's solitude rather than a crowd of faces as they might have.

He had to wonder: Did he love this place because it gave him something? Or just because it *asked* so little?

I never should have let my search for healing push away the person I loved first and longest and most. I always thought they were the ones begging me to find some cure for Mota's ears, pushing me out to search and search again even when my legs and shoulders ached for rest. Maybe not, though. Could be that was just my own will speaking, me fooling myself into the belief that I was loving them best by going out to hunt for answers they might not truly have wanted as much as they wanted me to be near.

Now I have neither them nor answers. But even without Mota and even without Pramél, I still have the glimmer of the stars to follow.

He'd studied the constellations outlined in the Echo Hall's Sanctuary hundreds of times before. Today, even with slashes of daylight falling through gaps in the ceiling, they looked purer than any night sky he'd ever seen, clearer than Cloud Lake on a windless day in summer.

The constellations looked like *glyphs*.

Etelier's mind sped through a score of ideas all at once.

They'd searched so long for a physical stack of tomes, a record written in paper, parchment, vellum, stone, something marked with *words*. But there were hundreds more diagrams and pictures they'd never stopped to consider. An entire library of Yulenic lore could be hidden in old maps or land markings. Disguised as architectural drawings or building plans. Perhaps simply coded in the pages and pages of maths the Lawrits used to calculate taxes and expenses. Or they could be shown in plain sight, masked as constellations in some star room Sanctuary.

The Citadel has one, Etelier thought. So does the North Hold barracks. And *the Divnum library* too, where *any* other glyphs could hide right under our fingers through all our subtle searches of the place. How could I have been so blind all this time?

But he supposed that was just what he was asking anyway.

He looked back at the walls, searching for any patterns he knew. His heart pounded in his chest and he found that his hands were sweaty despite the chill of the afternoon. For a moment he considered going himself, heading straight to the library. He'd be recognized in Divnum, though, where they'd be most alert anyway.

He froze in place, half turned to the door.

Hadn't he just told himself he'd looked for the wrong things all along? So he had to ask: Shouldn't I leave while I still can, while the Order's worried about Hirnu and I have a chance to get away undetected?

As always, his mind went back to his crushed ear, to how Mota's sickness cut her off from a world of laughter and birdsong and music.

One more search. For her. A final effort before I go.

With that in his mind, Etelier shut the empty Echo Hall behind him and ran to find Claravena.

WATCHING A WITCH

I'm starting to understand their fear of witches. My patched-up face is just one good reminder.

—The Witherclaw Witch; letter to Golkorun.

VARAN DIDN'T DECIDE what to do with Penaren until he'd shown her his witch contact's house and Varan saw the woman for herself. Wurelna, he called her. She had a long face and held one arm at her side as if it was stiff. Varan recognized her, even at a distance across the morning snow, as the witch at the Divnum walls on Perception Day, the one who'd killed Dlenar Tovóm. So Penaren had told the truth.

Varan wondered if she ought to use Penaren as a shield to approach the witch. But would this Wurelna even care if any harm were to come to him? The hideous thought came to Varan's mind that she could just kill Penaren and leave his body in a deep drift. She'd never killed anyone. Never even considered it. She rejected the very idea as soon as it entered her mind, but it came back like a fly seeking warmth in her hair. There was something in Penaren's eyes that looked like a corpse already, like nothing could truly hurt him. That alone made her consider killing him long enough that she felt a surge of shame ripple through her.

She left him bound and gagged in an alley while she dropped a message for Nomis outside the nearest Candleguard watch station.

"Now you can choose what to do next," she said, meeting Penaren's cold eyes once more.

He, in return, mumbled something quiet enough it might have been defiant. Just not defiant enough to frighten Varan.

"I don't want to decide anything for you," she said. "If you get free before my friend comes to arrest you, you'll have to choose what you do. I'll be right outside Wurelna's house. If you bring any Candles there, it will look like you turned on her. Also, the Divine will find out what I said in the note I just sent, and if you stay in Foneth, they *will* come looking for you."

Then you'll have three enemies to fear, Varan thought. The Order, the witches, and me.

Thought was the one indicator of life in Penaren's eyes. He had to have some measure of devious cognition in there, Optacrat that he was. So he wouldn't report her, wouldn't lead the Candleguard back to Wurelna. Instead, he'd choose whom he feared most—the Order, who had authority to tower over his, a witch, who might blame him if a score of warriors suddenly searched her neighborhood, or Varan, who *would* blame him. Varan bet on him weighing the odds carefully and choosing the safest path.

She didn't wait to find out what he'd try. She walked back through the snow for a closer look at the witch's home, leaving Penaren to think things over until someone came and freed him.

Wurelna's house was part of one of Belnum's southmost clusters of streets. Only a few tidy rows of homes lined the great sea of hills and plains beyond. Others rested alone in the snow, and Wurelna's was one of these, distant enough to be private while close enough not to be out of place. Varan knew she couldn't assume much, that she'd need to watch before making any move. So, after spending some of her last coins on a hot cup of soup, she found a tiny Sanctuary of wind-beaten boulders near enough to see Wurelna's house and sat to wait.

No one came in or out for several hours. More than once Varan had to move to warm herself up, and she never quite dispelled the chilly stiffness growing in her back. She kept her eyes on the house, though, waiting for that long face to appear again. On her first approach she'd seen that there was a back door now out of sight from where Varan sat, but thankfully there was no shelter or concealment there. When the witch emerged, Varan would know it.

It was getting into the afternoon when someone else walked by the Sanctuary without a glance in Varan's direction and entered

Wurelna's house. No clapping or waiting. Just walking right in. She had a sharply angled face almost as pale as Varan's own. Both she and Wurelna appeared behind the house almost immediately after, hurrying across the snow.

Did Penaren somehow warn them despite all Varan's precautions? Varan almost tripped as she stood to watch them go. Her feet had numbed after she last rubbed them for warmth. It was hard to walk, but she couldn't wait for them to go any farther.

Varan delayed as long as she dared to shake her leg and keep her distance. Then, when Wurelna and her companion were almost out of sight, she set out after them.

They made a winding path through the quiet south edges of Foneth. Their route took them through other little batches of houses and craft halls until two more figures joined them, wide-shouldered men. Varan recognized them; they'd been at the walls on Perception Day too, same as Wurelna had.

Four of them. Why didn't I bring someone to help me?

Varan kept following as Wurelna and the others hurried to the west edge of Belnum and on up the Great South Trade Road. Then Varan realized where they were going, because she'd come here before. The house of the wounded member of the Order, Suresni Medín.

A wave of dizziness almost overcame Varan then.

He couldn't be one of them. Not a Divine Mage. Giovel's friend, too, the only one he seemed to truly trust. God of Illumination, please let it not be so.

The four figures ducked into a clump of trees just off the road. They came out in Lance uniforms, half carrying the pale woman, who limped like a one-legged dog now. What now? Varan ignored her dizziness and circled closer.

They were talking to the three Lances guarding Suresni's house now. Saying something about a crowd. Something more. Injury—the one they called Tranin had an injury from the crowd. They couldn't stay, but could she wait there, safe with Suresni?

The Lances on guard didn't question. One opened Suresni's house and let Tranin in, while the other two dashed off in the direction Wurelna pointed. Ah, so that was their game. Not coming to meet Suresni as friends. Coming to divert his guards away, to get into his house, to be there with him in force while he was wounded and weak and unprotected. And Varan had just let his guards run away without a warning of the truth. The cold in her hands and feet seemed to sink deeper through her bones as she realized what was happening.

As soon as everyone was inside, she broke from her cover by the Trade Road and ran toward the little house. She hoped she hadn't waited too long.

IMPROVING THE PLAN

There's nothing quite like the feeling of being feared.
    —The Witherclaw Witch; letter to Drova.

As SOON AS she saw Etelier, Claravena noticed a glint of steel in his eyes. He was breathless, sweaty, looked as if he'd run across the Empty Hills to find her. But there was an earnestness to him, if anything. *Hopeful* again. It gave her enough pause to wait there in the Belnum street by Noru's house, wait and see what this was about.

"I'm surprised you'd even show your face now," she said as he leaned over to catch his breath. "I thought you'd quit when you started skipping meetings."

"I . . . found something," he gasped.

Ithilo emerged from Noru's house, grunting at the sight of Etelier. "Is *he* coming with us, Claravena?"

"No. What did you find that was worth running for?"

They couldn't delay long. The days were so short now that they'd only have four or five more hours of light at best and fewer if more clouds converged.

"The star room," he said between breaths. "Not just stars. Could be *glyphs*. At the library, that star room."

"What are you babbling about?" Ithilo asked. "Did you drink your ear salve, Etelier?"

"They can mark glyphs in the star room," he said. "At the library, or somewhere else. I think that's how they hide it."

A flood of cold shot through Claravena's body. She saw it in her mind now and couldn't believe she'd never imagined it before. But Etelier was right. It would be so *easy* to hide a glyph in plain sight, to mask it as a set of stars. And there were star rooms everywhere, including in the library. Come to think of it, she thought even the Candlespire might have one.

How much could they have hidden there, clear enough for anyone to see? Not enough to stop awakenings and change the laws, to be sure, but perhaps enough for Etelier, maybe even enough to balance out the Order's might.

"Have you been there yet?" Claravena asked, fighting the excitement in her own voice.

Etelier shook his head. He was still doubled over, heaving and clutching at his ribs as if he had a stitch. "Not yet."

She made a quick decision. "Then you should go. Now, while the rest of the plan is in motion. But we'll need one of the Divine to show us where best to look. Ithilo, go get Noru."

"You believe him, just like that?" Ithilo asked.

"I said *go get Noru.*"

Ithilo grunted then proceeded inside again.

"Tranin and Wurelna will be moving on Sur by now, and Ithilo and I are going after Ralden. You and Noru can get Giovel into that library and force him to show us what's hidden there."

"How do we get him there?" Etelier asked. "Is there a plan?"

He should have known the answer without her saying anything. If he'd merely come to the last few meetings, he'd know the plan over and under. Claravena fought down her impatience and said merely, "Noru can explain it along the way."

Ithilo was back, Noru walking behind him. "Is it time?" Noru asked. "And what's he doing here?"

"He's here to work with you," Claravena said.

Ithilo gritted his teeth. "Don't you think it's too late for us to change everything we've prepared for?"

"We're not going to change everything. We're going to improve the plan in two small ways. Noru, you'll be the one to take Giovel now. Instead of leading him back toward Wurelna and Tranin, you're going to take him to the Divnum Library."

"Giovel might recognize me," Noru argued.

"He won't have a choice. See, Etelier's going to bring his daughter to meet you there."

If this injunction surprised Etelier, he didn't show it. He just nodded. "Where is she now?"

Claravena handed him a scrap of parchment. "Follow these notes to find her. None of us have got close enough to spirit her out, and she might be guarded. I don't think she'll have enough protection to stop you, however."

"How can you trust him with this?" Ithilo growled. "Etelier's a heap of waste on all our backs."

Maybe so, Claravena thought. But the old thunder was still there, close to the surface. And he had his own daughter to think about once more, no matter how slim his hope might be of finding any healing glyphs for her. Parents were so easy to mold. They'd do the most deplorable things for their children, far worse than Ithilo or Noru or Claravena could ever do.

"Anything else I'll need to know before we divide?" Etelier asked.

"Once Giovel starts singing, kill him," Claravena replied. "We need to sink at least three of the Divine in Cold Lake today."

FORGETTING

It's surprisingly easy not to think about you.
—The Witherclaw Witch; letter to Golkorun.

THE FIRST QUESTION in Giovel's mind when a move began was whether he'd forgotten anything. Perhaps it was Banner Captain Piadu's training twenty years ago that seared it into his mind. Weapons? Orders? Maps? Companions? Do you know their parts as well as your own? Have you prepared for this contingency, considered that outcome? Piadu spent more time practicing this kind of mental preparation than they ever spent implementing his instruction. It stuck, though. So here Giovel was, huddled in a copse of leafless trees as rioters swarmed the Divnum walls, and his mind had the clarity to run through all the same questions anew, checking to make sure he hadn't forgotten any piece of the plan, pausing to savor the scent of woodsmoke from the watch station nearby even as he listened to shouts from beyond the woods. He was prepared.

"Do you really think the witches are responsible for this?" Elínla asked. She crouched behind a bush at his side, holding her cowl close as camouflage.

"Etelier spread the lie about gold in the walls," Giovel said. "If I had my own gold, I'd wager it against water that this is his move."

Now if only they knew why. Going after Hirnu would be obvious, of course. But why strike the walls now, when the witches finally had a reason to see real weakness in the Order?

Adni and Kanis were late. Adni had said to regroup by midday, and here it was two hours past, not much true daylight remaining. Giovel and Elínla breathed into their hands and stamped their feet softly for warmth, waiting while selfish fools attacked the Candleguard trying to secure the walls. The hours felt only longer because Elínla wouldn't meet Giovel's eyes, wouldn't say much more than she had to.

It was surprising how empty the copse felt even with her there. Giovel might as well have been alone. Some part of him had hoped Elínla would understand him and extend the trust she'd just started offering before he found out about Iremni.

Then again, he thought, I didn't realize I even *wanted* to be trusted until now. I've spent so much of my time pushing against the mountain and pulling against the wind. I assumed everyone else was doing the same behind all their plans and goals for their own power. If Elínla hadn't started trusting me, formerly at least, maybe I'd still think that. Or if Sur hadn't treated me like an equal. Or if Hirnu hadn't taken the time to sit and hurt with me. Or even if Adni hadn't told me how he really thinks behind his self-serving mask.

I suppose this *is* something I forgot before this move—to give back to them like they've slowly given me. Here I am alone because I never took the time for anyone else.

"They're only getting angrier," Elínla muttered, pointing.

Giovel looked back at the walls as someone in the throng hurled a rock at a tall member of the Candleguard, hitting her in the shoulder. Other Candles shouted back and moved in to cover their companion, but there was little they could do. They'd fight back or the dissidents would take the walls, sooner or later. Where *was* Adni?

"You look like you're going to bite your own tongue out," Elínla said.

Giovel turned, realizing his jaw was clamped shut hard. "Do you expect me to be calm about what's going on?"

"I don't expect much of anything from you."

Giovel turned toward her to argue but fell silent when he saw a Candle-marked messenger rushing toward them through the tangle of snow-buried shrub.

"Adni?" Giovel asked.

The messenger was a young girl, probably Inorovel's age. She crouched with them, her breath no longer steaming though she was clearly winded. "An attack," she stammered. "Redremel."

"That's a good ploy to lure these witches out," Elínla said. "When is it happening?"

"It's real, Lady Elínla," the messenger said, holding a short, inky note with the seal of Jinaten Teserot, Jade Commander. "Attacked the northeast scouting perimeter two days ago. Thousands of them."

Giovel snatched the note and read over it, but there was no more information on it. Not a hint of what resistance Jinaten's battalions had posed. Just that the attack happened as the girl said. Damn the Redremel forever.

"We need to find Adni *now*," Giovel said. The Lances would be withdrawing already, pouring northeast to fend off the Redremel. So much for their added presence in Foneth.

Elínla was on her feet. "This all smells like the witches knew when they'd attack—or know what we're up to. Run straight to the Candlespire, girl. If Lord Adni is there, tell him I'll be at Scout's Bridge looking for him. You stay here, Giovel."

The messenger ran as if she'd recovered herself completely, and Elínla followed. It left Giovel jittery with new nerves and itching to do like they did, to run, to move, to take an action while his heart beat faster and his blood felt warm. This was one contingency Piadu's training hadn't prepared him for, though.

A flood of Candles arrived all at once from the south, close to two hundred of them in all. It could have been all of Divnum's duty force coalescing here at once. They swooped toward the crowds at the walls, not breaking them apart but pushing them back with the shafts of their spears.

More thrown rocks. More impacts with Candleguard behind the line. Then a cluster of men climbed a tree and leaped onto the walls, pushing an older Candle off from fifteen paces up. He landed in the snow but didn't rise from the fall. Another Candle near where he'd stood whipped a sword out and slashed the two who'd pushed his companion. Giovel swore and almost ran out, despite his orders to wait for Adni.

More weapons drawn. More cries of pain. The smell of blood was like a dip in the valley, pulling everyone close to push and strike and shout.

Why are we like this? How can we let gold or anger or some fool witch convince us to turn on our own so quickly? We have an enemy just thirty leagues away, and here we are fighting those who should be our sisters and brothers.

Giovel shook himself and turned to look for any other messengers. No one was in sight. Maybe someone would have news at the nearby barracks, though it would probably be empty now, more Candles pouring out as the fighting intensified. Giovel gritted his teeth and started toward it just to be sure. He couldn't wait for Adni forever, not with Redremel, rebels, and witches to think about all at once.

When Giovel left the trees, he found a broad man in a red snow cloak approaching.

"Lord Giovel?"

He knew this man from somewhere, though he couldn't place the face. "Talk while I walk," he snapped. There was no time to be still.

The man didn't follow as Giovel brushed past. He simply said, "A confederate of mine has your daughter, Lord Giovel."

Inorovel.

Giovel missed a step and tripped on packed snow. He caught himself on one elbow and felt almost too weak to rise again. Hearing seemed to have left him. Let it all be a nightmare like those weeks alone.

"You will come with me," the man in the red snow cloak said.

Giovel tried once again and failed to push himself upright. He felt battered all over. His legs shook and the coldness returned to his hands with all the heaviness of lead and silver.

Then Giovel realized. After all my checking to see what this operation needed, to gather the pieces together . . . I had my weapons, my orders, my companion even. I kept my head when the messenger brought news. But I never even thought to warn Inorovel, to increase her guard, to move her somewhere safer.

So I did forget something. My daughter.

A VISIT TO THE RICH

I'm starting to like the reddish color of the sky here.
—The Witherclaw Witch; letter to Recia.

THE STREETS OF Belnum were clear and wide around Claravena. Someone had painstakingly moved the snow so cobbles and dirt alike were clean of slush or hardpack turned to ice. A street for people with money. The houses were bigger too, often with small Sanctuaries separating them—stretches of grass, rings of boulders, little ponds with frozen streams joining one to another. Afternoon sun streamed in the gaps between the buildings, though there was little warmth in it, even for people as rich as those living here. A few children played by the roads. There were no patrols. Perhaps because everyone had coin to secure their own property, or perhaps because the wealthy denizens of this corner of Foneth assumed no neighbor was low enough to be one of the witches, traitors, or hungry rats plaguing the rest of the city.

"You once lived near here, didn't you?" Claravena asked as they passed a house with a tower three times the height of the nearest building.

"That's right," Ithilo responded. "My family was close enough you could shout and they'd hear. Will hear, rather. My mother still lives there."

So maybe she'd hear more than yelling by the time they fulfilled their plan. Hopefully not, but Claravena had never killed a current member of the Divine Order before, let alone one of the most senior of them. Perhaps it was worth feeling nervous over. Instead Claravena felt an odd sense of calm, almost boredom.

It gave her pause.

Removing the Divine was so much of what she and the Starlit Order had worked for. Months of life, years for some of them. And there they were, ready to cut them to nothing in the course of an hour, if Claravena's plans went forward.

I should be elated, or at least so nervous I can't see straight. Instead I just feel like I'm walking against a biting wind, envying the wealth of the people who live in warmth on either side of me.

Why? Am I like Etelier now? Have I forgotten to care about anything but the task?

She tripped on an uneven cobble leading to one of the great houses. There was no snow to cushion her fall there, so she caught herself on the frozen ground, jamming hard against both wrists and one knee simultaneously.

"Watch where you step," Ithilo mumbled without even pausing.

She hesitated to push herself up. Not because of pain or injury, but because she realized she couldn't tell how she'd come here, what forces drove her to fight the Order and the Optacracy so hard for so long. She knew she hated every one of them. Knew her family had shattered because of them. Vengeance wasn't what led her on, though. So she had to wonder, *why* keep going?

Of course she hadn't always fought. When she and her sisters awakened, she'd tried everything she could to help them live with Yulena. They'd joined the Sept of the Southern Star together, hoping to find solace and self-mastery enough to temper their Yulena—and for Eronea, Lolen, Claravena and the others to overcome their own new terror of each other. It hadn't worked.

Then when Alene and Uro began experimenting, Claravena had buried herself in a study of every law and statute and policy related to awakening, weighing out what they were required to report, what not, what protections they could have if the Order came for them, whether the Grays could take them away, every piece she could think of. As it happened, the intricacy of law didn't matter. Alene and Lolen saw to that by killing one another long before anyone knew they had access to an illegal power.

So here we are, Claravena thought. Another sister hunted, another in the Grays, and me all alone and as lost now as I was when I started. So maybe it's not the Order I hate in the first place. Maybe it's Yulen itself.

But she loved it too, just as she still loved Eronea and their foolish older sisters. She was good at wielding Yulena, good enough to hide it for years now, to mask even the motion of invoking a spell. Maybe that was why she'd pushed so hard.

Not to burn the Order to the ground. Just to prove that it was the awakenings and the heart-link itself that were the real enemy. It was Claravena's deepest belief. The old theory often debated and never truly shown—that *something* caused these awakenings and pushed them all into the dead-end valley of knowing Yulen's voice. No one could validate that assertion; there was no evidence for it, no hidden Vindilic lore to explain awakenings like Etelier and Noru believed. But Claravena had held out for years with the hope of finding the hidden key somewhere.

In all likelihood, I won't be able to search again after this, she thought. We won't all survive this move against the Order. And then, what are we left with? No protection for future awakenings, no legal reform or retroactive recompense for others like us. Just our own conviction that Yulen itself is to blame, which is the only explanation we have for why we've awakened and others haven't.

So it's not anger at Erenoea that brought me this far. It's not vengeance for Adni Aman hunting Uro. Just the drive to show what I and my sister sisters were always made of. Yulen has robbed our bloodline of any respect we ever had, making us look weak as beetles and cold as the ground. That's not who we are. If I alone am left to prove that, then I swear by my sisters' names that I will.

"Are you coming?" Ithilo snapped.

He was almost fifteen paces ahead, peering back from the edge of the street. Claravena's wrists were starting to stiffen, still holding her up just above the cobbled street.

"You're going to have housewives flocking out to make sure you aren't a drunk vomiting on their grass," Ithilo said, now hurrying back to pull her upright. "Act dizzy if anyone approaches."

Sure enough, a woman in an embroidered cloak watched them from the lintel of a house across the way. Ithilo made a point of patting

Claravena on the shoulder and laughing it off as if she'd had an odd spell of melancholy.

"She's expecting in the spring," he called to the woman watching. "Do you have any hitherhop I could give her?"

"What are you doing?" Claravena hissed, recovering herself finally.

"What are *you* doing?" Ithilo hissed back. "You're acting like an imbecile, and it's going to risk us getting watched!"

His voice softened as the woman in the cloak hurried over to offer a measure of hitherhop and her congratulations on their coming child. Ithilo smiled and ushered Claravena off on his arm. He kept a hard grip on her until they were past the corner and out of sight.

"We're almost there," he said. "Ralden's house is the one at the end."

Claravena straightened. "No need to patronize me. I'm fine."

For our family, I'll be as fine as I have to be. And though everyone in this world might have forgotten my sisters, no one will ever forget me.

Two Candleguard lounged outside Ralden's house. "Are you sure you're ready for this?" Ithilo mumbled as they neared the house.

Claravena shushed him. "Stick to our plan."

Their plan was simple but relied on proximity to Ralden's house. Just to be sure it worked as anticipated, Claravena pulled a long parchment from her robe and approached the nearest of several houses on the same side of the street as Ralden's, if street sides even mattered in sections of the city as spacious as this. She and Ithilo clapped outside the first house, asking for signatures against Zuris Medín's ludicrous gambit to fortify the city. They had six signatures by the time they came to Ralden's door, and the two lazy Candleguard had relaxed even more upon seeing and hearing their supposed reason for approaching. They probably saw Claravena and Ithilo as nothing but a pair of nosy Optacrats. They were totally unprepared when Claravena shrieked and threw the parchment from her.

"WITCH!"

The big parchment fluttered to the ground, now glowing as a fully-formed glyph. And, fools that they were, the Candles reached for the spears and leveled them not at Claravena but at Ithilo. Ithilo threw his arms back in his tell, unleashing his spell on the nearer Candle. The Candle vanished, spirited off to somewhere nearby. Before his companion could recover himself, Ithilo turned to run.

Claravena screamed again. Ithilo sprinted for the edge of the street, and the remaining Candle followed, shouting after him. Now they had but to wait for any more hidden watchers to emerge as well.

Sure enough, two more Candles exited Ralden's house, sparing barely a glance at Claravena before running after their companion. A short Gray appeared from behind another house and ran out as well. Within fifty heartbeats, the street was clear except for people watching Ithilo run, and the front door to Ralden's house was unlocked. So many fools. All it took to divert their eyes was the very name of the thing they feared.

Claravena let herself in.

Ralden's house was opulent. Panels of wood stained a dark, purplish cherry lined the entrance. Only a few narrow textiles marked the walls, but they looked expensive enough to pay for Claravena's own home—narrow streams of silver cloth marked with a black so dark it seemed to absorb the glow of the silver. The hallway opened into a high-roofed Sanctuary with what looked like a small hill. Grass as green as flower bulbs sprouted in here, somehow thriving even in the late months of winter. Claravena saw no one nearby, though she heard footsteps echoing somewhere beyond the Sanctuary.

She took another risk and called, "Lady Ralden! We need to get you to safety!"

Would the woman know the voices of her guards? Hopefully not.

Sure enough, a voice called back, "Inia? Is that you? What's going on out there?"

Claravena crouched behind the Sanctuary hill to wait as the footsteps came nearer. They were slow. The steps of someone hobbling or limping, like Ralden must still be thanks to Wurelna's efforts almost three months before.

"Inia?" Ralden called. Her voice was close now, echoing inside the Sanctuary. Claravena sketched a Nettle and dove out from behind the hill.

Ralden wasn't alone, however. She had another Gray beside her, tablet already armed with what looked like a Rod. Almost as soon as Claravena showed herself, the Gray threw hands and feet forward in his tell. The Rod smashed into the grass right beside Claravena's feet. Claravena cast her Nettle back but missed wildly, shattering a gleaming window at the back of the Sanctuary.

"Out the back, Ralden," the Gray said calmly and unleashed another spell. Claravena rolled to the far side of the hill and drew another three glyphs in the dirt. One Flail, one Talon, one Reverse.

The Gray rounded the hill with his tablet raised. Claravena hurled a knife before firing a spell, hitting the Gray's tablet and nearly knocking it from his hands. Then she struck with the Reverse. The Gray immediately began to stagger, tripping over his own feet as he walked not toward but away from Claravena.

Ralden was gone already, but no matter. While the Gray cursed and tried to orient himself, Claravena hit him with the Flail, sending the tablet flying from the Gray's hands. Then she scooped it up, drew a backup Talon, and launched her previous glyph at the Gray's heart. It cut right through him, slashing the grassy hill with red.

The house's front door burst open then. Claravena lowered the tablet to strike, but it was only Ithilo, seemingly unharmed.

"I lost the Candles, killed one, spirited the Gray off too," he said quickly. "We won't have much time before they find their way back here. Where's Ralden?"

Claravena waved. "Stay back a few paces in case she has any more watchers hiding in here."

Best to be cautious, even with as little time as they had now the Candles knew they were here. The one Gray alone had surprised Claravena, and a house this big could hide many more.

Stars send that Eronea isn't among them.

The hallway behind the Sanctuary split off into six different rooms. With Ithilo watching her back, Claravena leaped into the first one and swung around to spot some sign of a trap. *Anything* in this room could mask one, though. Almost a score of bulky bookshelves lined the walls, with curtains and crevices between each. Large reading chairs broke the room into sections as well, affording even more hiding places. Worst of all, pale light flooded into the room from another doorway—a passage curving around toward the house's main entrance. There wasn't time to search all of this.

"Now we split up," Claravena said "You take the three rooms on the left, and I'll take this and the next two on the right."

She didn't wait for Ithilo to leave for his part. She simply started drawing, imbuing, and firing Dimmers into the room, knocking chairs over, pushing shelves free, blasting books through the air. One

Dimmer miscast and blackened Claravena's vision for a moment, but within the count of thirty she could see again and was sure Ralden hadn't hidden in there.

Two more rooms, fifteen or so more glyphs. Claravena demolished a dining hall almost as big as the Sanctuary and what appeared to be an office for Ralden's textile business—a cluttered room full of pattern swaths, color charts, fitting stools, and tiny looms, shears, flattening irons, and other tools. There wasn't much left but the hum of Yulena after a stream of spells did their work, but the splendor of the rooms still made Claravena wide-eyed.

It sounded as if Ithilo was finishing a sweep of the rooms across the hall when he found Ralden.

Wood splintered in the hallway walls as a massive spell punched into the siding. Ithilo dove out into the hall with his hands covering his head as two more spells followed the first. Claravena sketched a counter spell and ran close enough to loose it in at an angle, but the return glyphs continued quicker than she could draw. Fire and water, Ralden was *fast*.

"Together now," Claravena hissed at Ithilo. She sketched a Nettle while Ithilo scratched an Outpour in his field book. They met each other's eyes, then swiveled around on the smooth floor to strike into the last room simultaneously.

Claravena saw several things at once. A spray of golden light as another spell began inside the room. Showers of torn paper fluttering like snow. A row of paintings rattling against one wall. Stairwells arching upward in two directions at the back of the room. And in the stairs, not one but two women. Ralden and someone else, both holding sand tablets. Ralden sat, one hand clutching her bandaged side. The other woman was advancing past the stairs.

The doorway splintered open as a pair of spells hit its sides near where Claravena and Ithilo had shown their heads. They swiveled hard and fast enough to steer back into the hallway, missing anything but a tiny concussion wave from another glyph, but Claravena didn't stop moving. She crawled back to the next room for cover with a wild wave for Ithilo to follow. He had an open doorway between them now, no shelter to get across.

"There's another mage with her!" Claravena yelled to be heard over the impact of more spells. "Get back from there!"

Curse this rich woman that had not one but *three* Grays surrounding her like lapdogs. Claravena spun into the previous room on her side of the hall, dodging the wreckage from moments before. It looked like it had been a reception room, with fewer furnishings and a row of tall windows overlooking the hills behind the house. Claravena ran to a spot of wall that would put her near those stairwells, near Ralden, and began unleashing Flail after Flail. She'd never counted how many it would take to smash through an entire building. Hopefully less than the number of steps it would take that Gray to reach Ithilo.

Claravena had loosed six times when the wall buckled and blasted apart—not away from her but *toward* her, twin slashes of purple ripping through it from Ralden's direction.

An arrow of wood stabbed into Claravena's left arm. She dropped for cover. A piece of brick hit just above her eye as she went down, knocking her head back and scraping skin free as it ricocheted out into the room. Her sight pulsed dark, then painfully bright. Her eye felt whole, but the inside of her skull ached as if it had been shaken back and forth ten thousand times. She hit the ground, banging her head against wood even before the debris from the blast settled around her.

She could still see, could identify Raden hobbling toward the gaping gash in the wall, and behind her, her companion. Not a Gray, though. Hirnu Pala, the toughest mage alive. So she hadn't been deposed after all. Claravena wanted to laugh that she'd fallen for such a trap.

The sharp sound of an Ember made the two Divine turn abruptly. Ithilo. In that tiny moment, Claravena roared and pushed herself into a roll. She found her tablet under a layer of dust and splintered wood and scooped it up to start sketching another Dimmer. Ralden turned back and released a spell through the opened wall, but she couldn't get an angle from that close, so Claravena easily dodged aside. It hurt to move her neck, but nothing was broken that she could tell. She waited until another spell shot through the hole before she leaned back into sight and struck with her Dimmer.

The spell hit Ralden in the face, knocking her back into the stairwell at the back of the gallery. It wouldn't do much harm, but its blinding effect would have to be enough.

"We've got her!" someone shouted nearby. Not from the room with Hirnu. Claravena spun around to find three of the Candles from before. They were panting and sweaty, but they all had handbows leveled at her. And once again, the surprise made her want to laugh.

Well done, Divine Order. We knew you'd be ready for an attack, but you still outdid us with sheer numbers.

A scream echoed in the other room, a shrill, high-pitched shriek like a horse's in heat. Ithilo's voice. The Candles' attention flickered aside just long enough for Claravena to slash a single line onto her tablet. She hated experimental spellbuilding, but there was no time to do otherwise. She unleashed the one-line glyph, let it shoot free without her control, and ran at the tall windows in the back of the room.

One bolt shot past her face. Then a glyph through the opened wall, Hirnu baring her teeth from the hole. Claravena ignored it all and ran. Clanging sounds from her own spell followed as she leaped shoulder-first at the tall windows and crashed through to the snow and the biting air outside. It wasn't a long fall, just three paces into drifting powder. Claravena was back on her feet and curving around the front of the house almost as soon as she landed.

She didn't look back.

Whatever her glyph had done, it must have delayed the Candles. No more bolts followed. No more spells, either, though voices shouted after her. She strained her ears to listen for any more spell-impacts. When none came, she was sure Ithilo's scream had been his last.

At least it had been him and not Wurelna or Tranin. Or me, Claravena thought.

Time to forget losses and proceed where victory was still possible. Claravena spun behind the little cluster of streets by the wall and turned over the hills, toward the library.

The Divine might have tricked us here, she thought, but they only have one Hirnu. And we have a trick or two left in store as well.

THE GREAT DIVNUM LIBRARY

Mothers can be frightened too.
  —The Witherclaw Witch; letter to Inivar and Sil.

VARAN'S FIRST THOUGHT was to shout that a witch was here. Raising her voice would at least give Suresni or any remaining Lances warning that Wurelna and her friends had arrived. But no, better to have an advantage when she opened that door, to have some needle of surprise on her side. Varan didn't really know how to use the wrist-thrower strapped to each arm, and the only time she'd faced a witch alone she'd all but lost an ear. So she supposed she needed every advantage she could have this time.

Suresni's house had only a few rooms to each level. The sounds of creaking wood marked a stairwell in the back, probably where the 'wounded' witch friend Tranin was now approaching Suresni.

Varan walked in as if expected.

Two of Wurelna's companions appeared a breath later, peering down a narrow hallway at her. Varan threw her arms out like she'd seen others do, whipping her wrists back in a sharp motion to release the trigger mechanisms hooked to her middle fingers. Her darts shot almost directly to her sides, sticking to the walls by the door. The would-be Lances blinked at her in puzzlement.

So much for her surprise.

"It's the Witherclaw —" one of the pretend Lances started to say. He stopped, yelped and leaped back for cover as Varan twirled her arms and Quickened a pocket of air between him and his companion. The Quickened spot flashed orange. Then an explosion of smoke and heat shot through the hall with a bang like a door slammed shut. A dry patch of wall took flame, and both of Varan's targets darted into a stairwell to escape her.

"What's going on down there?" someone shouted overhead.

Before the others could respond, Varan shouted, "FIRE!"

"It's the Witherclaw," the fake Lance said again, this time raising his voice. Once again, his words morphed into a yelp as Varan opened her left-side wrist-thrower. Her dart took him in the open mouth this time.

The pretend Lance gagged, coughed, and staggered back. Varan Quickened every reaction she could think to speed the serum along—metabolic and respiratory. The witch-friend began to vomit blood onto his companion, who was fumbling for a short sword as Varan advanced and hurled another dart.

Pounding upstairs. Heavy footfalls, furniture moving. Varan Tempered hot air from her fire, spurring a gust of wind between the fake Lances and knocking them apart with a sound like cracking timber. Then she shouldered past and sprinted up a narrow stairwell to find Tranin and Suresni.

A series of blue flashes cut her off at the top of the staircase. Yulena.

Varan dropped to her hands and knees just below the top stair, dodging as a set of spells tore into the back walls and blasted holes into the cold sky. She caught a short glimpse of the witch behind the spells. Not Wurelna. Her sharp-faced friend Tranin. So they'd come in force, *two* witches for one wounded mage, not to mention the pair of bumbling fools downstairs, one who was now climbing behind Varan to flank her.

Varan spun around and leaped down the stairs, landing feet first on the shoulders of the witch-friend. He let out a sort of gurgle, probably losing his breath completely as her weight slammed him back down the stairwell. She landed with her knees on his ribcage, smacking his body against the wooden floor below the stairs. His companion was still there as well, trying to cough the dart from the side of his mouth.

Tranin ducked out of sight from the stairs, but Wurelna took her place and started pounding down the stairwell, clearing her way with another burst of Yulena. Varan jumped past the stairs and ran back up the narrow hallway for cover. Neither of the witches' wounded companions made a move to follow.

"He must have slipped out around us!" someone shouted overhead. Tranin.

Just my luck, Varan thought dourly. I come to help Suresni and he isn't even here to be helped.

Wurelna dropped down the last few steps and tripped over her fallen comrade just as Varan leaped into the tiny side room by the front door. No Suresni in here, either, but no way out while another spell shot by the entrance, shattering a little window by the door and spraying glass into the snow like flakes of ice in a storm.

"Witherclaw's cornered!" Wurelna called. "Come out with your hands on your face, Witherclaw. I don't want any more fire spraying from your eyes."

One hallway wall was still aflame, Varan realized, spreading toward the ceiling. Gods above. They'd be in a blaze fit for a feast if it caught into the old floorboards on the next level.

More footsteps on the stairs. Then Tranin's voice, "Where'd you hide Suresni, Witherclaw? Tell us and we won't kill your friends, the translator's daughter and her brood."

Varan froze in place.

Kirida. But no, they couldn't have her. Nomis would have her protected. That the witches knew about them was horrible enough, but Varan couldn't believe they'd taken Kirida, Progis, or tiny Chivi. If they did, though? Then it's all because of me, Varan thought.

"Let's see those hands," Wurelna yelled from somewhere nearby.

Kirida and her family weren't here. The only thing to do was to make sure no witch or messenger could reach them now, no matter what happened next.

So Varan screamed and leaped out, releasing both wrist-throwers once more and Tempering more hot air to blast her tiny darts out at the long-faced witch.

The hallway rattled as air buffeted the walls and pushed a narrow rug curling upward. Varan's serumed darts flew to the sides and pattered off the back walls, useless, but the sudden burst of air kicked up a discharge of dust and knocked Wurelna half off her feet. She staggered into Tranin, who now held a glowing mage tablet behind her, and they both stumbled for balance. Varan seized the moment to launch more darts, left, right, right again, one more from the left. The wrist-throwers sent a sharp pressure back into each of her elbows. She almost thought she'd snap her own bones using them, clumsy weapons. But she hit both witches in their sides before they recovered their feet.

"Drown in Cold Lake!" Tranin screamed. She made a spasmodic motion in her neck and shoulders. Her tell.

A flash of fire took the ceiling almost just as the witches began unleashing their spells at Varan. Maybe it was her burst of Tempered air fanning life back into the flames, but the prongs of fire whipped upward and blocked that exit just as silvery streams of Yulena began pounding into the walls and punching holes into the air outside. Varan dropped to the ground to evade Tranin's spells. Wurelna ran at her while she was down, seizing a fistful of Varan's hair before she could get back into the side room for cover. The witch yanked, pulling Varan into a hard slide that scraped her bad ear over rough planks of flooring.

Pain like clamping teeth. There was a flash of metal, a knife in the witch's hand. She leaned forward to swipe at Varan's neck.

Varan kicked off the nearby wall with so much force she lost a clump of hair to Wurelna's hand. The kick sent her own body spinning sideways, and Wurelna stumbled back as the hair came away, knife cutting into the floor barely a handsbreadth from Varan's shoulder. In the moment she had, Varan Enervated wildly in Wurelna's innards, trying to drain her energy and still her breath. Instead, the witch began belching like a swamp frog, head whipping back with each burst of gas from her mouth. Varan scampered back, Tempered the fire away from the front door, where she was ready to push her way through, burns or not.

Then something hit her hard in the shoulder, flipping her over and sending a hot, sweaty sensation shooting through her side. Her eyes began streaming water. Her mouth too, flooding like a dog's. Varan couldn't Enervate her own reflex to stop any of it. She just spat and sputtered and tried to regain her balance before the fire could take what was left of her hair.

Then the door swung open from the outside. Suresni stood there, badly dressed for the cold. He leaped over Varan to tackle the long-faced witch, ramming her knife-hand upward and grappling her away from Varan in the same motion. A stunned-looking Tranin paused in her jerking tell. It gave Varan just enough time to hurl two more darts past both Suresni and Wurelna, catching Tranin in the arm both times.

More Yulena. It looked like a spell had broken free from its caster, because the walls right beside Tranin ruptured in a globe of violet light almost in time with Tranin's tablet winking out. Stone cascaded outward, crunching the side wall together like a dried leaf smashed underfoot. A beam of wood toppled over Suresni and knocked him flat. Someone shouted, "Back!" Then the doorway by Varan pried upward from its posts, whipping into the air and scattering chunks of burning wood into the snow.

When Varan's eyes stopped streaming enough for her to blink, wipe her face, and find half her equilibrium, half of Suresni's house had toppled over, and Wurelna and Tranin were nowhere in sight. One of their fighters was still there, crumpled at the bottom of the stairwell where Varan had landed on him. No trace of the other except the thin trail of sick where he'd stood before. Suresni groaned and pushed himself upward, wincing and trying to rub his shoulder where the loose beam had struck.

"They ruined my house," was all he said, staring wide-eyed at the left side of the building, now wholly exposed to the frigid air of late afternoon.

Varan pushed herself upright. Her hair and clothes clung to her skin and her palms were clammy. Her throat and nose had dried out suddenly as well, as if all the moisture in them had leaked out after the witch's disgusting spell hit her.

But she was alive. Alive to chase after them.

"Are you hurt?" she asked, helping Suresni up from the wreckage. He didn't seem to be bandaged any more, but he moved stiffly as if just walking was new to him.

"Of course I'm hurt. Did you see that piece of wood that hit me?" He climbed over a chunk of broken wall to look for the witches. A small crowd had gathered in the streets, some mumbling and making warding signs, others stepping forward to investigate. And there were Tranin, her long-faced friend, and their companion, shuffling back toward the Trade Road, no longer wearing Lance gear.

"I see them," Varan said. "Can you send Lances after us to help when more of them arrive?" They couldn't go far. Not with rustwood serum in all three of them.

Suresni pulled a sand tablet and a coat from the tiny side room. "Forget Lances. I'll go after them myself."

Varan didn't argue. Just said, "I thought you were wounded."

"And I thought you disappeared. Come on. Those bastards can't get far like that."

The front lines of the crowd parted as Suresni showed himself. When they saw Varan with him, they shifted even wider apart.

Giovel never considered struggling. He probably could have broken free from the lone man who led away from the walls and off to the southeast part of Divnum. He was bound at the wrists, relieved of his weapons, but he knew how to fight with only his feet and the weight of his body. The thing was, he believed his captor's threat. It wouldn't have been so horrific except that Giovel knew he'd done nothing meaningful to prevent someone from finding Inorovel eventually.

They came after Iremni more than a year ago. I should have known they'd come back. So no struggle, no attempt to call for help or leave a sign for Elínla to follow. The Redremel are coming, the rebels are at the walls, but all I can do is cooperate now.

His captor took him to a wide part of the Iceflow near Bone Hill, where a woman waited with a tiny boat. She and Giovel's first captor rowed him south by the forests toward the Great Divnum Library. It was almost sunset when they arrived, and no archivists walked the lower hallways. Just another companion of Giovel's captors, who nodded, mumbled a few words, and led the way upstairs.

Giovel's guards pushed him into an almost lightless stack room on the third level of the building. Etelier sat there at a plain table, rubbing his hands together as if he were trying to get dirt off them without washing. He looked almost surprised when he saw Giovel, gray eyes widening.

"Got him," the one who'd first approached Giovel said. "One Divine Mage as planned. Can I keep his sand tablet?"

"If you want it," Etelier said. "The rest of you can leave us."

"You can't order me around."

"Fine. You stay, but those two leave, Noru."

The man behind Giovel pushed him forward hard. He tripped on the carpet and fell almost on his face, unable to catch himself except on one knee. When Etelier pulled him upright and shoved him into a chair, the other man and woman were gone.

"What do you want from me?" Giovel asked.

"I want a spell that can heal the damage done by drumfever," Etelier said.

What? "I don't know any spell like that."

The one called Noru slapped him in the back of the head. "Of course you don't, fishback. Word is you don't know any spells at all."

"We want to know where the Order's secret library is, what it's disguised as," Etelier said, now taking a chair on the other side of the table from Giovel. "I know you could hide glyphs in a hundred places here. The Star Room walls, for instance, or those old maps Ralden spent so much time studying before we killed her."

What in hellfire? Why did everyone think they had a secret library? And did they not know Ralden had survived? No, they must have. So unless Etelier was playing some bluff to scare him, Etelier was referring to something else. It made the pit in Giovel's stomach deepen.

There's a chance, he thought wildly. He could tell them the Order hid glyphs somewhere, show them, then wait as they killed themselves trying made-up spells. But they were just as likely to force *him* to cast any new glyphs he showed them, so he'd only get himself killed without Inorovel ever standing a chance to escape.

No lies this time.

"I don't know anything about a secret library," he said. "If there is one, the Order has never entrusted its location or nature to me."

Noru spat on him. "You think we're fools, do you?"

Etelier leaned forward over the table. "Let me make this clear, Giovel. We have your daughter bound and helpless and close by. The reason I want you here is for *my* daughter, who needs something only hidden Yulena is likely to give her. So. Father to father, you can be sure I'll do what it takes for my little girl, no matter the cost to yours."

The weight in Giovel's stomach seemed to expand into his knees, down into his feet. His sight swam for a moment as he tried to collect himself internally.

But I believe you, he thought. A father trying to help his child will push as hard and bend as low as anyone I can think of, except perhaps another father or mother.

"I'd tell you every spell I know if that could help you," Giovel said. "And I don't doubt that the Order has many more secrets I haven't learned. But I swear I don't know about any hidden library. Please. Just let Inorovel go. You can ransom me off to the Order—"

"Or what?" Etelier asked. "You'll break free? Kill us all? We know you're tamer than that. As it happens, we know you want us all alive. You see, we're aware you barely use Yulena, that you hate having anything to do with it. We also know about your wife, Iremni. Our companion Claravena spirited her some time ago, and we're given to understand you've been trying hard to find the responsible party since. You wouldn't turn and fight too hard now, would you? Now that you have us face to face with half a chance to get answers for what happened to her, what Claravena did to break her."

He had a name. He had half a confession. They felt empty.

Etelier went on. "We might know every weakness you have, Giovel Ullin. So we'll take some time to prick into them. Maybe hearing a scream or two from the other room will help you remember something."

"You'd show Inorovel to me if you had her here," Giovel said, voice rising almost to a shriek. "You're just talking from your ass now."

"Did we not let you see her? How stupid of us." Etelier stood, walked behind the next row of volumes, and dragged a chair into the dim light by the table.

Inorovel was bound to it, a thick chunk of cloth in her mouth, head angled to one side as if she was unconscious. Drugged. There was no mistaking her, though, even in the shadows of the little room.

Giovel's tiny spark of endurance dimmed to nothing.

My daughter. Captured by witches just as Iremni was before. And all because of *me*.

Claravena ran until she'd reached a side road by the river, a place her snow tracks across the hills would blend with mud, slush, and the thousands of other boot prints pressing into the ground. She found a wave of workers returning from Belnum with the sunset and attached herself to their parade, turning ever so slowly to look for pursuit.

Nothing.

Whether or not Ralden, Hirnu, or anyone else was behind her, however, the Divine would surely move in response to her attack. So she had to move too.

Fortunately, her plans always included emergency measures, steps to safeguard the Starlit Order in cases just like this. She had three paid message-runners within a mile, runners they could trust with silence and not just coin, so as soon as Claravena was sure no one tailed her, she left the crowd of tired workers, veered into the streets by Blue Tree, and found the first runner.

Her message was simple. The Order has their own trap. Meet at the Divnum Library directly, no matter who you have in hand. She sent the first runner to fetch the second from Scout's Bridge, where they'd split off to find Noru, Etelier, Tranin, and Wurelna.

They'd only have time to go for the most vulnerable now, and that meant Giovel. Claravena just prayed their intelligence about him was correct. If the Order was willing to lie so publicly and drastically about Hirnu turning on them, could be Giovel's weeks of depression and immobility were part of a long scheme too.

But the story of him hating Yulena? That one Claravena still believed. She had to trust that the old fool would still be vulnerable when it came right to it.

She was exhausted when she reached the library, cold with her own sweat while her toes burned and tingled. She'd spanned half of Divnum in only a few hours, and she hadn't eaten all day. It was dusk now, the snow turning blue in shadowed corners as the walls swallowed the sun, but it felt like the day had been twice as long as it should have been.

"Who all has arrived?" Claravena asked Noru's wife Dolidan, who stood on guard at the entrance of the library.

"Noru and Etelier are upstairs," Dolidan said. "They've got Giovel."

"And the daughter?"

"Her too."

At last something had gone right in their plans.

"Do you know whether Giovel's talked yet?" Claravena asked.

"They brought him in a short while back. That's all I know."

"Good enough. How many of you are down here?"

"Four, all told. And we've got two archivists tied in the back."

"Move the archivists outside and get the rest ready to leave. We won't be long with Giovel, and we need to divide as soon as he talks."

"Will you have time to get anything from him?" Dolidan asked with a frown.

"We will if we skip him and put the weight on his daughter first," Claravena said, ignoring her sweatiness and aching feet as she started up the rounded side of the library. "Have everyone ready to run, Dolidan."

They'd waited long enough. There was no time for patience tonight.

THE RAGE OF A FATHER OR A MOTHER

They say all kinds of things about me, maybe thinking I don't understand. I hate giving them any reason to think they were right.

—The Witherclaw Witch; letter to Golkorun.

THE WITCHES SLOWED before long, pausing to rest and swallow long drafts of something that made them gasp. Maybe peppermead to dampen the serum. Varan stayed back far enough to keep hidden. She'd considered simply darting them both again until they gave up and collapsed, but that was before she realized what an opportunity she had. They could lead her right to the rest of them. Maybe even to their keep.

"How did you know they were coming for me?" Suresni asked, making Varan jump. He limped to her hiding place at the icy corner of Ola's Gate where she peered from Belnum into Divnum.

"You should get help, if you're wounded," Varan said.

"It feels good to be on my feet for once. Where are all the Lances who were stationed at the gate?"

"I don't know."

The guardhouses built into the walls were dark, and the streets were empty. It looked as if any Lance assigned here had left for the day, even abandoning whatever night shifts they normally kept. The witches began to hobble again, grunting audibly.

"There's someone else with them," Suresni growled.

He was right. A thin man had appeared as if from nowhere, though he ran off after speaking to them for just a moment.

The witches changed direction. Where they'd been moving up the main road past the gate, they now turned south through the narrow rows of homes flanking Ola's Gate.

"How long did you intend to let them walk free?" Suresni asked.

"Until they can't walk anymore," Varan said.

"Fine with me. If that was a messenger we just saw, they might even lead us somewhere interesting."

"Shouldn't you stay somewhere safe?" Varan asked.

"It used to be that the Order guarded *you*, if I remember rightly. What ever happened to that arrangement? You can't command me not to follow anyone, witches least of all."

Varan bit back her impatience. "Don't slow me down."

"You sound like Giovel. Come on."

The witches managed to stay on their feet long after Varan thought was possible, probably due to whatever stimulant they kept bringing to their lips every hundred paces. And Suresni was right. They *did* lead somewhere interesting—to the dark round outline of the Great Divnum Library, where someone hailed them as friends and opened the main doorway for them. Varan and Suresni exchanged glances from the half cover of a few trees.

"There are no guard stations near here," Suresni mumbled. "Probably not a coincidence."

"I'm not waiting for Candles to come," Varan said.

"Then I'd better watch my own back," Suresni said, and pulled a sand tablet from his coat. "If we move around the south side, we won't be seen until we're close enough to spit on their friends at the doorway."

Varan followed Suresni in that direction.

The lamps smoked and sputtered in the room where they left Giovel. Etelier had gone almost as soon as he'd shown Inorovel, dragging the chair to which she was bound behind him and slamming the door shut. It left just Giovel, the dim glow of the lamps, Noru, and another man beside him.

After a moment of grumbling, Noru and his companion rummaged around the archives room and gathered a stack of documents. "We'll see if you've got some spells hidden even here," Noru said, spreading pages out across the table, his back to Giovel. His companion peered over his shoulder and mumbled questions.

It was as if Giovel was an afterthought. That was when he knew they didn't need him alive after all. They might keep him to see whether he talked, but they would doubtless be glad to have him dead. One less Divine Mage to thwart whatever it really was they wanted.

No matter what they wanted—killing him, finding some cure for drumfever, whatever else—Giovel finally knew who they were.

They're the ones who spirited Iremni. I've even got a name, this Claravena. So what now, now that I know even this much?

But he knew that too. He'd seen the paths crossing before him from the moment Etelier showed Inorovel.

It was all a great scale of things one could or couldn't control. Giovel's first option was to stay silent, give no information. He'd keep in command of himself, bide his time, wait for rescue, and stay true to the trust the Order had given him, little as that seemed to be. But this path would give him no control over *them*. They might get impatient and kill him or grow angry and kill Inorovel. In any case, they'd probably hurt one or both of them badly—and because Etelier knew the easiest way to hurt Giovel was through Inorovel, this option lent Giovel the least control over his circumstances.

The second option was to lie, to lead them along. It would give Giovel space to maneuver, perhaps to fabricate a situation where the balance shifted and he could escape. The problem was he'd still have very little control. The witches could split up—have one take Giovel wherever he claimed the secret library was while another held a knife to Inorovel's face. They could take *her* to investigate and leave Giovel behind. They'd find nothing, kill her, and come back to finish him next.

There were other options too. Giovel could stall all night and hope the witches didn't torture him, or just disavow the Order, beg for amnesty, claim that Inorovel had awakened, that she wanted to join them. But how could he control what she'd say or do when she awoke?

In the end, Giovel saw only one road that gave him control of the situation.

It was an option he didn't like. It was to cast two Talons. Kill both Noru and his companion and flee.

They were fools. They treated him like an old Optacrat, not a mage. They'd bound him, yes, but he could probably work himself free with time. And even if he couldn't right away, he could spell himself loose with Yulena. They'd done nothing but bind his arms and hands, as if that alone could stop a mage. Maybe it *would* stop mages like them, or maybe they simply thought he was too green, too fresh to know how to use Yulena against them.

They were wrong. And striking these two dead would give Giovel ultimate control over their actions. Dead men were entirely predictable.

The thing was, killing his captors also relinquished control he'd ached over since Iremni's spiriting. Because now he knew who'd done it. Now he had them close by. If he waited and the Order stormed the library and took them in, he could question them all and finally get some answers. If he held back, maybe just overpowered them, he could exert some small measure of power over their responses to his questions, just as they now did over him. But the more he tried to keep them alive, the more he risked losing himself and Inorovel.

Press for answers or forget whoever else is here and any secrets they hold about their uprising, Yulena, or Iremni's spiriting. Abandon vengeance to be one step forward when he fled.

In a way, it was choosing Inorovel—his own likeness and blood—or choosing Iremni, who'd betrayed the longest, deepest love he'd ever felt. So from the moment he'd seen his daughter, Giovel knew he couldn't be half-hearted now.

He chose Inorovel.

The witch and his companion had their backs to him across the table. Giovel pushed upward with one foot, leaning his chair slightly back, and rolled his weight hard to the left. His chair tipped slowly, then sped up and slapped him hard against the cold stone floor. His captors jumped and turned at the sound. Noru had a tablet raised, but he laughed when he realized Giovel was still bound, still stuck to his chair, just tipped so his face now pressed against the rough floor.

"You trying to break your neck before Claravena can do it for you?" the other one asked.

They turned again, facing the doorway and their chart.

Giovel's ropes held despite his motion, so he had nothing free to carve a glyph but his tongue. That would be enough. He leaned forward and licked a single Talon on the dry floor. Even with the cold he'd have to act quickly before his saliva dried. He'd made this shape hundreds, even thousands of times thanks to Hirnu, so many that he could do it without looking or wondering if his tongue was steady enough to make them true. He wished he could lick another Talon, one for each of his captors, but they stood so close together that one glyph might be enough, and Giovel couldn't wiggle far enough to lick another outline without breaking the first.

He imbued the glyph and cast it almost immediately, sharply inclining his neck and curling forward hard against the ropes. They could have stopped him if they'd only bound his head in place. But they had never seen him use Yulena, didn't know his tell.

The witch Noru sneezed just then, head rocking forward toward the table. Giovel's Talon took his companion in the throat, but it missed Noru by a hair, simply spraying blood into his face as his companion sagged onto him without even a chance to scream. Noru righted himself, met Giovel's eyes, his own wide with astonishment.

Noru snatched the paper from under his companion, sketching a glyph shape with his finger and his friend's own blood. He was too fast for Giovel to counter. No time for another glyph. No space to maneuver.

But Yulen's glow made the outline of the glyph visible through the thin paper, and it was a shape Giovel knew—another Talon. So Giovel seized control of the glyph just as Noru lifted his finger, releasing Noru's Talon straight into his own face.

Noru dropped as silently as his companion had. Giovel was ready to make another spell, either to strike again or to slash the legs off his chair so he could push himself forward to claim Noru's belt knife and cut his hands free. He didn't move, though. Time had halted in Giovel's consciousness.

Warmth and candlelight. Food after fasting. The thrill of Iremni's touch. Water on dry skin. Wind in summer. It was like every sensation Giovel ever treasured was welling through him all at once, bursting out to fill his body to the tips of his fingers and the crown of his head.

He wasn't sure how long the wave of feeling overcame him. It could have been a heartbeat or an hour for all he could tell. He realized he'd forgotten to breathe, that his eyes were shut. When he coughed and inhaled and looked up, he saw the witches' blood still pooling. So he'd lost almost no time. Just felt . . . something.

A word came to his mind, and he knew immediately what it meant. Sur had warned him.

Exhilaration.

It flooded out almost as quickly as it had arrived, but it left Giovel disoriented and acutely aware of every pain, desire, and sensation that remained. The burn of the ropes at his wrists, the ache in his face where he'd hit the floor, the itch by his now-dry tongue, the hunger for warm rice and sweet cream.

What under the stars happened to me?

The pressure on Giovel's face convinced him to keep moving forward. He fumbled through the red puddles on the floor until he could get one hand on Noru's knife and work himself free with it. He was sticky and nauseous when he finished, and he staggered back to get away from the witches' bodies.

No time to be silk-stomached now. No time to wonder what Sur meant or what had just transpired. Someone else might have heard the clatter, and Claravena and Etelier were still out there, with Inorovel nearby.

Giovel gritted his teeth, shook himself to clear his head, and scooped up the other witch's knife as well. He took both sand tablets too, stuffing one in his coat and marking the other with an Illumina.

I've hit with both glyphs I've used yet. Since Hirnu taught me to control twenty in a row without fail, I should have a few more spells in me yet.

More importantly, he'd made his choice. Now he just had to live with it.

Immediately after he'd shown Giovel his daughter, Etelier left to search the upper rooms of the library. He began with the star room Sanctuary directly above the entrance hall. It was immense for an interior Sanctuary, big enough for two or three hundred people to scatter through the black, dome-shaped room without blocking each other's paths. Where the Echo Hall's Sanctuary used bits of glass, the stars here were made of shimmering chips of snowshell, so the room shone like the sky on a winter night.

Etelier felt a fool as soon as he entered it.

There was the Dancing Crow. The Miser's Cup. The Halberdier. All constellations a child could name. Perhaps because of the cost of the snowshell, there were no patterns outside clear, known shapes mirroring the sky outside. No extra glyphs. No hidden spells. And even if there were, Etelier wasn't sure he'd be willing to cast them without instructions from the Divine.

He gritted his teeth and hurried to the maps room at the top level. There was more to search through here—the immense shape of Reiil that spanned nearly ten paces set on a dais at the room's center, shelves of maps of Lacia and Redrem and other far-off cities, stacks of rolled-up street charts of Belnum and North Holderím, as it had once been called. There was far too much to search through for any patterns. It would take *years* without guidance, if they could even remove this many items before the Azure, Jade, and Vermilion Commanders descended on them with five thousand Lances, forty Grays, and the rest of the Order.

All Etelier could do was shout into the empty room.

What was I expecting, though? For Giovel to guide us through every secret they've ever gathered? For the right maps to be marked with silver letters for anyone to read?

Giovel *would* talk. Of that Etelier was certain. But it meant it was time to wait again, time to hang his cloak, remove his boots, watch the sky change, and trust someone else to do a part he wished would just be done. He'd waited so long—for healers and cure-alls when Mota first fell sick, for witches promising new discoveries after that, for Noru to find Old Vindil, for some miracle like the Witherclaw's appearance, and now for this.

He supposed he'd waited so long Mota and Pramél had outgrown their need for him. Now, standing where he could see the scrolls and count the points that could be glyphs, waiting even one more hour felt like drinking poison while his body fought to spit.

He left the maps room and went back to see whether he could help Claravena with Giovel's daughter. He was just one floor above the entrance hall, following the curved, ramping balcony above, when he saw two newcomers enter below him. Tranin and Wurelna, both limping and gasping for breath as if they'd sprinted from Lilywater Lake to get here just now.

"Where's Claravena?" Tranin bellowed, dropping to sit on the stone floor. "We got her message."

"She's up here," Etelier called back. "What message?"

"The damn Order set a trap for us. They knew we were going after Sur somehow, and apparently they jumped Ithilo and Claravena too."

And yet she hadn't said a thing about this to *him* when she arrived. Just walked by to see Giovel's girl for herself. Etelier's rage stormed up again, this time at her as much as the delays.

"What happened?"

"We got darted like a sewing pad, that's what," Tranin said.

"By the Witherclaw," Wurelna added between gasps for breath.

So she *was* still with the Divine, despite all the rumors about her vanishing, turning on them. One more trap they'd laid and into which Claravena had led the so-called Starlit Order. No amount of waiting would fix blunders like this if the Divine were on to them.

"We need to get the hell out of here," Etelier said, starting down the stairs to reach the other two. "I say we take everything we can carry, slit Giovel's throat, and move on."

"Well you're not our leader anymore, are you?" Tranin growled. She shouldered past him to move upstairs. "I'm talking to Claravena before I run another step."

She and Wurelna vanished along the rows of shelves, moving toward the back of the building. Etelier considered going with them to demand some explanations. He thought he might just pull a knife if he did, though. Why was it so hard to hold himself back now?

The entrance doors swung wide again before Etelier made up his mind which way to go from the stairwell. He peered down and saw, outlined against the snow and Yulen's faint light, two more newcomers. He knew both of them as well. The first was Suresni Medín, alive and well. Funny that Wurelna and Tranin had also omitted any mention of that.

The second was the Witherclaw Witch.

And for the third time in moments, Etelier found his teeth grinding together, his jaw tightening, his heart beating faster as his fury spilled from his mind into his body. He almost thought he felt a new ache in his ruined ear.

"The Witherclaw's here!" he shouted.

He wouldn't have to wait anymore. Sure, she'd said she wouldn't heal his daughter, maybe even meant to say she *couldn't*, but that didn't matter anymore because Mota was long gone. Whatever came of their search for new magic, Etelier didn't mind paying the Witherclaw back for what she'd done to him.

His sand tablet was out before the Witherclaw seemed to realize what he'd shouted.

Claravena pushed Inorovel's chair into a tiny storage closet, leaving the door wide open. The walls were solid stone, and there was nothing there but a broom in one corner. Any sounds as she screamed would echo far beyond Giovel's hearing. Claravena wasn't sure what seeing it would do to him, but she had a feeling that hearing and wondering would make him talk quickly.

Claravena shoved a vial of revivifying salts under the girl's nose until she jerked awake enough to see where she was and try to shout for help. Only when she stopped struggling did Claravena cut the gag from her mouth.

"Do you know who I am?" she asked.

The girl froze, eyes wet, mouth half-open.

Well, it didn't matter anyway, did it? She'd scream just as audibly from pain as from fear once she realized who'd taken her. Claravena pulled a book from a nearby shelf, a thin volume with a wooden cover. She held it in front of Giovel's daughter for a long moment, waiting to see if the girl came to her wits and said anything. Then she swung it hard across the girl's face.

"My father is Lord Giovel—"

"Your father's tied up in the other room," Claravena cut in. She struck again, shutting her own eyes on time with the blow. It was hard to put strength into it, even now. The girl screamed in time with the impact.

Claravena pulled her knife out again, bracing herself to give the girl a real taste of pain, when she heard Etelier shouting below.

"The Witherclaw's here!"

What?

Claravena swiveled out of the doorway. Then something smashed into her shoulder, hurling her several paces back and pushing her side with so much force she found herself spinning around and facing right back where she'd looked before, toward the archive rooms. Where Giovel stood, with a tablet in his hands.

Ah. His show of doing no magic was yet another prong of the Divine Order's trap. A long ruse played out patiently, curse every Divine Mage.

Another spell shot straight at Claravena. She dove to the ground, flattening herself below the spell and whipping out her own tablet as she pushed herself upright. She barely had time to sketch her own glyph before Giovel released another one, this one a Talon from the looks of it. It slashed through a bookshelf beside the wall, sending torn pages fluttering through the air like a coat of snow.

"To me!" Claravena shouted, pushing forward to block the entrance to the little closet where Giovel's daughter still sat.

But who would come? Etelier, maybe, if the Witherclaw wasn't too close to him already. Noru? Giovel had likely evaded or captured him somehow, though Claravena couldn't imagine how. Then again, she hadn't believed he'd use Yulena, and now he wielded it not only angrily but with skill.

Wurelna and Tranin appeared from nearby lanes of tomes, emerging on either side of Giovel with their own tablets out and red with glyphs drawn. Luck at last. Claravena spun around to be sure no one else was nearby—some secret guard who might have freed Giovel, perhaps? She found no one, so she cleared the short distance to the closet and raised her knife to level at the girl.

Giovel ignored Wurelna and Tranin and came straight at Claravena. His neck launched forward as part of a hideous tell, and a Rod from his tablet slammed into Claravena's extending wrist.

A snap. Pain like a horse's kick. Then an intense rush of dizziness. Claravena staggered back, trying to hold her broken wrist, struggling to keep a hand on her tablet. She scraped her knee on the wooden floor by the upper stairs, realizing she'd fallen over and not noticed. Stars above but it ached.

Giovel was down as well when she recovered herself enough to look up. Wurelna held back in the shelves like a frightened mouse while Tranin leaped on him with a dagger, the fool. Giovel caught Tranin midair with one leg kicking out at her stomach. She halted completely before collapsing on her side, breathless. He threw another spell back at Wurelna as she released a Nettle in his direction, tearing a section of the wood flooring apart in the process.

More dizziness. More aching, some in odd places like Claravena's neck and back and feet. What the hell was wrong with her? Her spinning head cleared enough for her to stand, to cradle her bad wrist toward her despite the agony it was to move her arm at all. Then, for the first time since she'd made this grand plan to crush the Divine Order in a day, she considered: It might be time to take off the cloak and make a run for it.

Two more of Ithilo's strongarms appeared on the stairs, rushing at Giovel. He caught one in the shoulder with Tranin's dagger, batted Wurelna out of sight with another glyph, and ran to meet the second strongarm, hurling himself at him like a mountain goat.

"To me!" Claravena shouted again.

But she began her withdrawal, stepping back, looking for another way down, then turning to run when she saw the strongarm holding Giovel back for a moment.

There were crashes below, flares of Yulena and what looked like fire. Fire. That might work to cover her tracks *and* cut Giovel off.

Claravena darted behind the nearest row of books, pulled a flint from her pouch, and struck it against her knife blade. A few sparks was all it took to light a tome from the shelf at waist-level. Claravena breathed into her ember, let it spread, and slid the book between a few others when she was sure it wouldn't smother out.

Half the shelf was ablaze a moment later.

Claravena ran deeper into the rows of books, putting the flames between her and Giovel and whoever else was there. She'd made up her mind. It *was* time to run.

A witch rained Yulena down at Varan, half-covered by the twist of the stairwell where he stood. Suresni leaped for cover, and Varan found herself scurrying to the shadowed edge of the hallway in search of protection as well.

The spells came relentlessly, furiously. Bolts of what looked like clear glass pounded into the floor, smashing stone panels apart. An arrow of red cut through a tapestry hanging just behind Varan as she ran for cover. Twisted spears of light slashed into the walls, scoring the ancient stone as if it were made of wet clay.

Varan whipped her wrist out to hurl a few darts toward the witch, but she was too far to keep them flying true. She Quickened air toward the stairwell next. The curved frame of the girding blocked any impact that it might have on the witch.

She'd have to get closer.

Suresni unleashed his own spells from the opposite end of the wide entrance room. His spells struck within an armlength of the witch, pushing him back for a moment. The witch was faster, though, creating and releasing two glyphs for every one Suresni seemed to manage. Suresni's efforts did, however, take the witch's attention off Varan long enough for her to run to the back side of the stairwell where she Quickened air once more, hitting the witch hard in the back. He tumbled face-first into the stairs above him, losing his tablet for a moment.

More spells shot down from the second level—this time from Tranin, who stood almost directly opposite Varan on the open second level of the library. Something hit Varan in the leg, making her go shaky and numb so suddenly she almost pitched over onto her face.

"In here!" Suresni shouted, waving into a side room off the round entrance hall.

He loosed another glyph, this one sending a flare of white light at the stairwell. In that moment of illumination, Varan noticed the features of the witch recovering himself there. He was tall. Gray-eyed. His left-ear was little more than a scab.

Etelier.

The moment she saw him, she felt like she saw herself.

My ear is ruined, a casualty of a power we both hate and never asked for; maybe I brought it on myself for chasing you alone, and maybe you brought it on *yourself* for trying to take me in. The people I love are beyond my reach, just like yours—mine because you brought me here, and yours because Yulena only kills and never heals. What we want can't be so different, can it?

And that's how I see myself reflected in the rage behind your glyphs. I know it for what it is because your rage is mine too. It's the rage of a father or a mother—anger on behalf of someone who needs your hand more than anything else but to whom you can offer *nothing* because of that damn orb in the sky.

We are the same.

Rather than following Suresni for cover, Varan roared into the wide room, Tempered Tranin's last spell aside and Quickened a plume of fire on the stairs by Etelier. He stumbled again, this time swiping to try beating back flames as they took hold of his clothes. Varan spun her hands around, Quickening again on the shelves at the top of the stairs, stirring up a wall of fire to block any route of retreat. Etelier was too quick for her to trap, but not so quick as to escape unscathed. He cried out as a jet of orange licked his arm when he reached the top of the stairs.

Varan followed, Tempering the flames away just long enough to reach the next level. Etelier was already gone, hidden by black walls of shelves. So she Quickened more fires to strip away his hiding places.

Giovel broke free of the witch's guard by stomping on his toes. It wouldn't keep him back long, but it was long enough for Giovel to run at the witch who'd tried tackling him before. She had her back open now, facing the entrance hall to hurl spells into it. Giovel threw his right shoulder at hers, knocking her right over the railing and out two paces into the open air. One of her own glyphs snapped free and hit her in the neck before she plunged downward. Giovel didn't wait to see how she landed. He pulled his second stolen tablet from his coat, hit the guard with a Tremor, and began drawing again to fight the long-faced witch.

She was nowhere to be seen now. Both she and her companion had moved so slowly, so tentatively, as if they were poisoned or drunk. Which meant she wouldn't get far in this spreading inferno the red-haired witch with no tell had caused. And even if she could, Giovel had determined where to go next, because he'd heard the direction from which Inorovel shouted his name.

All this time since Iremni died, he'd run straight at the witches, hounded them any chance he had. He'd left his doors open while he skipped duties, forgot to watch Inorovel in his haste to bite at the witches' boots. Today, however, he wouldn't make that mistake again.

So he ignored the red-headed witch, forgot the long-faced one, didn't wait to see whether the other was injured from her fall, didn't even turn to see if Sur and the Witherclaw could stop Etelier below.

He followed the sound of Inorovel's voice to a tiny closet at the edge of the flames. She sat in a wooden chair, bound ankles, knees, waist, shoulders, and hands. But she was *alive*, and her eyes lit up like lamps when she saw him reaching toward her.

"Hold very still," he said quickly, and began hacking through the ropes with the witch's dagger. Its grip was like the rope knife he'd once thought to use on Adni.

This is a better use, I think.

An arm of fire slapped near the doorway, and waves of black smoke already filled the stacks nearby. Giovel doubted the second level would last long, and there was little to keep the flames from rising now. But that wasn't his concern. Inorovel was.

He cut her free, scooped her up, and darted back toward the stairwell the guards had climbed moments before. No one was there to stop him now as he held Inorovel close and raced between columns of fire.

I'm done here, he thought. I have the person I love most who's still alive. That's enough today.

NO TELL AND NO GLYPHS

I think you'd be ashamed of me now.
    —The Witherclaw Witch; letter to Recia.

THE FLAMES FORCED Etelier away from the railed hall lining the center of the second level. Spears of fire filled the book stacks now, almost as if another blaze had broken out before Varan's began to spread. With smoke billowing upward and rows of shelves already alight, the only place Etelier could find to run was deeper into the corridors at the shadowed heart of the library.

Was there another way out? An east doorway? Etelier hadn't visited the place in nearly a year, since early in his search for the Divine's secret records. He couldn't remember enough to be sure he wasn't walling himself in where Varan could incinerate him more easily.

Well. For every inch of skin she'd taken from his face, he'd taken his own. He could do it again, perhaps, if he got half a moment to calm his breathing, draw a single glyph, and take aim at her.

Into the rows of shelves it was.

Etelier thought his heart would stop when he found two of Claravena's fools running toward him. They wore Lance uniforms with tabards for the Jade Army, fooling Etelier with their disguise until he was close enough to recognize their faces.

"Split up and cover my back!" he ordered, rushing right past the two of them.

He couldn't run much longer, so he slid to a halt behind a thick row of Optacracy records. His legs felt weak from fatigue, and his breath came in ragged gasps now. It should have been chilly through the whole library, but sweat like honey made Etelier's clothes stick to him.

Claravena's guards rushed ahead to do as Etelier had told them, one moving in each direction. Suresni Medín cut the left one off, vaulting out of nowhere to grab the guard's arm and ram it back against a shelf. The guard punched at Suresni's side and fended him off, but Suresni had a sword out a moment later and backed her away with the blade at her throat.

"I'll cut her open if you don't come out, Etelier," he called.

Would he? Of any Divine Mage, he might just. Etelier turned to run again because he couldn't do anything to save the woman now.

He'd gone down five more rows, each increasingly black, when a flare of light announced that Varan was nearby, igniting more shelves. She'd burn them all alive, the witch. Unless she burned first.

Claravena's second guard took her from behind, grabbing her by the neck as if he meant to snap her in half with nothing but his hands. Varan gave a garbled cry then fell back, silently struggling. A flash of silver shot past her head. Suresni, stabbing into her attacker's eye with a boot knife. The man howled, dropped Varan, and slashed back at Suresni with his own blade, catching him hard in the leg. Etelier found himself drawing a glyph, ready to strike while Varan was on the floor and Suresni was vulnerable.

But then they'll see me, they'll follow.

He left the glyph half-made on his tablet and ran deeper into the darkness.

It came to Claravena that she'd been huddled in the corner a long time, hugging her knees to her chin, gripping her own feet. Her left arm throbbed and ached and seemed to vanish from her senses all in the span of a moment, but she must have been motionless for minutes, trying to stay hidden.

Giovel wasn't coming for her. No one was. It was just her in the west corner of the library's third level, waiting as smoke moved upward and choked out whatever clear air remained.

It was odd. She ought to feel relieved, even hopeful. The halls below had almost quieted, though echoes of footsteps and the dull roar of fire were still there. Instead of feeling safe for her moment of refuge, Claravena found herself almost wishing someone had harried her more closely.

It wasn't a new wish. It was one she'd lived with since Erenoea left to join the Grays.

I'm the last sister, aren't I?

The flames below would never be put out. They'd spread too far and too fast with nothing to impede them. All the Divine's secrets, burned away in moments. Claravena supposed she'd burn too, trapped on the third level if she didn't move soon, so she forced herself upright, gritted her teeth against the searing pain in her wrist and her arm and everywhere else, and hurried to the western stairwell.

The end of the second level was almost quiet there, with faint slants of light emerging from a few windows right above the entrance hall, and the orange haze of the fire blocked by hundreds of rows of close-set wooden shelves. There was no way farther down, though, not without moving back toward the blaze.

Up a row of silent tables. Past more archive rooms. All the way to the open middle of the entrance, where half the railed level was burned black and the flames were hot and blinding. Claravena saw motion below and almost ducked to hide, but it was just Wurelna, trying to drag a limp Tranin across the entrance hall toward the door while ash and red pages fluttered down behind her.

The stairs on this side of the hall smoldered with embers and small tongues of blue fire. Another stairwell stood, untouched, far across the open center of the great room, but it was close to the glaring fire now, close to the sounds of crashing shelves, footsteps, and what could only be Yulena. Was that where Giovel was? Or the Witherclaw Witch, if Etelier had been right about her arriving?

Claravena steeled herself, pulled her bad hand close to keep it from jostling as she went, and circled toward that remaining stairwell.

She was nearly there when an immense gout of flame erupted in the rows of tomes. Glass casements shattered by the score. A concussion wave hurled scrolls and volumes in all directions. Bits of char and even unburned wood exploded outward, clattering against the walls or the low ceiling where the stacks pressed into the next level. Claravena froze, enveloped by the searing wave of heat from the inferno. And there, behind it all, stood the Witherclaw, arms spinning at her sides, head thrown forward. Her tell was oddly similar to Giovel's.

Just beyond the ring of new fire, Etelier ran to a window and threw himself forward. His cape was on fire. He must be mad from the heat. The window was far above the ground—fifteen paces at least. He'd be luckier if he *did* die from a fall of that height.

As soon as he was gone, the Witherclaw swiveled around. Her eyes —black as charcoal—fell on Claravena.

And there's something I can fear more than the flames, Claravena thought before she made a run for the stairs.

Varan's own fires stopped her from getting to the window where Etelier had escaped. She supposed she could Temper them away or perhaps Enervate them down, but it would take time. Etelier would likely be dead now. And if he'd survived the fall, he'd be gone before Varan could fight through her own blaze. So she ran after the red-haired woman instead.

Varan recognized her. Not a witch, if she was right, but she'd been there at the Croen Estate months before. And more importantly, she was probably the last one left in this fiery maze.

"Varan!" Suresni called from an aisle over.

Varan turned. He was cut off, surrounded by flames, and hurt again what was more. He clutched one side with his own cape, trying to staunch a bleeding gash.

"Turn around and come this way!" Varan shouted over the roar of fire. She Tempered the smaller conflagration on her right side, clearing a path for a moment or two. The fires were untamable, though, reeking of wet and moldy wood, spewing smoke like volcanoes.

Suresni stumbled through the tiny break in the walls of flame, shielding his eyes as he came near more dancing arms of red and blue at the tops of the bookshelves. Varan Tempered as much as she could while he went, cursing that the red-haired woman had any moment more to escape.

Her luck held. The red-headed woman was just clambering down the stairs, moving gingerly as if she had a broken bone in her arm, when Varan reached the stairwell above her. Varan threw herself forward in an Enervating motion, pushing away the woman's breath. Breathless or not, the witch somehow spun around and struck with a spell that flowered from her tablet like a fountain of violet stars and blasted hard into Varan's torso before she could duck out of the way. Varan's whole body flailed in place, shaking so badly she fell over. The effect was gone almost as quickly as it had come, but it set Varan's teeth on edge.

So the red-haired woman *was* a witch. One more of them, still ready to fight even with one bad hand.

"Stay back, Suresni!" Varan called.

"Damn it, there's nowhere to go but down now!" Suresni yelled. Flames flared behind him, spreading into a long carpet that ran the length of the rail over the entrance hall. He was right, Varan saw. The whole level was done for, with no ways out but this single staircase now, since the other had burned from the fires she'd unleashed on Etelier.

Varan cursed and raced ahead of him, trying to Enervate the witch's breath once more. The witch was moving already, tracing another glyph while she ran behind a display case of old manuscripts. Another violet spell shot out, catching Varan once again in the chest so she shook like a droplet of water trying to hold onto a windswept branch of a tree. Losing her footing, Varan slid onto one ankle and hit the floor hard. Before she could recover herself this time, the witch sent another spell at Suresni. He dove down the stairs, just avoiding the attack and tumbling headlong onto his wounded side for it. He cried out in pain and rammed to a halt, folded oddly with his knees against his shoulders.

"Stay back or I'll Talon him open!" the witch snarled from behind her cover.

Varan couldn't even see her hair. And where she couldn't see, she couldn't Temper, couldn't Enervate, couldn't do much of anything. So she took a chance and Quickened another exploding wave of flame against the old display case, hoping to blast it out of the way. The shelves ripped free, flinging burning pages upward. The case itself held in place, but the witch gasped and leaped forward, exposing herself on the way back into the low-ceilinged, narrow rows of shelves behind the entrance hall. A place Varan knew she'd be trapped.

"Go for help, Suresni!" Varan called and raced after the witch without waiting to see whether Suresni could move at all.

Despite the roar of fire above, the ground-floor stacks were dark as a grave plot. There were stone shelves here—not just wooden ones—and great metal shields likely built to keep flames at bay. These must be some of the library's most irreplaceable volumes. A wealth of knowledge, hiding a wounded witch somewhere nearby.

The witch's footsteps stopped abruptly, echoing oddly between the stone, metal, and wood. So she was smart enough to hide by slowing her feet, or stupid enough not to run while she had the chance. Perhaps she'd be stupid enough to goad out of hiding as well.

"I've wanted to meet you for a long time, witch," Varan called into the dark rows.

Her ploy worked. The witch called back, "And why's that?"

Her voice echoed oddly, masking the angle of its origin. Varan twisted around the corner of a stone column, squinting into the shadows. Nothing. No glow of Yulen glyphs, no movement, just long, black rows of books.

"I've been studying Medín just so I could ask why you spirited me here," Varan said.

"I'd tell you why if it was me."

The witch was somewhere . . . left, Varan thought. She inched that direction, turning so the light off her skin wouldn't give her own position away too clearly.

"Who, then?" Varan called. "Etelier? Or another one of you?"

"We spirit so many that it's hard to be sure."

Hot iron on bare skin. Varan couldn't imagine any words that would stoke her anger more than the witch's just had. She spun around another stone corner, hoping to see some stir of motion where she'd thought the witch's voice originated. Nothing.

"You know, I hate to duel you like this," the witch said. A speaking voice. She was so close, somewhere between these shelves. "It's not really an even pairing. You see, I can use Yulena without any tell."

And now, just as quickly as she'd made Varan seethe, she'd made her laugh. Varan turned one more corner.

There. I see you now. And you're looking in the wrong direction.

Varan leaned back before the witch could look in her direction. "Maybe we're equal," she said. "You don't have a mage's tell, and I don't need glyphs."

She ran forward, Quickening air and fire together to send flames whipping into the narrow lanes between the shelves. She saw red hair swinging around, then the wide-eyed look on the witch's face, and wondered: Is it because you didn't think I'd find you? Or because for all this time, you never knew my cursed, worthless power isn't part of Yulena to begin with?

The witch hurled herself to one side. Not fast enough to avoid some burns, Varan was sure, but she put a stone shelf between the two of them before Varan could reach the next juncture and strike again. The witch hurled spells back, too, creating them quickly despite having only one good arm. A bolt of something hit the ceiling just above Varan's head. A silvery bubble splashed against her knee, sending waves of heat through her body. She cried out, threw herself forward and Tempered more fire.

Two more glyphs, hurtling past her head.

A burst of flame engulfing one of the shelves, lighting the aisle beside the witch so Varan glimpsed her red hair twisting around a corner once more.

Varan clutched her throbbing knees where the witch had just struck, fighting to stay upright as a searing sensation spread outward. But the witch's back was turned, and Varan could still move. So she ran on.

One more corner. Three more spells, one that grazed Varan's face and made her feel like she'd been scored to the bone of her right cheek. She could still see, could still walk, so she Tempered a thermic synthesis in the witch, flooding heat through her just as her glyph had done to Varan.

The witch stumbled into a shelf and fell back on her side, crying out when she landed badly on her bad arm. She released one more spell, though—perhaps miscast it. It split off the tablet like a flash of light from a signal mirror, crashing into the ceiling and ripping through wooden rafters, dry brick, stone plates.

There was a mighty crack, and the whole ceiling seemed to shift downward. Two great spikes of stone and red, burning wood plummeted from above, followed by an avalanche of flaming rubble, roaring timbers, blazing pages, and leather binding. Varan staggered back as a room-sized chunk of the second level collapsed around her, smashing the shelves of the lower stacks and sending massive sprays of sparks in every direction. A heavy wave of heat followed, hotter than the spell that had grazed Varan's face.

The hall rumbled like a drum when the stone and wood settled. Then there was just the tidal sound of fire and the witch screaming beyond it.

She screamed words Varan didn't know. Maybe they were curses. But the way she said them made Varan think not. Names, more like.

"Help me!" the witch shouted then. "I'll tell you anything you want, Witherclaw!"

Varan couldn't see her. The extent of the rubble and the burning hell from the collapse of the level above made her sure the witch was truly trapped. Varan doubted she *could* show mercy now.

"How do you undo a spiriting?" she called.

"What?"

"How do you *undo a spiriting?*"

Another crack. More beams coming down. The witch screamed once more, then howled as if she were stuck under something. More words Varan didn't know. More names.

"CAN YOU DO IT?" Varan shouted.

"I don't know how!" the witch shouted. Then her voice cut off in a cough. Smoke spilled across the wreckage, so thick Varan could hardly see the gold of the inferno.

"Help me!"

The ceiling creaked over Varan's head. She looked upward, glanced just once over the fire, then turned to run from it.

Could she help? She didn't know. She'd never Tempered flames and air like this or used her powers as weapons before she woke up in Foneth. For all she knew, she held more power to calm a blaze than she might think. The real question was whether she would, whether she *wanted to try*. And she didn't.

You have nothing for me. I have nothing for you.

Varan raced back toward the entrance, stumbling in the dark, tripping over loose stones, limping from bruises and sweating and vomiting suddenly, though she didn't know how she had anything left in her stomach. The witch's screams echoed behind Varan until she reached the entrance hall, dragged Suresni's unconscious body from the stairs, and hurried out into the unsettling cold.

Spirals of fire burst from the few windows in the great stone dome that was the Divnum Library.

Varan's mind was far from the fires, though. It was with Golkorun, Inivar, and Sil. Because, for the first time since her spiriting, she doubted she'd see them again.

A GOODBYE

Mothers can also be lonely.
    —The Witherclaw Witch; letter to Inivar and Sil.

ETELIER WAS LUCKY. He landed in powder, crunching one arm at a strange angle but not breaking anything. A single tiny shard of glass stuck from his chin, and smoke rose from his clothes where they'd burned before he leaped.

But he was alive. One more night for Etelier.

And Etelier knew what he'd do with that winter night. It was the clearest his mind had felt in weeks, months maybe. He'd leave Foneth with this one more span of hours, as if it were to be his last. Better to use it searching for Mota and Pramél, turned in the direction he wished to the stars he'd been looking all along.

Could be I'll never find them. Could be they'll make sure I don't.

Somehow that didn't bother him now.

He abandoned his burned cloak, dug himself from the drift by the library's edge, and rubbed his arms for warmth. Then he began to walk, not too quickly, not as restlessly as before. Steadily.

The hills by the library were empty, but scores and hundreds of Lances lined the streets by Tovóm's Passage and the Trade Road, hurrying every way with hand lamps. There must be thousands in Foneth now, trying to unravel what had happened during the wall attacks. More ran toward the library when it became clear, even from the distance, that it was aflame.

Maybe in the morning I'll be far enough away not to see the smoke, Etelier thought. Or maybe I'll just keep my eyes away, no matter how far I do or don't make it. There's nothing to look back to and everything to look away for.

He went back home for the final time. It struck him that there was no Yulenic hum here, no trail of old spells. Or perhaps he just couldn't hear it since he'd lost an ear.

He changed out of his sweaty, singed, soot-stained clothes and put on a clean set. Probably a set that had sat clean since before Pramél left, maybe even washed with her own hands. He thought of her golden skin and deep green eyes as he sat in the Sanctuary, the one room she loved in this tiny house. Moss still covered the little stone shelf, with a few dried leaves hanging where she'd put them out of Mota's reach.

Before leaving, he took a moment in the other rooms too—the narrow kitchen where he'd first told Pramél he'd awakened. Their tiny room, where they'd shaken with cold and sweltered in summers, where they'd held each other and made love and forgotten to love each other all over again.

Then to Mota's room, which seemed all the smaller with her gone. More like a closet—a few paces of creaking floorboards and one child-sized bed. The bed was stripped clean, no pillow or blankets anymore. No laughing voice and tiny hands that could barely reach around one of Etelier's thumbs.

He thought he might have a tear for that room. The Witherclaw's fires had left him dry as ash, though, so he just touched the posts of the bed, imagined Mota's voice and face, and shut the door behind him.

The world out there is so much bigger than this place. I'll never know which way to turn. There's no path ahead of me, no trail they've marked for me to follow. I might never see them if I spend the rest of my life searching, and I don't know if I have the patience to hunt like that. My patience with Yulena bled out after only a few years.

Beyond all his questions, he knew two things.

He *would* search for them. And he would never come back to Foneth.

TRUTH

I should have stuck to selling herbs.

—The Witherclaw Witch; letter to Drova.

GIOVEL'S BACK GAVE out a few hundred paces from the library. He collapsed beside the road, gasping for breath, grunting in pain, and trying to hold Inorovel close despite his body's ache to rest.

"I'm not hurt," Inorovel said over and over again.

It was so dark Giovel could barely see her face, even with bright snow surrounding them. Her skin glinted with tears.

"Come on," Giovel said. "A little farther yet."

"What about the others in the library? Do you need to go back? Go for help?"

"Soon enough."

"I can walk. You don't have to carry me."

He was relieved to hear it. His days of carrying her like a child should have ended years before. Not because his back and shoulders couldn't do it any longer. Just because Inorovel had stopped *being* a child years before Iremni left them. Giovel hoped he hadn't missed too much since then.

They went directly to the Candlespire, where only a few nervous greenleafs stood guard, surprised and relieved to see Giovel coming.

"Lord Adni's out," they said. "And Lady Elínla."

"The Lances?" Giovel asked.

"Gone to reinforce the Redremel scouting perimeter, sir."

"Are any Grays here?"

"One inside."

He'd have to stay, wait with Inorovel himself until the witches were dead or routed or more Grays could recongregate. So be it. He didn't want to leave anyway, so he gave quick orders calling reserve fighters to the library and sending messengers to find the other members of the Order. That done, he took Inorovel to the council hall and bolted the doors from the inside.

"Don't you have to leave me now?" Inorovel asked.

"I'll wait for the rest of the Order to come to us instead."

Inorovel nodded quietly. She dropped into a seat at the dark table of the Divine Order. So brave, though. Giovel sat beside her and took one of her hands, finding his whole arm shaking as he did so.

"Are you cold?" Inorovel asked. "You feel like a wind chime."

He laughed, shaking all the harder. The cold felt mild now, and his bone-breaking weariness was leaving already. He was just relieved. Resolved.

"Can you tell me what happened to you?" he asked.

Inorovel's face seemed to darken.

"If you're ready to explain, that is," Giovel said.

Another nod. "I think so. The men in the library found me on my own at the middle of the day. They forced something into my nose and I sort of fainted. They must have brought me to the library. The next thing I really knew, a witch had me tied up. That's when you came."

She hadn't answered the question he didn't ask, didn't want to ask. What else did they do to you? How did they hurt you? There was a bruise or two on the left side of her face, and her eyes were angry red, perhaps from cold, perhaps from whatever substance they'd used to drug her. Iremni hadn't looked all that much worse when they found her all those months before.

But Giovel had found Inorovel faster, thank every star.

"I'm alright," Inorovel said, now squeezing his shaking hand. "Are you? You're the one who fought off all those witches."

He laughed again, perhaps from giddy disbelief that he'd even survived the encounter. Despite wanting to ask Inorovel more, he just let the exhausted laugh come until it was spent, pushing his questions down and gripping her hand back in the cold quiet of a safe room.

There were shouts outside, feet hurrying this way and that. Giovel didn't stir even to watch from the windows. He just sat and waited, close to his daughter.

She was asleep, he realized, slumped over in her chair like an old Lawrit waiting for minutes to be read. Giovel draped his coat over her and let her rest while she could.

The night felt long.

Three different Grays came to check on Giovel. They all brought whispers of riots and attacks on the walls, witches striking at Ralden and Sur and others. Nothing was firm or clear, and Giovel couldn't add to the reports other than what he'd seen near Ola's Gate and at the library after the witches had taken him. Then Ind Telen himself appeared, the small, round-faced old man who was the Lances' Azure Commander. His news was even less substantial—that he'd sent fifteen hundred spears to help the Jade battalions with the Redremel and was waiting for news again.

"I'd hoped the Order would know more," Telen said.

Giovel didn't respond. Just wondered how much of the Order would be left after tonight.

There were clashes of blades below sometime near dawn. Shouts. Giovel drew a Flail glyph and stood to face the door. The sounds died down almost as quickly as they'd broken out.

"What was it?" Giovel whispered when a Gray called for him.

"Three rogue Optacrats tried to storm the spire just now. They resisted arrest—even with fifty Lances on them. I think they're all dead."

Giovel set his tablet on the table, thanked the Gray, and barred the doors again.

He didn't sleep, nor did he leave. There was no word from the library and nothing from the remainder of the Order. For a few terrified moments Giovel considered that more of them or *all* of them might have died during the attacks of the last day and night. They'd taken him so easily, and he'd been alert and on-guard. What if they'd found Hirnu as well? Or Adni? Or Kanis, the newest and least-protected of them all?

As it happened, Kanis was the first of the Order to arrive. He came covered in mud, a wide, haunted look to his eyes. No sign of any real injury, though.

"Where's Elínla?" Giovel asked, keeping his voice low and motioning back outside the council chamber for Inorovel's sake. "And Adni?"

"I thought Elínla was with you," Kanis said, still breathing hard as if he'd run some distance to get to the Candlespire. His eyes went wider still when he noticed Inorovel, asleep against the council chamber's table, just before Giovel closed the door.

"Elínla and I split as soon as we heard about the Redremel sighting. She was looking for the two of you at Scout's Bridge."

"Redremel sighting?"

Perhaps Kanis knew even less than Giovel did, then.

"I'll explain later. Where did you last see Adni?"

Kanis swallowed. "Adni's dead."

Giovel waited for some wave of feeling. He had time to wonder whether it would be shock, fear, relief, or pure joy that hit him first. Instead, he felt nothing but the soreness of his ankles where his boots were starting to chafe. No clear emotion for the loss of an Illumined Knight.

Do I have that much control of myself? Or am I simply that cold-hearted?

"Tell me what happened," Giovel said.

"But what about these Redremel you mentioned?"

"The Lances have already mustered to counter it. There's nothing we can do but regroup and make sure we've accounted for the witches —or whoever they set against the walls."

Kanis rubbed sweat and trails of dirt from his face. He looked younger than ever, scarcely older than Inorovel was. Yulen had forced them to grow quickly, Giovel supposed.

"Adni and I went straight to Ola's Gate when we heard about fighting there," Kanis began slowly. "There were already a few hundred people fighting when we arrived, with just a score or two of Candles and Lances trying to fend them off. I thought Adni was just worried about witches and all, but it was like he went mad when we saw what was happening."

"The fighting, you mean?"

"No," Kanis said. "The way they tried to destroy the walls. There were workers of all kinds with mattocks and shovels and slate wedges. It was like they meant to topple the walls right there, with Lances still on them and everything. Adni started shouting and waving when we got there, but I don't think anyone even heard him. Then he started turning spells on the crowds, almost without any warning. He killed a few people before I even realized what was happening."

The emotion Giovel had looked for at first caught up to him, and it wasn't shock or relief now. Just anger. One moment he'd been wondering whether these people at the walls were wild with terror at the hint of a Redremel incursion—wondering if they'd even heard about it before they started battering the walls. Now cold wrath at Adni Aman pushed his questions away.

"What happened to him after that?" Giovel asked.

"People were already throwing things at the Lances, stones and tools and such. When some of them realized Adni was there, they started to turn and fight him instead. I couldn't get to Adni in time to do anything. I think a brick hit him in the head. When I got close enough to help, he was already dead."

Years of training and practice with Yulena, yet a thrown stone was all it took to bring Adni down.

"Could it have been a witch that hit him?" Giovel asked, forcing his face to stay placid.

"I didn't see any obvious spells except Adni's. If a witch did it, I think they must have been the most accurate witch in the world."

Could *you* have done it, Giovel wanted to ask.

"Hirnu's outside," Kanis said. "We can ask her if she saw any spells when Adni went down."

"She was there?"

"She showed up just as the throng started turning on Adni. I think they might have come after me too, if she hadn't been there. She was amazing, though. She used some sort of spell to catch everyone's attention and then organized some Grays and the Lances and Candles to get things calmed down. They obeyed Hirnu like she was the Optate herself then."

Hirnu was supposed to be with Ralden. What could have pulled her all the way to Ola's Gate? Questions for later, though. Just hearing that she was there set Giovel's mind at ease about Kanis's account. Kanis couldn't have suddenly turned witch on Adni without Hirnu realizing it. Or maybe Giovel was simply glad for an excuse not to mistrust one more member of the Order. He'd lost enough for not trusting them—and perhaps they had too, for not trusting him.

Amber sunlight crested the distant walls of the city, faintly visible from the windows outside the council hall. Giovel had a stir from inside the room.

"What happened to you?" Kanis asked. He was somehow still wide-eyed even after recounting his own happenings.

"I'll tell you all as soon as I can. I need to see to my daughter first."

Kanis nodded. "I'll go tell Hirnu you're safe, at least."

Giovel mumbled his thanks as he turned back into the council hall. That any of them were safe felt like a victory now—Hirnu especially.

He found Inorovel rubbing her face inside the council hall, looking around in a daze.

"Is it morning?" she asked.

"The earliest I've seen you awake in thirteen years," Giovel replied. He yawned himself, stretching against the protest in his knees and sides and back. "I think I can take you home now."

"Wait. What happened last night?"

Where even to begin? "A group of people attacked the city walls while the witches had us. Redrem made a push at the border too."

"They were working with those witches?"

"I don't know. No one seems sure of anything yet."

Inorovel's mouth hung a quarter open. She appeared on the verge of speaking again but stopped herself short.

"Let's at least go downstairs and find something to eat," Giovel suggested.

"Is it safe?"

"Lady Hirnu and a new member of the Order are both downstairs. I think it will be safe now." And I'll be with you this time, unfailingly.

He walked back out the doorway, surprised what a relief it was to be leaving after the tortuous day and night behind him. He'd taken several steps before he realized Inorovel had paused at the door.

Just when I thought I'd never leave her side again.

"Wait," she mumbled.

Giovel waited.

"I want to ask you something," Inorovel said.

"What is it?"

She pressed her lips together at first as if she wasn't sure how to phrase her question. Her eyes were locked on his though, with an intensity to her stare that made her look more like him than he'd ever realized was possible. So much of Iremni, but some spark of Giovel showing too.

"You're not like you were," Inorovel said after a long pause. "The last time we even talked to each other."

All at once he saw himself as if through another's eyes, shouting at her, attacking their table, destroying the only home she knew. Yes, he'd been different then.

"You never said what was going on, why you were like that," she continued. "Can you tell me?"

He thought about lying, or at least obfuscating the truth. It would be easy; between the witches' threat, trouble with Adni, the painful slowness of watching Varan, guilt at not doing it well, and the darkness of winter itself, he had plenty of concerns and fears and defeats he could share to explain his collapse. The thing was, he was at a loss to explain his recovery without the whole truth.

And Inorovel should know. She shouldn't have to wonder about her da, not when she's already been left in the shadows about her mother.

So Giovel told the truth.

"I learned that your mother had awakened."

For all he'd said, Inorovel looked as if she might not have heard him.

"She was a known awakening, being watched by Grays, or the Divine, or someone working for the Optate herself," Giovel said. "Her description was on a list. It's possible she was a witch herself, maybe for months, maybe for years. Somehow the witches I've been hunting found out about her. They were spiriting awakenings all over Foneth, and she was one of them. They were likely trying to recruit her."

No response. Inorovel's eyes were empty.

Giovel stepped toward her, took her hand once more and held on until she moved to wipe one eye.

"I should have told you when I found out," he said simply.

"Are you sure about her?"

He wished it were harder to answer. "I'm sure."

Inorovel pulled her hand from his, wiping tears from both eyes now. So Giovel stood beside her once more, waiting and listening though she had no more questions and no more words. Voices echoed below them, and the Candlespire stairs clattered with boots coming and going, but Giovel and Inorovel stood there until the sun and low-hanging clouds and smoke from the corner of Divnum fully blocked out the night's stars.

ILLUMINED

So far as I can remember, there's nothing in common between their maps and ours.
  —The Witherclaw Witch; a letter to Recia.

IT WAS AN odd week. First there were reports from every group Giovel could imagine—guilds, dignitaries from Yeren, Tovómil vassals who claimed to have been hired to attack the walls. Sorting through the dozens and then hundreds of documents took Giovel, Hirnu, and Elínla nearly every waking hour for the first few days after the attacks.

For every report there was a question, of course. How many witches are left for those we got? Where is the body of their leader, Etelier? How do we try the fools he tricked into striking the walls and killing Adni? Should the Witherclaw be tried with them for burning the Great Divnum Library to charcoal? Were the Redremel behind any of this?

Another question that bobbed at the surface like twigs in the river: Who will replace Adni?

To Giovel there were three true consolations amid so many questions.

First, there was hope in the Lances' seeming success against the Redremel. Half of Ind Telen's Azure Lances returned to Foneth just two days after departing, bringing news of victory at the northeast scouting perimeter. Reports from Jinaten Teserot said that Redrem had paid a steep price for every Lance lost. The real question was how long a break in the fighting would last and how to fend them off the next time; spring was almost here, when they could come in true force. Optate Olura promptly issued several decrees to increase watches along Foneth's borders, to establish defensible gathering points in each district, and to expedite Zuris's plans as much as could be done without sacrificing soldiers. So the war was far from over. But the beginning, after months of waiting, was a painful relief, like having a splinter pulled from the pad of a hand.

Second, that the spiritings seemed to have halted. Whether they were over forever or simply paused by the witches' defeat was unclear, but no spiritings were reported that entire week—a first since Perception Day, nearly four months before.

And third, that four known witches were dead, with the red-haired woman Claravena among them. Only Etelier's body hadn't turned up. Elínla had found the long-faced woman Wurelna—a former member of the Gray Order as it happened—and brought her in wounded but alive. They'd found Tranin's body abandoned in the snow near Wurelna, crushed dead most likely from her fall in the library. Giovel himself had dispatched Noru, and Hirnu and Ralden had killed one more during an attack on Ralden's home.

Five witches, all told, in exchange for one Divine Mage. Giovel might once have thought it a fair trade. Any trade of blood felt worthless now, even one for Adni.

One other consolation emerged as the days passed. The riots at the walls did not return, despite the rage of those the Lances and Candleguard had managed to subdue there. The thing was, no one found gold there or anywhere else. Perhaps because no one found *anything* in the old, spell-made walls. Just stone and dry mortar, bits of moss, twigs hammered in by centuries of rainfall. The Lances themselves ordered a search, and it returned nothing. The lack of evidence seemed to sway the treasure-hungry rebels. Either that or a week eating plain rice and dried carrots while sitting in holding cells.

Eight days after the attacks, an entourage arrived at the Candlespire with an announcement: Optate Olura Medín, Protector and Servant of Foneth, High Governor herself was coming to meet with her Divine Order of Mages.

"It's not as bad as it sounds," Sur told Giovel while they waited at the base of the Candlespire. He leaned on a heavy cane to support himself as he recovered from his new wounds, but he looked almost as happy as Giovel had ever seen him. "Shaving and putting on clean cowls is about all she really expects."

"But what do her sycophantic followers expect?" Giovel mumbled. "They're the ones who cling to their positions long after the elections."

"Don't tell me you're afraid of what people think of you now. Just let Hirnu do all the talking. She's the only one Olura cares about now that Adni's dead."

"How can you be so glib about this? We faked Hirnu's deposition, if you recall. We said she'd found *Renma's lost glyph*. And we never consulted the Optate about it."

"No, no. *Adni* did that, and he's not around to be punished for it anymore."

"We can't blame a dead man for the destruction of the most valuable building in the known world."

"Well, that was my plan," Sur said.

The other junior members of the Order seemed even more nervous than Giovel felt. Sweat coated Elínla's face visibly before Olura arrived, and Kanis seemed the most terrified of all, shaking in place as he tried to brush wrinkles out of his new gray cowl.

"At least you had people watching when you played your part," Sur said, slapping him on the shoulder. "It's the rest of us who have only our own word to defend ourselves."

By all accounts, Kanis had acquitted himself admirably, using both forbearance and skill to protect the Divnum walls when Adni went livid with rage. Hirnu went so far as to say she saw a future leader of the Order in him. So perhaps Adni had been right in one small thing. Perhaps he *did* know whom to choose for the Order. He'd left them varied, strong, and—unless Giovel was mistaken—united. Odd that any leader could do that by pitting his people against himself.

"I actually look forward to seeing Olura," Ralden said. Unlike Sur she stood of her own accord and looked as composed as ever, hair combed back, clothes clean enough to be used as napkins. "I have a few ideas for building a new Divnum library, and I think she'll like to hear them."

As it happened, there was no formal reprimand, though, no hammer fall of discipline for the immense costs the Order might have mitigated. Instead, Olura arrived with a massive train of followers but no real fanfare, said in a quiet voice that she'd like to speak with Hirnu alone, and followed her to the council chamber with no one but a single woman-at-arms as an escort. It was almost like welcoming any other person to the Candlespire. Olura looked much older than the last time Giovel had seen her, though. It had only been two years since her election, hadn't it? But he'd been a fresh Banner Captain in the Candleguard back then. So much had changed.

The Optate's meeting with Hirnu was remarkably short. Hirnu emerged alone just moments later.

"So you're our new Illumined Knight, are you?" Sur asked. "Would you rather we congratulate you or offer our pity first?"

"I refused," Hirnu said simply. "She wants to see you, Ralden."

"You *what?*" Elínla burst out. "What's wrong with you?"

"I'm content where I am," Hirnu said and took a standing position beside Sur.

Giovel found himself smiling. He also liked where she stood and was proud, almost for the first time, to stand across from her.

To no one's surprise, the meeting with Ralden went perhaps twenty times as long. Olura finally emerged herself, descending the stairs of the Candlespire and stepping out into the snow to announce that she had named Ralden as Councilor to the Optate, Illumined Knight of the Divine Order.

"I expect you to trust her judgment, advise her with clarity, and render your best diligence to the efforts she directs," Olura said. "That is all."

"Tell Rosir I said hello," Sur offered as she walked by. "Oh, and Aunt Gida."

Olura walked on as if she hadn't heard him speak at all.

Ralden spared no time in telling them seven of her new plans, all devised to increase their efficiency and reduce wasted time and process. She also assured them she'd have three new members of the Order appointed within the next three days, wildly ambitious though that was given how long finding even *one* had taken Adni.

But Giovel wondered. No matter the attention she gave her guild, Ralden had fought bravely against the witches and had never promised him what she couldn't dispatch. He didn't know anyone who worked with more zeal than she did. Furthermore, no other

Divine Mage had championed regulation, compliance to law, and reigning in of the Order's authority as Ralden had in the past year — even in her efforts to shield Varan from unscrupulous study. She might be just the tempering influence they needed, Giovel himself as much as the others. So perhaps Adni wasn't the only one who chose leaders well.

Kanis and Elínla sighed in relief as the Optate's entourage processed away from the Candlespire, and Ralden led them inside for their first meeting under her leadership. Giovel touched Elínla's shoulder.

"You'll get your chance, someday."

She frowned. "I didn't exactly want Olura to pick me, if that's what you mean."

"I know that. I meant you'll get your chance as Observer of the Order someday."

Her frown softened ever so slightly. "I forgot I ever mentioned that to you. To anyone."

"You'll be good at it, when that day comes."

Maybe that's why I'm proud to be part of the Order now, he said to himself. Because I'm starting to believe in the people around me.

True to her word, Ralden had her three appointees within three days, growing the Order's size from six to nine. It put Giovel in the Order's middle in seniority, right where he felt most comfortable.

Everyone in Foneth seemed to know who Varan was now. If it had been burdensome before, when her hair and eyes were different enough to mark her as an odd outsider, now it was a parade of lodestones rolling behind her wherever she tried to go. Incinerating one of the city's oldest buildings hadn't helped. Then again, saving Suresni Medín and defeating three or four witches more or less on her own hardly quelled the embers of her growing fame either. Everywhere she went, people stared and whispered anew.

She heard enough to be sure it wasn't all admiring. Plenty of Foneth's people stared out of fear, speculating over what this Witherclaw Witch wanted from them or whom she'd kill next.

You don't understand. I never killed anyone. Or never meant to.

She found anger in some of the eyes that followed her. There were many reasons she, at least, could imagine for the people of Foneth to be upset. She was a witch to them, yet she walked free, somehow, while others did not.

"The Optate herself has offered you a commendation," Kirida said on the ninth day since the fire at the library. They sat on cushioned chairs in front of Kirida's house, watching the lake and enjoying an uncommonly warm sun.

Varan fought Progis's little hands out of her good ear while she asked, "What does that mean?"

"It means they don't have any money to give you as a reward," Nomis said, rocking a blanketed Chivi in his arms. "Typical. You'd be rich as Ralden if there weren't a war on."

"Then . . . they're not going to punish me?" Varan asked.

"Not publicly, anyway," Nomis said. "Optacrats can always find other ways to prick you, though."

"He's fooling," Kirida said.

"Am not, sadly. We can't pretend you didn't make enemies, Varan. A lot of people are unhappy with how things have happened."

"That's the witches' fault—not hers," Kirida said.

Not fully, though. Varan knew she had to share in the blame, for fleeing the Order at the very least, no matter how valuable her contribution might have been in the end. It just remained to be seen when or how much blame she'd be given. And since that was beyond her control, she tried to put it from her mind and, while she could, embrace the warmth of an early spring day and the companionship of people who were not afraid of her.

Another five days passed, and Giovel sent a message to her.

Varan,

Can you meet me at the Candlespire at midday? It won't take long.

Your friend,

Giovel

Should I be afraid to go, she wondered? Should I make my run for freedom while I can? Not even the Optate's commendation can protect me from Foneth's laws regarding magic. If the Order rules me a witch, there's no power likely to overturn their decision. I'll be trapped here forever.

She stared at Giovel's message a long time before deciding how she'd respond. He could have sent Grays after her directly, she supposed. But then again, inviting her in as if nothing was wrong could be his way of disarming her. She had hardly seen Giovel in two months, and even before then she wasn't sure that she'd ever really come to trust him. His wounds had been too fresh for her ever to understand him.

She thought of Progis, Chivi, Nomis, Kirida, even Uri. For their sake and safety, she decided to comply.

Giovel met her just outside the Candlespire. Elínla was with him, scowling behind her jagged tattoo and pacing back and forth as Varan approached. Giovel, at least, wore no weapon, and he looked genuinely at ease—something Varan didn't think she'd ever seen before.

"Hello, Varan."

"Giovel."

"Thank you for coming when I called. Would you like to talk inside?"

The air was warm again today, warm enough to begin thawing the months' worth of snow piled high by every lake and river in Foneth, so Varan shook her head. "We can talk here." If the topic of conversation allowed it, at least.

"Of course," Giovel said. "Elínla and I have a few things we thought you should hear."

Varan's training as a heal-all, not to mention four years of parenting, kept her from showing the sudden spike of panic in her chest. "Go on."

"We've interrogated the surviving witch," Elínla said. "We can't be sure she's told us all she could, but she's confessed enough to be confident she didn't spirit you here."

The surge of energy in Varan's body seemed to flatten like souring milk. "You believe her."

"Her account fits what we know about Yulena and about every other spiriting we've recorded. If she lied to us, she did it well. We were even willing to offer her some clemency if she helped us find where you came from and reverse your spiriting."

And she had refused. They'd tell Varan otherwise.

Varan swallowed the nauseating lump growing in her throat. "What did she say that convinced you?"

"She told us they can't spirit someone without seeing them."

Varan blinked and looked from Elínla to Giovel and back. That was it?

"Yulena isn't like your power," Elínla went on, eyes following Varan's. "The witch Wurelna's intelligence matches what we've experienced trying to control even known spells. It's highly unlikely anyone could control a spell like this spiriting glyph without knowing exactly whom they were targeting, where that person stood, and what the distance was between them. If they could have spirited people like you at random, we believe there would have been more from far away."

"But there's only me," Varan said, nodding.

"Wurelna doesn't believe any of her fellow witches could have done it, either by chance or purpose," Giovel said quietly. "We'll continue to interrogate her and to coax anything else we can. We at least have the shape of the spiriting glyph now, and Hirnu Pala has promised to study it. But that will take time. Years even."

"And we'd be lying if we said she could reverse a glyph's effect," Elínla added. "She will try, but mages have never really been able to do that."

Mages who used Yulena, at least.

Varan realized her legs were locked. A rush of dizziness coursed into her head. She took an unsteady step and tried to find equilibrium.

Nothing.

"If a witch didn't spirit me, then who?"

"Wurelna claims she doesn't know where this spiriting spell comes from," Elínla said. "It's possible the witches who first discovered it are still out there. We just don't know."

"The Order, then," Varan said, voice rising. "You said they'd want my power, Giovel."

"I wish I could answer that," he said now. "But every member of the Order was seen in Divnum the day you arrived except for Dlenar

—and he returned the next day. If, somehow, he knew where you were, watched you, even spirited you, he would have had to return here as fast as you did."

"If someone could spirit me, they could spirit him back too," Varan said. "He could have . . . could have done . . ."

Her eyes were wet. A hand touched her shoulder, lighter than Giovel's. Elínla had the decency not to dismiss Varan's words or tell her she was wrong, that she was reaching for sand at the bottom of an ocean. Elínla just stood there a moment and let Varan try forming more thoughts in Medín, until her thoughts ran out and she stepped back to recover herself.

All those weeks and months learning the words and asking the questions, searching just to find out who *had* the answer, let alone how to make this spiriting right. And now Varan couldn't help but feel it had all been a waste.

"I've known this witch a long time," Elínla said after a long moment. "She was once my superior in the Grays. No matter her crimes in turning on the Optacracy, I believe she has told us the truth about the spiriting glyph and its limits."

By the time Varan cleared her eyes of hot tears, Elínla was gone. Giovel turned away, looking across the brown grass near Cloud Lake. "Why don't you walk with me, like we walked before?"

Varan stepped ahead, numb all over. "There's more you want to talk about, isn't there? My punishment."

"Punishment?"

"The library. The deaths of the witches you meant to capture. Running from you."

"Ah. So you've heard some of the talk about Foneth. Then you've probably heard by now, but the Lawrits and six different guilds of archivists have pressed us about the Divnum Library. To put it bluntly, they want someone to be held responsible for the fires."

Yes, she had heard those rumors, though no one had ever confirmed them in her hearing. Striving once again to calm her face, despite the agonizing acceleration in her heartbeat, Varan said, "I understand why."

"It's ridiculous, of course. Especially since Claravena started the fire in the first place, and you were only doing your part to fend her and Etelier off."

"You don't have to cover what I did. The fire was my doing. I Quickened it to stop Etelier, but it was more than I could keep under control."

"Varan, what are you talking about? I *saw* Claravena spark a flame in the stacks. I was tailing her at the moment."

If Giovel too was trying to hide his emotions, he did it skillfully, better than Varan thought he ever could.

". . . Truly?" she asked.

"Yes, of course." His gaze softened. "I won't lie to you about what's happening."

She could think of a lot of reasons a lie might fit, though. To protect himself, to protect her, if he cared half a spit what became of her. To paint the witches the color he wanted them to be. Even just to placate powers like these archivists whom he might want on his side. But in the end, Varan found herself almost laughing because she believed Giovel.

"Stars above. You really thought it was your fault, didn't you?" he asked. "And you still came to talk when I asked you?"

Varan let out a stored-up breath. "I didn't know Claravena started any fires too." No wonder the flames had spread so quickly on the library's second level, though. It sent a tide of relief through Varan. Not that it meant she was safe. Just that it meant—to her—that someone else shared the weight of accountability for what happened.

"I've told them what I just told you," Giovel said. "Now not everyone cares who did what, maybe because you're still around to be punished whereas Claravena isn't. The sum of things is that they've asked for legal retribution on grounds of witchcraft, and the Order has refused to pursue it."

Dizziness again. Yet another surge of energy in her chest. "What are you saying?"

"We've dropped the whole pointless matter. As far as the Order's concerned, you're free to go and do as you wish."

Varan found her mind at a loss for the right words to respond, at least words Giovel could understand. After a long moment she said, "Thank you."

"We all owe you our thanks too, Varan, especially after what happened in the library. Sur swears he'd be twice-dead that day if you hadn't come for him. I might have been overpowered too, especially if you *and* Sur hadn't arrived when you did—and Inorovel likely would have been hurt even worse if not killed outright."

"Inorovel was there?"

"The witches captured her. You didn't know?"

No she hadn't. No one had ever told her.

"It doesn't hurt having Ralden indebted to you either," Giovel added. "I assume you've heard that she's the new Illumined Knight? She probably could have handled the archivists and Lawrits by herself now, and she would have done it to stand for you. Ralden actually argued to let you go free from the day she learned about your arrival here. None of us doubts that you're our ally."

"So . . . you don't think I'm a witch anymore."

"Some of us never did."

And once again, Varan believed Giovel when he said it, because for all his wounds and distraction and anger as he'd guarded her, Giovel had looked at her with understanding and not revulsion. She'd almost forgotten that now.

The reminder brought a calm she'd missed for months.

"Actually, Ralden raised the idea of appointing you to be a member of the Order," Giovel said.

"What? Me?"

"Of course, she shares plenty of ideas that never breathe the air of another morning. The point is, you don't owe us anything. That's really why Ralden didn't ask you to join us. She wants you to make your own way, and we all agreed that was best. So. What do you think you'll do now?"

She didn't have to think to answer. "I need to leave Foneth."

Giovel's face fell ever so slightly. "To search for your home."

"I need to go somewhere beyond what's on your maps." Despite having no direction, no clear picture where to go next.

"Then I hope with all my heart that you're successful," Giovel said.

More reports. More plans from Ralden. Another skirmish with Redremel scouts fifty leagues from North Hold.

The witch Wurelna, along with Varan's captured Optacrat, confessed that Birenlu was an informant for Etelier and the others.

Giovel had little choice but to share what he knew, for good or ill, which gave evidence enough for Birenlu to be arrested. She met Giovel's eyes as the Candles took her away. There was no anger in her own gaze. Just a great sorrow that Giovel thought he could share.

Two days later, Giovel and Inorovel followed Uri, Nomis, Kirida, and their two little boys, as they went to see Varan off from Ola's Gate. They halted at the north edge of Divnum, where Belnum spilled into it by the broad roads running east to west. Before anyone said much, Varan busied herself checking over her well-laden packhorse—a gift from Sur and Ralden together. She wore a Witherclaw dress once again.

May someone recognize its pattern soon, Giovel thought.

Nomis's and Kirida's son Progis was too young to realize what goodbye truly meant, but he hugged Varan's legs and waved before she even turned to leave. The others embraced her in turn, even Inorovel who barely knew Varan.

Giovel supposed they could have summoned an honor guard, maybe got half the Order to see her off, but Varan seemed content just to have any people there, people she might miss.

She'd given herself so completely to Uri's little family. Even in his little time with them, Giovel had seen Varan love those two boys as if they were her own. How had she learned to focus so much on *here* while she yearned for somewhere else?

If I knew that, though, I wouldn't have lost so much time *here* with Inorovel.

"Which direction will you go first, Varan?" Kirida asked.

Although a few maps stuck out between folds in the saddlebags, Varan made no motion to consult them. "I'll start north," she said.

Away from Yulen.

She set off walking beside her packhorse, following the roads toward the Old Lacia Trail. She paused to wave once and didn't look back after that.

"How will she find where she came from?" Inorovel asked.

"Luck and magery, most likely," Nomis said.

"She has a lot more than that to guide her," Uri said.

Giovel agreed.

AWAKE AND AWAKENED

I'm coming home to you. I promise.
  —The Witherclaw Witch; letter to Golkorun, Inivar, and Sil.

IT WAS ODD how the work of a lifetime seemed to move so quickly. Zuris's plan to fortify Foneth made for a good example, showing clear progress just in the fifth month since they'd begun. Most of those were snow-laden winter months as well, so it was impressive that the undertaking had seen any progress at all. Foneth was changing, though, reshaping as surely as a hammer made an impression in heated gold.

A week into spring, Giovel surveyed the new Lilywater Dam, the cleared streets beside Mintleaf Forest, and emptied homes on the east side of the Coldwood. Three distinct fingers to the great hand of relocation. Each had taken thousands of hours of labor and fortunes in costs, yet to Giovel the work was just a blink or two removed from the last times he'd seen these places. One day people lived there. The next, their homes had been stripped of usable materials, their roads had been deepened to let water wash through, and the people who'd made whole lives there now resided somewhere within Divnum's walls.

The truth was, hundreds were glad for a reason to put the ruined city of North Hold behind them. They wanted protection. The events of that year alone made Giovel understand why.

So he had to wonder: Will the next year be different? Will the Redremel replace the witches' cloud of fear? Will I see as many of my fellow Divine Mages direly wounded—even killed? Or will I be the one they watch fall this time?

Maybe not, now I've found my way with Yulena.

He thought about it again and again as he watched a new work crew leveling budding forest near the Ironroot Shrine. Cutting down places Redremel raiding parties might have hidden someday. It was a crisp, windless day, with sunlight warming the ground just enough that Giovel could pull back his hood. A day of renewed promise, too, since the latest stretch of work was funded half by the Optate and half by a metallurgy guild, thanks to Ralden's influence in incentivizing the movement of new populations into Divnum. Her way to grow the city while tearing it open. Still, Giovel had to shake himself not to feel cold with loss for the scores of Sanctuaries being destroyed to make Foneth more defensible.

Elínla walked to his side and sat on the grass, sipping from a flask. "You were right, I think."

"Hmm? About what?"

"About Zuris and his plan. You were right that it's our future," Elínla said. "The more time I spend out here, the clearer it is that we could never defend so much. We almost lost the city to a band of rabble and ten witches. Think about what fifteen or twenty thousand Redremel will do."

"As it happens, I'm trying not to think of anything like it."

No success in his attempt, though. It was a worm eating its way to the back of his mind, settling deeper each day.

"How are your Grays?" he asked.

"Recovering. I've promoted Eronea Dohn to train the new initiates. Her sister was one of the witches killed in the library."

Giovel nodded sadly. "I'd heard."

"I have a question for you as well," Elínla said.

She almost never asked him anything. Giovel raised an eyebrow and said, "Go ahead."

"It's about your weeks of withdrawal."

Ah. Then don't ask after all, he wanted to say. But he couldn't pretend they hadn't happened—especially not to someone who had stayed strong when she needed allies most. So, steeling himself, Giovel motioned for her to continue.

"What happened to you, Giovel? I thought you'd finally hit your target in the Order, then you vanished on us all at once. And we needed you then more than ever."

Her voice was calm, but Giovel couldn't imagine her ire had subsided completely. Nor did he blame her if it hadn't, because she was right. The Order had needed him, and he had been in some winter funk, useless.

"Do you remember Adni's list? Of awakenings?" he asked.

"Of course. I remember you saying your wife was on it, the day you came back. You really hadn't known before?"

"No."

"Neither had I."

Elínla's eyes followed him as he looked at the grass, which was just beginning to smell like spring grass should. She said nothing more. Just stared.

Then, "I really came to ask how you shook yourself free from that," she said.

"Hirnu visited me. She stayed nearby and made me feel as if she understood. Which I suppose she did, in a way."

"Because of her son, Joruni?"

"She told you about him?"

"No. But there have been rumors for years, even back when I was a new Gray. The story is that Joruni killed himself when Hirnu joined the Order."

Giovel tried to decide whether the truth—that she'd been the one to end his life—was sadder or not. He couldn't tell.

"It's odd," Elínla said after another sip from her flask. "Hirnu, of all people, having the right words to say to you when she says so little to anyone. Or even odder, you finding answers in Yulena when you'd used it so little before."

"What do you mean by that?"

"Giovel, I understand why you once kept from even glancing at your tablet. The whole Order knew how much you hated Yulena."

"That's not what I was asking. What was it you said about finding answers? What answers?"

She looked away as if the question embarrassed her. "Weren't you trying to avoid remembering more about Iremni? But now you've awakened, *truly* awakened to what Yulena can feel like. To the pleasure of making it your own. You can never go back from that kind of awakening. So in a way, now you have a chance to understand Iremni better than you ever did before."

Her words hit him like a barrel of ice. Like a needle shocking him from the edge of rest. And she was right again. In the moment Elínla said it, Giovel saw more of Iremni's mind and heart than he'd ever understood before.

Because he *had* awakened. Because he now knew firsthand what Sur had tried to describe all those months before—Yulena's exhilarating secret. That its power was an exultation, a joy to wield and to hold close. It hadn't been long since Giovel discovered it, and he had scarcely touched Yulena since the battle in the Divnum library, but the triumph of the sensation was there all the same, making him itch for even his practices with Hirnu or any other chance to tame the river of power Yulena offered him.

Iremni must have felt this too, he thought. No wonder she was torn and broken and aloof. She was *starving*, and she couldn't satisfy both Yulen and me because I was a Divine Mage.

He saw and resaw as many moments then as he'd seen in his weeks of aloofness. Every motion of her hands and shoulders and mouth took on new meaning. Not just concealing her own awakening but living in some tidal war. She'd had her own thrilling power and *him* pulling in different directions with all their might.

And now I understand why that alone was enough to break her, Giovel thought.

He realized his eyes were wet. His chin, too. It felt odd, but he couldn't recall weeping like this at any moment in his life, though he knew he must have at least as a child. He couldn't tell whether he was newly afraid of his own awakening now, grief-stricken for Iremni, or overcome with relief just to understand that tiny piece of her at long last.

I swear I wanted to understand sooner, Iremni.

He lowered his face to his hands, shaking all over. The tears held strong until his eyes burned and his breathing rasped. Even then his shoulders shook with great sobs he couldn't keep inside. Elínla put one hand on his shoulder, then her other on his own tear-streaked arm, gripping him and helping him stay in place.

"Sur warned me this would happen," he managed to say as his own weeping finally began to wane. "Not that I'd cry like a raincloud, I mean. About Yulena. He didn't think you understood, though."

Once again Elínla looked away. "I think everyone who awakens comes to understand Yulena's pull eventually."

"Well. Here I am."

Elínla stood, brushing grass from her cowl. "But now you can be sure it's not you and you alone, Giovel. You have friends who trust you, who'd risk themselves to watch your back as many times as you ask. Sur's one of them, Hirnu too. I'd wager even Ralden is. And I hope we can count each other friends like that as well."

He wiped his eyes, feeling more clear-sighted than he'd been in over a year.

"I think we can."

Giovel stayed by Ironroot Shrine until the sun began dimming and the work crew left for the day. Perhaps he should have been seeing to his new duties training and organizing Grays for shifts guarding the Optate. The work would wait one day, though, and the smells and colors of early spring might not.

As he rode Boulder back to Divnum, Giovel found a name for the sensation left behind when his tears ran out. It wasn't what he'd expected a bout of weeping to bring. It was a wave of love for the woman with whom he'd spent his life.

There in those moments of clarity he'd found some round, empty place of mind and memory where they could stand together, the two of them as he recollected, and where the new Yulen-cursed Giovel and Iremni could stand as well. It was a place where he could treasure her years of warmth, work, laughter, passion, tears for him and tears of her own, care in their quietest moments, and every other tiny facet that made her fill his life—where he could see and reconcile each piece with an Iremni who loved Yulena too, so much that she never even told him. It was a place those two Iremnis could stand, without shattering, as one.

He couldn't say whether either Iremni in that hollow of his mind was the real one. But did any person truly know any other like that?

He left Boulder at the Candlespire and went straight home. Then he burned dinner, and Inorovel laughed at him because it was the thousandth time. She told him about her studies and her friends and the cut she'd given herself trying to shape a piece of broken glass. When other fathers would be sending their children to sleep, Giovel asked if she'd like to walk by the Candlespire or Keep Hatahad. So they walked into the cool night, visiting the spot by Bone Hill where they'd scattered Iremni's ashes to feed new lifetimes of Sanctuaries.

And for the first time, Giovel stood in the place they'd said their farewells and saw a narrow opening in the weeks and months of fog-like grief, with clear starlight glimmering beyond.

ACKNOWLEDGEMENTS

Like most creative endeavors, this book needed lifelines from a village of smart and caring people. Many thanks to the first batch of readers who saw the manuscript: My brother William Taylor, whose sharp questions shed light on the weakest points in early drafts so readers wouldn't have to think as hard in the following iterations; Tori Tigges and Josh Stamper, both who brought fresh perspectives from their reading in the genre and gave encouragement at times when it was much needed.

Big props are also due to the members of my writing group: Jason Dodge, Logan Davis, Sarah Tigges, and Alex Tigges. Your unique takes on the book helped me zoom out and see it more clearly. Just as valuable, your commitment to your own craft helped me believe I wasn't a fool to keep writing.

The expert work of my editor Shelli Gustafson is mostly invisible by design. That alone makes them invaluable in my mind, and I'm deeply grateful for the insight and attention to detail she brought to the project.

I feel very lucky to have had the support of my family. Particular thanks to Samee Taylor, Rebekah Taylor, and Mary Cragun, all who took me seriously (enough) and somehow kept from blanching the numerous times I asked them to read a few (or several) hundred pages on my behalf.

I can't say enough to thank my wife and best friend Delaney. Delaney swapped computers many times, let me requisition an entire closet as a writing sanctuary, read the roughest draft of all and helped make it better, and not only supported but consistently safeguarded the time it took me to write. I'd lack more than just a novel if it weren't for her.

SELECT LIST OF CHARACTERS

Adni Aman: Councilor to the Optate and Illumined Knight of the Divine Order of Mages; former member of the Gray Order, most well known for his defeat of the Worenthi Witch.

Alene Dohn: An awakening; sister of Claravena, Eronea, Lolen, and Uro Dohn.

Aried Pala: Niece of Hirnu Pala; cousin of Joruni Pala.

Claravena Dohn: A witch, notable for her lack of tell when using Yulena; sister of Alene, Eronea, Lolen, and Uro Dohn.

Dalenchivor Asann: Son of Kirida and Nomis Asann; grandson of Uri Risdarol; brother of Progis Asann.

Deleos Tovóm: A leading member of House Tovóm, widely known for his extravagant lifestyle and frequent gambling losses; nephew of Dlenar Tovóm.

Dlenar Tovóm: A member of the Divine Order of Mages, chiefly responsible for gathering intelligence on awakenings and witch sightings; uncle of Deleos Tovóm.

Dolidan Sifio: A frequent strongarm for the allied witches; wife of Noru Sifio.

Drova Felekas: Mother of Varan Witherclaw and Recia Lujir; grandmother of Edisilu and Inivar Pir.

Edisilu (Sil) Pir: Son of Varan Witherclaw and Golkorun Pir; brother of Inivar Pir.

Elínla Nodan: A member of the Divine Order of Mages and the Sept of Blue Heaven; former member of the Gray Order, well regarded for her prodigious skill with Yulena and her rapid rise to the Gray Order's leadership prior to her appointment to the Divine Order.

Eronea Dohn: A member of the Gray Order; sister of Claravena, Eronea, Lolen, and Uro Dohn.

Etelier Finar: A witch; leader of allied witches; husband of Pramél Finar; father of Mota Finar.

Frenico Gedio: A Cloudblade; former squad brother of Giovel Ullin.

Furapar Hurot: A former witch who died in a spellbuilding accident.

Gameldisar Jada: A former Banner Captain in the Candleguard who was killed by a witch.

Giovel Ullin: The juniormost member of the Divine Order of Mages; former District Commander, Cloudblade, and Banner Captain in the Candleguard; husband of Iremni Ullin; father of Inorovel Ullin.

Golkorun Pir: Calligrapher; husband of Varan Witherclaw; father of Inivar and Edisilu Pir.

Hirnu Pala: A member of the Divine Order of Mages serving as Observer for the Order, with sole authority to research and build new spells on behalf of the Optate; aunt of Aried Pala; mother of Joruni Pala.

Ind Telen: Azure Commander of the Lances.

Inivar Pir: Son of Varan Witherclaw and Golkorun Pir; brother of Edisilu Pir.

Inorovel Ullin: Daughter of Iremni and Giovel Ullin.

Ithilo Wolénd: A witch; primary recruiter for allied witches.

Jinaten 'Tenswords' Teserot: Jade Commander of the Lances; well known for breaking numerous swords while holding the northern line in the battle of the Dancing Crow.

Joruni Pala: Son of Hirnu Pala; cousin of Aried Pala.

Kanis Delirot: An awakening discovered by Adni Aman.

Kirida Asann: A former logistician for the Vermilion Lances; wife of Nomis Asann; daughter of Uri Risdarol; mother of Progis and Dalenchivor Asann.

Kraza Legosi: Former Lawrit and High Optate, most remembered for instituting and promoting various laws to restrict the use of Yulena outside the Divine Order's work to prevent spellbuilding.

Lolen Dohn: An awakening; sister of Alene, Claravena, Eronea, and Uro Dohn.

Luciron Inian: An Optacrat responsible for allocation of Candleguard funding.

Mota Finar: Daughter of Pramél and Etelier Finar.

Nomis Asann: A Candleguard; husband of Kirida Asann; father of Progis and Dalenchivor Asann.

Noru Sifio: A witch; deeply interested in Vindilic lore and the search for Vindil's ruins; husband of Dolidan Sifio.

Olinos Vada: A Banner Captain in the Candleguard; former Banner Captain of Giovel Ullin.

Olura Medín: High Optate; Protector and Servant of Foneth; High Governor; aunt of Suresni Medín; second cousin of Zuris Medín.

Órkol Lanirot: A witch.

Piatém Jada: A witch.

Pramél Finar: Wife of Etelier; mother of Mota.

Progis Asann: Son of Kirida and Nomis; grandson of Uri; brother of Dalenchivor.

Raf Zotan: A witch.

Ralden Esgirot: A member of the Divine Order of Mages, principally responsible for adherence to Order protocols and regulations; leader of the Still Heron Textile Guild.

Recia Lujir: Sister of Varan Witherclaw; daughter of Drova Felekas; aunt of Inivar and Edisilu Pir.

Riddin Cligio: A member of the Jade Lances.

Sironis Lun: A retired member of the Divine Order of Mages; often outspoken in favor of lighter penalties for first-time spellbuilding.

Suresni (Sur) Medín: A member of the Divine Order of Mages, chiefly responsible for apprehending known witches; a former Jade Lance; nephew of Olura Medín; third cousin of Zuris Medín.

Tranin Ve: A witch; leader of allied witches' spiriting efforts.

Uri Risdarol: A translator for the Optacracy; mother of Kirida Asann; grandmother of Progis and Dalenchivor Asann; friend of Iremni Ullin.

Uro Dohn: An awakening; sister of Alene, Claravena, Eronea, and Lolen Dohn.

Varan Witherclaw: A spiriting; Witherclaw herbalist; wife of Golkorun Pir; mother of Inivar and Edisilu Pir; daughter of Drova Felekas; sister of Recia Lujir.

Wurelna Tenemot: A witch; former member of the Gray Order.

Yilitha Dar: Senior member of the Gray Order.

Zuris Medín: Vermilion Commander of the Lances; former logistician for Azure Lances; second cousin of Olura Medín; third cousin of Suresni Medín.

SELECT LIST OF GLYPHS

The Talon: Widely regarded as the oldest existing spell to be named, the Talon strikes with a piercing wave of energy much like a jagged dagger. It has remained highly popular for nearly seven hundred years, despite being difficult to control. Discovery attributed to Renma Ot.

The Tremor: A spell that causes prolonged, vigorous shaking in its targets. The Tremor is unique in that its effect is observably identical in both living and non-living targets. Discovery attributed to Renma Ot.

The Vice: A spell unleashing a small crushing bolt of force, often enough to break bones or destroy organs in living targets. Discovery attributed to Renma Ot.

The Ember: A spell with a kick-like effect that leaves mild, lingering burns on living targets. Many mages attempted to ignite fires with the Ember early after its discovery, but no trustworthy records indicate success. Discovery attributed to Renma Ot.

The Bellows: A distinctly complicated spell utilizing a glyph that can rarely be drawn by a single mage in less than an hour. The Bellows initiates an unfocused wave of force somewhat like a powerful gust of wind. This spell often merely pushes living things back from its glyph of origin, not striking with enough coordinated force to damage them directly. The Bellows has no observable effect on non-living objects. Discovery attributed to Renma Ot.

The Needle: A spell loosing a precise line of energy. If cast correctly, the Needle can pierce a finger-width into almost any substance, but it is rarely forceful enough to be valuable. The Needle fell out of use for several centuries before being brought back as a cooking tool during the era of Optate Noyro Jada. Discovery attributed to Renma Ot.

The Hawk: An imperceptibly quick spell that strikes with modest power but--due to its speed--is almost impossible to evade even when cast by a mage with an obvious tell. Discovery attributed to Renma Ot.

The Flail: An inaccurate spell striking with significant force and causing targets to twitch and flail wildly, often losing their balance and dropping things on their person. Its use as a disarming spell made it extremely common in the two hundred years between the founding of the Divine Order and the outlawing of Yulena as a tool of war. Discovery attributed to Jejari Nodan.

The Sour: A spell prompting gagging and vomiting from a variety of living targets. Numerous Observers have claimed that the Sour is oddly ineffective against young children, though none have ever explained how they know this. Discovery attributed to Jejari Nodan.

The Mace: A short-range spell exerting massive force across a shallow arc near the glyph of origin, often crushing anything in its direct path. Attributed to Jejari Nodan. Forbidden from use by the Divine Order.

The Flare: A spell issuing a flare of bright, sustained light which blossoms over a distance from the glyph of origin. While typically useless as a combat spell, the Flare is remarkably easy to control while also utilizing a simple glyph. These attributes have made it popular as a signaling spell. Discovery attributed to Kestirali Dar.

The Outpour: A spell with rapid dehydrating effect, causing living targets to sweat, weep, piss, or otherwise expel liquids at uncontrollable rates. Discovery attributed to Lorso Anivar.

The Rod: A spell that strikes with a direct, blunt application of force much like the swinging of a rod. The Divine and Gray Orders immediately adopted the Rod, at the time of its discovery, as a primary spell for subduing witches. Discovery attributed to Murdoni Tovóm.

The Lance: A spell releasing twin silver blade-like bursts of energy that tend to cut through a variety of obstacles. The Lance's name was attributed first to its piercing nature, but later scholarship argues that this spell received its name when Murdoni Tovóm used it to publicly kill a Lance who'd angered her. Discovery attributed to Murdoni Tovóm.

The Gag: An unreliable but popular glyph shown to cause various muscles to lock in place in living targets. The Gag is often directed toward the neck or upper chest in an attempt to restrict the muscles used in verbalization, thus silencing a target. Discovery attributed to Murdoni Tovóm.

The Sleeper: A spell with an extremely narrow breadth of effect, often causing muscles to go numb in living targets. It was first considered a step toward medicinal Yulena, but the number of Sleeper glyphs required to numb a person for even simple medical operations showed it to be ineffective. Discovery attributed to Murdoni Tovóm.

The Adze: A forceful but slow-moving spell given its name because it appears to move in a distinctly curved trajectory no matter what a mage does to control it. Discovery attributed to Murdoni Tovóm. Forbidden from use by the Divine Order.

The Net: A spell releasing a weak outward force in nearly every direction around the glyph of origin. The Net is singular in how its outward path of motion seems to expand around the glyph, as if growing only after it clears a certain distance. Early experiments showed that a mage could completely avoid its effect by standing near the glyph of origin, making it a relatively safe spell for its caster--though dangerous in other uses since its expansion often hurls aside or damages objects or living things nearby. Discovery attributed to Murdoni Tovóm. Forbidden from use by the Divine Order.

The Torch: A spell causing a cloud-like outflow that somehow emits intense heat without radiating energy beyond the immediate vicinity of its motion. Elemental philosophers once worked with the Divine Order to try containing some of the substance shown by this spell, but it evaded isolation by any means they could employ, and several were badly burned in the process, losing skin and muscle alike to the searing effect of the Torch. Discovery attributed to Murdoni Tovóm. Forbidden from use by the Divine Order.

The Stonecutter: A reliably short-range spell that slashes out with a single stroke much like the fall of an axe. This spell was known to cleave an entire horse and rider simultaneously before Kraza Legosi saw it in action and campaigned successfully to outlaw its use. Discovery attributed to Murdoni Tovóm. Forbidden from use by the Divine Order.

The Pillar: A highly predictable glyph that releases a compressed plume of energy from the glyph of origin. The Pillar almost always shoots directly upward from its glyph. Records indicate that some mages once used this spell as a battering ram by engraving glyphs on objects that rested perpendicular to the ground, but these accounts are almost surely false since the force the Pillar effuses usually leaves a crater behind and would certainly crush a sand tablet or similar object used to initiate it. Discovery attributed to Murdoni Tovóm. Forbidden from use by the Divine Order.

The Hailstorm: A spell resulting in a series of bursts at seemingly random intervals, with various sizes and angles of impact. Bright flashes of pale blue light make this spell's effect appear almost like hail falling. Discovery attributed to Siresa Jada.

The Ballista: A staggeringly powerful spell that is also notably difficult to control and aim. The Ballista was named such when its discoverer miscast it, resulting in his immediate death. Discovery attributed to Kilio Tovóm. Forbidden from use by the Divine Order.

The Bowstring: A spell resulting in great force applied precisely in two opposite directions, often across very long and direct trajectories. The Bowstring's name came from a foolish attempt to use it to train archers to shoot more accurately. Discovery attributed to Kilio Tovóm. Forbidden from use by the Divine Order.

The Illumina: A spell with almost no detectable effect but a startling flash of white, which often leaves spotty sight for anyone looking toward its glyph of origin. Discovery attributed to Sironis Lun.

The Pull: A short-range spell showing little apparent force but eliciting a lethargic feeling in living targets, often slowing them down substantially for minutes at a time. Discovery attributed to Hirnu Pala.

The Whip: A spell that lashes out with great force but tends to snap back near or against the mage using it, often resulting in injury and, in at least two known cases, in the mage's death. Discovery attributed to the Worenthi Witch. Forbidden from use by the Divine Order.

The Dimmer: A spell utilizing a remarkably simple glyph to strike with mild force and greatly diminish sight in living targets for a short time. Discovery attributed to Wurelna Tenemot.

The Reverse: An accurate spell eliciting an overpowering muddling effect in living targets, causing them to confuse their sense of direction and balance for a few moments. Discovery attributed to Wurelna Tenemot.

The Nettle: A spell resulting in acute itching all over a living target. The effect fades remarkably quickly. Discovery attributed to Wurelna Tenemot.

The Hammer: A simple glyph discharging a strong blunt force, much like the Rod. Discovery unknown.

The Glass: An uncommonly unreliable spell, generally causing a living target to see double for several minutes. Recorded effects have also been said to include nausea, euphoria, and partial paralysis. Discovery unknown.

ABOUT THE AUTHOR

Stephen Taylor writes for fun. His fiction has appeared in *The Future Fire*, *MYTHIC*, *The Colored Lens* and other publications. When he's not writing he's often making music with his family. He lives in North Carolina. Lean more about the author at www.stephenjtaylor.com.

www.ingramcontent.com/pod-product-compliance
Lightning Source LLC
Chambersburg PA
CBHW070306310726

48976CB00005B/1592